"What don't you want me to do, Romi, my sweet virgin?"

Why did those words sound so hot in Max's voice?

"Turn you on? You weren't complaining a second ago."

She couldn't deny it. Wasn't sure she wanted to, even if she could. "Neither were you."

But he'd stopped and she hadn't even thought to try. Darn him.

"No, and I never will."

Why did he have to say things like that? Things that could make her hope when hope and this man did not go together. "We still want different things."

"Are you so sure? If I hadn't stopped you would have let me take you, here and now."

He was talking about sex when she was referring to a relationship. And he knew it. "Do you get some thrill out of reminding me of my own weakness?"

"It's not a weakness, *milaya*."

Lucy Monroe's

RUTHLESS RUSSIANS

Passion is in their blood

As boys, they came from Russia to America to make
their fortunes. Now formidable opponents in the
boardroom, Viktor Beck and Maxwell Black are
about to make the biggest acquisitions of their lives
by marrying two of San Francisco's most notorious
heiresses! Beneath their suave American exteriors
beat the passionate hearts of fearsome Cossack
warriors—and their intended brides are about to
give them the battle of their lives!

In **AN HEIRESS FOR HIS EMPIRE**
October 2014

A tabloid sex scandal means Viktor Beck can put his
plan in motion and marry heiress Madison Archer—the
key to taking over her father's business and building
his empire. But even this ruthless Russian is not
prepared for his wild bride to be a virgin!

In **A VIRGIN FOR HIS PRIZE**
November 2014

Formidable CEO Maxwell Black is about to
make his ultimate acquisition—socialite
Romi Grayson! She has something he wants,
and his need for control—in all areas—means he
won't rest until his ring is on her finger and the
innocent Romi is warm and willing in his bed!

A VIRGIN
FOR HIS PRIZE

BY
LUCY MONROE

MILLS &
BOON

Published in Great Britain 2014
by Mills & Boon, an imprint of Harlequin (UK) Limited,
Eton House, 18-24 Paradise Road, Richmond, Surrey, TW9 1SR

© 2014 Lucy Monroe

ISBN: 978-0-263-25025-1

Harlequin (UK) Limited's policy is to use papers that are natural,
renewable and recyclable products and made from wood grown in
sustainable forests. The logging and manufacturing processes conform
to the legal environmental regulations of the country of origin.

Printed and bound in Spain
by Blackprint CPI, Barcelona

Lucy Monroe started reading at the age of four. After going through the children's books at home, she was caught by her mother reading adult novels pilfered from the higher shelves on the bookcase... Alas, it was nine years before she got her hands on a Mills & Boon® romance her older sister had brought home. She loves to create the strong alpha males and independent women who people Mills & Boon® books. When she's not immersed in a romance novel (whether reading or writing it), she enjoys travel with her family, having tea with the neighbours, gardening, and visits from her numerous nieces and nephews.

Lucy loves to hear from her readers:
email LucyMonroe@LucyMonroe.com,
or visit www.LucyMonroe.com

Recent titles by the same author:

AN HEIRESS FOR HIS EMPIRE *(Ruthless Russians)*
SHEIKH'S SCANDAL *(The Chatsfield)*
MILLION DOLLAR CHRISTMAS PROPOSAL
PRINCE OF SECRETS *(By His Royal Decree)*

Did you know these are also available as eBooks?
Visit www.millsandboon.co.uk

In honor of The Gathering Place and the two amazing families who have created this wonderful sanctuary they so generously share with those blessed enough to call them both friend and family. I have never written a book in a more peaceful and love-filled environment. Thank you!

CHAPTER ONE

FURY FIGHTING WITH the pain of betrayal, Romi Grayson set her phone down on the table beside her with careful movements. The temptation to throw the mobile device across the room was staggering.

That lying, manipulative, opportunistic *tycoon!*

Maxwell Black had made it very clear to Romi that he wasn't in the market for a long-term relationship, but that hadn't meant he wasn't interested in something else. His generosity in and out of bed with his lovers had been the fodder for gossip for years. As were the unexpectedly amicable breakups.

Max had promised Romi sexual pleasure beyond the scope of her imagination.

He'd said she would be the sole focus of his interest.

Until he was done with her.

The *über*-wealthy tycoon-playboy had offered Romi absolute fidelity *with a time limit.*

She'd walked away.

From the promise. From the possibilities. From the certainty of a broken heart.

They'd only dated a few times, but he'd sparked a depth of emotion in her that was both immediate and frightening. Terrifying for its intensity, Romi had had no doubts that she wouldn't survive a breakup down the road with her heart intact.

Walking away after their short, almost platonic association had been painful enough. *Almost* being the operative word. Max had given Romi her first taste of sexual pleasure with a partner.

Awed by the sensations he evoked, she'd been close to giving in to Max's offer.

Ultimately, she'd had no choice, though. Not with his attitude.

For all her "free-spirited" ways, Romi was a traditionalist at heart. She wanted a home, a family and the man she loved to be looking at the future, not the expiry date on their relationship.

That same man had been prepared to *marry* Romi's sister-by-choice, Madison Archer.

For a payoff!

Shares in Archer International Holdings and the prospect of taking over when Jeremy Archer retired had tempted Maxwell Black to break his "no commitments" rule.

The mercenary *cad*.

It was an old-fashioned word, but man, it *fit*.

"Ramona!" Her dad's wavering call came from the den he spent most of his time in these days.

He only made it into the office about two days a week, his longtime director of operations running Grayson Enterprises in everything but name.

Some might have expected Romi to take over the family business, but not her dad. Harry Grayson had always made it clear he expected his daughter to follow her own dreams.

Filtered sunlight from the single window on the north side cast the den in gray light. Her father sat on the sofa facing the dark screen of a wall-mounted big-screen television. The highball glass in his hand was empty but for a couple of ice cubes. Bloodshot, red-rimmed hazel eyes testified to the fact it hadn't been empty for long, or often in the past hours.

She walked forward and took the glass from his unresisting fingers. "It's only afternoon, Daddy. You don't need this."

There was a time when he hadn't picked up a drink with alcohol in it before the cocktail hour. He'd drunk steadily from that point so that he went to bed every night so inebriated, walking up the stairs was a danger.

But the drinking hadn't gone on during the day.

Over the past few years, the drinking had gotten worse while she was away at school. Her father now started at lunchtime with a glass of wine that often became a bottle.

But drinking hard liquor this early in the day was still something new.

Recognition took seconds to register in his rheumy gaze. "Ramona."

"Yes, Daddy. You called me." Something he never would have done sober.

Graysons did not do *common* things like shout through the house for one another. They used the intercom system.

But Harry Grayson didn't look in any shape to cross the room to the intercom. His brows drew together in an exaggerated effort at concentrating. "I did?"

"Yes, Daddy, you did."

He looked with confusion around the room, like the answer might leap out at him. "I think I lost the remote."

Romi bent down and picked up the small electronic device from the floor at his feet. "Here it is."

"Oh, thank you." He frowned. "It's not working."

She swiped her hand on the screen and spoke the command to turn the TV on. The sound of afternoon news commentary filled the room from the surround-sound speakers.

"It's working just fine."

"Wouldn't turn on for me," her father slurred.

She wasn't surprised. The remote was programmed to take voice instruction with recognizable commands, not speech blurred by alcohol.

"You look upset, kitten."

That was the thing about her dad. Even with his brain pickled by too much drink, he cared about her. He paid attention. She had no trouble remembering that even drunk, her dad was twice the father than a man like Maddie's dad could ever hope to be.

"I'm okay."

"No, you're not." He was careful to enunciate every word.

And for some reason that made Romi feel like crying. "It's nothing, really."

"No, I know it's something." For just a moment, her dad wasn't a drunk bent on destroying his liver.

He was the man who had loved her mother so much, he'd married her against his own family's wishes. He was the guy who raised Romi from the time she was three, refusing the easy road of allowing other family members to take on her care.

"It's an old story." And she'd fallen for it.

"Tell me."

"I fell for a man."

"You didn't tell me."

Romi ignored that, incapable of coming up with a response that wouldn't hurt one of them. "He told me he didn't do commitment."

"And you found out he's married?" her dad asked, looking as angry as emotions dulled by overimbibing would allow.

"No, but I did find out he's willing to get married. For the right price."

"The cad!"

She couldn't help smiling at how her father's word echoed her own thoughts just a few minutes before. "Exactly."

"You're better off without him."

"Of course." If only she could convince her heart as easily as her head.

Maxwell Black was bored. Attending these functions rarely provided anything but a few mind-numbing hours interspersed with brief moments of useful networking.

Oh, he believed in the cause. Tonight's gala was dedicated to raising funds for and awareness of the plight of hunger among school-age children.

Considering the focus of the evening, he might have an opportunity to indulge in one of his favorite pastimes. Watching Romi Grayson.

Touching her was more satisfying, but she'd turned down his offer of a liaison in no uncertain terms.

In a rare show of restraint, he hadn't continued the pursuit.

There was something different…almost *special*…about the old-money San Francisco heiress, a vulnerability he was unwilling to exploit.

A first for him—he'd stayed away from her as much out of self-preservation as anything else.

He felt protective toward her in ways he did not understand, ways that could be manipulated if she knew about them. So, she would never find out.

Even so, plans and intentions changed and he was coming to the conclusion that he and Romi might have a future after all. So long as Maxwell dictated the terms.

The soft scent of jasmine and vanilla he always associated with the heiress activist reached him before she did.

"Well, well, well, if it isn't Maxwell Black, *master* tycoon."

Squelching the urge to turn quickly, he slowly faced her.

Black, silky chin-length hair framed Romi's pixie-like features, her bow-shaped lips set in an uncustomary flat line. Her makeup was dramatic tonight, bringing out the gentian blue of her eyes. Eyes that snapped with accusation he did not understand.

Or perhaps he did.

"Good evening, Romi. You look lovely tonight."

The elegant peacock-blue evening gown accented her modest curves, highlighting Romi's particular brand of delicate femininity. Fragility at odds with her gung-ho approach to life. Romi didn't consider any cause too great, or any opponent too intimidating to take on.

Borderline petite at five foot five, with a personality that more than made up for her smaller stature, Maxwell had found Ramona Grayson intriguing from their first meeting.

"Thank you." She frowned at him, but offered grudgingly, "You're very handsome yourself tonight. Not a designer I recognize. A tuxedo from one of the tailors on Savile Row?"

He smiled, impressed by her powers of observation. Having his clothing made to fit could be considered a luxury by some, but for Maxwell it was more than that. Tailored designer brands impressed, but having a *bespoke* suit, patterned and constructed entirely to his specifications, made another kind of impression, one in line with Maxwell's reputation for utter control in and out of the boardroom.

"My suit-maker is local, but he apprenticed with a Savile Row tailor."

"Of course. I notice you don't give his name."

"Why? Are you looking for a new tailor for your father?" Not that Maxwell thought his would take on Grayson.

The tailor was both expensive and extremely discerning about his clientele. An alcoholic on the verge of taking his company down to the bottom of a whiskey bottle had no chance.

Romi's barely there grimace was quickly masked. "No."

"The waiting list for his services is a year out." Maxwell found himself offering the truth as an excuse, an unaccustomed effort to spare her feelings.

"No doubt you subverted it somehow."

Maxwell smiled. "Not a chance. The man's a martinet about his schedule and his client standards."

"Still, I'm surprised," Romi said, *her* intent to bait him obvious.

Something was definitely bothering her. "Are you?"

"You're a very opportunistic man." The edge to her voice was sharper than a chef's cleaver.

He couldn't deny it, didn't want to. His ability to identify and take advantage of opportunities was something that had helped Maxwell to build his business and his fortune to what they were today. A multimillionaire personally, his company, Black Information Technologies, or BIT, was valued at ten times his personal assets.

Not bad for a thirty-two-year-old bastard having no acknowledged ties to wealth, like Romi had been born with.

However, it was clear something about that character trait had upset Romi. Recently, if he wasn't mistaken. Since there was no way she could know about the plans he'd been considering for her father's company, it had to be something else.

Mentally going back through the events of the past week that others were aware of, Maxwell thought he might know. "You've spoken to Madison Archer."

"I talk to Maddie every day, several times a day." The increased annoyance in Romi's voice left no doubt he was on the right track.

Though he still was not sure *why* Romi would be upset with Maxwell for being offered the marriage-based business contract by Jeremy Archer.

"I can hardly be held accountable for her father's actions." Though he wouldn't hesitate to take advantage of the auspicious conditions Archer had provided, even if not for the opportunities the president of AIH had intended.

Romi crossed her arms, leaning back in a classic pose of annoyance. "Only your willingness to participate in them."

He took a moment to appreciate the way her stance pressed her small breasts together to create a shadow of tempting cleavage. Everything about her body turned him on. Thin, with modest curves, she was nevertheless one-hundred-percent enticing woman.

"I went to a meeting where Jeremy Archer offered a very

lucrative contract and your so-called sister-by-choice held her own very well." Though he wasn't prepared to tell Romi *how* Madison had kept her father in line.

Maxwell had plans for that information. Because he *was* an opportunistic bastard. Literally and figuratively.

Unless he'd misread Madison Archer, she had not shared her actions with her best friend.

Which created leverage for Maxwell with Romi. She would do anything to prevent her SBC from being harmed in any way. Even by Madison's own precipitous actions.

"You were willing to break your own rules for a price," Romi sneered.

Ah. Now he understood. Maxwell was actually a little surprised that Madison had shared his offer with Romi. The Archer heiress had never seriously considered it and he hadn't expected her to. That didn't mean he would deny himself the opportunity to give Viktor Beck a few seconds of doubt.

They'd been friends and competitors since early childhood.

Still, Romi was upset Maxwell had made the counteroffer. That might bode well for his own plans where she was concerned.

"And that price wasn't *love*." He laced the last word with his own brand of disgust.

The overly emotional and incredibly naive heiress thought that sentiment the only motivation worthy of note. Even after the loss of that *love* had nearly destroyed her own father and what remained of their family.

"More like thirty pieces of silver." Her blue gaze snapped with fire he wanted in his bed.

The small taste he'd had of her had only whetted an appetite Maxwell had come to accept would not be satisfied by anything but unfettered access to this woman alone.

"Your inference would imply I betrayed someone. I

didn't." He and Romi had gone their separate ways nearly a year ago.

"Your own integrity maybe."

"What is dishonest about a business deal where the terms are laid bare for everyone involved?"

"So, your 'no commitment' rule was only for me?" Romi's voice betrayed pained disappointment.

He didn't like hearing that from her. Even less than he'd liked the sound of "no thank you" spoken with a catch of desperation in her voice. "I didn't offer Madison the kind of commitment you believe you need."

"You offered to marry her."

"I offered a business arrangement without conjugal rights or the promise of fidelity."

"That's horrible." Romi was getting genuinely upset, her voice rising in agitation.

Soon, those around them would notice.

He took her by her elbow and began leading her toward the balcony doors. He was hoping the evening drop in temperature would mean it was deserted.

"Where are we going?" she asked, though she didn't try to pull away.

"Someplace more private than here."

Memory slashed across his brain…a similar question, an almost identical answer, but for a very different purpose.

He'd wanted to kiss her.

She'd been seething with an emotion very different from anger that time. She'd wanted the kiss, too.

Her response had nearly caused him to lose control of his own body for the first time since his initial foray into sex.

The balcony was as deserted as he'd hoped it would be, with only one other couple tucked away in the corner shadows at the opposite end. The low-level lighting and thirty feet separating the two couples insured a certain level of privacy so long as he and Romi did not raise their voices.

She shivered in the cool air and he moved them into the

corner, where strategically placed potted greenery acted as both a privacy screen and wind barrier.

Anyone looking closely would see them, but only from certain angles. The other couple was not at that angle.

Even without the wind, the evening air was still chilly.

He removed his jacket and tucked it around Romi like a cape. "Better?" he asked.

Nodding, Romi bit her lip in a gesture of vulnerability that nearly derailed his intention to *talk*.

"You didn't need to give me your coat." She pulled it closer, a clearly unconscious action in direct opposition to the words she spoke. "We won't be out here long. I'm not even sure why I came with you in the first place."

"Because you are angry I considered Jeremy Archer's business proposal and we need to talk about that."

"I don't know why."

He merely waited in silence.

Romi huffed out a sigh. "Maddie deserves better than a business marriage." She glared up at Maxwell with a mix of emotions he couldn't quite read. "You do, too."

"I do not find Madison particularly attractive. Foregoing conjugal rights would not have been a great sacrifice."

"She's beautiful."

"I find beauty in a different package." The red-headed Archer heiress was undeniably pleasing to the eye, but she did nothing for Maxwell personally.

He liked willowy figures, usually going for taller women because of his own six-foot-five-inch height. Though despite the foot difference in their height, Romi fit with him surprisingly well. He preferred dark hair and found her black tresses particularly appealing. Sharp elfin features were also unexpectedly attractive.

Before Romi, he'd never been drawn to blue eyes, but hers were so striking, so expressive, he found them intensely alluring. He liked knowing everything his sexual partners were feeling and thinking. Romi's eyes revealed what her charming verbal honesty did not.

And unlike her SBC, who rarely blushed at all, Romi's frequently pink cheeks—at least in his presence—that had nothing to do with her makeup were equally expressive.

"I just don't understand how you were willing to marry her." With a sound of frustration, Romi put her hand over her mouth, a sure sign she wished she hadn't said that out loud.

"I was willing to entertain the idea, but she wasn't interested in me as her future husband and I knew that before I ever made the offer of a marriage in name only."

"What? How did you know?"

"Madison Archer may be better at hiding her emotions than you, but there can be no doubt that only one man in that conference room had the remotest of chances in fulfilling the contract her father had drawn up."

Romi's smile was soft. "They're good together."

"Let's hope so." Viktor and Madison's engagement had already been announced, along with the whirlwind date set for their wedding.

He didn't know Madison Archer well, but what he knew of her, he respected and liked. And while many would look on Viktor as Maxwell's lifelong rival, the man who shared his Russian heritage was one of a select few Maxwell called friend.

Considering the fact that both people appeared to be entering the agreement with poorly hidden—to him at least—romantic aspirations and a long-term future together as their goal, Maxwell hoped it worked out for them.

He didn't believe in permanent romantic ties. He considered marriage like any other contract—to be kept in place for the duration of the benefit of both parties.

His mother had taught him from an early age to see romantic relationships as a means to an end. Natalya Black had always told her son that love was the biggest fairy tale of all.

She'd believed in Maxwell and told him he could do anything he set his mind to, but never give in to "so-called" love. It only weakened the afflicted and made them lose their focus.

Maxwell didn't know where his mother's life lessons had come from, but he knew his own and he'd discovered early on she was right.

Leaving Russia and her disapproving relatives for a new start in America had not included Natalya giving up her tendency to line her nest with the golden straw of cleverly chosen bed partners of defined duration.

The transience of the men in his mother's life had taught him one thing. There was no such thing as forever and anyone who believed in it was a fool.

They'd only come close one time. One man had made Natalya glow with something besides satisfaction in a well-chosen partner. The man had also taken a paternal interest in Maxwell as none of his mother's other affairs ever had or been allowed to.

For three years, Maxwell had a father figure show up at his activities, someone as interested in teaching him what it was to be a boy raised in America as his mother and those at the cultural center had been in exposing him to bits of his Russian heritage, someone besides a neighbor the school could call when Maxwell needed to go home early with the flu.

Then Carlyle's estranged wife had returned, along with his real son and daughter, and Maxwell never saw the man again. Natalya lost her glow, but not her determination to give Maxwell every chance life in America had to offer.

"Madison said she thought something about Perry's claims intrigued you." Romi frowned, her gaze searching.

Broken out of the unexpected reverie, Maxwell took a

moment to catch up. Then he said, "You know I like control in bed."

"I figured."

Yes, he hadn't hidden his preferences during their kisses and the touching. "I had no desire to take her to bed, therefore it follows my preference for control wasn't my reason for intrigue."

"Oh." Romi's frown turned to puzzlement. "Then why?"

"I found it interesting that Perry made the claims he did."

"The more salacious the story, the more money they would pay for it." The lovely heiress's tone dripped cynicism.

Maxwell's was a bit more derisive when he said, "Perry Timwater isn't capable of upholding a more dominant role in sex."

"How would you know?"

"I've met him." And what Maxwell had seen of the other man had neither impressed, nor inspired a desire to further their association. "He has neither the confidence, nor the attention to the needs of others to succeed in that role."

"I'm sure he's a selfish lover," Romi said with her customary direct honesty. "He was a very selfish friend."

"You are probably right." Maxwell felt his lips quirking as they often did in her presence.

Romi Grayson always entertained him, even when she didn't mean to. She intrigued him as much because of the attraction he felt for her as the fact she was so unlike him. He didn't understand her.

That was not something Maxwell was used to.

Understanding what motivated people was what made him so good in the business world. He knew how to identify a need and exploit it, without compromising his own sense of honor.

It might not be as shiny and uncomplicated as Viktor's, but Maxwell did have one.

Romi's mercurial nature made her an enigma. He'd been sure she would go for his offer of monogamy of limited duration, but she hadn't. Even more inexplicably, her reaction had told him the offer had hurt her in some way, which he hadn't expected and found he did not like.

"So, why *were* you intrigued?"

"Why do you think?" he prodded, wondering how much she'd really learned about him during their brief time of dating.

She paused and thought, which wasn't something anyone else would have expected from her. She came off as passionate and impetuous, but he'd learned that as much as she might appear to act without thought, Romi rarely ever did.

Finally, she said, "You've got more curiosity than any man I've ever met. The situation didn't make sense to you, something you aren't really on a first-name basis with. So you wanted to understand it."

He nodded, not really surprised she guessed his reaction so easily. He'd learned that she studied him with as much attention as he had any business rival in his career.

"The stories themselves were a puzzle," Maxwell agreed. "Despite both you and Madison Archer's penchant for making it into the media spotlight, neither of you are known for sexual exploits."

Something he should have paid closer attention to before making his offer to her. He should have realized that the reason her sex life was never speculated on in the media was because she didn't have one.

That innocence wasn't going to leave her open to the kind of liaison Maxwell was used to negotiating with his lovers.

Which meant that if he wanted Romi, and the year apart had shown him that at present no one else would suffice, he would have to figure out a different arrangement.

One they could both live with.

If his plans included a measure of what he thought might well be irresistible persuasion, well, his honor didn't require a level playing field.

Winning was key. Full stop.

CHAPTER TWO

"AND YOU FOUND *that* intriguing?" Romi demanded.

Max was amused by the fact she and Madison weren't known for their sexual promiscuity, no doubt following that particular line of reasoning to its correct conclusion. They weren't known for it because they'd never been sexually promiscuous.

The most experience Romi had in that regard had been with Max himself.

"Not so much, no." Max actually managed to look more or less abashed. "It brought to light some home truths. That's all."

"What do you mean?" Like she didn't know.

He *had* worked it out. If there had been anything to write about her or Madison's sex life, media vultures would have done it. Therefore there was *nothing* to write about.

Max's gorgeous features twisted with a cynical smile. "Do you really want me to spell it out for you?"

"Maybe not." Romi stifled a sigh, the certainty that she spent a little too much of her life avoiding those home truths he was talking about pricking at her until it drew blood.

She wanted to talk about the reason her nonexistent lovers were never discussed in the media even less than she wanted to discuss her father's deteriorating condition. Even with Maddie. If Romi pretended everything was okay, maybe it would be.

The fact that she spent a great deal of her waking hours

trying to right injustices and excesses of the world she lived in, but could not face her own family's brokenness, did not escape her.

"What is the matter?" Max asked in a tone she would have called genuine concern from anyone else.

From him? It probably indicated that moment his inner shark smelled blood in the water.

"Nothing."

"That is not true."

"Does it matter?" she asked with a heavy dose of skepticism.

He adjusted her closer. "Yes."

They were just standing there. No enemies, or even pernicious media in sight. And yet, his big, handsome body felt like a shield between her and the rest of the world. That was one of the most dangerous things about Maxwell Black: how safe she felt in his presence.

He was a full-on predator, but he made her feel protected.

Talk about a rich and active fantasy life.

"Why?" Why would her feelings make any difference to him?

How could they? She wasn't anything to him. Not anything at all.

His pewter gaze trapped hers. "You matter to me."

"No. I don't believe you." As a potential bed partner she might have had some value, but they hadn't been anything like friends.

"You will."

"What? Wait…" He was talking like they had a future.

"You look confused, my sweet little activist."

"I'm not *your* anything." And if she needed reminding as much, or more, than he did, well…she wasn't admitting anything out loud.

"Aren't you?"

"No."

"So, you've been dating."

She opened her mouth to say of course she had, but couldn't force word one of the untruth past her lips. Romi might be a professional at avoidance, but tongue-tied only began to describe what happened to her when she tried to tell a bald-faced lie.

Especially to people she cared about. Prevaricate? Yes. Obfuscate? Definitely. Sidestep? She had the full bag of tricks. Out-and-out lie? Not a chance.

"My dating life is none of your business."

"You don't have one."

"So you say." Right. Turn it back on him without confirming or denying. She would have a made a good spy.

Except for that whole "inability to lie" thing.

"I do say. Name one man you have dated since you turned down my offer."

She glared up at Max, wanting so much just to pull a name out of the air. Any name. But she could not do it.

It just wasn't in her. Her dad said she got that trait from her mother. Romi wished she could remember Jenna Grayson, but she'd only been three when her mom died.

"I bet you could name a hundred." Redirection was her friend.

"Not even a half dozen."

He was still a handful ahead of her. "You work too many hours."

It was a problem.

"You think so?"

"I know so." She'd seen the evidence in the short time they'd been dating.

He didn't move, but suddenly he felt closer, like he was taking up more of the space between them than he had been. "Running a company like BIT cannot be done in a forty-hour work week."

"It could if you weren't so intent on being king of the world." She found herself wanting to lean into him and just let him hold her.

How crazy was that?

Max's laughter washed through her, warming in a way even his tuxedo jacket did not. "I promise, I am not trying to be king of the world."

"Just your part of it."

"Well, I have competition."

"So you say." She wasn't sure she believed it.

Maxwell had a ruthless streak that meant he would always be top dog, even if it meant a dirty, bloody battle to get there.

"None of the women I have dated in the past year rated a callback audition."

"Poor them."

Max's smile was predatory and just a little bit devastating. "You think so."

She knew so. Walking away from him had been one of the most difficult things Romi had ever done, but no way was she giving him a chance to own her heart only to break it.

As he was guaranteed to do.

"I enjoyed dating you." A huge understatement, it still came out easily because it was also the truth.

"As I enjoyed our time together."

"Good?" Embarrassed the word had come out more a question than statement, Romi felt a blush crawl up her neck.

"Not good. You turned me down."

"We wanted different things." And apparently she hadn't thought to offer him part of a company to get what she wanted.

Visions of doing just that caused a bubble of hysterical laughter to nearly burst out.

It was all she could do to hold the humor in.

She couldn't hold back a few mocking words however. "Too bad my dad wasn't selling my hand in marriage, huh?"

Max tugged her close, his head tipping down. "I was thinking that exact thing."

"You jerk." She was laughing as she said the words, not meaning them, just responding in kind to his sarcasm.

But it meant her lips were parted when his mouth landed against hers.

Heat suffused her as her traitorous body melted into his without forethought or even permission from the thinking part of her brain. Forced suddenly into blatant recognition of a year's long starvation of her senses, she returned his kiss with a hunger she'd done her best to pretend did not exist.

Voracious now, she had no hope of holding back the tide of feeling crashing over her.

It was the cost of ignoring emotions rather than facing them.

She wanted this man with every fiber of her being, no matter how much her brain told her it was a bad idea.

A spectacularly, out-of-this-world, *really* bad idea.

Her lips did not agree as they moved against his, her tongue eager as it met his, her body pliant to his touch.

She skimmed her hands up his hard chest, mapping the shape of muscles honed by workouts that would make a tri-athlete pause. Singeing her fingertips with electric warmth, the heat of his body translated through the smooth fabric of his dress shirt.

She brushed over tiny, hardened nubs and she reveled in the proof of her effect on him.

With a feral groan, Max flexed his lower body toward hers and she had even more potent proof in the press of his clearly excited, intimidatingly large shaft against her. It couldn't be comfortable for him to be trapped in his clothes in that condition, but he didn't complain or pull away.

Unheeded, his expensive, handmade tuxedo jacket fell from her shoulders as she wrapped her hands around his neck and pressed into him, chest to thigh. Was it possible to feel sparks in every single nerve ending of where her body met his?

She didn't know if it was some kind of domino effect, but that's what it felt like to her.

As her body exploded with delight in that simple but very intimate touch, the kiss went nuclear.

Their mouths ate at each other, his hands moved over her back, down along her sides, over her bottom...everywhere. Hers locked behind his head as she undulated against him—giving friction, receiving the stimulation she needed. It was insane. The way she responded to his nearness, the unending and increasing desire for more and more and more.

Sensations she'd dreamt about almost nightly and pretended to forget in the morning, but hadn't experienced in a year, roared through her in a conflagration as unstoppable as the brush fires that raged in the south every summer.

It burned the walls of her defenses to cinders. All she could do was hold on and hope not to be consumed completely.

It was Max that broke the kiss, Max that took a step back, Max that held her away from him when she would have followed.

Feeling too much desire to be embarrassed, Romi demanded, "Why?"

He wanted her. She'd felt it. If she looked down, she'd see it, even in the dim shadows of the balcony.

"The next time we have sex, it will be in a bed and I won't stop until you've climaxed with me inside you." His breath panted in irregular intervals, but his deep voice was infused with absolute certainty.

She barely bit back the *when* that wanted to pop out of her mouth.

Oh, wow. Yeah. Not a good idea.

But she wanted it. So bad. She shook with the need to continue what they started, for just the experience of being held in his arms again.

"That can't happen." She wished her voice had even a modicum of certainty in it.

Some little bit of the self-preservation that lay in ashes around her.

"That's a lie and you don't do those."

She opened her mouth to deny his words, but darned if he wasn't right. "Please, don't do this to me, Max."

"What don't you want me to do, Romi, my sweet virgin?" Why did those words sound so hot in his voice? "Turn you on? You weren't complaining a second ago."

She couldn't deny it. Wasn't sure she wanted to, even if she could. "Neither were you."

But he'd stopped and she hadn't even thought to try. Darn him.

"No, and I never will."

Why did he have to say things like that? Things that could make her hope when hope and this man did *not* go together. "We still want different things."

"Are you so sure? If I hadn't stopped, you would have let me take you here and now."

He was talking about sex when she was referring to a relationship. And he knew it. "Do you get some sick thrill out of rubbing in my own weakness to me?"

"It's not a weakness, *milaya*."

"So you say." Her words lacked conviction, but he knew what using his Russian endearments on her did to Romi.

It wasn't just the fact he called her lovely, but his possessive claim on her and how he only used this word on her. She'd asked him, annoyed when she thought he was just calling her the same thing he did every other woman he slept with.

He'd admitted he never used the Russian endearments with other women.

She hadn't asked why because he had seemed less than thrilled about the realization and she hadn't wanted him to stop.

Now she wished she had.

"So I know," he responded, no lack of conviction in *his* tone. "Your passion is amazing."

"You stopped." It couldn't have been that amazing.

"Because I want something better for your first time."

"You're making some big assumptions there."

"Are you going to try to deny your innocence?"

"No." And they were back to this again because this man never let Romi run her repertoire of avoidance techniques about the important stuff. "My first time isn't going to be with a man who puts a sell-by date on his girlfriends before the relationship even starts."

"And yet your first time *will* be with me."

"I was talking about you," she informed him sarcastically.

"No. You were talking about a circumstance, not a man."

She stepped away from him and hated how cold that made her feel, and not just because of the goose bumps on her arms. "Are you trying to confuse me on purpose?"

"No, *milaya*. Not at all. I'm just telling the truth."

"And what truth is that?" She was going to regret asking, she just knew it.

"That you will be in my bed very soon."

"Without a sell-by date?" she asked with a tiny kernel of hope that felt almost like a betrayal.

But could he really have spent the last year wanting her like she'd been wanting him, enough to break his own set-in-cement rules?

"Not as a boyfriend."

"What does *that* mean?" Was he trying to say he didn't want any commitment at all?

A one-night stand? For the loss of her virginity? And why was that even a little bit tempting?

He never answered her question, just picked up his suit jacket and shook it out before putting it back on. Quality cut and fabric showed almost no effect from its sojourn on the balcony floor.

Somehow she found herself back inside dancing with the man, ignoring the glares of envy sent her way and doing her best to do the same to her own body's weakness in the face of Max's nearness.

He set out to entertain and charm, succeeding to the point that she let him drive her home instead of calling for her father's car and driver.

He pulled the Maserati, a different one than he'd been driving the year before, to a purring halt in front of her dad's mansion. This one had a backseat.

"Still living with your father?" he asked, though he had to know, or why else would they be here?

"Yes."

Max nodded. "No desire to live on your own?"

"He needs me." It was an admission, but not one that would surprise an American tycoon with surprisingly deep Russian roots.

Romi didn't even share with Maddie how bad things had gotten for her dad, but a year ago? She'd told Maxwell Black.

On their second date. Maybe that was why he'd put the sell-by date on their relationship after their third one.

But no, that was just the way Max ran his love life, or sex life really. The man didn't believe in love. Well, that wasn't quite accurate.

He believed the emotion was real enough, just refused to ever let himself feel it.

Romi wished *she* had the ability to turn her heart off.

But it was never going to happen.

"You are a good daughter." His pewter eyes warmed with sincerity.

It was almost surreal. "What, no admonishment to leave him to work it out on his own?"

"What have I ever said that implied I did not take the obligations of family seriously?" Max actually sounded a little offended.

Feeling convicted for letting her own insecurities spill over onto him, Romi said, "Nothing."

She knew he cared deeply for his mother.

Max had never been hesitant to admit he supported Natalya Black financially. They might live separately, but Romi had no doubt that if his mother needed to live with him, they would be sharing a residence right now. No questions, no lesser options.

"We share a dedication to family."

"What we have of them," she agreed.

Romi didn't know why, but Max and his mother had no connection to their family back in Russia. He'd never mentioned his father, much less the man's family, so Romi had always assumed they were either all gone or like her father's family.

Estranged.

"I still see my mom's family yearly." Unlike the Graysons, who had turned their back on Harry when he'd married a woman from a decidedly middle-class background instead of old money, the Lawtons had remained in their daughter's life and that of her husband and child.

Albeit on a more limited basis than Romi had always wanted.

"Why only once a year?" Max asked, like he was reading her mind.

She shrugged, looking away from him. "They only came to visit when my mom was alive. Since then, I've gone to stay with my grandparents for a couple of weeks every summer."

But she and her father had never been invited to share the major holidays with them. Romi didn't know if that was because he'd made it clear in some way he wasn't interested, or if they weren't, and she'd never really tried to find out.

It was enough she got a taste of the family that had made her mom the person she'd been. Even if that person was someone Romi would never know.

She'd enjoyed the different kind of living, sharing a room
with the sewing machine and her grandmother's craft projects, sleeping on the floor in the family room with her cousins when they stayed over. No servants, no cars and drivers,
no shopping in exclusive boutiques.

Lots of summer barbecues, playing in a yard maintained
better by her grandfather than any gardener her dad had
ever employed.

"Why don't any of them come to visit you?" Max asked.

She didn't really know, but had made her own internal
excuses. "It's a long trip."

"A few hours by plane."

"Still."

"It's a different world for them, isn't it?"

She nodded. She'd finally come to realize as an adult that
her mom's family found her life as an heiress—her bedroom
that was a three-room suite in a multimillion-dollar mansion, all of the trappings of wealth—too foreign for comfort.

She thought maybe they hadn't been any happier that
Jenna had married Harry than the Graysons. The Lawtons
just hadn't turned their backs on their daughter.

Her grandparents were political activists like Romi, but
unlike her, they had little affection or respect for the people
that had populated Romi's life since birth.

Old money wealth, *big business*, they were dirty words
to her grandparents.

Romi had always wanted to make a difference, but she'd
never felt the need to destroy the system to rebuild it.

Her grandparents had spent a month living in a tent during Occupy Wall Street. Her aunts and uncles weren't as
antiwealth and antiestablishment, but made no bones about
the fact they preferred their suburban lives over Romi's in
San Francisco.

"Your cousins could come to visit, couldn't they?" Max
asked, like it mattered to him.

She didn't know why it should. Romi shrugged. "I'm not as close with them as I was when I was little."

Not like they were to each other.

Her mother had been the youngest and all of her cousins were at least five years older than Romi. Most were married with children, all were established in careers and lives that did not lend themselves to visiting a single cousin cross country that they barely knew.

Max made a sound that in anyone else would have been a sigh. He made it seem more like a nonverbal admission. "My family turned their back on my mother because she chose to break with tradition."

"She married an American?"

"No."

"But Black…"

"Is not a Russian name. She changed it from Blokov when she immigrated with me. She wanted no reminder of the family who found it so easy to reject her because she lived her life differently than they wanted her to."

"I'm sorry. She's a pretty neat lady."

Romi had met Natalya Black at more than one charity function she'd attended with her son. Romi had found the older Russian woman still quite beautiful and very charming.

"She is pragmatic."

"She raised you. I imagine she is." Romi had never known anyone as compartmentalized and rationally logical as Max.

Max quirked his brow. "Is that a compliment or a complaint?"

"Neither, really." Romi grinned cheekily. "It just is."

"Now, you sound like a proper Russian pragmatist."

"What about your dad?" Romi asked, surprised at herself.

But she'd regretted all the questions she hadn't asked a year ago too much to make the same mistake again.

"My mother has never named him, though I have often thought his name must be something similar to mine, as Maxwell is hardly Russian."

"Maybe she just wanted to break away from her home-land and embrace her new life in America."

"We emigrated when I was a year old."

"Oh."

He smiled, no indication the discussion hurt him. "Some things just are, right?"

"Right." But somehow she was sure this man would never allow a child of his to grow up not even knowing his name.

They said good-night, with Max's assertion he would see her again soon sounding more like a threat than a promise.

CHAPTER THREE

MAXWELL DRANK A glass of very good champagne and watched Romi Grayson fulfill her role as maid of honor for Madison Beck, née Archer, with her usual flair.

Adorned with a tiara every bit as ornate, if significantly smaller than Madison's, Romi's smooth bob of hair glistened in a fall of black silk around her face. Large but tasteful diamonds in a classic setting twinkled in her earlobes. She wore no other jewelry with the designer silk gown of blue that exactly matched her pretty eyes and was cut to complement Madison's 1950s vintage gown.

Romi flicked a look at him and he made no effort to hide the fact he watched her. Pleasure zinged through him at the blush that tinted her cheeks.

She looked away, but her azure gaze returned to meet his almost immediately.

He let one eyelid slide closed in a slow wink, allowing his lips to almost tilt into a smile.

The blush darkened and he could see the breath she took. Imagining he could hear the soft gasp of air that followed, he started across the room toward her.

A hand landed on his arm and he barely broke stride to shake his head decisively at a woman he'd flirted with previously on a couple of occasions. The sister of a man who owned one of the major companies in Silicon Valley, she was a contact worth cultivating.

But not right now.

Romi had not moved so much as an inch since he'd started toward her, waiting as if she stood inside a bubble of her own.

No one approached her when she'd spent the last hours talking to *everyone*. But there was something ethereal about her in that moment and Maxwell knew he wasn't the only one who felt it.

He stopped in front of her, his hand out. "Dance with me."

This time he heard the small catch of air. "I…"

"You know you want to."

"We don't always want what is best for us."

He shook his head, not buying it. "No word games right now, Romi. Just dance with me."

"You are demanding."

He shrugged and pulled her into his arms, not surprised when she didn't object and not even a little shocked when her body unhesitatingly molded to his. They reacted to each other in a physical way that was almost mystical.

If he believed in that sort of thing.

The music was slow and he pulled her body close into the shelter of his own so they could move together in a special kind of intimacy.

"Did you enjoy the wedding?" she asked in the soft tone that haunted his dreams.

"How did you know I was in attendance?" The invitation to the reception had not surprised Maxwell, but the invite to the wedding had.

He knew it was Viktor's doing. Or perhaps the older Becks. They considered Maxwell *family* by dint of their shared heritage and years spent as friendly neighbors.

"I seem to have some kind of homing device where you are concerned," Romi admitted in a voice that didn't sound either particularly happy or bothered by that reality. "I'm pretty sure Maddie didn't know you were there."

"It was predominately family." The other heiress wouldn't have been looking for his face among her other guests.

"Yes." It was a statement, but with a question underlying the agreement.

"I grew up with Viktor."

"I didn't know that." Romi looked up, her blue eyes searching his face. "It should be hard to imagine you as a child, but it isn't."

"I do not know why. Everyone is a child at some point."

"Are you sure?" she teased.

He frowned, but he wasn't actually even a little annoyed. "I spent time in diapers and playing in sandboxes just like anyone else. I promise."

"No popping fully formed into existence as a corporate tycoon?" she taunted.

"You are feeling feisty, aren't you?"

She shrugged. "I just like teasing you."

"I noticed." No one else but his mother ever had.

And Natalya Black was too practical to be playful all that often, even with her only child.

"I was a child like everyone else," he assured her. "You said yourself you could picture it."

Her smile was nothing short of wicked. "A child surely, but not like everyone else. Not you."

"I was. I even wanted to be a fireman when I was a little boy." A common aspiration among his classmates.

Romi grinned. "I wanted to be a princess."

He was charmed. "Right now, you look like you got your wish."

She laughed, the sound joyous and instantly addictive. He couldn't help but join her.

"Did you really say something so naff?"

"What is naff about it?" But he knew. In any other instance, he'd think another man telling a woman she looked like a princess was completely cheesy.

The truth made it something else.

"You said I look like a princess," she pointed out with patent disbelief and a lot of leftover humor.

"I did."

Her eyes widened innocently, and she asked, "Aren't you even a little embarrassed?"

"Corporate kings don't get embarrassed, didn't you know that? Especially when we speak the truth."

She gasped and went silent for several seconds before asking, "When did you realize you'd rather be king than a firefighter?"

Oh, she did like avoiding things that made her uncomfortable. He only let her get away with it sometimes. This would be one of them.

It should be an easy question to answer, but Maxwell realized he wasn't sure when he'd given up his aspirations of saving lives and instead decided he wanted a different kind of power. "Somewhere between wanting to be a super hero and realizing Batman had to be as rich as the royal family to do the things he did."

"Did you ever stop wanting to be a superhero?"

"Corporate kings don't save the world."

"Don't they?" She was very serious all of a sudden. "Black Information Technologies is one of the most sustainable of the Fortune 500 companies."

"It's a matter of practicality."

"Why did I know you'd say something like that?"

"Because I grew out of my desire to be Batman."

"Good. His backstory is too dark anyway."

He laughed, once again delighted by her outlook.

Romi grew serious. "I can't imagine a company like BIT springing up out of a half-baked idea and a lot of ingenuity."

"No. I planned the start of the company and its trajectory very carefully from the very beginning." He'd begun the plans the day he learned of the final concession his mother had negotiated from his father.

A multimillion-dollar settlement for Maxwell on his eighteenth birthday.

Maxwell wasn't supposed to know who his father was. Growing up, all he'd been able to guess was the man had been rich and powerful enough to facilitate his former mistress's immigration to America.

Maxwell had assumed his father had been American as well, though his mother's plans to move to this country could well have had nothing to do with the homeland of her son's father. Maxwell had learned he was right when he'd hired Sebastian Hawk's international security and detective agency to find out who the man was.

Hawk's agency was *the* organization to go to for security and information. Maxwell had gone to them when he'd first opened his company and had met the owner a year later. Sebastian Hawk was a self-made millionaire who still took an interest in how his company was run.

Maxwell had more than doubled his initial capital and wanted to return the settlement to the father who had never had an interest in meeting, much less recognizing, his son.

Maxwell had discovered his father was a high-ranking diplomat from a very powerful and obscenely wealthy American family with public servant ties back to the revolutionary era. Married, with children older than his illegitimate son, the man had had a great deal to lose if Maxwell's existence came to light.

Pointedly changing the direction of his own thoughts, Maxwell said, "I stopped wanting to be a fireman after visiting the fire station on a school field trip."

"That's funny." Romi tilted her head to the side and observed him with interest even as her body moved against his to the rhythm of the music. "That's when kids usually decide they want to be one."

"Most of the other children in my class did. I've never wanted to be part of a crowd."

"So you decided you couldn't be a fireman because everyone else wanted to be one?" she asked, humor lacing her lovely voice.

"Exactly."

She grinned. "You wanted to be special."

"Are you saying I am not?"

"Oh, no, Your Majesty," she said facetiously. "You are definitely in a class all by yourself."

"Not alone maybe, but not like *everyone* else."

"Firefighters are actually a very small percentage of our population." She pointed out that fact like maybe he didn't know.

"Yes, they are a rarified breed as well, and definitely to be admired and respected. However, I like control far too much to have a job dealing with either nature's vagaries or that of human error, which I have no power to prevent."

"There is that." Romi shook her head. "Have you always been such a control freak?"

"My mother would say yes."

Romi didn't appear bothered by that admission. "I kind of like you this way."

He wondered if she would say that after he laid out his latest plan for her.

"I am glad," he said.

"Although I think the more appropriate term would be *Corporate Tsar* rather than *King*."

"You think so? Because I was born in Russia?"

"Because you have the heart of a tsar, I think."

He could not deny it.

He kept her in his arms by the simple expedient of continuing to dance for another thirty minutes. Even during the faster music and she never complained.

A couple of men tried to cut in, but Maxwell refused to offer the polite retreat and simply danced her away. When a woman tried the same, wanting to dance with him, he turned her down as well.

"You really aren't controlled by social niceties, are you?" Romi asked after the last one.

"You knew this about me."

She nodded with something like satisfaction. "I'll admit, I don't mind in this instance."

"I'm glad to hear that, but admit to being curious as to why." Just something about the way she'd spoken, he thought there was a story behind her words.

"Have you ever danced with JD?" she asked, referring to the last man Maxwell had simply ignored in his attempt to partner Romi.

Maxwell gave a short bark of laughter. "No."

"He's grabby. Though I suppose if he danced with you he wouldn't be." Her giggle was very smug.

"You think you are funny, don't you?"

"Why yes, I do."

Maxwell's eyes narrowed. "You're saying he tried to touch you?"

"Nothing serious. He just pretends he doesn't realize my waist is several inches above the curve of my behind."

"I'll break his hand." Maxwell was shocked by the words. Not the sentiment. He knew he was unacceptably protective of this woman, but to express it out loud wasn't something he usually did.

"Not necessary." She snuggled in. "I can be a very klutzy dancer when I need to be."

The effort it took to hold back further imprecations did not make him happy.

Romi allowed herself to relax in Maxwell's arms while they danced longer than she probably should have. But it felt so good, so *safe*.

Eventually, she had to look up and scan the room for her dad.

He was talking to Jeremy Archer, his movements animated, on the verge of exaggerated, and his expression belligerent.

Not good.

Stifling her regret at the action, Romi pushed herself away from Max. "I need to go check on my father."

The self-made tycoon didn't argue, for which she was grateful.

She wasn't sure how she felt a second later, though, when he said, "I'll come with you."

"That's not necessary," she said by rote rather than from feeling.

He didn't bother to reply, just took her arm and started toward Jeremy and Romi's dad.

Harry Grayson's voice was elevated, his speech slightly slurred. "I don't need your advice, Jeremy. One of us actually grieved the passing of his wife. It's affected my business, but I'm far from bankrupt."

This was not good. Anytime her dad started talking about Romi's deceased mother, things had a way of sliding downhill fast.

Preparing to intervene, Romi was nonplussed when Max's deep voice dropped into the tense silence. "Good evening, gentlemen. May I offer my congratulations, Jeremy? Madison makes a beautiful bride and Viktor Beck is a very good man."

His eyes widened in surprise, but the business mogul nodded his gray head in acknowledgement. "Thank you, Black."

Romi ignored Jeremy Archer in favor of her own father, and not just because it was clear the time had come to go. But she hadn't forgiven Jeremy for the way he treated Madison when the whole Perry debacle happened.

Romi had never thought the man was much of a father before that, but her opinion of him had dropped even lower.

"Dad," she said to Harry Grayson, "I'm getting tired. I'd like to go, if that's all right."

Her father turned a confused gaze on her. "You were having fun dancing."

"But I wore her out," Max smoothly inserted, with one of those conspiratorial smiles men seemed so adept at giving each other.

Particularly the men she knew.

Her dad gave Jeremy an angry look and then nodded at Romi. "Okay, kitten. I'll call for the car."

"No need. I'm happy to drop you both off."

"In your Maserati?" While he no longer drove the two-door, purely sporty model, and this one had a backseat, Max had been drinking champagne before they started dancing.

"I've got a car and driver and I've already texted him. He'll be waiting for us when we get outside."

"You're very efficient." And Romi wasn't sure she meant that as a compliment.

The wry twist to Max's lips said he guessed that. "Oh, I am."

"A little too coldly efficient, if you ask me," Jeremy Archer had the audacity to say.

"Says the man with antifreeze instead of blood pumping through his veins," her dad said with surprising clarity, both of thought and speech.

Jeremy's face contorted with annoyance. "You need to go home and let your daughter pour you into bed, Gray."

"What I need—" her father started to say.

"We'll chalk this conversation up to the tactlessness that can come from longstanding friendship," Max said in a tone that warned his patience was not limitless. "Agreed?"

In a move that shocked Romi, both her dad and Jeremy nodded. Grudgingly, but they agreed all the same.

"Good." Max gave Jeremy a look that Romi couldn't quite interpret. "From now on, you don't need to worry about the viability of Grayson Enterprises. It is not up for grabs, nor will it be facing bankruptcy anytime in the near or distant future."

Wow. That was quiet a promise. And an odd one for Max to make.

Her dad hadn't said anything about BIT and Grayson going into business together, but his expression didn't look nearly as confused as Romi felt.

In fact, the expression he'd turned toward his oldest friend and sometimes rival was nothing short of triumphant. "That's right, and Romi's not *my* investment capital in this deal, either."

What deal? What had her father and Max been talking about?

Jeremy looked first startled and then concerned. "You're merging?"

But her dad didn't answer, finally showing some sense of discretion. He even congratulated Jeremy on his daughter's marriage. "They're a good, solid couple, no matter how they got together."

Romi believed that, too. It was the only reason she'd accepted Maddie's request to be her maid of honor. Her SBC deserved the best and a chance at true happiness.

Romi believed Viktor Beck was that for Maddie.

Maddie didn't try to convince her to stay longer when Romi told her they were leaving. She didn't even voice concern at the fact Romi and her father were doing so in the company of Maxwell Black.

Maddie just hugged her hard and thanked Romi for being the best sister a woman could ever choose *or* be born with.

When they arrived at her home, Max walked to the door with Romi and her father.

He stopped outside. "I'm not going to come in tonight, but I'll be by tomorrow morning to talk."

Romi wasn't sure if he was talking to her or her dad, but Harry nodded so she figured it was him.

"I'll look forward to it," her dad said before stepping inside.

Max nodded, his masculine lips set in a firm line. Then

he turned to Romi. "I would like to take you to lunch afterward."

"Oh, I—"

"The time for running is done, Ramona. We have things we need to discuss."

She didn't bother telling him she didn't like being addressed by her full name. That minor annoyance was nothing compared to the threat of *talking*. "We did all our discussing a year ago."

"Circumstances change."

She wrapped her arms around herself, trying to hold the heat in. "I'm pretty sure ours haven't."

"And yet I am requesting your company all the same." He reached out and tucked her wrap more tightly around her.

"Sounds more like a demand to me."

He shrugged. "I have been accused."

"Yeah. That's believable."

"Then believe me when I tell you that we have things, important things, we need to discuss." He brushed the back of his fingers down her cheek.

Romi shivered, but not from the cold this time. "What are they?"

"I'm sure you can guess."

"Max…" But she didn't know what she wanted to say, where she wanted *this* conversation to go.

She'd spent a year doing her best to forget Maxwell Black and it hadn't worked.

The silence stretched between them before he leaned down and kissed her firmly, but quickly. "Tomorrow, Romi. Block out your afternoon."

"For lunch?" she asked breathlessly and unable to do a thing about that fact.

"For me."

"I'm not making any promises, Max."

"I am, Romi. Both to myself and to you. You will be mine."

The words should have made her nervous. Should have scared her right of her wits really, but Romi liked them too much. Her secret fantasies all revolved around this man.

She touched her lips, still tingling from the kiss. "Tomorrow."

Without another word, Max turned and went down the steps with a purposeful stride.

Romi moved restlessly in her bed. She'd left her father sleeping on the sofa in his study, the usual wool throw covering him.

She should be thinking about her best friend and the irrevocable step Maddie had taken in marrying Viktor Beck. Or if not that, Romi should be worrying about the problems with her dad's company that Jeremy Archer clearly felt worth accosting her father over at his own daughter's wedding reception.

But all of that bubbled in its own cauldron of stress at the periphery of the thoughts consuming her.

Maxwell Black said she was going to be his.

He knew she wanted a commitment. The hope of a future, not a guarantee, but at least the possibility. Okay *probability*. But she wasn't looking for promises as much as the likelihood of them being made down the road.

None of which had he been willing to offer a year ago.

No, he'd presented the possibility of six months to a year of sexual pleasure and intermittent companionship, with the clear and nonnegotiable understanding that they would go their separate ways after a year.

She'd turned him down flat.

And it had not been easy, though she'd tried very hard not to let Max see just how difficult she'd found it to utter that single-syllable word. *No.*

But her heart had been on the line and she was smart enough to know it.

She hadn't suddenly gone stupid, so why had she agreed to meet with Max?

Romi didn't have a reason, at least not a good one.

She still wanted him. She still found him the most intriguing and attractive man she'd ever met.

Maxwell Black was her Kryptonite and that scared the willies out of her.

Some people, after growing up the way she had, watching her dad pine for her dead mother and slowly come apart, would have been determined never to go through that themselves.

Romi had taken the opposite view. She wanted that kind of devotion directed at her. She knew what it was to be loved.

Her dad was flawed. Some might even say weak, but he loved Romi with the best that was in him.

His drinking had taken its toll, but it hadn't all been bad. Harry Grayson had given his daughter the finest he had to give and she was grateful.

His company might have suffered, but she'd never once doubted her dad's love.

She was determined that the man she married one day would love her with that same kind of devotion. Hopefully *without* a past grief to overcome and an addiction to alcohol.

Max's intensity and dedication to her pleasure had tricked her into thinking once that he might just be that guy.

He'd disabused her of that belief. With prejudice. No matter how he saw it.

So, why was she meeting him tomorrow?

Because she couldn't help herself.

For the daughter of an alcoholic that was not just a little worrisome.

That was terrifying.

She had to wrest back control of her life.

Because she *wasn't* her dad.

Romi was her own person, with her own strengths and

her own weaknesses. She wasn't going to let Max be one of them.

Even if she craved him with a desire embedded to the very marrow of her bones.

Maybe what she needed was her own deal.

Her own offer with a set of parameters that weren't going to leave her heart bleeding out when he walked away.

CHAPTER FOUR

MAXWELL WALKED INTO Harry Grayson's study, with the certain knowledge that he was looking forward to his lunch meeting with Romi much more.

However, this one was necessary if he wanted the next one to end the way he planned for it to.

Dressed casually in a sweater over his dress shirt and tie, his trousers creased perfectly, Harry Grayson's slightly reddened eyes were the only indicator of his excesses the night before. "Good morning, Maxwell. Have a seat. I'll ring for coffee."

"Thank you." In other circumstances, Maxwell might have refused the offer of hospitality, but he was sure the older man could do with a shot of caffeine.

Maxwell was actually a little relieved that things hadn't progressed to the point where Grayson had offered him a drink at nine in the morning. He waited quietly while Grayson called his housekeeper and ordered a tray of the hot beverage.

Grayson's hand trembled only slightly as he hung up the phone. "I looked over the contract you sent over."

"Good." That was another positive sign.

"It's a favorable contract."

"To both parties." Maxwell didn't do charity when it came to business.

"Why?"

"What?"

"Why Grayson Enterprises? Surely there are better companies for this sort of merger. Black Information Technologies isn't just solvent. You're growing with ROIs other companies would kill for in this climate."

"Yes." Maxwell didn't deny it.

There was no point. He'd worked hard, and smart, to make his company what it was today.

"So, you have nearly unlimited options for this kind of merger. I'm not so blind I don't realize my company probably isn't the best of them."

"I plan to marry your daughter."

The stark words hit the older man like a blow. He sat back in his chair like Maxwell's strike had been physical rather than verbal. "I'm not Jeremy Archer. I'm not selling my daughter to insure the future of my company."

"And I am not trying to buy her." Not that Maxwell considered Viktor's marriage to Madison in that light.

The man wanted control of AIH, but he wanted the woman, too.

"Do you love her?" Grayson demanded.

"That is between Romi and myself."

"She's my daughter. I want her to be happy."

"Do you?"

"Of course I do. How can you ask that? I'm no Jeremy Archer," he said again, like that particular point was one that needed making. Maybe it was. To him. "I'm not selling Romi to save a company that isn't on the brink of bankruptcy, no matter what that bastard likes to imply."

Maxwell didn't bother reminding Grayson he'd already said as much. No matter how together he *looked*, going to bed drunk night after night took its toll on the man's thought processes.

"But you are vulnerable to takeover." The fact Maxwell didn't have to be here making a merger offer could be left unspoken.

Grayson wasn't stupid, even if he wasn't thinking with the same sharp reasoning he'd once been known for.

Just nearly constantly inebriated.

"Romi isn't part of this deal."

Did he think if he kept saying it that would make it truer? "No, she isn't, but your sobriety is."

"What? That wasn't in the contract." Grayson looked down at the contract Maxwell's office had sent over two days before like it might jump up and attack.

Maxwell pulled a sheaf of papers from his briefcase. "No, it's in the codicil I've got here."

Last night he'd realized that Romi might well need more than the impetus he'd arranged for her acquiescence to his plans. If he wanted to give Romi something more than just saving her father's company from the other predators, he would keep that particular motivation to himself.

Grayson paled sickly as he read the codicil. "I don't have to agree to this. My life is my business."

"And yet I've decided to make it *my* business."

"Like my company."

"Would you rather be having this discussion with Jeremy Archer?"

"More like Viktor Beck."

"Viktor wouldn't consider the merger. He'd go for the takeover." Because in his own way, Viktor Beck was every bit as ruthless as Maxwell Black.

"I'm not going into rehab."

Maxwell didn't argue. He knew better.

Instead, he asked, "Have you considered how much your death from alcoholism-related disease will hurt your daughter?"

"She's an adult."

"Who would grieve your loss, with guilt she would never let go of. She's got a very tender heart."

"You don't have to tell me that." Grayson glared, fraying around the edges. "She's *my* daughter."

"Then you should know how your actions affect her."

"I'm not her responsibility. That's not how it works." But his words lacked conviction.

As well they should. Romi took care of her father and if he didn't see that, Grayson was being willfully blind.

"Are you saying you consider her yours?" he asked the older man.

"Yes, of course."

"Even though she's an adult?"

"Yes," the other man ground out.

"Then you owe her your sobriety."

"It's not that easy."

"Life never is."

"I miss her mother, damn it."

Maxwell *didn't* say that the older man spent too much of his time pickled with alcohol to miss anyone. Though he thought it. Or maybe it was the constant inebriation that made it impossible for the older Grayson to move on with his life.

His maudlin inability to move beyond his grief might well be fed by the alcoholism and not just vice versa.

But all Maxwell said was, "The deal depends on you going into rehab and staying until the doctor releases you."

"That's not going to happen." Grayson tossed the papers on his desk with a jerky movement. "There's not even a time limit."

"No, there isn't. You're staying until you have developed a new way to handle your grief."

"It's not just about grief. Not anymore," Grayson surprised Maxwell by admitting.

He'd known that, but he had not realized the older man was that self-aware.

"All the more reason to fix the problem now." Maxwell wasn't offering an out.

"It's not just a problem you can *fix*."

"I disagree."

"Then you go to rehab."

"I don't need it. You do." The man didn't need coddling.

He got enough of that and sweet understanding from his daughter. It was time for Harry Grayson to be the man Romi thought he was.

Grayson said with a lousy attempt at defiance, "I don't have to sign this contract."

"And I don't have to merge with your company. I can take it over without your cooperation. That's not what's at stake here."

"What is?"

"Visiting time with Romi."

"What the hell are you talking about?"

"You aren't going to keep hurting her. One way or another." Maxwell was under no illusion it would be easy to stage an intervention in Romi's life with her dad, but she was strong.

She would want Harry Grayson healthy more than her own comfort, no matter how much she might rather avoid the problem.

"She won't let you take her away from me." The words were strong, but the worried expression that accompanied them said Grayson wasn't as confident as they sounded.

"You underestimate my powers of persuasion." Maxwell, on the other hand, had no doubts about his own abilities.

"You underestimate her loyalty and strength of love."

"She won't be the one saying goodbye. *You* will."

Showing his brain still functioned, Grayson stopped arguing. "You'll do whatever you have to do to get your way."

"You know my reputation."

"I do. It's why your offer of a merger surprised me."

"Accept what I offer."

"Why? So you don't have to *take* what you want?"

"For Romi's sake."

The other man's face crumpled. "She's a good daughter."

"She deserves a healthy father."

"You must care about her or you wouldn't be pushing this."

Maxwell didn't know if Grayson was trying to convince himself or Maxwell, and he didn't care. He simply waited for the older man to agree to Maxwell's terms.

"Fine. I'll sign the contract. And the codicil."

"Good."

Maxwell made a call and his bodyguard and personal administrative assistant came in to witness the contract. As a licensed notary, his secondary assistant notarized the contract, too.

Cold-bloodedly efficient? Maybe.

But it worked for him.

"You're almost scarily resourceful."

Maxwell didn't deny it.

Grayson was cursing that truth fifteen minutes later when his bags were packed and Maxwell assigned him a bodyguard-babysitter that would make sure the other man would end up in the rehab center and stay there.

Romi breezed into the house at five minutes after noon, feeling anything but breezy.

But living by the mantra Never Let Them See You Sweat, she strove for nonchalance as she walked into the living room, where Mrs. K had told Romi she would find *Mr. Black* waiting for her.

His suit jacket removed and tossed over the back of a chair, his tie loosened and tailored slacks stretched attractively across his muscular thighs, Max relaxed on the sofa. The Grayson family photo albums covered the coffee table in front of him.

Max looked up from the one open in his lap. "Your mother was a beautiful woman."

"Yes, she was." Romi set her handbag down and crossed the room.

"You take after her." He offered her a view of the album that required she sit beside him to see it.

It would have been churlish to refuse, so she didn't. Tugging the hem of her tunic dress into place, Romi settled next to him. "Thank you, but most people think I look like my dad's side of the family."

"No." Maxwell gave a decisive shake of his head. "Your eyes are not only the same color as hers, but the same almond shape as well."

"She was a brunette." Romi's hair was the same color as her Grandmother Grayson's had been in her youth. Not that she'd ever met the family matriarch.

"You can see that it was the same fine texture. Like silk…" Max made the words a caress. "And it was straight like yours."

He grasped some strands of her hair between thumb and forefinger before sliding them down, maybe to show how *silky* her hair was?

For all the time Romi had spent studying the pictures of her mom, she'd never seen the things Max pointed out.

"I'm a shrimp compared to her." Four inches taller than her daughter, Jenna Grayson had been a willowy beauty.

"Same pixie-shaped face." He pointed to the pointed line of her mom's jaw. "See?"

Romi found herself nodding, caught by his sincerity.

"You also have the same way of holding your head when you are amused. Look at this picture, and this one." He grabbed one of the other albums.

"You really have been studying these. How long have you been waiting for me?" she asked, touched in a way she didn't want to admit.

Max set the album down and gave Romi a look she didn't understand, like he was trying to read something in her face. "Your father and I finished our business nearly two hours ago."

"And you waited all that time for me?"

"Yes."

"Why not leave and come back?" Or at least work on his table here? Why spend the time going through her family's photo history?

"I found enough to occupy myself."

He had, but certainly nothing she would have considered Maxwell Black spending his morning doing. It was just so *domestic*. And of all the words she'd used to describe this man, *domestic* was not one of them.

No matter how much he might care about his mother, she'd never thought of him as a *family* guy.

The strange intimacy of the moment getting to her, Romi stood up. "Let me just check in with my dad and then we can go to lunch." She didn't offer to change her clothes.

She'd worn a 1960s-inspired tunic dress in a bright pattern of yellow and white circles on a black background with leggings in the same shade of yellow when she left the house this morning. She'd had a strategy meeting with the local chapter of her favorite environmentalist group early that morning and then coffee with a woman instrumental in starting a series of successful charter schools around the country.

She couldn't believe her and Maddie's dream of starting their own charter school was so close to realization. Viktor Beck had offered to buy them a building as a wedding gift to Maddie.

Pretty wonderful, really.

Another reason Romi thought the guy might well be the right one for her best friend.

If her clothes were good enough for her meetings, they were good enough for Max.

She wasn't going to try to sex up the outfit.

Max stood as well. "Your father is not here."

"What?" He'd gone into the office? Today? "I thought—"

"You know we had a business discussion today."

"Yes."

"It went well."

"Good." She didn't have much else to add. "I don't really have much to do with Grayson Enterprises."

In case he didn't already realize that, but her dad had never once suggested Romi give up activism and her dream of running a charter school for the corporate world.

Max nodded, but he said, "I think in this instance, you will be interested in the outcome."

"Why?"

"Because it will affect you."

"I don't think so." Not in any way that really mattered.

Romi didn't have anything like the Madison family trust, but her Grandfather Grayson had left her enough money to help finance her dream of the school. She'd been shocked when the lawyers contacted her when she was a sophomore in college, but not too proud to take the money.

Even back then, she and Maddie had been talking dreams and Romi had known she needed money to get them off the ground.

Her dad had started his own trust for her on her birth.

She wasn't the heiress Maddie was, but Romi couldn't care less if her dad sold off his company. He didn't spend enough time there anymore for her to think it really mattered to him, either.

"I don't really care if he sells the business to you outright."

"Madison Beck cares what happens to Grayson Enterprises, very much in fact." Max's words came out in a warning tone.

"What?" Romi shook her head, but the words made no sense. "What in the world does that mean? Maddie doesn't care about business any more than I do."

"No, but she cares a great deal for you."

"I know that." They were sisters in everything but blood.

"And you care about her."

"You know I do."

Maxwell nodded his head, his pewter eyes reflecting both satisfaction and certainty. Or was that determination?

Whatever it was, it sent a frisson of something up Romi's spine. She couldn't call it fear because it felt way too much like anticipation.

Maddie always said Romi had an overdeveloped sense of adventure. Coming from Madcap Madison, the risk-taking heiress, that was saying something.

"Are you ready for lunch?" Max asked, as if he hadn't just been making cryptic comments latent with portent about her father's company and Romi's SBC.

"I think so?"

"Is that a question or a statement?" he prodded with some amusement.

"I'm not sure." In fact, she was fairly sure this lunch idea was a bad one, but she *had* come up with her deal and now was as good a time as any to proffer it to him. "You're an enigmatic guy, Max."

"And you wear your every thought on your lovely face."

"Opposites attract?"

His laughter was real and warm, a sound she knew very few ever heard. She treasured the moment despite her sense of confusion.

"Let's go. We will eat lunch."

"And talk." He'd said so.

"Yes."

"I have a deal for you," she offered, to show he wasn't the only one with plans for the future the other didn't know about.

"Do you?" he asked, still half-amused, but also clearly intrigued.

"Yep."

"You'll have to tell me about it in the car."

She considered talking about what she wanted to in the car. "Did you drive yourself?"

"Didn't you see the Maserati outside?"

"I wasn't really paying attention." She'd been thinking about what she was going to offer Max and practicing her nonchalance.

"I drove myself."

"Then we can talk in the car."

"So this deal has a private component?" he asked in a teasing tone.

She didn't hesitate to admit, "Very private."

"Interesting."

Here was hoping.

She'd noticed the other night that the Maserati was new, not the same car he'd had when they were dating before. More differences were apparent in the light of day.

His previous car had been luxurious, but this one was gorgeous and a little bigger. Was that just because it was a four-door?

"Please tell me you don't trade your cars as often as your bed partners."

He laughed as he pulled out of the circular drive in front of her home. "Not at all. I had my last car for five years before I bought this one."

"Wow, that's actually a long time. So, you are capable of longer-term commitment."

He didn't laugh like she expected. "A car is an investment, not a commitment."

So he still didn't like the *C* word. She wasn't surprised. "A sports car is an indulgence is what it is."

"The Maserati is an extremely well-made car."

"With impressive racing lines and an *über*-powerful engine." Even she was impressed by it.

He shrugged. "I don't mind the luxury, either."

"You'd be kinder to the environment if you drove a hybrid."

He actually shuddered. "No thank you."

She bit back laughter. "Many of the newer hybrids are more powerful than the earliest models."

"I will make you a deal, Romi."

"Yes."

"When Maserati designs a hybrid, I will buy it."

She smiled. "Deal."

"Until then, we'll settle for their foray into the more environmentally conscious diesel engine."

"This is a diesel?"

"Yes."

"Hybrid would be better." Many environmentalists would actually disagree and she was sure he knew it, but she couldn't stop herself teasing him.

"Says you. We will have to agree to leave it up to you to drive the *greener* vehicles."

"I don't have a car at all."

"Your father's driver is at your disposal and if I am not mistaken, your father has a Daimler."

"I ride public transport most of the time. I only use Dad's car and driver when I have to dress up."

"What?" Max demanded, his tone sharp. "You ride public transport?"

"Yes." She grinned, feeling a little smug at his reaction.

"At night?" he asked with credible horror.

"Sometimes."

His jaw looked hewn from granite. "That is not safe."

"We aren't the Rockefeller branch of the Graysons, you know? Dad and I don't even have bodyguards."

Max swore. In Russian. It was kind of cute.

"Don't worry about it. San Francisco has a very confusing transportation system, but I've got it down. I know the fastest route everywhere I need to get in the city."

"You need a keeper." He didn't sound like he was joking.

"Are you applying for the job?"

He swore again. This time in English.

"Is that a *no?*" she pressed, really enjoying this more than she should be.

The sound that came out of his throat could have been a growl.

She giggled.

"Tell me about this deal you have for me," he instructed in a tight voice as they traversed familiar streets.

"I want you. That's no secret."

His nostrils flared, his eyes narrowing in shock. "No, it is not."

So, he hadn't been expecting this conversation, either. Nice. The Maxwell Blacks of the world could do with a little more of the unexpected in their lives. "And you want me."

"I do." Firm, unequivocal.

"Right. Only, I'm not interested in an affair."

"So you said a year ago."

Oh, she definitely had. And he'd listened.

Maybe it was the fact he *had* that made her capable of putting forth the offer she was about to. "But I'm also not particularly keen to remain a twenty-four-year-old virgin."

He flicked a quick glance at her, his expression now more than shocked. He didn't look superhappy with her pronouncement, either. "What do you plan to do about that?"

"That's what my deal is about."

"You want to make a deal for your virginity?" he demanded, sounding almost impressed.

"Not for, *about*. One night. You and me." He could read between the lines and get what she was offering.

"You want to have sex for one night?" he clarified, his voice strained.

"Yes."

"And then what?"

"And then we go our separate ways."

"Why only one night?"

"Because I don't want my heart broken." She just might survive a single night with him.

Any longer and she was going to be lost to love. How could she help it? Just looking at him told her he was her ideal man, but she had the taste of pleasure from a year ago to back that up.

"You are too honest for your own good."

"Am I?"

"Yes."

"You're not going to pretend that you didn't know I was falling hard for you a year ago." She would be so disappointed if he tried to prevaricate on that point.

"No."

Good. "So, there wouldn't be any point in lying about it."

"No, I don't suppose there is." He turned on a familiar street and she realized they weren't headed to any of his usual haunts.

"So, what do you say?"

"To one night of sex?"

"Yes." Yikes, what else were they talking about?

"I say no."

"Good, so…" Her voice trailed off as his denial registered. "What? After all that…*are you kidding me?*"

He wanted her. She knew he did. He hadn't denied it, either. What was wrong with him?

"I assure you, I would not joke about this."

"Well, why the heck not?"

"One night would be in direct conflict with my own plans. I have my own deal for you to consider."

"What is it?" she asked with very little grace and even less patience.

"Marriage."

She was still choking on her own breath in shock when they turned into the parking garage for his apartment building.

CHAPTER FIVE

ROMI WAS STILL trying to come to terms with the bombshell Max had dropped in the car as he gave her a tour of his penthouse apartment.

She'd say he realized she needed time to collect herself, but that would be attributing a level of consideration she would never have accused him of in the past.

Not that he'd ever been *inconsiderate* with her, but he could change his name to Ruthless and it would so fit.

With a master suite that included a home office and a spa-sized bathroom, two guest bedrooms and a truly enormous living area that boasted a full-size living room, billiard area and dining room that merged into the kitchen, his home took up the entire top floor of his building.

Decorated in warm browns, coppers and brass accents, it was a very masculine space, but not at all utilitarian-feeling.

While the décor registered, his words sort of skated over her head. Her own thoughts were too scattered to settle in understanding, her hands cold and clammy where they were fisted at her sides.

Had he said *marriage* in the car?

Food was laid on the shiny mahogany table: small plates topped with Caesar salad, silver dome-covered entrée plates off to the side and a basket of Parmesan-crusted flatbread placed strategically between the two place settings. The tangy scent of Caesar dressing and garlic tickled her nose, even from the middle of the living room.

The setting was romantic, the Tiffany box on the table a glaring testament to the fact Max had *not* been joking in the car.

"Lunch smells good." She moved toward the table and then spun to face him, unable to hold it in any longer. *"You want to marry me?"*

"Now you react. I thought you might not have heard me." The humor in his tone was matched by the glint in his gorgeous gray eyes.

"I thought I had to have misheard you. Maybe you said *carriage*." It was as likely as what he actually had said. "Or *suffrage*, or *masonage*."

"Is that even a word?"

"Maybe? I don't know. The Masons are a real thing right, so *Masonage*." It should be a word.

In a move that would have appalled Helene Archer, who had been a free spirit in many ways, but firmly traditional when it came to proper manners, Romi rubbed her palms against the cotton knit of her leggings, getting rid of unwanted moisture.

His lips quirked at the corner. "I think perhaps you are in shock. Sit down. I will pour you a glass of wine."

"Shouldn't it be champagne?" she asked snarkily, but let him lead her to the table, where she settled into a chair with nothing like grace.

She just sort of plopped. Gobsmacked. That *was* a word, right? Kim from England, who had organized the clean air march back in April, said it sometimes.

Romi liked her. She was smart.

Oh, crap. Her mind was rabbiting all over the place to avoid that Tiffany box on the table.

"You don't want to marry me," she told him, sure she was right. "You don't want to get married at all."

"You are mistaken."

Finally, something other than total annihilating confusion pushed at Romi's brain. Anger suffused her. "A year ago, you were pretty clear that you weren't looking for a lifetime."

"No one can promise that." Oh, he sounded so superior.

"You are wrong, Max. I know that's hard for you to comprehend, but in this? You are totally off-base." She crossed her arms and glared up at all six feet five inches of him. "Millions of people make just those kinds of promises all the time."

He wasn't impressed. The flat line of his lips and equally flat look in his pewter eyes told her that. "And break them as often as not."

"They still make them." And if Max made a promise?

He would keep it. Ruthless he might be, but he kept his word. It was why he didn't give it very often.

"That meeting I attended with Madison and her father was very illuminating," Max said, apropos of nothing.

Romi continued to glare at him, letting her annoyance show. "Are you determined to keep me off balance?"

"It is a good negotiation tactic."

"Am I a competitor you are hoping to *absorb* or *defeat?*" she asked, sounding downright cranky.

Which she was on the verge of being. So, okay. Yeah. Really irritated. He was talking about marriage like it was a business deal and that was just a really raw wound right now, after everything Maddie had been through lately.

"No, you are the woman I intend to marry."

"You aren't making any sense. You do know that, right?" Seriously. He had to know it.

"I am speaking English."

"Mostly. You did curse in Russian."

He shrugged and she didn't belabor the point. She was getting side-tracked again and even she knew she needed to rein in her wayward thoughts.

"You don't love me." That was something she was very sure of.

He almost looked regretful. "Love is not in my emotional repertoire."

"Tell your mom that."

"Familial love is not the same as romantic love as you are well aware."

This man! He would test the patience of Santa Claus and Romi was no children's benevolent holiday trope. "They come from the same place."

"So you say."

She rolled her eyes. "Pretty much everyone agrees that love—all kinds of love—comes from the heart."

"My heart beats blood, not bloody-minded emotion." Spoken with his typical certainty, the claim focused on the concrete rather than the concept.

"You're being obtuse on purpose."

"No." Oh, he just oozed sincerity and certainty. "We simply do not agree on this point."

"When I marry it will be to a man who loves me as much as my father loved my mother." Of that she was very sure.

She settled her once cold, now shaking, hands in her lap, unwilling to admit how much she'd hoped that might be him at one time.

Max looked supremely unconvinced. "I have no desire to be a carbon copy of your father."

"He's not weak." That's not what Max had said, but she knew what he meant.

"He is, but he is also intelligent, loyal and willing to dig for the inner strength he has not utilized in too long."

"Wow, I don't know what to say to that." She was all set to just be mad at this man and then he showed so much humanity, she couldn't ignore it.

"Say you will hear me out, with an open mind."

She sighed, wishing this conversation could actually go somewhere meaningful. "Some things are not negotiable, Max."

Leaning toward her, he cupped her cheeks with gentle

firmness. "And sometimes we are surprised by the compromises we are willing to make."

She wanted to say his touch made her weak, but what it really did was make her feel things that made her doubt her own convictions. Was that just another definition of weakness? Or something more?

"This marriage idea is a compromise for you." He desired her enough to offer it and that blew her mind really, but that kind of physical passion without love was just lust.

And lust made a lousy basis for a marriage. The divorce rate and tabloid headlines made that reality clear pretty much every day.

"My dad did not offer you part of Grayson Enterprises to marry me." She knew that without a doubt.

"No, but his company is involved."

She moved her head away from that too-inspiring touch and he let her go.

"How?" she asked.

"Did Madison tell you her father threatened your father's company in order to try to force her into Jeremy's plans for her marriage?"

"Maddie married Viktor to save my dad's company?" Romi asked, feeling like all the air was slowly being sucked from the room.

"Oh, no. Your sister-by-choice is a formidable opponent." Max's admiration was clear.

Regardless of the very unfamiliar sting of jealousy, particularly directed at her SBC, Romi said, "Maddie is amazing."

"She gave your father a very limited opportunity to take the threat off the table."

"But he didn't." Romi knew Jeremy Archer well enough to guess that.

"No."

"What did Maddie do?" If she hadn't given in to her dad's bullying, she'd done something big to make him back off.

"Madison told Archer that if your father's company was under threat on her twenty-fifth birthday, all of the shares to AIH in her trust fund would be transferred to your father personally."

"What? No. She can't do that!"

"I assure you it has been done. She signed the paperwork that afternoon."

"How do you know?"

"Do you really need to ask?"

No. If this man wanted information, he would get it. "But you're going into business with my father. Even AIH can't touch him."

"Our contract is written in such a way that his company will be under threat by *me* if certain conditions are not met." He didn't sound triumphant *or* guilty. Just matter-of-fact.

"What conditions?"

"Do you really want details? Suffice to say, measurables over which I will have full control for the next six months."

"You wouldn't manipulate things so my dad lost his company. You just wouldn't." That was so...ruthless.

Oh, man. He *would* do it because this man had a ruthless streak about as wide as the Golden Gate Bridge.

"I don't plan to, no. I *intend* to rebuild your father's company and use it as a springboard for other things." No modesty in that statement.

"Provided I go along with your *deal*."

Max nodded, no ambivalence about that reality evident in his manner. "That is part of it, yes."

"What is the other part?"

"Your father in rehab."

"What? How?" She'd tried, but it was too hard.

Too hard to hold her dad accountable, too hard to push when she was better at avoidance and she loved him so much.

She'd change the world, but it wouldn't start at home.

"It's part of our contract. However, although your father

has signed everything and is as we speak on his way to a very exclusive, very discreet rehabilitation facility with a success rate of over seventy percent, I haven't signed the contract yet."

"And you won't if I don't marry you?" She could barely believe the mercenary tactic. "How could you hold his health hostage like that? That's monstrous, Max. You have to know that."

"You forget, I'm holding his company, too."

"I don't care."

"I realized that."

"So, you adjusted your plans accordingly." The man *was* a monster.

But he *wasn't*. Darn it. She knew Max better than that. He *was* ruthless and pragmatic to the point of emotionlessness about some things.

But he wasn't a monster.

Just a very determined shark who didn't mind getting some blood in the water if that meant feasting.

"What are the terms of the marriage?" There had to be some.

A man like Maxwell Black didn't make this kind of offer without covering all the contingencies.

"The usual terms, I would imagine, with a well-structured prenuptial agreement."

"Because you don't anticipate it lasting."

"No." Brutal honesty.

But then, could she expect anything else with this man?

"Is there an expiration date?" she asked.

"Not exactly."

"What does that mean?" A year ago, he'd had a very definitive end date in mind for their affair.

"Either of us can end the marriage at any time."

"But there will be consequences as laid out in the prenup?"

"Naturally."

"For both of us." She didn't know why she was so sure of that, particularly considering the conversation so far, but she was.

"Absolutely."

"Why, Max?"

"Because contrary to your unexpected and rather inexplicable offer, you don't believe in uncommitted sex." He began to eat like their discussion was no more earth-shattering than planning a follow-on date.

Maybe for him, it wasn't.

Only she didn't believe that, either.

She pulled some of her earlier nonchalance around her as she began to eat as well. He didn't have to know it was a facade over roiling emotions and cacophonous thought. "As you said, people change."

"No, I said circumstances change. It takes a lot more to change people."

"How can you be so smart about some stuff and so ignorant about other things?" she wondered aloud, not even really asking him, just astonished by the reality.

"What am I ignorant about?"

"Love."

"The refusal to succumb is not ignorance, it is an informed decision." Max sighed, sounding as close to tired as she'd ever heard him. "You know I don't believe in forever, this gives you the trappings of commitment you need."

"With an out clause for you."

"Since divorce law in this country allows the eventual dissolution of any marriage so long as the party seeking dissolution is committed to her course, that is already an out clause."

For the most part, that was true. "You must have a time line you believe our so-called marriage will fall into."

"There will be nothing *so-called* about it. You will be mine, Romi. Make no mistake. And I will be yours in every way the law dictates."

"You sound like a caveman right now." And she liked it. Way too much. "Or a throwback tsar."

"Sue me."

She almost laughed, but couldn't quite release the tension. "How long?"

"Until?"

"The sell-by date."

"That is crass."

"The *time line* then."

"Most negative repercussions outlined in the prenup are nullified at the ten-year mark."

"Ten years?"

"Is practically a lifetime."

"Not even close." But married to someone incapable of love? She very much feared he would be right.

"So, let me get this straight. You want sex with me?"

"Yes."

"And you're willing to blackmail me into marrying you?" He offered her a piece of flatbread. "Yes."

"No complaint about the terminology." She accepted the bread, a sense of unreality surrounding her.

He shrugged. "Much of business is done in the same way. Terms don't change realities."

"I offered you a night of sex." And he'd turned her down.

"I want more than a night."

Right. "You want ten years."

"Maybe more."

"And maybe less."

"You may be ready to walk away before I am." He didn't sound concerned about that, but he also didn't sound like they were just words to placate.

Idiot. Really. Mr. Brilliant Businessman-Corporate Tsar had no clue.

"But fidelity until divorce?" she asked, that sense of unreality nearly drowning her.

"Nonnegotiable."

"What about children?"

"Children?" he asked, like he'd never heard the word before.

"You know, the little people that call you dad."

"Papa. Russian children call their fathers *papa*."

It was such a curious mix, the bits of his heritage he refused to let go and the elements to his character and life that were purely American.

"Well, do you want any babies that will grow up to call you papa?"

He went completely still, a bite partway to his mouth. She wasn't even sure he was still breathing. His expression was indescribable, but something about what she'd said had struck a chord deep inside him.

"My mother would like a grandchild." The words did not match the awed tone in his voice.

He resumed eating, but she wasn't fooled. He was no more nonchalant about this conversation than she was, if for very different reasons. Or maybe just fewer reasons. The idea of having his children unraveled something inside her.

"What about *you*? Would *you* like a child?" she pressed.

A new emotion flickered in Maxwell's gray eyes. Yearning. "Yes. I would like a child."

"Would having a child change the sell-by date on the marriage?" She wanted to know.

"People with children divorce all the time."

That was not what she'd wanted to hear, true as it might be. "Would you want to see your child only a couple of weekends a month?"

"We would share custody." But he didn't sound any more enthusiastic about that prospect than she felt.

Romi narrowed her eyes and challenged, "Would we?"

"Perhaps we should consider remaining married until our child goes to college."

"What if we have more than one?"

"Would you want to?" The awe was there again.

And it touched her when she wanted very much to keep her wits about her. "I'd always hoped to have more than one child." Hardly a secret, it wasn't hard to admit. "I would have loved to have a sibling that actually lived with me."

"As opposed to your sister-by-choice."

"You don't know how many times I wished Maddie had been my sister by birth. We agreed a long time ago we wanted more than one child because we wanted something different for our own families."

"How many children do you want?" he asked cautiously.

"At least two, maybe more." She shared Maddie's dream of possibly adopting at some point.

Max didn't look upset by her answer. Far from it, he appeared intrigued. "Russians put a premium on family."

"And yours was truncated."

"Exactly."

"So, you are saying you want more than one child." From the man who *still* considered *commitment* a dirty word, despite his claim he wanted to marry her.

For him, a wedding really was just a piece of paper—a contract that could be adhered to, or broken with consequences.

Even so…

"This conversation is beyond surreal," she said helplessly.

Surely he could see that.

"I do not agree. It is the conversation we should have had a year ago, I think." He laid his silverware on his plate, clearly done with his salad.

"Are you kidding me? After a few dates?" Put that way, it didn't make a whole lot more sense *now*.

"I knew I wanted you. You made your terms clear."

"I wasn't negotiating terms when we broke up." Was it a breakup when the number of dates wouldn't count all the fingers on one hand?

"Nevertheless, you revealed what it would take to get you into my bed."

"I *revealed* that on the way over here."

His brows rose, his disbelief clear. "Do you honestly believe one night would be enough for us?"

"That's not the point."

"What is the point?"

He wanted honesty? She'd give him some truth. "The whole point of one night is because no *limited* time would ever be enough. I was falling for you a year ago and my heart doesn't have very far to go before we hit the place of no return. I do not want to fall in love with a man who considers it a weakness, can't you understand that?"

"Are you so sure you have a choice?"

Crap. That hurt. She gasped with a real live physical pain as the truth of *his* words sank in.

Nevertheless, she wasn't taking that lying down. "I think you don't have a lot to say about an emotion you refuse to feel."

"We are different people, Romi."

"No kidding."

Rather than annoying him, her sarcasm made him smile. And that irritated *her*.

"You wear your heart on your sleeve."

"At least I have a heart," she retorted, stung.

"Yes, you do. A generous one."

"How can you sound so admiring when you've made it clear it's a trait you don't actually admire?"

"I never said I found your ability to love a weakness."

"But for you it would be?" she asked, confused.

"As I said, we are different people. You are willing to risk the pain of eventual separation for the benefit of the temporary emotion."

"What if it isn't temporary? What if it never goes away?" That was what scared her the most with him.

Maxwell Black could end up being her one true love. As cheesy as some might consider that, Romi believed in soul mates. Her parents had been.

And while Romi wanted nothing more than to have that kind of love for herself, she did not want to spend the rest of her life grieving for a lost love. Particularly one who had simply walked away.

"There is no actual expiration on the marriage," he pointed out. "Read the contract."

"No, because it's not what you have on paper that worries me. It's what is going on inside *you*, Max. You expect to get bored eventually. You expect to walk away."

"No."

"But, you said—"

"I acknowledge the *probability* that our marriage will not last. I do not demand that it end at some point."

Which was actually a huge departure from his attitude the year before. "I just don't understand what you hope to get out of this."

"Your body."

All the air really left the room this time, Romi's vision going black around the edges.

With a muttered Russian imprecation, Max jumped up and then he was there, holding her so she would not slide sideways out of her chair.

Her fuzzy gaze settled on the Tiffany ring box. *That* did not help her sense of disorientation.

"You need to finish eating. We will continue this discussion after you have done so."

"You think I'm suffering low blood sugar?" she asked with a near hysterical laugh.

First of all, she was almost finished with her salad—even if it had been appetizer-sized—and a piece of flatbread. Second of all, his words were the problem. Not the food, or the fact she hadn't eaten all of it.

"You are suffering something. Now, eat." He removed the dome covering her plate and traded it for the salad plate before going around the table to do the same for his own lunch.

Certain she couldn't eat any more, half of Romi's artichoke-and-egg-white quiche and its accompanying slice of melon was gone before she realized she was wrong.

She stared across the table at Max, unaccountably cranky that he might have been right. Sometimes she needed protein and the fact he'd taken note of that during their brief time together made her feel strange.

That didn't make the topic of their conversation any more normal, either. "So, if I don't marry you, you're going to take my father's company, thereby triggering Maddie's crazy fail-safe and just in case that's not enough, you'll revoke your support of my dad going into rehab?"

Repeating it didn't make the threat any less outrageous than when he'd made it, or any easier to understand.

Max didn't even flicker an eyelid. "Yes."

"What does that make you?"

"The winner."

CHAPTER SIX

"Is that all that matters to you?" she asked with shock, when really, she had no reason to be surprised. She made no effort to hide her unease with the idea. "That you win?"

"I *never* go into a fight without the intention of doing just that and the certainty I can do so."

"Have you ever lost?" she wondered out loud.

"I lost my Russian family before I knew what it meant to have anyone in my life besides my mother."

"That wasn't your fight. It was your mom's." And while the loss was very real, and no doubt impacting, even to an emotionless tycoon who relegated marriage to a business deal, it wasn't an example of Max being defeated.

"She won her independence and the life she wanted for me at great cost. Mama still misses her family."

"So, you were raised not to count the cost, but to weigh the victory." It was the attitude of strength, one that made no allowance for fear.

She was impressed despite herself.

"That is a very good way to put it." He smiled. "Mama would be proud."

"Don't think I haven't noticed that you didn't answer my question." One thing a professional at avoidance like Romi could do was recognize the tactic.

"I have never come out the loser in a business deal."

No doubt, but that wasn't exactly what she was asking. Since Romi didn't actually see marriage as a business deal.

"What about personally?" Though she couldn't imagine him really fighting for anything on a personal basis.

Before today anyway.

He certainly hadn't fought to keep seeing her a year ago. She'd told him no and he'd accepted her word without trying to change her mind. She'd vacillated between relief and disappointment.

The relief had been unwarranted emotion, she now realized. Maxwell Black didn't give up. He just regrouped.

"Not since I became an adult."

"Your mom's family does not count, we've already said."

"Every loss counts," he responded implacably.

And he said he had no heart. For the first time since meeting him, Romi wondered if the heart he claimed not to be guided by was just buried *really* deep.

"Then you shouldn't have any trouble remembering them."

Rather than answer, he stood and indicated the living room with a tip of his head. "Would you like to move this discussion somewhere more comfortable?"

They ended up side by side on the big brown leather sectional even though there were several seating options that would not have required such close proximity.

He settled back into the corner, his arm along the back, his gaze holding hers. "Despite having a relationship with my mother that lasted more than two years, my father walked away from me without a backward glance."

"You don't know that." She kicked her ballet flats off and tucked one foot under her, turning to face him more squarely.

"I do."

"Have you spoken to him?" She tried to picture that conversation and couldn't quite do it.

"No."

"Then you don't know what regrets are still open wounds

in his heart." She could not fathom any parent *not* regretting being a nonentity in Max's life.

Ruthless the man might be, but he was a son to be proud of.

"He offered money and bringing his influence to bear to facilitate our immigration in exchange for silence on my mother's part. Both about her relationship with him and about my existence. She was never even allowed to name him."

"That could be because his choices were limited, not because he didn't want you." She didn't know why it was so important to her to convince Max of that.

"Your heart is too tender." He reached out to brush her hair behind her ear. "You need someone to watch over you and make sure the world does not rip it to shreds."

"Like you're trying to do?"

He let his hand fall away. "Not even close. I'm offering you a place in my life, not coming after you with a scalpel directed at your heart."

"Nice image." No way was she going to admit she missed the warmth of his hand.

"I am Russian. Imagery is in my blood."

"Russians are also known for their passionate natures."

"You have reason to believe that of me." His meaning was clear.

He was equating passion to sex while she'd been talking about emotion. Nothing new about that, but maybe it wasn't the epic misunderstanding she'd always considered it.

He was willing to acknowledge his sexual nature and need. Could that be a way to his heart?

And did she have the courage to even try?

Did she even want to? Was the remote possibility of finding a way to his deeper emotions worth putting hers at risk?

She could walk away right now and it would hurt, but she would get over him.

Eventually.

The past year had at least shown her the former if not the latter.

But he wasn't just asking her to take a chance on dating, on a relationship. He wasn't *asking* anything.

He was blackmailing her and because Max saw the whole thing as some kind of business deal with fringe benefits, he didn't even think there was anything wrong with that.

"The fringe benefits, as you call them, go both directions," he said, a sardonic twist to his mouth.

"I said that out loud, didn't I?" Darn it.

He smirked, his hand gliding along her thigh suggestively. "Yes."

Romi did her best to ignore the sparks dancing along her nerve endings from his touch. "So, you're not going to tell me about the loss that proved to you that love was weakness, are you?"

"You believe I've suffered some trauma that left me incapable of letting my emotions control me?" He left his hand resting on her thigh, but stilled its movement.

"Have you?"

"I learned early that romantic love didn't count for much when other more important considerations were on the table, but it wasn't anything my mother hadn't been telling me since before I could walk."

Romi couldn't take her eyes off that large masculine hand covering her thigh. "Your mom doesn't believe in love?"

"With good reason. No affection ever lasted beyond the point at which she became an inconvenience."

"She doesn't seem bitter." While Romi had only met her a handful of times, she'd never gotten the impression that Natalya Black was one of those cynical women that made everyone bleed with their bitterness.

"She is not. She is a realist."

Who had taught her son to see erotic love as a weakness. "And she wanted to protect you from heartache."

"Yes." He looked a little surprised by the idea and his own agreement to it.

"How old were you when you learned this lesson?" The idea of him in love hurt her in some indefinable way, especially if he'd been a vulnerable teen, risking his heart.

"Ten."

"So not a personal loss?" Surprise, surprise.

"It was very personal."

"But the romance was between your mother and her lover." No way had Max been in love at such a young age.

"*Batya* made Mama glow for three years."

"He was Russian?"

"No. He was American. *Batya* is a Russian nickname for father. It is what I called him."

And Max hadn't reverted to using the man's given name later. That said something about how deeply the hurt went. How ingrained that role had been in Max's heart.

"And you?"

"He lived with us, though I realized later it must only have seemed that way. Our home was not his, but he was *there* every evening, adding a sense of security to our small house. *Batya* took me to ball games, came to my school and culture center activities. He sat at the head of our table on holidays and took us out for our birthdays."

In other words, he'd *been* Max's dad. For a little while anyway. "But it didn't last."

"No."

"Why?"

"Does it matter?"

"Probably not." The lesson here was that Max had clearly opened his heart to this man who had acted like a father, only to have it crushed when the man walked away.

"Have you ever been in love?"

"No chance." The words were spoken with such quiet vehemence, she knew he had never been that vulnerable teenager she worried about.

Max truly had learned his lessons early and he'd taken them to heart until no one would accuse him of having one.

"Me, either." And honestly?

She wasn't keen to fall right now, but every minute spent in this man's company was undermining Romi's belief she had any say in the matter.

She wasn't sure what it was about that sad little story that got to her so much, but no way could she ever see Max as a monster. No matter what pressures he brought to bear for his marriage plan.

"You really hedged your bets with this marriage thing, didn't you?" she asked, needing to move away from the emotional morass their discussion had become for her.

"If by that you mean I considered every contingency, you would be right."

"Maddie is out of town on her honeymoon. You know I don't want to interrupt her with a call to ask about her contingency plan."

"You do not trust me regarding the details?"

"Should I?"

He considered that for a moment. "Perhaps not, but I have never lied to you, nor will I ever."

"I'm not sure you telling me that in the same conversation you admit to setting up a truly untenable situation for me can carry much weight for me."

Max's eyes narrowed. "Call Jeremy Archer."

"He lies."

"If anything, he would be tempted to deny it, yes?"

"Yes. So, why would *you* trust him to back you up?"

Max shrugged. "Few businessmen in this town would cross me without very strong provocation. Viktor maybe, but Jeremy? He's too wrapped up in his company to risk it by lying about me."

"Without compelling cause."

"Precisely."

"How do I know my dad is in rehab?" She wasn't sure

what was pushing her to question the reliability of everything he claimed, but she had this irresistible urge to prick the bubble of his confidence.

Even if only a little.

Rather than appear in the list "pricked," Max looked smugly satisfied by his planning. "He will get a single phone call before going into immersion therapy, during which he will be allowed no external contact. Not with family. Not for his business."

"That works in your favor."

"It is my habit to make sure most things do."

"Wow, the arrogance level just skyrocketed in here."

Max smiled, amusement glinting in his gray eyes. "Arrogance is defined as excessive confidence. Mine, on the other hand, is well-founded."

"I won't argue that."

"I would not expect you to. You are far too intelligent to take on the hopeless cause."

"Oh, I don't know. According to a lot of men in your position, my activism on behalf of the environment is exactly that."

"I do not agree."

And that should give her hope, shouldn't it? How pragmatic was it to be a CEO so committed to sustainability? She was sure he would say very pragmatic, but only if you had an eye and a *heart* for the future.

Was he closer? He seemed closer. "Tell me something."

"Anything." The heat of his hand burned through the fabric of her leggings.

"I wish you meant that, but I won't push it." The temptation to lean into him was huge and growing. She fought it, trying to stay focused on what needed saying. "I just need confirmation of something."

"Yes?"

"Would you ever walk away from your child as your father and your mother's lover did with you?"

"No." The word fell with the weight of a boulder between them, every ounce of lust in his expression transforming to determination.

No doubt he meant it.

It made her doubt his willingness to walk away from her as well. He thought he could and most likely would, but she wasn't so sure. Especially if they decided to have children together.

If he didn't let himself love her, he wasn't going to fall for someone else, either. And no other power but love was going to make this man rip the fabric of his family.

No matter what he told himself, or her, for that matter.

"You are just a mass of contradictions, aren't you?"

"Not at all," he said with a different kind of force and obvious horror at the very idea.

She laid down her own line in the sand. "I'm not agreeing to anything today." She waited for him to take that in.

If his first reaction was to try to obliterate it, they were done here. No matter what extra aces he'd slipped into his hand, she wasn't playing.

"Today?" he asked with emphasis on the single word.

"Today."

"This is not an indefinite offer."

"Oh, I know, but you're smart enough to realize that little box isn't getting opened this afternoon." She flicked her head toward the dining table and the Tiffany box still sitting unopened near her now empty plate.

Max's head tilted, a predatory light growing in his eyes. "I thought it was."

"Well, I guess even Corporate Tsars can be wrong sometimes."

"Perhaps." Nothing in his expression or relaxed posture indicated that bothered him.

He seemed…well, turned on. And that wasn't what she was expecting in reaction to her statement. Though it certainly didn't hurt in regard to how she wanted to spend the rest of their afternoon.

"Tonight, today…whatever, we go with *my* plan."

"That entails…?" he asked with the air of a man who already knew.

Maybe he did. Or maybe, he was just so good at exuding confidence, it came naturally—even when he was in the dark.

"You and I test out our sexual compatibility in a bed and with complete follow-through." He had to know what that meant because she wasn't spelling it out. "I talk to my dad when he calls. Tomorrow, I talk to Jeremy Archer. Depending on that conversation, I decide whether I need to interrupt my SBC's honeymoon."

"You will not." Max sounded so sure of that fact.

But then, as Romi had already acknowledged, he always did. Uncertainty wasn't in Max's repertoire any more than love was. Since calling Maddie was on the very bottom of the list of things Romi wanted to do right now, she wasn't going to argue regardless.

"Tomorrow night, I eat dinner alone. I think about what you are offering and what you are threatening and if I can reconcile the two."

Or if she could live with the consequences of not doing so. Romi was pretty sure that didn't need saying.

Apparently Max agreed with her, because he merely nodded. "We will have lunch again the day after."

"You can bring your little blue box. It will either get opened, or not."

He shifted so he was very much in her personal space, his body surrounding hers as one arm slid around her waist and the one on the back of the couch moved to rest behind her head. "You show very little curiosity regarding a piece of jewelry you will be wearing for some time to come."

"Jewelry isn't going to sway me." But his nearness might.

"No more than the salvation of your father's company."

"Right." But the salvation of her father?

That was something else entirely. It was everything. And Max had set it in motion, no matter what his supposed motivations for doing so were.

"You're taking this delay really well," she breathed, his face almost close enough to kiss. Realization came over her slowly. "You knew I would ask for time."

"I had hoped you would make a quick decision, but I was prepared to give a week." However, he had expected her to open the ring box.

He would learn that for all the trappings of wealth that surrounded her, Romi wasn't all that interested in them.

"And I only asked for three days."

"A decent compromise."

She almost laughed at the idea of Maxwell Black compromising with anyone, but the truth was that he considered the entire marriage idea a compromise. And he *had* allowed a counteroffer.

For time at least.

Max hadn't said no about the sex. From the way he was sitting and the alpha male pheromones saturating the air around them, she didn't think he was going to, either.

Romi wasn't sure why that was so important, but it was. She needed to link with him intimately before making a decision.

At this point, she wasn't looking for logic or reason. Romi's instincts were telling her she needed the physical connection and she wasn't going to ignore them.

Maxwell did not need convincing when it came to giving in to Romi's desire to give herself to him fully.

No, she clearly did *not* see it that way, but she had never allowed another man the same level of intimacy.

Maxwell could not figure out why she was offering the gift to him now, without things settled between them. But then, that was no new situation for him with her. Her mind worked in ways his did not.

Perhaps it was as simple as her needing a sense of some control over the situation.

He wasn't averse to giving her that.

Was in fact ridiculously eager to do so. It was just that she had looked so damn vulnerable when she'd found out about her father's rehab.

Maxwell had not cared for the feeling that he was doing something wrong. He knew he was not.

Maxwell had not put Madison's shares up for grabs as a bargaining tool. His willingness to use that situation did not make him a villain. It made him smart.

And *he* had not led Harry Grayson down the path of functioning alcoholism. Maxwell had in fact convinced the older man to go somewhere he could get help with his addiction.

Was he willing to follow through on his threat to back out of the deal? Yes.

Had Maxwell ever considered, even for a moment, it would come to that? No.

He wasn't the monster Romi seemed to think him.

No matter what she might think, Maxwell wanted her to accept the terms of his deal, not simply give in to them.

If his successful years in business had taught him one thing, it was that voluntary partners worked harder to make the venture work. It wasn't always a luxury he could afford himself, but when possible, Maxwell maneuvered his rivals into wanting the mergers he chose to pursue.

Something niggled at considering his marriage proposal just another business merger, but that was essentially exactly what it was. Right?

Pushing aside the uncomfortable thoughts, he considered his next move. No question it involved making love to Romi, but did he start here and take her to the bedroom?

Considering his hair trigger where she was concerned,

if they began here—even with the most basic of kisses—
chances were, this is where Romi would gift him her virginity.

She deserved more ceremony than that.

He would take her to his bed, not the guest room where
he conducted most of his sexual trysts. His wrought-iron
bed, imported from the ironmasters in Russia, had never
been occupied by anyone but him.

Using more control than he realized would be necessary, he pulled away from the allure of her body and stood.
Maxwell put his hand out to Romi. "Come, we will have
your sexual taste test."

She burst out laughing, all traces of the overly emotional,
dangerously vulnerable woman drowning under her sweet
humor. "That is not what I said."

"But it is what you meant?"

"Maybe I'm just ready to lose my virginity."

"Maybe there is something going on here *neither* of us
understands." He liked that idea much better than him being
the only one in the dark.

"Oooh, the Corporate Tsar doesn't know everything.
How disconcerting that must be for you."

"I am used to that unfortunate turn of events around
you."

"I confuse you?" she asked, sounding really far too happy
about the possibility.

"Do you doubt it? Have we not established that we are
very different people?"

"You're nothing like Jeremy Archer, or my dad for that
matter, but you understand them. Don't try to pretend you
don't."

"You, Romi, are an enigma."

She preened. "Well, that's nice to know."

He shook his head. "Like right now. I do not understand
why this is so satisfying *and* amusing to you."

"You are a very dangerous man to me, Maxwell Black,"

she said with a lot more serious mien than she had shown only a second before. "It's good to know you don't have it all easy with me."

"I would call you anything but easy, *milaya*."

Her blue gaze sparked with heat as she placed her hand in his and stood. "You know I love when you use Russian endearments."

He *did* know it. Though once again, he was not sure he understood why. But it was easier to use Russian endearments than English for him.

His mother had never used the English terms and while he would admit it aloud only under the threat of his company's dissolution, Russian was the language of what passed for his heart.

Unlike her silent and rather bemused response to his tour earlier, Romi commented on the décor on the way to his bedroom, seemingly surprised it felt like a home rather than a hotel room.

"Why would my home feel like a hotel?" he had to ask.

"Well, because decorators often go generic when they do places for men like you."

"Men like me?" He pressed against the door to his study with his back, pushing it open wide enough for them to enter.

"Corporate Tsars," she said with the tiniest bit of sarcasm lacing the second word.

Her allusion to his royal attitude was not lost on Maxwell, but he refused to pretend to be other than what he was. A man who knew what he wanted and had a decided talent for figuring out how to get it.

"If I wanted to live in a place that looked like a hotel, I would live in one." If he wanted to live in a palace, he'd live in one of those, too.

"See, that's the way I always thought. You should have heard me and Maddie when Jeremy had his mansion redecorated."

"It is not the warmest of abodes." There was nothing wrong with the mansion if you wanted to live in luxury without personality.

The designer who had redone the Archer house had obviously been very knowledgeable in his or her field—talented even—but it was a cold place with no evidence a family lived there.

Though Maxwell supposed with just Jeremy Archer in residence, a *family* didn't. "It's a showplace for a megarich tycoon who likes to impress and intimidate with his surroundings as much as his money."

Maxwell's own strategy for how his home came across to visitors was more subtle. His penthouse reflected him and his wealth in a way that let others know he was not afraid for them to know who he was.

Of course, that was because nothing of manipulative value could be discovered visiting the main areas of his home. His favorite colors? His preference for dark wood? Yes.

Even his Russian heritage and wholesale acceptance of the country of his second citizenship, America.

What no one saw, unless they were looking very closely and knew how to read such things—not a common occurrence—was his desire for control or his genuine affection for his mother.

There was only a single formal picture of her in the living area. His bedroom suite was different.

There, much of what made Maxwell the man he was could be seen on display.

Hence the dearth of invitations to that sanctum.

He did not invite women to the bed in which he slept for a reason. The only friend who had been in his personal office in memory was Viktor Beck, and the only people who had seen every room in his apartment were his mother and his cleaning staff.

Before today.

Today, Maxwell brought Romi into his private sanctuary without hesitation.

She seemed to realize the enormity of it when they stepped over the threshold into his office. She stopped and drew in a shocked breath. "You are in here."

"I am indeed."

"No, I know." She rolled her eyes. "You're so droll. I mean, I can see *you* in this room. I thought your apartment was so much *your* home, but this? This is like a glimpse at your heart."

"You are assuming on that heart thing again."

She shook her head, not even cracking a smile. "Thank you for bringing me here."

"It was part of your deal."

"No, sex was my deal. That could have happened in a guest room."

He winced.

Her eyes narrowed. "That's where you take your lovers, isn't it?"

He shrugged. She'd guessed. There was no point in confirming it.

"You know if I do marry you, we'll be buying *all* new furniture for those rooms, right?"

"Whatever you want."

"I'm pretty sure that's not how things work with you. I may not have gotten the full meal, but the taste I had was not a man who gave his partner whatever she wanted."

"On the contrary, I am very good at determining what it is you *really* want and giving it."

"You were a year ago, that's for sure." Her blue eyes glowed with remembered passion.

CHAPTER SEVEN

ROMI GAZED AT him with nothing less than adoration. "Other men aren't like you."

"You tested this theory?" Maxwell demanded even as he basked unashamedly in her evident approval of his sexual prowess.

"You know I didn't."

"Then how do you know?"

She blushed. "I just do."

He found her innocence charming when the same in other women had acted as a huge red flag for Maxwell.

He stopped in the middle of his office, and brushed his hand along her heated cheek. "Yes, but how, sweet little Romi?"

"I may be a virgin, but that doesn't mean I've never done anything with other guys."

"Like?" he pressed, wondering if she realized they were engaged in foreplay.

She rolled her expressive eyes. "I've kissed other men."

"And on the basis of kissing alone..." He leaned down and pressed his lips to hers, taking advantage of her surprised gasp for a small taste before lifting his head. "You have determined I am unique?"

She blinked up at him.

He smiled.

"You're starting now, aren't you?" she asked.

"I began in the living room."

She looked like she was realigning her thoughts based on his claim and then she nodded. "Like I said. No one like you."

"Did you do more than kiss with other men?" he asked, allowing his breath to caress her lips.

Her pupils dilated, her expression going dreamy. "Hmmm?"

"Other men," he reminded her. "Your experience with them."

"Some touching."

"Here?" he asked, brushing along her back.

"What? I don't..." She swayed toward him. "Maybe? I think so."

He liked this proof she could not think clearly from the simple touches. His own libido was already in overdrive.

"What about here?" he asked as he cupped her nape and ran his thumb down to her pulse point.

She moaned, leaning into a kiss he kept brief by necessity. They *would* make it to the bedroom.

"No one ever took over like you do." Her words weren't an answer to his teasing.

But they were exactly what Maxwell wanted to hear. "And no one ever made you feel like I did, either."

"Not even close." Her desire to be near him screamed from every line of her willing body.

He shook his head at his own stupidity and her stubbornness. They could have had *this* for the last year. "Yet you broke it off with me."

"Because you offered a definitive ending date."

"And that wasn't something you wanted." She was really hung up on that concept.

He needed to remember that.

"No."

He didn't point out he was offering something very different this time. She knew it.

Just as he knew that ultimately, she would agree to marry him.

The draw between them was irresistible. He'd provided a way for them to meet, to connect, but one way or another, they would have come together again. It had been inevitable.

One day she might even admit that.

He forced himself to step back, to create physical space between them. He wanted her surrender, but if he accepted too early, they weren't going to make it the steps it would take to go from his office to his bedroom.

Romi seemed to understand that instinctively as well, as she looked around his personal space with dazed eyes that slowly cleared.

She moved to the photos gracing one of the built-in bookshelves. "Oh, my gosh…this is you as a little boy. With your mom."

She reached out and touched the photo with the same delicacy her hands showed on his body.

Pleasure shuddered through him. "I told you I was a child once."

"And an adorable one at that." He wasn't sure what the wistfulness in her voice was about.

"Mama thought so."

Romi threw him a smile over her shoulder before going back to the pictures. "This man, he's the one isn't he? The one that went away?"

He knew the photo she was talking about. It was of Natalya, Maxwell and the man he had called *Batya* for three years. They were on a harbor tour about a year after *Batya* had come into their lives.

Maxwell could remember *Batya* pointing out the landmarks and telling his eight-year-old self things the guide didn't mention. It had been a magical day.

"I'm surprised you have it out." Romi's voice was soft, her sympathy not grating like it would be from someone else.

"It is part of my history." A part he had never allowed himself to forget. Not the good times, not the way he'd felt when *Batya* simply wasn't there any longer, nor the years that followed.

"And putting it away wouldn't change that."

"No. Besides, it was a good day."

"Have you ever spoken to him since he left?"

"He died. No one told us. Why would they? Mama saw the obituary and told me. He was barely fifty."

"Oh, Max." That look on her face. It should have been like sandpaper on a raw wound, but he felt something warm unfurl inside him instead.

She crossed to him and walked right into his embrace, no sexual overtones to her actions, just a pure compassion that could only come from a pure heart like hers.

Romi's hands locked behind his neck, her head tilted back. "Do you know how old I was when Maddie and I decided to be sisters?"

He shook his head, strangely reluctant to speak, shocked at the fact he wasn't kissing her despite their positions. No other woman could derail his libidinous nature to something softer.

She said he was dangerous to her, but really, the opposite was just as true. He might never have the honesty to admit it, but he wasn't a fool to hide from reality, either.

"Five," she said, answering her own question.

"That is a long time ago." His voice came out oddly scratchy.

"Yes." Guileless blue eyes met his. "Almost twenty years."

He nodded.

"When I care about someone, I stay in his or her life. I don't give up because it's uncomfortable, or inconvenient." Those same blue eyes compelled him to believe in something other than the past.

He found himself wanting to and that only made him

more wary. "She did not have another family she had to give you up to keep."

"No, but if you think living with my dad the past few years has been a picnic, you're wrong. Or even being best friends with Madcap Madison. That girl scares the crap out of me sometimes, but I will never just walk out of her life."

Maxwell opened his mouth to tell her that their relationship wasn't the same, but closed it again without speaking.

One year ago, Romi had turned down his offer of a liaison with a time limit, but not once in the past twelve months had she tried to avoid him. If she saw him at an event, she spoke to him. She answered the phone when he called, though she'd made it clear it wasn't easy on her when he did call.

The queen of avoidance didn't avoid people.

It was an important realization to make.

"You are very special," he told her.

Her smile was luminescent. "I'm just me, but I've got to tell you, Max, I'm learning more about you in an afternoon than I have in all the time I've known you."

"You're going to marry me. You should know me."

"Arrogant much?" she mocked.

"We've already discussed this."

She sighed, but didn't look annoyed. Just accepting. "Make love to me, Max. I want to know what I'll learn about you then."

He didn't think there was much more for her to learn, but he wasn't about to turn her down.

He'd only said *no* in the car because in no dimension of time was one night going to be enough between the two of them.

Romi gasped out a laugh as Maxwell lifted her into his arms to carry her through to the bedroom.

"What are you doing?" she demanded breathlessly.

"My patience is at an end and we are going to do this right."

"I'm not your bride." Not yet.

"I am making you mine tonight. If that is not marriage, what is?"

She almost snarked that she thought it was a business contract where he was concerned, but the expression in his dark gray eyes stopped her.

There was no humor there, no uncertainty, just burning possession and desire. She'd known he was like this. Had found it almost impossible to resist and just as difficult to forget.

"We're making you mine, too, right?"

"Oh, yes, *milaya*, this is a two-sided promise we are making with our bodies."

"You've had sex with lots of women."

"More than a couple," he admitted without shame.

"You didn't claim them."

"For the hours we spent together their bodies were mine to pleasure, but the connection lasted only as long as the sex." He carried her into the bedroom and the moment felt as profound as he claimed.

She reflexively tightened her arms around his neck. "You're staking a different kind of claim on me."

"I did so a year ago."

"Did you really?"

"Oh, yes."

She believed him. Had no space to deny it. If she were honest with herself, she'd acknowledge she'd felt the claim and had lived with the hope that time would dull it into extinction.

Only now could she admit that hadn't happened with anything like speed or success. And he was intent on renewing that claim, taking it to the natural conclusion.

A claim she was pretty sure she would never be able to

dismiss again. Even with her best techniques at ignoring realities she did not want to face.

"You said you dated." If the claim went both ways, that shouldn't have happened.

Should it?

"I didn't say those dates ended in sex."

Shock coursed through Romi. "You haven't been celibate a year."

"I haven't?"

"Don't tease me. Just tell me." She needed it spelled out in that voice of his she knew never lied to her.

"Yes, Ramona. A year ago, you claimed my body and it wants only you now. Does that make you happy?" He sure didn't seem thrilled by the knowledge.

But Romi? She was a lot happier about it than his blackmail marriage proposal. "You know I didn't want anyone else, either."

"So, now we give in to the irresistible force."

"I thought that was *you*," she teased.

"So did I, before you engendered a burning desire in me that would not be quenched."

The kiss that followed sent fire licking through her and touched to the depths of her soul as his mouth claimed hers with a marauder's enthusiasm. When it ended, she was lying on the center of his huge bed, her clothes rumpled by his insistence on connecting with skin.

Gray irises almost swallowed completely by black, he perused her form with blatant possession and undeniable passion. Shoes gone, trousers open at the waist, Max's shirt was unbuttoned to reveal the dark whorls of hair on his muscular chest.

Moving to sit up, he reached out and she found both her hands caught in his. She looked down at their laced fingers and then back up to his handsome face.

His expression was borderline stunned, something about

the moment beyond what he had clearly expected. That was okay. Romi wasn't feeling all that steady herself.

"This is my pledge to you," he said and her heart stopped.

A pledge was a vow, a promise from a man who didn't break his word. She wasn't ready for promises, but couldn't find the words to deny him the moment.

"For as long as we are together, there will be no other," he said, all promise, no hesitation. "Any children we have will call *me* papa and be secure in my presence in their lives until the day I die."

Tears burned at the back of her eyes. "You're not being fair."

Pledges like this could not be dismissed the next day like cobwebs on the wind. Not even when a lesser man made them, much less a man of Maxwell Black's character.

"For as long as you belong to me, I will belong to you," he continued as if she had not spoken. "Your well-being will be my priority, your pleasure my desire, your happiness my goal."

"Even while you're blackmailing me with my dad's health?" she asked helplessly.

Gray eyes burned with certainty. "Even then."

"Stop making me promises." *Please stop*, her heart cried. "Just…just make love to me."

"You can deny it, but the truth will not change. This…" He pulled one hand away to point between the two of them. "This is bigger than sex, this is bigger than a single night's mind-blowing passion."

"That almost sounds like you are admitting to having a heart."

"Nyet," he denied in uncompromising Russian. "But a soul? Yes, that I have. Somehow, Ramona Grayson, you have found the way to touch it."

Even if he thought that would end one day, that their marriage wasn't about being soul mates, that admission right there was a better reason to take a chance on this man than all the blackmail in the world.

The kiss that followed was another promise in itself. A vow between the two of them that could not be pretended or ignored away. No matter what tomorrow brought, this moment would change Romi fundamentally and not just because she was taking her first lover.

The kiss didn't just hint, but it *vowed* the kind of passion a person could go her entire life without experiencing.

He lifted his lips from hers, but kept his body close, his gaze intent and determined in the way she remembered. "Tell me."

She remembered that demand, too, but somehow she knew that right now it meant more than playing a sensual game.

Max had made his promises. Now he would have hers.

"Yours."

"Only mine."

"Only yours."

He didn't ask for more, didn't demand she guarantee to be a good or even present mother. It was all covered in that single declaration, minimal words laden with complicated and far-reaching commitments. And she could not make herself regret that truth.

Whatever tomorrow might bring.

They undressed one another like old lovers, though they'd never been fully naked together before. When they'd dated, their times of intimacy had been explosive and unplanned.

Which wasn't to say they hadn't been intense, amazing and ultimately absolutely unforgettable.

But they'd never come to his penthouse to make love. She'd known where he lived, had even been in his building to wait for him, but never in his home, and definitely not his bedroom.

It felt so natural, though, to push his shirt off his shoulders, to tug his dangling belt from the loops on his trousers, that she did it all without any real thought.

And when he drew her tunic mini off, she didn't try to cover her small breasts, which were encased in a white silk bra designed to lift them into prominence. Not because she'd worn it for the very purpose of enticing him, either, but because she felt no need to hide. No desire for false barriers between them.

Max's eyes flared with heat as he traced the path of the lace covering the upper swells with one masculine finger. "Very pretty. I don't remember your lingerie being this sexy."

"I knew what I wanted." She didn't even blush when she said it.

She'd had plans for this afternoon and that shouldn't come as a shock to the unparalleled tsar of plan making.

The air around them vibrated with sensual hunger as her words seemed to impact him in a wholly favorable way.

"I like it." He leaned down and placed a kiss on the tip of her nipple, the heat from his breath drawing it into a tight bead. "Very much."

"Thank you."

"But it too must come off." Suiting action to words, he unclasped her bra and drew the silk away from her body.

She shivered in reaction to the feel of air on her nipples and his fingertips on her skin.

"You are so responsive," he said with masculine satisfaction.

"To you."

"As it should be." He cupped her breasts, his big hands holding her gently but with unmistakable possession. "Here? Have others touched you like this?"

"What?" Why was he asking her that?

"You said I am not like other men. I asked you how you knew," he reminded her, like he could read her confusion on her face.

Probably, he could.

"I...not like this. Under my shirt. Not my bra." The words shivered out of her as he squeezed carefully, kneading her breasts and pulling more pleasure from her.

"I am different from other men, but *milaya*, I think your response to me is unique as well, yes?"

"Oh, yes," she breathed softly.

"I will erase the touch of any other man, no matter how intimate."

How did she tell him he didn't need to erase what had never been there? She wasn't a total novice, or at least had always told herself the kissing and clothed petting meant she wasn't one. But Romi had been fooling herself.

This was sexual foreplay that would change her.

The other touches had left no lasting impact.

She tried to tell him that, but the words came out disjointed as Max removed her leggings and panties in one deft movement before tossing them aside.

"Shh...I understand. You are mine. I am yours. It is good." He pressed his finger to her lips, but then followed it almost immediately with his lips.

The kiss wasn't long, but it was thorough and she was squirming with passion's renewal when he pulled back.

His smile was full primeval predator. "It goes both ways, never doubt it."

"You're erasing the memory of other women in your bed?"

"No."

She couldn't stifle the sound of hurt.

He pressed her naked body to his still partially clothed one. "You cannot erase what has never been."

The words were an eerie match to her own thoughts only seconds before and an atavistic shiver trembled through her, but he could not mean them. "You've been with lots of other women."

"Never in this bed. Never with the knowledge that they owned my future."

No matter how fleeting that ownership might be, Romi couldn't help appreciating the sentiment. "Good."

He nodded, but he wasn't done. "Never has a woman responded to me like you do. Never has my own control been so tested, in the bedroom or out of it."

He'd said things like that before, but she'd never taken it to mean much. Now she realized it really was important to him. It helped explain why he'd overcome his own relationship boundaries to offer marriage, even marriage with a time-relative, easy-out clause.

"I like testing your control."

His laughter was deep and sexy. "No doubt."

Max stepped off the bed to remove the rest of his clothes and she didn't insist she get to do it. One thing she'd learned a year ago was she got extremely excited by his take-charge attitude in the bedroom. It had bothered her a year ago and maybe that was part of the reason she *hadn't* been willing to compromise her own ideas about relationships even though she'd wanted to so badly.

He didn't return to the bed immediately once he'd stripped, but stood in proud nudity and allowed her to look her fill. Like he knew she was craving just the sight of him.

Considering how well he'd known her every desire a year ago, she guessed he probably did.

Women were supposed to be less visual than men. Romi wasn't sure who had decided that. All she knew was that the sight of Max was as tantalizing as a touch for her.

She loved his height, the definition of his muscles, the contrast of his fair Russian skin to his dark hair, the way he held himself with such confidence. And she adored the way his chest was covered in short, dark, silky curls. The hair narrowed to a *V* and then followed a tapered trail that led to the patch surrounding his engorged sex. Flushed with blood, it stood out from his body in truly impressive proportions.

"You are devouring me with your eyes, *milaya*."

Was she? "You're a beautiful man." No other word fit as perfectly the work of art that Maxwell Black was naked.

From the dark hair that tempted her fingers to run through it, to the features she saw in her dreams and fantasies both, to a body covered in muscle from shoulders, to eight-pack rippling down his stomach, to thighs and calves that would make a professional athlete proud, he was complete and utter masculine perfection.

Perfection who claimed she touched something in his soul.

How soon before the feelings inside her coalesced into love so indomitable it would never end?

She didn't know, but she refused to allow her fear of that kind of inescapable emotion stop her from reveling in every incredible sensation this moment had to offer.

"You lay there like a goddess and call me beautiful?" There was that dark, sexy laugh again.

"Hardly a goddess."

"You inflame my senses." There was not an ounce of sarcasm or cheesy innuendo in his tone.

Romi rolled to her side facing him and propped her head on her hand. "That's pretty poetic for a business tycoon."

She bent her knee and let it rest on the bed, her upper thigh crossing her lower one, giving her best "sexy goddess" imitation, which was very close to one of her favorite yoga poses.

His gray eyes sparked with approval. "I thought we agreed I am a Corporate Tsar."

"And tsars are poetic in bed?" she wondered aloud.

"This one is, apparently."

Privately, she agreed, pretty sure that under all those tycoon smarts and ruthlessness, lived the soul of a poet.

She brushed her hand up her own thigh and over her hip. "Are you coming back to bed?"

"Are you so sure you want to poke the bear?" he asked in a very bearlike rumble.

"If it gets you closer to me? Oh, yes." She liked looking, but now she wanted to touch.

To be touched.

"You know what they say…"

"Be careful what you wish for," she said.

In a smooth movement worthy of a jungle cat—no lumbering bear—Max joined her on the bed. "You just might get it."

He pressed against her shoulder so she fell back, adjusted her legs so there was room for him between them and blanketed her with his body, every maneuver confident and determined.

They both stilled so only their breathing caused the slightest movement. He felt so right over her, his body big and strong, fitting perfectly against hers.

Max's head dipped until their foreheads touched, their breaths mingling in excited pants. "I want to consume you."

"Yes, please." This is what she *wanted*, had wanted for a lot longer than she'd admitted to herself.

His kiss was beyond consuming; it was voracious and domineering and filled with unbearable need. Not only was she helpless to deny that need, but Romi could also not help matching it. Desire whooshed through in a wildfire that nothing but full and total consummation and satisfaction would have any hope of putting out.

Her hands roamed restlessly over him, mapping him with touch everywhere she could reach, the heat of his body translating back to hers. Every caress only fed her need to touch him more so that her hunger increased into a conflagration of unsatisfied longing.

He held her head in place as their mouths continued to meet in a passion so strong, it obliterated everything else.

The world around them ceased to exist as lips and tongues tangoed to a sensual tune old as time and fresh as an infant's first smile.

At some point, he took hold of her hands and drew them upward until they rested over her head. Her initial inclination to fight the restriction drowned under the onslaught of desire that washed through her in response to him taking control.

Holding her wrists together with one hand, Max began to touch her in ways she remembered and others she did not.

There was no limit to the intimacy of his caresses, no spot on her body too private, and so many unexpected erogenous zones that elicited astonishing increases in her ardor. He explored her body, provoking reaction with every brush of his fingertips, bringing every single nerve ending online until her body was screaming with the demand for more.

"Maxwell," she gasped, not sure exactly what she was asking for, but knowing she needed *more*.

He lifted away from her and that was *not* what she wanted. She tried to reach for him, but he still had her wrists pinned.

She made a sound of frustration she'd never heard from herself before. "What are you doing?" Oh, gosh…she was *whining*.

Romi did not whine. Never had.

He didn't seem annoyed, though. His expression was too intent for any other emotion than desire. "I want to give you pleasure beyond your wildest imagining."

"I'm pretty sure we're already there."

"I want more. Don't you, *dorogaya*?"

"You know I do." He was the one who had moved away. "Then you must trust me."

She opened her mouth and found herself bewilderingly bereft of answer. He didn't seem to notice as he released her hands and stepped back from the bed.

He turned away and opened a drawer in a dark wood

cabinet. When he turned back, he had a pile of cerulean blue silk in his hand.

"What is that for?" she asked in a voice roughened by passion.

He shook out the fabric and she saw that it was two long scarves, the silk so fine it rippled on the air with the slightest movement.

CHAPTER EIGHT

"I BOUGHT THESE months ago," Max replied in a musing tone. "I should have known then."

"Known what?" Romi asked.

"That you were not going to get out of my head."

"Okay." Assimilating the fact that the silk was the exact shade of her eyes when she was happy, Romi chewed on her bottom lip. "Um, what are they for?"

"Your pleasure."

"You want to tie me up." She shouldn't have been startled.

He had given her tremendous pleasure before by accepting control and using it to her benefit. She *wasn't* shocked. Not really.

She also wasn't sure *how* she felt about the scarves.

He must have read the ambivalence in her face because he said persuasively, "Just your hands."

"Not this time." She wasn't sure why, but she knew those scarves represented something between them that wasn't there yet.

He reeled back, as if her words *had* shocked him, maybe even *hurt* him. "You enjoyed me being in control very much a year ago."

"Yes." There was no denying it.

Romi wouldn't even try to deny that she got a special sexual thrill out of the attention he gave her, the way she became his entire focus when that happened. But she wasn't ready for the scarves, either.

She *really* wasn't sure why. One time, when they'd been dating, he'd used his tie to bind her hands behind her back while he touched her. She'd loved it.

He'd brought her to a mind-shattering climax, quickly followed by another.

And still, she wasn't going for the scarves right now.

He sat beside her, running the silk over her body, bringing forth shivers of sensation she made no attempt to stifle. "A year ago, you would not have hesitated."

"I know."

"So?" he prompted, clearly expecting her to change her mind.

It was that confidence that coalesced at least a partial understanding of her hesitancy for that type of game right now.

"Maybe I trusted you more before you offered my father's sobriety only to turn around and threaten it, or before you threatened to take advantage of my best friend's desire to protect me from her dad." Romi wasn't accusing, or trying to pick a fight, just stating the facts.

And maybe the fact he was trying to blackmail her into his version of marriage bothered her more than she'd realized. She *didn't* accept that he was a monster, but that didn't mean he couldn't hurt her with his single-minded view of the world and insistence of having his own way.

In fact, she was pretty sure he *could*.

The silk pooled on her stomach in a pile of fabric so light she barely felt it.

Frowning, he ran his hands down her body in a move that seemed wholly unconscious, hurt he probably didn't even realize was there shadowing his gray gaze. "The one has nothing to do with the other."

That hurt gave her hope, but didn't sway her certainty that she had hold firm on this. "You are too intelligent and understanding of human nature to believe that."

"*Dorogaya*, your pleasure is my top priority."

"You've never used that word before," she said because she'd rather focus on that than his claim. A claim she believed, but was not the point. "What does it mean?"

"Sweetheart."

"So, more intimate than *milaya*?" She hoped she'd pronounced that right.

"Yes. Why? Does it matter?"

"You know it does."

His use of this new Russian endearment was no coincidence, but was it by design or necessity to satisfy the poet in his soul?

He nodded, acknowledging that it did matter. "You do not wish me to use the scarves?"

"No."

"I have never used them with another woman."

She liked hearing that more than she would ever admit. "That isn't why I don't want to use them right now."

"You do not trust me."

"I'm not sure."

"You are punishing me."

"I don't think so." But she wouldn't give an unequivocal denial because she wasn't sure if she wasn't. At least a little.

He studied her measuringly for several long seconds before scooping up the silk, his fingers brushing over her abdomen with a clearly deliberate movement. "We will leave the restraints in the drawer for now."

"Okay."

"You know you only ever have to say *no* if you want me to stop doing *anything*."

"I believe you." They'd never needed a safe word.

Romi had once asked him if he ever played that way and he'd told her sex was not a game to him.

Despite the undeniable sensual games he played, she believed that. He wouldn't want a safe word because to Maxwell Black, respecting the word *no* was as important as keeping his word.

"I will know you trust me when you pull them out." And there was that hurt again, but he seemed no more aware of it.

She nodded, her throat suddenly gone too dry to answer.

He took the blue silk away and part of her regretted it, but not enough to stop him.

If her refusal bothered him on a conscious level, it didn't show. His erection had not flagged, his expression as filled with primal desire as ever. He came back to her, but didn't blanket her with his body as he'd done before.

Instead, he leaned over her to adjust her hands above her head, one clasping the other wrist. "Okay?" he asked.

She jerked her head in affirmative. "Mmm-hmm."

"Keep them there." It wasn't a question.

She answered anyway. "All right."

With a gentle, but inexorable touch, he separated her thighs, opening her in unambiguous familiarity. She was *his*. "You are so very lovely."

"Thank you." Her voice was husky. So strange. So not like her usual perky tones.

He brushed his fingers through the curls at the apex of her thighs and she jolted. Who knew her *hair* could be sensitive, but did that feel *good*? It felt amazing.

He leaned down and breathed in deeply. "I want the fragrance of your desire."

"Um, okay," she practically whispered. She felt like maybe she should be embarrassed, but there was no room for that kind of reaction between them.

There was too much honest need.

"There is a school of sexual thought that claims there are four different areas of the foot that are particularly sexually stimulating. Did you know that?" he asked as he gently pressed into one that sent a sensual frisson straight up her inner thigh and into her core.

"No, oh...ohhh..." Her answer tailed off into a moan as he found another.

"I'm an eclectic learner," he said almost conversationally, but the forceful desire in his dark metallic-gray eyes removed any casual feel to the words.

"Ye-esss?"

"I studied the pressure points of the body with a master of Dim Mak who had made it his life's work to also discover the unexpected areas of the body that could give the most pleasure."

"Aren't pressure points about pain?" she asked uncertainly.

"Knowing them is as important for avoidance as knowing those touches that can bring the greatest pleasure. I will never take you over that edge between pleasure and pain, though sometimes the ecstasy is going to be so great, you will wonder how close you are."

"Oh." She stared at him in shock, which she knew reflected her own innocence. "You studied how to have sex?"

"Not just sex, *dorogaya*, but amazing, mind-melting sex."

"The kind that makes you feel like you've had an out-of-body experience." She could remember that from a year ago and they hadn't even had intercourse.

His smile was both pleased and predatory. "Yes."

"But you're a Corporate Tsar. When did you have time?"

"Everyone needs a hobby. Naturally, my teacher also trained me in traditional kung fu."

No wonder his body was so buff. "It was part of your exercise regimen then." Even so, it was a little mind-boggling that Max had made a study of sex.

"Yes."

"That's a lot of work for part-time lovers." Her words rose and fell several octaves as his touch grew more intimate, moving up to her inner thighs.

He shrugged, but she saw something in his eyes.

And she had her answer. Or at least part of it. Just as she was excited by him taking control, Max got something out of it, too. "Your pleasure comes from controlling that of your partner."

"Part of it, yes."

Of course it would. A man like him, whose whole life was focused on control. Sex would be no different.

"Maybe you were just practicing for me?" She liked that thought more than that he'd given *this* part of himself to others before her.

It was *hers*. She wasn't sure where that possessive thought came from, but she did nothing to squelch it. Evidence to the contrary, it wasn't as if he could read her mind anyway.

His sexy chuckle didn't sound even a little mocking. "I think perhaps you are right."

When he bypassed her most intimate flesh to move up her body, she wasn't surprised. He'd done this a year ago. Built her pleasure until she was aching for touches her innocent body had never known.

Even so, she couldn't hold back a sound of protest.

"Shh…" His caress moved up her waist, his expression so hot it burned. "We will get there, but you only have one first time."

He was going to tease her more than before?

She realized the words had come out in a plaintive wail when he shook his head decisively. "I am not teasing you, *dorogaya*. I am *pleasuring* you."

"Tom-ay-to, to-mah-to," she gasped out as his thumbs skimmed over her rigid nipples.

Her breasts were small, but they had discovered together that the peaks were extremely sensitive.

"No, no, no…it is not just a different way of saying the same thing," he assured her. "To tease is to make your partner wonder if you will ever give the bliss craved and you know I will."

"On your time frame," she gasped out.

"That is my way." He said it with that Russian pragmatism she found both appalling and ridiculously appealing by turns.

"Sometime, maybe you should let *me* use the blue scarves." Oh, gosh…every word required effort as his caresses grew more and more tantalizing.

He stopped, his entire being arrested by her comment. He looked down at her, an unreadable expression on his face. "I have never been open to another lover doing so."

"But me?" she asked, knowing his answer mattered very much, though not at all sure why.

After all, she didn't really want to use the scarves on him; she much preferred it the other way around.

"Yes." Their gazes locked, as intimate as any caress. "Sometime, yes."

Elation filled her, but she just *knew* if he saw it, he would mistake it for triumph. Which isn't how she felt at all, so she did her best to simply nod and say, "I think I might like that."

"We will see, won't we?"

Yes, they would. But not today. Today, they would make love his way and she would give him the gift of her innocence. She didn't care if that was an old-fashioned way to look at it, she suspected he saw it the same way.

He kissed her then, whether it was to stop the conversation, or simply because that was the next step in her very willing seduction, she didn't know. What she did know was that it short-circuited her brain, which was already overloaded with pleasure.

His mouth possessed hers with the power of any tsar laying claim to his territory. Thrillingly. Absolutely. And with unmistakable intent.

Max's caresses became more zealous, taking on a feverish edge and increasing the delight to her senses when she would have said the latter was impossible. But something deep inside her basked in the tangible proof of the knowledge he wanted to make her his own.

She wasn't sure when her hands moved from above her head so she could wrap her arms around him, doing a little claiming of her own. Instead of stopping, as he might have done a year ago, Max's touches turned even more passionate and less controlled.

Part of her reveled in that, but the rest of her just enjoyed the next level of sexual delight it inspired.

Romi's hands lost purchase on Max as he moved to follow the touch of his hands with that of his mouth. Masculine lips, talented tongue and careful teeth teased already sensitive flesh until she was whimpering with need.

And not in the least embarrassed by that fact.

He nuzzled into the apex of her thighs, making a fully masculine sound of satisfaction. Then he parted her with his fingers before flicking his tongue against her clitoris and she tried to come up off the bed.

Her cry echoed around them as he continued to kiss her in the most intimate way possible. His fingers slipped inside her, the only flesh besides her doctor's that had ever been *inside* Romi's body.

There was no impediment to his deep finger thrusting. There wouldn't be after years in gymnastics.

The only area she and Maddie had diverged. Maddie had played soccer and softball. Romi had competed in gymnastics until her height decreed she would be able to take those aspirations no further.

Along the way, her inner barrier had stretched and finally broken, she was sure.

All thoughts of the whys and wherefores exploded in a cataclysm of bliss that had her shaking and screaming.

He gentled her through the climax and took her beyond to another layer of pleasure on the cusp of orgasm. Again.

Only then did he move to settle between her thighs, his swollen member pressing against the entrance to her body.

His expression was every bit as possessive as his position. "This is mine, *dorogaya*. Your innocence will never belong to another."

She wouldn't, either, in any way, she was sure of it. But there was no point in telling him. He was still laboring under the mistaken impression that if they married, it would be a temporary if years-long condition.

She knew better. Right then, she knew to the very depths of her soul *and* heart that this man would always be hers and vice versa. He might never let himself love her and that would inevitably bring pain with it.

But their souls were already entwined.

He didn't ask if she was ready. He didn't say anything at all. He just looked down at her with eyes that claimed, demanded and pleaded all at the same time.

The demand excited her in a way others might not understand, but the pleading she was sure he had no knowledge of. That decided her beyond a shadow of any possible doubt that the time had come to join their bodies.

"Please," she said to and for Max.

He nodded and began pushing inside, the wide girth of his shaft stretching her as she had never been stretched before. It felt so right, the link between their souls causing her body to accommodate his, his big frame surrounding her to make that connection even more intimate and perfect.

Romi didn't realize how long it had been since she felt truly safe until the moment when any sense of being alone and having to protect herself and those around her was gone completely.

Maxwell wasn't a tsar. He was her own personal Cossack. Bloodthirsty in his face to the world, but a wall between her and anything that might hurt her.

Even his own threats.

Where that certainty came from, she again did not know, but her inner conviction was absolute.

He made love to her with care, but also with a passion that grew increasingly unbridled until they strained together in an act millions of others engaged in every day, but still felt unique to them.

Special.

No one else would ever affect her as he did.

And no other woman would draw this lack of control, this unplanned, unmeasured movement and reaction from Maxwell Black.

Her pleasure built in proportion to the emotional intimacy she felt despite the lack of love words between them. She wasn't ready to acknowledge that feeling if it did reside in her heart. However, the invisible threads this intimate act was building between them went deeper than romance.

They were stronger than any words, even *I love you*. She would never live another day of her life without feeling a bond with this man.

Even if they didn't live in the same house and never again shared their bodies.

Was that because she was a virgin? She didn't know and didn't care.

It simply was.

Rapture built between them, their breathing growing more erratic, a sheen of sweat washing over their bodies, the physical heat between them growing by degrees. Her own heart was beating so fast and hard, she could feel it in her ears. She knew his tempo would mirror hers if she laid her hand against his heart, but holding onto his shoulders as they mated was taking all her coordination.

Suddenly that feeling, that ecstasy only he had brought forth, was right there, ready to burst inside her.

"Maxwell," she cried as she thrust up to meet him.

"Give it to me, *dorogaya*. Now." His voice was fractured and harsh with need.

She had no thought to deny him, bliss shattering through her, destroying the last defense she may have had between them.

And then his big body went rigid, his throat corded, his jaw clenched, before he gave a loud shout and came, too.

It was the most profound moment of her life. She had never felt this close to anyone. Not to her family, not to her SBC, not to anyone.

"Dorogaya." Max collapsed on top of her, whispering Russian into Romi's hair.

She welcomed the weight, not really caring how hard it was to breathe in that moment. She didn't know what he was saying, but she recognized the endearments he'd used with her and wallowed in the emotional warmth that poured through her with each utterance.

Sometime later, Max lifted away only enough to come down beside her, wrapping his body possessively around hers.

"That was amazing," she said, though it was probably pretty obvious to him that he'd melted her brain along with her nerve endings.

"It was." He sounded a little surprised by his own admission.

She didn't say anything, just snuggled in, feeling like she couldn't get close enough.

"We did not use a condom," he said, no regret in his tone, just stating a fact.

"No, we didn't."

"We will in future, but for your first time there should be no barriers between us."

And he said he had no romance in his soul. "I could still get pregnant," she pointed out, but with no heat.

"If you do, you do. We are getting married regardless. If you do not, we will wait some time for our first child."

"You think that's your decision to make alone?" she asked, not upset, because she *didn't* and he'd figure that out, but wondering.

"No. Do you disagree?"

"No."

"I thought not."

Hmmm…maybe he just *knew* some things, too.

"Which is not to be taken as an agreement from me on your highly irregular marriage proposal," she reminded him.

"Duly noted." He flipped her onto her back and looked down at her, his eyes dark with an unexpected renewed passion. "But for now, let's keep on testing our physical compatibility."

Oh, man, as if that was in any kind of question. She didn't say anything like that, though. Romi just returned kiss for kiss and this time around he seemed content for her to return caress for caress, too.

Later, she was grateful for his height and strength as they showered together. Her legs were as rubberized as if she'd run a full-length marathon.

Other muscles felt just as used, too.

She sure wasn't going to feel bad about missing her evening workout for the day.

He made dinner and it wasn't just soup out of a tin, either. He grilled chicken on the balcony to his penthouse, while rice finished in the cooker, and then sautéed asparagus in olive oil and garlic.

She smiled at him as they ate. "I'm impressed."

"That I can cook?"

"Yes. I'm pretty sure it's not your typical skill set for a Corporate Tsar."

He shrugged. "I don't like keeping staff on site. Besides, cooking relaxes me."

"I've heard that." She wasn't sure she saw the appeal.

"Don't you cook?"

"Nope. We always had a housekeeper." Mrs. K had come to work for them when Romi was in primary school, but there had never been a time when her father didn't employ someone in the position.

Romi was definitely no one's idea of a domestic goddess.

"We didn't."

She sidled up to him, enjoying the way his arm came out to automatically pull her into his side. "You don't sound like that bothers you."

"It doesn't, but since I wasn't raised with them, I'm more apt to find household help intrusive than not."

"You don't do your own cleaning." No way.

His smile was sardonic. "No."

"I didn't think so."

"Is it going to bother you?" Max asked her.

"What?"

"Not having live-in domestic help?"

"Is it going to bother you to do the cooking when we haven't arranged for a meal?" She didn't mind cleaning, or making her own bed, though admittedly she didn't very often, but that sort of thing was in her skill set.

Cooking wasn't.

"No."

"Then, no."

Later, Romi savored a bite of asparagus perfectly prepared. "I might have to take a cooking class someday. This is really delicious." Maybe Maddie would take the class with her.

"I am glad you like it." He ate his own food with little attention, his focus entirely on her. "I don't expect you to learn to cook. My housekeeper comes in daily and prepares most evening meals ahead of time."

"Good to know. *If* I decide to marry you."

He didn't get angry. In fact, humor played at the corners of his mouth. "Marriage will bring sufficient changes to your life without cooking."

"You don't say." She flicked him a flirtatious glance.

"Besides having a hell of a lot of sex, smart aleck."

"Did I say anything about sex?" Unaccountably, heat washed through her cheeks. She would have thought herself incapable of embarrassment about these things after their very long afternoon of lovemaking.

"You have a charming blush."

"Thanks?"

"You're not sure you appreciate my observation?"

"Not really, no. I think someone with more tact would have simply ignored my pink cheeks."

"I am not known for my tact."

"No, I don't imagine you are." She sipped at the crisp white wine he'd served with dinner. "So, you said *other* changes."

"You will have a security detail assigned to you."

"I'm sure that's not necessary."

He smiled, though there was very little humor in it. "I'm sure that it is."

"I can't attend, much less speak at a rally for lower CO2 emissions with a bunch of security guys following me around."

"You can dress them in T-shirts with conservation slogans, but your team will be with you at all times you are away from home." He made it sound like that was going to start immediately.

She frowned. "You don't always have a detail."

"I do."

"What about last night? There was no gun-toting gorilla in the car with us."

"No, but there was a two-man team of highly trained professional personal security agents in the car behind us. They parked at the end of the driveway."

"Oh. Were they in the ballroom?"

"No. Viktor had security covered for the reception. My detail got a couple of hours to do what they wanted. They didn't leave the hotel, though."

"Oh." So, that argument had gone nowhere. "Does your mom have security?"

"Mama has a bodyguard."

"Natalya wouldn't agree to a full detail, would she?"

Max's frown said it all.

That was more promising. "Couldn't I just have a bodyguard, too?"

"I prefer a two-man detail when you are away from home."

Or not. "Isn't that a ridiculous expenditure?"

"Nothing like paying out a ten-million-dollar ransom."

"Like you'd pay that to get me back." Seriously.

Max just looked at her.

No. He couldn't mean it. He had to be talking out of his hat. "Why would you?" Did they even have kidnapping insurance that went that high?

"You're talking like this is a done deal." His look wasn't quite a smile, but it was definitely triumphant.

Still, she recognized Max's conversational tactic. She'd used it herself. "I know what you are doing."

Max didn't want to answer her and so pushed the conversation in a direction he knew she didn't want to go.

"You'll be spending the night." He looked at her clothes, or lack thereof significantly.

She'd donned one of his dress shirts after dinner. Burgundy silk, it felt good against her skin and well, she *liked* the fact that it was Max's.

Romi had been wearing it since before Max started cooking, the fact he brought it up now indicated he *really* didn't want to talk about the fact he would pay such a ridiculously high sum to get her back.

Nevertheless, she stored that bit of information away, along with how matter-of-fact he'd been about it. He hadn't hesitated for a moment and that meant something, didn't it?

CHAPTER NINE

AFTER DINNER, ROMI texted Jeremy Archer and asked if she could schedule a phone call with him the next day.

He must have forwarded the text to his administrative assistant because that's who sent a time for the phone call to Romi.

Romi couldn't help comparing the response to how her dad would have reacted to a text from Maddie. First, Maddie *wouldn't* have had to schedule the phone call, not even back in the day when he was working at Grayson Enterprises full-time.

Second, if Romi's dad had been that busy, *he* would have texted to say so and schedule the time.

Even with the drinking, she much preferred Harry Grayson as a parent over Jeremy Archer.

Warm hands slid around to settle on her stomach and Max's hard body pressed against her back. "What are you thinking?"

She told him.

"You really mean that, don't you?" Max asked, sounding surprised.

She turned in his arms. "Parenting is about more than providing money for the best schools and someone to cook nutritious meals."

"I agree."

"Good."

"My mother set a very good example."

"Well, you may not believe it, but my dad did, too."

"I would not discount your childhood memories because your father has slid so deeply into the bottle in recent years."

"Thank you." She smiled. "So, we agree…children deserve their parents to be fully engaged in parenting."

"Yes."

"My dad did a great job raising me without my mom."

"And my mother did a stellar job without my sperm donor," he replied drily.

"But if we make babies together, they get both of us."

"Absolutely."

"Even if we don't stay together." She would say it so he didn't have to.

His muscles contracted around her, pulling her close against him. "Especially then."

He didn't seem to notice how tight he was holding her. An unconscious reaction to her words? Maybe.

Maybe Max didn't like thinking about ending the marriage she hadn't agreed to yet any more than she did.

She looked up at him through her lashes and leered playfully. "Wanna do some more compatibility testing?"

His eyes going molten, Max didn't even crack a smile. His answer was to simply bend down and lift her into his arms, heading toward the bedroom without delay. She hooked one arm around his broad shoulders and leaned forward to place soft little kisses against the side of his neck.

She inhaled deeply of his masculine scent. He'd shaved again before dinner and the faint traces of his aftershave added a woodsy fragrance.

Nuzzling into the scent, she flicked her tongue out to taste his skin. Salty and clean, it was all Max. The one man she wanted above all others.

Now, look who was being naff. But really? This man was it for her and she knew it.

The changing light indicated they'd come into the bedroom. Romi squirmed out of his arms before they could land on the bed together.

"What?" he demanded.

She pointed to the oversized brown leather armchair with matching ottoman in the corner. "Sit down over there."

He questioned her with his eyes, but he didn't argue. The chair was easily large enough to hold them both and yet he didn't look dwarfed in it at all.

His presence was so real, so overwhelming.

Corporate Tsar? Definitely. Maxwell Black would dominate the most ornate throne, not the other way around.

And she liked that with shameless enthusiasm.

She started to nudge the ottoman out of the way with her knee and suddenly it was sliding to the side, Max's foot shoving against it.

"Thank you," she told him.

He merely shrugged.

She tugged at the hem of his undershirt. "Here, let's take this off."

He'd put on a pair of sleep pants and black-ribbed man's tank top after their shower.

She loved the way the shirt clung to his muscles and exposed the hair she enjoyed so much, but she wanted him naked and this was the first, very necessary, step.

Max peeled it off and tossed the undershirt to the side. He gripped the waistband of his flannel sweats. "These, too, hmm?"

She nodded, happy he was on board with her plan. He might even know what her endgame was.

When he was naked, sitting on the chair, she dropped to her knees in front of him. Nostrils flaring, his jaw locked, bringing to mind that Cossack she'd likened him to earlier.

"You like me in this position," she tried teasing, but her own voice was husky with desire and anticipation.

Molten pewter locked onto her with laser intensity. "I like you any way I can get you."

"I believe you." And didn't that just make her want to do this more? Pressing against his knees, she asked, "Widen your legs for me?"

"You want to be in charge this time?" he asked, not sounding bothered by the fact. And not merely curious, either. More like intrigued.

"I want to experiment." Did that sound bad? "You're not just an experiment for me," she hastened to add.

"I know that." He let his thighs fall open, giving her an unhindered view of his rapidly growing erection and heavy balls below it. "I am at your disposal."

"So polite." Any mockery she'd meant to infuse her tone with was lost in her delight at his clear willingness to let her explore.

"For you."

"It's always just for me, isn't it?"

"Oh, yes." No doubt in his tone or expression.

She was special to him and despite his jaundiced view of relationships, he didn't hesitate to let her know it.

How was she going to keep any part of her heart from fixating on this man?

Unable to hold back any longer, Romi reached out and ran her finger down the hardening shaft and over the wrinkled skin lightly dusted with hair below. "It's so soft."

"This is what you call soft?" he asked teasingly, running his own hand over his engorged member. "It feels pretty hard to me."

Her breath caught at the sight. "I didn't mean that."

"No?" He let his hand fall away and laid both hands to rest on the arms of the chair, opening his body in an even more blatant invitation to her touch.

She shook her head, unable to form a verbal answer.

He was so perfect. So delicious. And so incredibly tempting. A temptation she had no impetus to hold back from giving in to.

Romi reached out to touch him again, this time like he

had. She curled her fingers around his steel-hard shaft. She loved the way he filled her hand, how his silky smooth skin felt so hot against the palm of her hand and pads of her fingers.

Running her hand up and down the intimate column of flesh, she elicited a low groan from him.

"I like touching you."

His grin was feral, triumphant, not amused. "I know, *dorogaya*."

She really loved the way he'd shifted to the more intimate endearment when they were making love.

And this was making love every bit as much as when he was buried inside her body. For her anyway.

She didn't know how he saw it, but she felt that same soul-deep connection.

Romi continued to run her hand up and down his erection until he was moaning steadily, tilting his hips up in silent supplication. She totally understood in that moment how exciting he could find giving pleasure to his lovers.

To her.

Seeing him react to *her* touch impacted her own desire like a matchstick to a bucket of gasoline.

Drunk on the power in a way wine never impacted her, she leaned forward and kissed the tip of his erection. Pearly liquid had formed and smeared on her lips. She flicked her tongue out to taste it. He groaned and swore in Russian.

"I like how you taste." She licked the remaining pearly liquid from her lips.

"I'm glad."

She dipped her head and did it again, this time tasting directly from the source. Salty. Sweet. *Maxwell*. A moment of intimacy she never wanted to know with another man.

Which said a lot about the *choice* she insisted she hadn't yet made.

Ignoring that thought, she took the head into her mouth, swirling her tongue around the circumference.

The sound that came out of Max was pure, visceral, primitive *need*. So, she kept doing just that, laving his bulbous tip with her tongue, bringing forth more sounds of passion and masculine pleasure.

"Move your hand on the shaft and suck." It was both masculine demand and plea.

Never had Romi heard instructions given in a tone of such raw desire.

No thought of denial entered her head. She gave him exactly what he asked for and discovered she enjoyed doing it. Very much.

No surprise there. She loved everything about touching this man.

Suddenly his hands were in her hair, tugging at her head. "Stop, Romi…please, *dorogaya*. You must stop."

She pulled back with reluctance and looked up at him. He shook his head, like he couldn't quite believe what was happening. "I'm too close to coming."

"Uh-huh." That was the point, wasn't it?

"You aren't ready for that. You may never want to taste me to that extent."

"Oh." She'd liked it so far, but she'd heard that a man's ejaculate was bitter.

Maybe it was a stronger flavor when he came?

She stopped her musing when he took both lapels of the silk dress shirt she wore in his hands and very deliberately, very slowly, pulled them apart so buttons and fabric gave.

Unbearably turned on, she did not move as he reached out to cup her small breasts, abrading her nipples with his thumbs. "You were made just for me."

That wasn't something she would ever deny. She wasn't the one who thought it was inevitable they would one day separate.

He sure wasn't thinking of separating right now.

He was thinking about her, his pewter gaze filled with desire *for* her, like she was all he could see.

With impressive strength that turned her on even more, he lifted her into his lap. Romi's knees fell to the sides of his thighs, his hands on her bottom holding her exactly where he wanted. Her own hands landed against his chest and she perched there, her body exposed for him.

He tugged her close to rub her soft, wet intimate flesh against his imposing hardness. Her clitoris met that hard masculine column of flesh, and pleasure jolted through her. He rocked his pelvis, stimulating the bundle of nerve endings until her breath was sobbing in and out in a vain effort to keep up with the speed of her heart.

She could climax like this, too easily. But that wasn't what she wanted.

Romi shifted with intent…Max lifted and tilted her…and then she was sliding down over him, her body once again stretching to accommodate his size. Encasing him in her most tender flesh, Romi held Max inside her, their physical connection complete.

The only sound between them their harsh breathing, hard fingers guided her hips into movement. "Come on, *dorogaya*. Move for me."

She obeyed because she couldn't do anything else, lifting and lowering her hips with jerky enthusiasm. Romi let him lead her into a rhythm that pleasured them both, bringing little bursts of ecstasy with every downward thrust of her hips and long moaning pleasure with every rise upward.

He praised her efforts until they climaxed again almost simultaneously, his rigidity and loss of control sending her over the edge into pure, unadulterated ecstasy. They froze there together in a tableau of rapture, her body slick with sweat, his pupils blown from sensation.

She didn't know how long they were like that, but eventually, Romi let herself fall forward and he caught her. Like she knew he would.

Max cradled her close against his body, his breathing still as harsh as her own. "We forgot the condom."

"Again," she panted.

"The first time we did not forget."

She didn't quibble. *She* had forgotten. He'd been looking to give her what she needed the first time they made love.

"Hopefully, it will be okay. It's the wrong time in my cycle." Her period had just ended a couple of days ago. She shouldn't be ovulating yet. She remembered that much from health class.

"We will be more careful."

She nodded against his chest. "Maybe we should keep condoms around the bedroom."

"Around the penthouse, more like."

She grinned where he could not see her, inordinately proud of herself. He thought they would lose control in just any room at any time. From a man of his controlling temperament, that was the ultimate compliment.

"You're pleased with yourself, aren't you?" he asked, a smile in his own voice.

"Well, your vaunted control hasn't been so much in evidence," she said modestly.

He laughed and it was only as she heard the rich sound and felt it rumble in his chest did she realize how wrongly he could have taken her words, or simply how offended he could have gotten. Because control really was a thing for this man.

"You put my control to the test. That is true."

"Does that make us *very* compatible or not very?" she asked, tongue in cheek, certain of the answer, not even a little bit worried.

"As if you did not know." He tilted her head up so their gazes met. "You're a handful, you know that?"

"I'm aware."

"Your father spoiled you."

"Sweet, not rotten. That's what Dad always said. He spoiled me sweet, not rotten."

Max's warm smile said he might just agree with the older Grayson.

Harry Grayson called at nine and cried when he spoke to Romi, but he made a promise, too. He promised to dry out and to try to make the program work.

"I know it's hard for you," she offered.

He made a sound of disagreement that surprised her until the words that followed. "Not as hard as losing my daughter to my weakness would be."

"I'm not going anywhere."

"At some point watching me destroy myself would hurt too much to stay."

His words shocked her. "No."

"Yes." He sighed, clearly trying to get ahold of himself. "Listen, kitten. All I've ever wanted for you was happiness."

"I know."

"You aren't going to be happy if I kill myself slowly with bourbon, no matter how good the year."

"Um, yeah…I could really care less how high-quality your liquor cabinet is."

"I know. You care about me." There was something in her dad's tone—an echo of the man who had raised her before his drinking had become such a consuming pastime.

"I love you, Daddy."

"I love you, too, kitten." Enough to try to get and stay sober.

He didn't have to say the words aloud. She heard them anyway and they gave her hope for the future with her dad she hadn't had in a long time.

They rang off and Max took her to bed, where he cuddled her for a long time before making love to her with such passion she forgot her own name right along with the phone call from her dad.

* * *

Max and Romi made love again the next morning before sharing breakfast and him insisting on driving Romi home before going into BIT.

He got out and came around to open her door with the kind of courtesy that usually either annoyed her or came off as fake. With Max it felt natural and she didn't mind it. Appreciated the gesture even.

He stopped at her door like he had the other night. "I will not come in." He smiled more naturally than she'd ever seen him, a tinge of mischief lighting the gorgeous dark gray of his eyes. "My schedule is too full this morning for a late start."

She shamelessly fluttered her lashes at him with a confidence born of their new intimacy. "Are you saying you can't resist me?"

"If I could resist you, I would not have spent a year pining."

Talk about exaggeration. If anyone had been pining, it had been her. Her best efforts to forget him notwithstanding. "Oh, be real, Max. Men like you don't pine."

"Call it what you like, but don't call it resisting you."

She nodded, touched in a way she was sure he had not intended. But that admission wasn't just about sex, no matter how he fooled himself.

Romi should know. She had spent her life avoiding things she didn't want to face. She recognized the signs.

But then maybe he wasn't trying to fool himself. He'd as good as said it was more than sex the day before. Not love. Oh, no. Not love for Maxwell Black, but it was definitely more than sex.

"I will pick you up for a late dinner," he said as he turned to go.

"We agreed. I need tonight to think." Not that she hadn't pretty much made up her mind, but he didn't need to know that.

He turned to face her at the bottom step. "You can think after dinner."

"That's not what we agreed."

"We didn't say no contact while you did your thinking."

"It was implied."

"No."

She opened her mouth to argue, but the words wouldn't come. To claim she didn't want to see him would be a lie. "Fine. But I'm not waiting until nine to eat. I'll expect you at seven."

His lips flatlined, but he nodded.

"Okay, see you then." She wasn't sure what to do with herself.

She should just turn around and go back inside, but she didn't want to. How pathetic would it be to stand there and watch him drive away?

Pretty pathetic, she figured, but that was what she was going to do anyway.

He'd have to get used to her foibles if he wanted to marry her, even if he planned to divorce her down the line.

Max's eyes narrowed, his jaw going hard, and then he was striding back up the steps. He didn't stop when he reached her, but took her into his arms and gave her a very thorough, very possessive kiss. "Seven o'clock. Pack an overnight bag."

"That's not the deal." But she was talking to his back and he didn't acknowledge the words before climbing back into the Maserati and driving away.

The phone call with Jeremy Archer was more than a little stilted. Romi was still angry with the corporate shark that treated his daughter like a bargaining chip on his game board.

"Where did you hear that?" he demanded after she'd asked if Maddie had made the threat to give her shares over to Harry Grayson.

"Does it matter?"

"My daughter didn't tell you. She wouldn't."

"If you know her that well, why didn't you know her well enough to handle this whole thing differently?"

"I don't need parenting advice from a child."

"You need it from someone," she told him with tactless honesty and not even a smidgen of guilt.

"She made the threat," he confirmed. "Why? Are you planning to capitalize on it?" he sneered. "It won't happen. That drunk isn't getting his hands on my company."

It was only twenty-five percent, but Romi didn't quibble particulars. She was too furious. "My dad is not a drunk!"

Jeremy's bark of laughter was harsh, clearly unconvinced.

It infuriated her. Her dad was an alcoholic, but he wasn't a waste of space, like this heartless man implied. "You were friends once."

"We still are," Jeremy said, sounding surprised she'd say that.

"You know the old saying, with *friends* like you, my dad doesn't need enemies."

"Don't presume to judge what you don't understand. Neither you nor my daughter ever showed the least interest in business. You have no idea how our world works."

"I know that my dad's world is one worth living in and yours isn't."

She wasn't surprised by the hangup that followed. Nor was she tempted to call back. Romi had gotten the information she'd wanted.

Maddie *had* made the threat. Whatever the particulars were, Romi didn't know and wasn't about to interrupt her SBC's honeymoon to find out.

Maddie hadn't told her because she knew Romi would have demanded she tear up the paperwork. To no avail. Romi had no doubts on that score.

Maddie could be more obdurate than executives in the oil industry denying the existence of global warming.

Even if Romi told Maddie of Max's threat, the redhead wouldn't alter the paperwork. In a month maybe, when she was happily married and sure that Viktor would keep a tight rein on Jeremy. But until then? Maddie would not consider losing the shares worth backing down from her father.

Oh, Romi planned to talk to her SBC about it anyway. When she got back from her honeymoon, but since the threat to her shares wasn't the main reason Romi planned to say *yes* to Max's proposal, it wasn't a priority.

She wasn't going to say yes because of his threat to her father's sobriety either. Harry Grayson wasn't going to *stay* sober if he couldn't remain in the program without the motivation of Max's merger. Romi was honest enough to admit to herself that she hoped this thing worked for her dad both in the short and long term, but she wasn't marrying Max and signing his ridiculously long prenuptial agreement for her dad's sake.

She was going to say yes to the blackmail proposal because she couldn't imagine her life without Max in it.

Did that mean she'd done the one thing she'd been determined not to and fallen in love with the Corporate Tsar?

She thought probably it did.

Surprisingly, that knowledge did not make her want to bury her head in the sand or run. In fact, there was a certain amount of freedom in acknowledging that there was no point in fighting something that had already happened.

She loved Maxwell Black and had every intention of taking a chance on marriage to him. Romi was primarily a positive person. She hoped for the best and for the most part believed it would come to pass.

She'd broken things off with Max a year ago because he had put a definitive sell-by date on their relationship.

There was nothing to hope for when he'd been adamant he only wanted six months to a year.

The prenup he'd given her to read over made it clear he didn't expect the marriage to last past ten years, but there was no *requirement* they divorce at that time. Regardless of the language of the contract, Max was going into this with a different attitude.

For one thing, he wanted children with her. Enough that he'd lost his vaunted control enough to make love to her without protection. Subconsciously, he wasn't afraid of creating that permanent bond between them.

After his own childhood, he wasn't *ever* walking away from his children, even if he thought he might walk away from her.

It might be wishful thinking, but Romi doubted that outcome, too.

A lifetime wouldn't be enough to grow bored or grow apart. They shared a soul even if he didn't see it that way and she thought maybe he was starting to get an inkling.

Romi had never been a person to be dictated by what others believed. *She* believed in soul mates and, she realized now, she believed Maxwell Black was hers.

How could she *not* take the chance on marriage to him?

When he came by for dinner, she'd have an overnight bag packed and an answer to his proposal.

CHAPTER TEN

MAXWELL CURSED THE tail end of rush-hour traffic as he drove toward the exclusive neighborhood where Harry Grayson had purchased his house before Romi had ever been born.

Maxwell would be cutting it fine, but he had every intention of arriving by the seven o'clock deadline.

If another lover had required an earlier time for dinner, he would have simply canceled. The fact he hadn't even considered doing so with Romi was somewhat disconcerting, but perhaps not so shocking.

He planned to make her his wife. That would require different concessions on his part.

The type of concessions he had made for no one but his mother and she rarely asked of him. He had no doubts Romi wouldn't be nearly as accommodating.

He might have no direct personal experience with that kind of thing, but Maxwell had always assumed a wife would be more demanding of his time and attention than any of his lovers.

Hence his lack of desire to ever enter the wedded state. Before this.

He wanted Romi, though. And she required more than a short-term affair. Though she'd tried to talk him into a one-night stand. For her *first* time.

He could not believe she'd thought a single night would be enough for them.

They were not just combustible in bed, he and Romi were an atom separating with nuclear force. Only they generated that kind of power when they came together.

The housekeeper led him into the living room, where Romi was sitting on the sofa looking through the same photo albums that had so fascinated him. Her father's drinking problem and loss of her mother aside, Romi had lived a clearly happy childhood.

The photographic evidence had shown that and so much more. Those albums revealed Harry Grayson's deep love for his daughter and for the woman he had married and lost.

Looking through them had made Maxwell question for the first time whether domestic bliss was truly an oxymoron.

Romi looked up when he came into the room, her gaze not quite focused, her thoughts clearly in the past. "Max. You're here."

"As you see," he replied wryly.

She smiled, her attention fixing more firmly on him. "On time. I'm impressed."

"You said seven."

"I did." She closed and stacked the albums. "I thought we could eat here before going back to your place."

So, she wasn't going to fight spending the night with him. Good.

The relief he felt in response to that knowledge was not acute. He was simply glad to avoid that particular argument.

They had more important things to do with their time. "I have reservations." At one of San Francisco's best restaurants.

It also happened to be one he knew Romi enjoyed.

Romi smiled at him persuasively. "Mrs. K made her famous spinach lasagna."

"Famous with whom?" he asked, not averse to the more private setting for their conversation.

Romi shrugged, self-deprecation in her tone. "Maddie and me."

"Then, by all means, I must taste this famous lasagna."

Romi's smile was blinding then and he made no effort to squelch the urge to kiss the happily curved lips.

Afterward, while Romi put away the photo albums, he called and canceled his reservations.

The table in the formal dining room was large enough for sixteen, but only one end was set, shrinking the large space to friendly dimensions. The white linen and candles set a tone that he hoped boded well for Romi's decision.

He pulled the light blue ring box out of his pocket and set it beside the place setting meant for Romi.

Her eyes tracked his movements, her expression for once not revealing even the smallest detail of what she was thinking. "I thought you were bringing that to dinner tomorrow."

"I will then, too, if that is necessary." But after last night, what were the chances Romi was really going to deny him?

Pretty low.

Maxwell spent his days assessing decisions just like this one and he rarely made a mistake. The emotional component existed in business as well.

The only true unknown entity was the way Romi's mind worked. Her reactions were guided by a set of rules he did not understand. He was still nearly one-hundred-percent sure of the outcome.

For one thing, there was the possibility, no matter how remote, that she was pregnant.

Ramona Grayson wasn't the type of woman to dismiss that as unimportant.

For another, she had wanted to give him her innocence. That was a gift of unparalleled importance in either of their worlds and would factor into her decision, even if she refused to acknowledge that truth to herself.

Romi didn't answer his implied question, but took her

seat. He joined her, unsurprised when Mrs. K came in with the salad course immediately.

"Tell me about your day," he said to Romi as he spread his napkin in his lap.

She didn't hesitate, opening up with frustrated candor about her phone call with Jeremy Archer. "He's just so cold."

"Business is all he knows."

Romi dismissed that with a wave of her hand, her fork thankfully empty. "Some people would the say the same about you, but you're not like him."

"You don't think so?" he asked, surprised by the observation.

He and the president of AIH had a lot in common. Though Maxwell was better at business than the older man. His killer instincts were more refined and his focus wasn't caught up with how he looked to others. Maxwell did whatever the hell he wanted and didn't worry if old-money San Francisco business approved.

Romi's expression took on a rare implacability. "You wouldn't make your daughter the pawn in a business proposal."

"No." Though how Romi had realized that truth in the face of what he *would* do, he couldn't quite figure.

Maxwell shook his head.

"What?"

"You don't make sense to me," he admitted.

"So you've said."

Touché. "One day I'm going to figure you out."

"Good luck with that. *I'm* not always sure why I do or think the things I do." She winked and gave him a wry smile.

Now, that did *not* surprise him. "Archer and I both do whatever we need to get what we want."

"No. You've already admitted you wouldn't use your child, so you don't do *whatever*. You do what you think is expedient and gives you the most control."

She, on the other hand, understood *him* all too well.

"Some things are easier to control than others," he informed her.

"You mean like people."

"Yes." Like her.

"Like me," she said, echoing his thoughts.

"Like you." It was something he was only beginning to come to terms with.

"Good. I don't think I could consider marrying you if that weren't true."

He'd never considered his inability to control her would be a benefit where she was concerned. He should have. Which only showed how off his usual game he was when it came to Ramona Grayson.

He had to admit, if only to himself, he enjoyed the fact she was so difficult to pin down as well.

Regardless, he already knew she was considering his proposal; he wanted to know if she was going to accept it. "Have you come to any conclusions?"

"I'm going to turn down the director position for LZO."

Okay, not what he'd been asking, but she knew that. "What is LZO?"

"A start-up environmental group."

"And you're turning down the directorship why?" He would have thought that kind of thing fit Romi to a *T*.

Romi waited to answer until she'd eaten another bite and taken a sip of her Australian Shiraz. "Maddie and I are starting a charter school for kids that need a break."

"I didn't know that." And it chagrined him that he didn't.

"Viktor is buying us a building as a wedding gift for Maddie. With the income from her trust and my Grayson inheritance and savings, we can swing operating expenses until we get the donor roll established."

"I thought environmentalism was your thing." Maxwell didn't examine his annoyance at the thought of Viktor feeding Romi's dream, even if it was one she shared with the man's wife.

"And children. It's all about making the world a better place for the generations to come, right?"

He wasn't sure, but he liked the outlook. "I'm impressed."

"Thanks."

"I will dedicate fifty percent of BIT's corporate giving to the school on a yearly basis." He didn't need to take time to think about it.

He believed in giving back and not because he was a bleeding heart like Romi, but there were very few charitable options Maxwell felt a personal connection to. Anything related to Romi would be one of them.

Romi gasped. "That's…" She trailed off, clearly speechless.

"About three million a year." And better than a building, even if the building cost more up front.

"I don't know what to say."

"Say yes."

"It's reliant on me marrying you?" she asked.

He couldn't tell if the idea disappointed or upset her. Maxwell didn't know what to think of this new ability to hide her emotions from him. He didn't like it, though.

He shook his head, making an instant decision and taking a gamble. "No, Romi. I believe in the next generation, too."

Which was nothing but the truth.

She stared at him, like she was trying to read his sincerity.

He lifted his brow in query. "Do you want it in writing before you give me your decision?"

"No." She ducked her head as Mrs. K brought in their dinner plates.

When the housekeeper was gone, Romi looked up at him. "I believe you."

She might think she didn't trust him, but she did. And

his risk had paid off because he'd made her realize it, even if only a little.

"Thank you." Her words were soft, but the look in her eyes?

Pure hero worship.

And he loved it.

"You are welcome," he replied. "I will have my corporate-giving coordinator contact you next week."

"Actually, we've got a lot of paperwork to fill out, permits to file, et cetera, before we're a fully functioning nonprofit."

No doubt. "I have someone who can help you with that."

"Maddie was going to use her trust's lawyers."

"The school's financial picture will look better with a lawyer that doesn't charge fifteen hundred an hour." The old-money lawyers in San Francisco didn't do pro bono and they charged three times as much as decent corporate lawyers with less prestigious clientele and addresses.

"True."

"I'll text you the firm's name and contact information. I'll let them know to expect your call."

"I'll talk to Maddie about it when she gets back from her honeymoon."

"Palm Springs? What kind of honeymoon is that?" He liked the city himself, but it was hardly the exotic locale most would consider for a wealthy businessman and his heiress wife's honeymoon.

"One tailored to the woman who loves that city above all others."

"Really?"

"It holds good memories for her."

"What about you?"

Romi shrugged. "I like it. She and I have been there together many times."

Was his soon-to-be fiancée being deliberately obtuse? "Is it *your* ideal honeymoon spot?"

"Not really." One of Romi's charming blushes pinkened her cheeks.

Intriguing. "Where would you want to go?"

"Europe would be nice."

"But not where you were thinking of. Come on, *milaya*, spill."

She bit her lip and then sighed. "Building a house with one of the organizations that provide homes for people and families in need. You know, something like that. Something we could look back on and say we started our lives together giving a family a home."

Okay. That was unexpected.

"We could not simply buy a house for some deserving family?" he asked faintly, excitement not his first reaction to the idea.

"It's not the same, is it?" Romi asked. She shrugged dismissively. "It doesn't matter. Just a dream. We wouldn't have a honeymoon anyway.

"Why not?" He really didn't understand the way her mind worked.

Didn't Romi want a honeymoon?

She shrugged again and then looked down at her dinner, cutting a precise bite of the lasagna. "I mean, it's not like we're a romantic couple."

They were something and it wasn't a couple who was going to skip their honeymoon.

"Madison and Viktor are?" he asked with sarcasm.

Romi's head snapped up and her eyes were filled with fervor. "They are. I mean, they both act like it's all about the deal and protecting Maddie's reputation and our dream for the charter school while Viktor gets to take over AIH, but they're so in love it's sickening."

"Are you sure you aren't seeing things that aren't there?" Maxwell's old friend had looked besotted at the wedding and reception, though.

"No. They'll both figure it out eventually. Until then,

things are going to be a little tense. You know with the whole, 'you married me to get my dad's company' thing between them."

"Maybe Archer was just playing matchmaker."

"I don't think so." Romi grimaced. "He offered the contract to you, too."

Romi really didn't like Jeremy Archer.

"Madison was never going to consider anyone but Viktor."

"Her dad didn't know that."

"Maybe he did." Archer wasn't an idiot after all.

"Yeah, you go on believing that."

"You hold a grudge, don't you?"

Romi looked surprised. "Actually, it takes a lot to make me mad, but then…yes, I suppose it takes a *lot* more to change that. And I'm really protective of the people I love."

"I've noticed."

"Yes, well…"

"It's an admirable trait. I, too, am protective of the people important to me." His list was just much, much shorter.

Up to the point he'd met Romi, it had had one name on it. Natalya Black.

He thought Romi probably had quite a few friends that had tasted her fierce loyalty, even if they weren't as close to her as Harry Grayson or Madison Beck.

Romi dropped all pretense of eating and met his gaze, her own beautiful blue eyes filled with serious lights. "Would your wife be important to you?"

Relieved that he could admit to the uncommon protectiveness without acknowledging whatever nebulous feelings might drive it, he nodded. "Naturally."

"At least as long as we're married."

He considered her words and how wrong they felt. "I think that once we have been married, you will always be on my short list of those who can claim my protection."

Provided the divorce was amicable, but he'd never had

a bad breakup. Of course just the thought of Romi walking away from him annoyed Maxwell.

Not something they had to discuss right now however. "Tell me about building houses in Haiti."

"It could be anywhere in the world really, but Maddie and I did it three summers in a row in Mexico. We always said we wanted to participate in a Haiti build, though."

"I'm having a hard time picturing Madcap Madison and Romi Grayson, well-known activist heiress, building houses in the Mexican heat."

"It was the most amazing experience. Everyone works like dogs to get these really simple dwellings built in a week, but the families are so grateful. The children…they're incredible. I loved working with them even more than working on the house team."

He could well imagine and said so.

She smiled, mischief glinting in her gaze. "You know what I can't imagine?"

"What?"

"You pouring concrete in the Haitian sun wearing scrubs and a sun hat."

Neither could he. Surely he could wear something else.

She must have read his look because she laughed. "Some people wear jeans and long-sleeved T-shirts, but scrubs are the most comfortable. They let air circulate and are easy to get clean. Both are important."

He wondered if his tailor did scrubs. "I see."

"So, what about you?"

"What about me?" He'd never had dreams of building a house in Haiti, that was for sure.

"What would your ideal honeymoon be?"

He liked that she asked, so he told her the truth. "I would like to visit Russia, meet the family that turned their backs on my mother and show them the success she raised without their help."

"I bet they regret pushing her away and miss her."

"If they do, they've never contacted her to say so."

Romi frowned. "Maybe they don't know how. Did she tell them she was emigrating to the United States?"

"I do not know."

"She changed her name, right?"

"Yes."

"So, neither of you would have been easy to find."

He refused to let them off the hook of responsibility so easily. "Where there is a will, there is a way."

"For men like you? Absolutely. For lesser mortals, not so much."

He didn't want to discuss his mother's estranged family any longer. He didn't even consider them his relatives. "Tell me you made your decision."

"I won't say I don't care about Maddie's shares."

"But…" he offered, because her tone implied it.

Damn. Was she going to say *no?* He did not believe it.

She fiddled with her silverware, looking down at the table before meeting his gaze, her own filled with certainty. "And you know how important my dad's health is to me."

"Yes."

"*But* I won't let you use either to blackmail me into marriage."

"You won't." A flurry of curse words fought to come out of his mouth. Maxwell bit them back.

Romi reached out and picked up the ring box. "So, you're going to have to deal with the fact that I'm agreeing because I can't imagine living the rest of my life without you in it."

Everything inside of Maxwell went still. "What?"

Romi's gaze warmed with emotion he refused to name. "I will marry you."

Totally unexpected and extremely unfamiliar panic filled him. "I don't love you. I won't love you." Double damn. Why did his code of honor insist on rearing its head right now?

"So you've said."

"And you are okay with that?" he asked, his mouth spilling words his brain had not authorized.

"Does it matter?"

She should ask. He'd been willing to give her compelling motivation to do what he wanted.

But this…this offer of herself because she wanted to do it? He had no frame of reference for it, zero sense of control with it.

"It does," he admitted shortly.

"You don't sound happy about that."

"I don't like the rules of the game to change."

"Unless you're the one doing the changing?"

"That goes without saying."

"I'll sign the prenup," she offered, like a lollipop to a crying child.

He frowned. "Yes, you will."

She grinned. "Feel better?"

"I did not *feel* badly to begin with. You are accepting my deal, whatever your reasons." That was exactly what he wanted.

"Yes, I am."

Why did he feel like that was entirely on her terms and because it was what *she* wanted? She'd agreed to sign the prenup. She'd agreed to the marriage. His plan had led to exactly the outcome he wanted, but somehow it had become her plan, too.

Was that what it meant to marry rather than take a lover? No other woman had ever influenced Maxwell's plans.

He sipped his wine, almost enjoying the sense of being off-kilter. It was so foreign to him. Maybe when the source was the woman who had blown his mind in bed the night before, it wasn't such a bad thing.

"I told your father I was going to marry you," Maxwell informed her.

Romi cast Maxwell a wary glance. "You were right."

"He seemed to think it would only happen if you wanted it to."

Romi grinned. "He was right, too."

For the first time in adult memory, Maxwell did not know what to say. She had chosen him even though he didn't love her like her father had loved her mother. What did that mean? Did she see an expiration date on their relationship?

Was the sex that good?

Did she plan to find the love of her life *after* Maxwell?

Anger washed over him at the idea.

Romi handed him the Tiffany box.

He took it with a silent question.

"I'd like to tell our children about the moment their father proposed."

That did not sound like a woman planning to move on to someone else later. Still, he couldn't let her think this was a romantic moment between two people who believed in forever. "I am not going on one knee."

"Fine." She stared at him expectantly, the vibrant blue of her eyes glowing with it.

"You already agreed to marry me."

"Yes." She sighed, some of the expectation dimming and along with it the glow. "Do you really want me to put the ring on myself?"

"No!" Damn. Where had *that* come from?

Her expression lightened and only then did he realize hurt had begun to shadow her blue gaze. That's where the glow had gone.

The Russian curse words that flowed through his mind in that moment put the others to shame.

He stood and moved around the table until he stood beside her chair. Leaning down, he gripped the back of the chair and turned it so she faced him.

Her eyes had gone round, her mouth dropping open in surprise. "Max?"

"There should be a story for our children." Russians understood family stories, the history that really mattered.

It wasn't about promising love for a lifetime.

He dropped to one knee, flipped the ring box open and offered it to Romi. "Will you marry me, Ramona Grayson?"

Beautiful blue eyes glistening suspiciously, she nodded her head really fast.

"Words, *dorogaya*. Give me the words. For your children." And for him, though he would never say so.

"Yes, Maxwell Black, I will marry you and I don't care how airtight that book you call a prenuptial agreement is, you'll have a heck of a time getting rid of me."

He didn't argue with her. Maxwell didn't want to dwell on invoking the clauses in the contract.

He took the ring from the box and put his hand out imperiously for hers. She gave it to him without hesitation, placing her left hand into his.

He slid the custom-designed engagement ring onto her finger and only then did she look down at it.

The ten-karat blue sapphire was the same shade as her eyes, the large diamonds on either side sparkling with Romi's effervescence. Set in a vintage-style Russian gold filigree band, he was very pleased with the Tiffany master jeweler's design.

"It's beautiful," she said in an emotion-laden voice.

"I had it designed for you."

"You're a planner."

"I am." No need to tell her the designers had been working on the ring since well before Jeremy Archer's marriage contract offer for his daughter.

"It's really big."

"But it fits you." And he didn't mean the size. Naturally, he'd gotten that right.

She choked out a laugh. "It does. I should be all about how ostentatious it is, but I love it."

"It sparkles like you do."

"Ooh, you really do say some of the cheesiest things and make them sound way too romantic."

He shrugged. "It's a gift."

That had only manifested for this woman, but who was keeping track?

"Are you ready to go home?" he asked.

Romi's face contorted with emotion. "Other than college dorms, I've never lived anywhere but here."

"You like the penthouse."

"I do."

"But this is home."

"Dad needed me for so long, I couldn't think of living anywhere else."

"Even so, you love this house, don't you?"

Romi nodded but smiled as she stood, no reluctance evident in her manner. "I'm ready to go."

They hadn't finished dinner, but he didn't think either of them was worried about that right now.

He wanted to go back to the penthouse and consummate Romi's promise to be his and he was certain she wanted the same.

CHAPTER ELEVEN

KNOWING MAX WOULD want it as much as she did, Romi had packed for a much longer stay than overnight.

Triumph had flashed in his gaze when he'd seen her suitcases and matching carryall. He'd smiled, too. "Lime green with white polka dots?"

"I suppose your luggage is black."

"No." He winked. "It's brown leather."

She melted at the wink and poured herself into the passenger seat of his growling predator of a car.

He shocked her by insisting she unpack before doing anything else, but when her last pair of bright purple jeans was hanging in his walk-in closet, which was the size of a small bedroom—and empty on one side for her—he carried her off to bed and they made love.

She'd thought maybe the night before had been so beyond the known universe because it was her first time, but she'd soon discovered it was just being with this man.

He rocked her world and by every indication she did the same for him.

Maddie returned from her honeymoon in high spirits and ready to find a building for the charter school. She and Romi spent hours trailing after Viktor's incredibly competent Realtor.

Not really sure why she did it, Romi hid her engagement ring in her purse whenever they were together. She didn't tell her SBC that Romi's father was in rehab and Romi herself was living with the man she intended to marry.

"Would you like to have Madison and Viktor over?" Max asked as she curled into his side while they watched his favorite crime drama one evening after Maddie's return to town.

They shared similar taste in music and most television shows. Their workout regimens were complementary and they had the same favorite area restaurants.

But she wasn't a huge fan of the crime drama they were watching, so she'd been texting with Maddie while it played.

"Huh? What?"

He turned down the television, a one-hundred-and-twenty-eight-inch screen that dropped down from the ceiling. "I said, you should invite Viktor and Madison over for dinner."

No, he'd asked if she wanted to. Apparently, to Max it was the same thing. "Uh…"

"We'll have it catered if you like."

Romi actually liked Max's housekeeper's cooking. She was no Mrs. K, but the woman was really talented at dinners that did well straight from the fridge or with an easy reheat. "That's not…I mean…Maddie doesn't know about us."

Max gave her ring a disbelieving look. "How can she not?"

"I…uh…I didn't tell her?"

"Are you asking me, or telling me?"

"Telling you."

"How did she miss the ring?" he asked, his tone carefully neutral.

"Um…I took it off."

Max picked up the remote and pressed a button. The television turned off and the screen lifted slowly toward the ceiling with a soft whir.

"Was your program over?" Romi asked, pretty sure it hadn't been, but she hadn't been paying attention.

"No."

"Oh, um…"

"That's a lot of ums for a woman who rarely feels the need for the word."

She didn't have an answer for that. He was right, she wasn't used to stumbling over her words.

He turned so their gazes caught. "Why haven't you told your sister-by-choice that you are engaged to be married and living with your fiancé?" Max's lips thinned and he did not sound happy.

"I…"

"You are not thinking about backing out."

"No."

"You said you wanted this."

"I do." Couldn't he tell how much she enjoyed being with him?

Dark gray eyes narrowed. "Then why?"

"They just got back from their honeymoon." It sounded lame, even to her own ears.

He wasn't impressed, either. "Nearly two weeks ago."

Romi had been hiding her ring and new living situation for weeks? It hadn't seemed that long. "Maddie is still settling into being married, though."

"And you sharing your own plans would somehow impede that?" Disbelief laced his tone.

"No. I don't know." Romi didn't really know why she didn't want to tell Maddie about Max.

"Viktor knows."

"What?" Romi demanded, sitting up in agitation. "How?"

"I told him."

"Why would you?"

"We are friends. More to the point why *wouldn't* you?"

"I…" Romi's gaze skittered around the room, seeking inspiration.

She'd discovered her whole avoidance thing didn't work with Max. Not only was he like a pit bull with a meaty bone when it came to discussing stuff he thought was important, but she also found herself wanting, even needing to deal with the real stuff when that real stuff included him.

Only not when it came to telling her SBC apparently.

"She's going to have to know or how will you ask her to be your matron of honor?" Max asked reasonably.

"For a courthouse wedding?" That was one thing Romi hadn't been worried about. "That's a little over-the-top."

He frowned. "Who said we were getting married in a courthouse?"

"Where else would we get married?"

"Holy Virgin Cathedral." His tone said he didn't understand why that hadn't been obvious to her.

"What? I thought…it's a business thing for you."

"It's a marriage and we're having a traditional Russian wedding. Mama is coming over tomorrow evening to discuss plans."

"Tomorrow?" Had he lost his mind? "No. That's impossible."

"Are you backing out?" he asked again.

"No!" Where did he get his ideas? "I told you I wasn't having second thoughts. It's just, I barely know your mother."

"All the more reason to have her for dinner. You can invite Madison and Viktor to join us."

"Get off the invite-them-to-dinner kick. When were you going to tell me your mother was coming?"

"I just did."

"That's not what I meant."

He made a visible grab for patience. "Romi, my mother wishes to get to know you."

"She's already met me."

"And yet you barely know her," he said, throwing her words back at her.

"Fine. So, she's coming for dinner. I'm not inviting Maddie."

"Why not?"

Romi thought about it, even as the sheer panic going through her did not abate, and realized she could think of no better buffer for this dinner with her future mother-in-law than her SBC.

Darn it. "She's going to be mad I didn't tell her." Really mad.

And Romi wouldn't blame her SBC, not even a little. She should have said something. Romi didn't understand why it was so hard for her, but she wasn't backing out and that meant telling Maddie about her upcoming marriage.

"She'll forgive you."

"I'm not ready to tell her."

He didn't ask why, just waited for her to say something.

"I always said I'd only marry a man who loved me as much as my dad loved my mom."

"I know," Max replied warily, like love was this really scary topic that could get up and bite him.

"She's going to think you love me."

"Is that a bad thing?"

"It's a lie." And Romi didn't want to lie to Maddie, but she wasn't willing to tell her SBC the truth, either.

That Romi was marrying a man she loved with every fiber of her being but who didn't believe in the emotion.

"What are you planning to do then? Wait to tell her when our first child is on the way?" Max asked with no small amount of exasperation. "I'm pretty sure Viktor will spill the beans before that."

"We aren't planning to get pregnant right away. We agreed."

"I was being facetious."

"Well, don't." Humor wasn't registering right now.

Max sighed and scooted closer, pulling Romi into his arms. "Madison married Viktor for reasons unrelated to love. She is not going to judge you."

"I know, but she won't understand, either. I'm not being

coerced." Even if Max had done his best to put the black-mail bid on the table.

He was silent for a few seconds and then he asked, "Does she know Harry is undergoing treatment for his alcoholism?"

"No."

"Don't you think she deserves to?"

"Yes, of course she does."

"So, tell her."

"It's not so easy."

"Why not?"

"Because I'm waiting for you to change your mind," she burst out and then covered her mouth with her hand, shocked by her own words.

"About what?" he asked. "The merger with Grayson Enterprises is a done deal. Your dad isn't leaving the treatment facility."

"That's not what I'm worried about."

"What then?"

"What if you decide you don't want to marry me?" she asked, stunned as the words revealed the worries she hadn't realized were plaguing her.

Max didn't look shocked. He looked patient. Aargh.

"Romi, *dorogaya*, I am the one who blackmailed you. Remember?" He tugged until she was straddling his lap.

She pressed close. "I like it when you call me that, not just in the bedroom."

"I will remember as you should how you came to be wearing my ring and it was not some great feminine plot that I'm going to wiggle out of soon."

"Right." Because they'd already signed the prenup and applied for the license.

Only she was getting almost everything she'd ever dreamed of. She was marrying the man of her dreams. They were planning a family together. Her dad was on his way to healthy. It was all so good, she was terrified everything was going to fall apart.

"You are mine, *dorogaya*. I am not letting you go."

She wanted to believe that. So much. "I thought we were just waiting to get married until my dad was out of treatment." At the courthouse. No fanfare.

Fanfare. A church wedding. That all just made it real. And real things could be destroyed or lost.

"We are."

"But you want a big wedding."

"Yes."

"At the church."

"Naturally."

"So, we have to set a date." She knew that only a *significant* donation to the restoration fund had gotten Maddie and Viktor their wedding date.

"Yes."

"Your mother wants to help plan the wedding."

"I am her only child."

"I haven't had a mother in six years." And her dad was in no condition to plan a wedding.

Though she very much wanted him to give her away.

Max cocked his head to one side. "I thought Jenna died when you were three."

"She did, but Madison's mom took over. Helene Archer was my mother like Maddie is my sister."

"By choice."

"Yes. She loved me."

"Mama will adore you as well."

"Chance would be a fine thing." It was another thing her friend Kim from the U.K. said.

Sometimes those Britishisms were more fitting than anything else she could think to say.

He laughed. The jerk. Was still laughing.

"Stop. It's not funny."

"This panic? Is hilarious. My mother will adore you. Madison will be thrilled for you. We *will* be married."

"Oh." She blinked up at him, biting her lower lip. "Maybe you could say it again."

"We will be married in exactly five weeks, three days."

"What? You said we were waiting for my dad."

"He'll get a day pass and we'll have a dry reception."

"You would do that for him?"

Max rolled his eyes. "Where is all this coming from?"

"I don't know." The knowledge she was falling deeper and deeper in love every day and he was just as committed today as he'd been a year ago to keeping that emotion out of his repertoire?

Max tugged her into his lap and tilted her face up toward his with a hand under chin. "You are mine, Ramona Grayson. You can't take that promise back. We will marry in the cathedral and proclaim this truth before our friends and family."

"Doesn't sound much like a business arrangement."

"I am at heart still a Russian man."

"So, you have a soul even if you are a corporate shark."

"I thought tsar?" he teased.

"That, too. Maybe they're the same."

"Could be. Some of the tsars were known for their bloodthirsty ruthlessness."

"You are ruthless." And why *that* didn't scare her when the happiness within her grasp did was one of life's little mysteries.

"But you are in my circle of protection."

"So, I have nothing to fear from you."

"No."

If only that were true. "I love you, Max."

Sometimes, she just had to say it out loud. Though, come to think of it, this might be the first time she'd said those three little words to him.

The way he stopped moving and talking and just stared

at her indicated that might actually be the case. She said, "I do, you know."

"You did say you couldn't imagine your life without me in it."

Which was as good as an admission. "Yes, I did."

"I will treasure your love."

"Will you?" How could he if he thought it was a weak emotion.

"It is a gift I will not take for granted."

"Even if you can't return it."

He winced. "Yes."

"Okay."

"So, tell your SBC."

"I will."

"Good."

He sealed her promise with his lips.

She returned the kiss with enthusiasm, helping him when nimble masculine fingers began unbuttoning the oversized tie-dyed men's-style dress shirt worn with her leggings.

His Armani sweater was an easy tug and off, and then there was just the black silk T-shirt, which followed with a ripple of his muscles.

She explored his chest, rubbing her body against his. This was always good. No matter when, how often or what they did together, it was good. Better than good. Incredible.

Their sexual compatibility couldn't be questioned. So, why couldn't he take the next step and love her?

If he wanted to know why she didn't want to have dinner with his mother? Maybe it was because Romi would rather smack the woman for teaching Max to eschew love in favor of pragmatism and carefully cultivated ruthlessness.

He showed that ruthlessness now, teasing Romi to the point of whimpering need, before lifting her and sliding her onto his condom-covered erection. She was on top, but he drove the coupling, thrusting up into her and hitting that spot inside that made fireworks go off inside Romi's head.

He held her hips in place, controlling the depth and angle of his thrusts.

They never broke eye contact through the long minutes of coupling and intense pleasure. She saw the way his skin flushed with the increased blood pressure that came before climax.

He could easily see the way her hair grew damp around her face from perspiration.

Bottomless pools, dark and mysterious, his eyes bored into hers, speaking messages she couldn't decipher, but that increased her bliss all the same.

She'd learned to appreciate the scent of his desire and even more so their combined musk. It was a heady fragrance that added to her desire, but also her security in their intimacy.

This was theirs alone. No one else combined with him for the exact same perfume of lust.

The way he inhaled deeply showed he enjoyed it just as much.

"My love," she gasped as her body hovered on the precipice of ultimate pleasure.

That dark gaze flared with something intense and his thrusting grew stronger and erratic.

"You like that word," she said with wonder.

"On your lips."

But not on his own. She refused to let that dampen the moment between them.

She simply reveled in the joy of intimacy and how much he clearly liked knowing he owned her heart.

"You are mine," he said, reflecting her thoughts.

"You are mine, too." She needed them both to acknowledge that fact.

"Yes."

She nodded, satisfaction and pleasure warring for supremacy in her heart. "With no expiration date."

He didn't reply, just increased his pace, his expression so intent, it sent shivers throughout her oversensitized body.

With knowing fingers, he shifted her and changed his own angle so his pelvic bone pressed into her pleasure spot on every upward piston of his hips.

Mini explosions of delight accompanied each movement, pleasure spiraling inside until it released in a cataclysm that made her scream and bow her body in shattering ecstasy.

They were cuddled in the bed after their shower, his body an octopus around her like she'd grown accustomed to, her breathing even and shallow as she hovered at the edge of sleep.

"You are mine," he whispered into her hair. "No expirations."

It was a huge admission, even if he made it when he thought she'd already fallen under the influence of the sandman.

Maddie took the news of Romi's engagement way better than she expected. "I thought there was something between you and that guy."

"Something big."

"You love him."

"I do."

"It's catching."

"So, you finally admitted it to yourself?" Romi asked her SBC.

"I did." She glowed with the kind of happiness Romi had rarely witnessed in her life. "He loves me, too."

"Oh, honey. That's wonderful. I mean I knew it, I just didn't know he'd admit it so quickly." Romi ignored the flicker of regret that she couldn't say the same, her genuine joy for her SBC big enough to cover it easily.

"Yeah, well something happened with my dad."

"Tell me about it," Romi demanded.

"He threatened to have me committed...to stop me from

taking control of my inheritance from the Madison Trust when I turn twenty-five."

Romi was shocked. Even Jeremy Archer wasn't that awful. "That jerk!"

"That's kind of what I thought."

Romi experienced a guilty twinge. "I think I know why he made the threat."

"Why?" Maddie asked.

"Because I asked him about the paperwork you signed that spelled out my dad would get the shares to AIH in the Madison Family Trust once you gained control in a couple of weeks."

"How did you find out about it?"

"Max told me."

"Oh." Maddie didn't look too worried, definitely no inkling Max might have used the situation as leverage with Romi. "I don't know why that would set my dad off. I mean he knows half the shares are going to you regardless."

"Max didn't tell me that!"

"Why not, I wonder?"

"Anyway, only my dad would have triggered the shares going to your dad. So, unless he wanted to take over Grayson Enterprises, his shares were safe. I didn't think he wanted the company that badly."

"Even if he did, it wasn't going to happen. My dad and Max signed a merger contract. Grayson Enterprises is now a subsidiary of BIT."

"That's great. He's protecting you already."

That was one way to look at it. Was in fact how Romi chose to see Max's actions. "He got Dad to go into treatment."

Maddie's eyes filled with tears and she hugged Romi. "I'm so glad, sweetie."

"Me, too." But something about what Maddie said had Romi thinking.

"So your dad was the only one who could trigger the

share dump from the trust?" Romi asked, trying to understand.

"Yes. I was protecting your dad's company from him."

"But…" That wasn't what Max had said.

To be fair, he could have misunderstood. Unlikely, but possible.

Not that it mattered. Romi hadn't made her decision about marrying him because of the shares.

"Wait a minute, you're giving me half of your shares?" she asked as that fact registered completely.

No. No way.

"Yeah, but you and I both know you'll just put the money back into the school. My dad needed to understand that he couldn't threaten you with impunity." Maddie so clearly didn't care about the wealth involved.

Romi was appalled. "But he threatened to have you committed."

"That was never going to happen." Maddie sounded so confident. "I'm not mentally fragile and even if he could get that self-serving doctor to say I was, Vik would never have let him get away with it."

"It's nice to know you have backup, isn't it?" Romi wasn't sure Maxwell Black would be as protective of her as Viktor Beck was of Maddie, but she knew he had her back in a way no one other than Maddie had in too many years to think about.

His deal with her dad showed that, no matter what justifications Max put on it.

"Yes. We've always been there for each other, but for a long time, we didn't have the power." Maddie was obviously as pleased by the turn their lives had taken as Romi was.

Romi's smile was still wry. "Not being corporate sharks in the making and all."

"It's…I'm…I'm just so happy," Maddie said, sounding a little flabbergasted by that reality.

Romi hugged her again. "And I'm incredibly happy for you."

"Ditto, sis, ditto."

Maddie assumed Romi was marrying for love and Romi let her keep thinking that. She'd spent her life protecting the people she loved and she wasn't going to stop now.

Besides, it wasn't a lie. Romi *was* marrying Max because she loved him and that was a truth that covered pretty much everything else.

"So, you'll come to dinner?" she pressed Maddie.

Her SBC nodded firmly. "Of course we will."

"Good. Max's mom is going to be there."

"She'll love you. How can she help herself?"

Romi laughed. "You're biased."

"Family should be." Maddie's grin was conspiratorial.

And Romi returned it in kind. "Yes, they should be."

Neither mentioned how that *didn't* work with Jeremy Archer.

CHAPTER TWELVE

"DID YOU MAKE this, Ramona?" Natalya asked Maxwell's fiancée.

Romi shook her head. "I'm afraid not."

His mama looked up at him with a fond smile. "Did you cook, *mishka?*"

"No, *Mama*. We ordered in."

"Oh." She frowned. "Ramona does not cook?"

"She's too busy saving the world," Madison said with a laugh.

His mother turned her attention to Viktor's wife. "Yes? I would think something might be left over for home."

"Mama," Max said in a tone he knew would get her attention. "I am not marrying Romi for her cooking skills. I employ a housekeeper for a reason and have more than one catering service on call."

"Well, yes, of course."

"Too bad Mrs. K won't be coming with Romi. That woman is a domestic goddess, but the only person she's more committed to taking care of than Romi is Harry," Madison said with a smile.

"She's besotted, but he'll never see it." Romi's laugh was a welcome sound.

She'd grown increasingly brittle in his mother's company. He didn't know why Natalya was behaving like this, but he was beginning to question the wisdom of asking her to help plan the wedding.

Madison nodded. "It's too bad, too."

"Can you imagine my father and Mrs. K?" Romi asked with still overflowing amusement.

"You believe your father should not consider his domestic staff in a romantic way?" his mother asked with some bite.

Maxwell stifled the urge to roll his eyes.

"Under most circumstances, it would be very bad form," Romi said with no give in her tone. "Making a pass at one's employees is not acceptable behavior and my father has too much honor to do such a thing."

"Does he?" Natalya asked, sounding unconvinced.

Maxwell wondered how long before he could offer to take her home. She did not like to drive and preferred his company over a car and driver.

"Yes," Romi replied with exaggerated patience. "But in this case, I'm sure Mrs. K would welcome his interest."

"She's a law unto herself," Madison agreed. "Mrs. K would run rings around him and I don't think she'd give up her job."

Maxwell's mother sniffed. "Surely she would be happy to keep home for him as his wife rather than housekeeper."

Instead of looking even a little offended, Romi's expression turned thoughtful. "You know, Natalya, I believe you are right. She might just keep him on the straight and narrow, too."

"Matchmaking thoughts?" Madison teased.

Romi made no effort to deny it. "I can't believe I didn't think of it before."

"You wanted the best for Mrs. K and your dad was too lost in his grief and the bottle to be that." Madison showed none of Romi's tendency to ignore the tougher subjects.

Romi considered her friend's words. "He still could be... lost in his grief."

"No. He's going to get better and come out of this treatment stronger. I just know it," Madison said with certainty. "Right, Vik?"

Viktor nodded. "I am sure you are right."

He didn't even sound a little like he was just humoring his wife. The besotted look he gave her however, put anything he said in agreement under the light of suspicion.

The man had succumbed and there was no doubt about it.

"Alcoholism is a genetic trait," Natalya pointed out with overt significance and a complete lack of tact.

Romi flinched and Maxwell stood without thought. "*Mam*, I will call for the car. Please gather your things."

"What, *mishka*? What do you mean? I am not finished with my dinner." She pointed to her only half-eaten plate.

He did not care. "You are."

"I was just pointing out that you might not be choosing from the strongest gene pool for your future progeny," she said as if that should make her thoughtless words acceptable.

The look he gave his mother was one he could never remember turning on her. "Romi is the woman I am going to marry, the only woman I have *ever* considered having children with and the only one I ever will."

"I didn't say—"

"I know exactly what you said and so does everyone here. If you hope for an invitation to return, you will apologize to Romi before we leave."

"But, my son—"

"What does *mishka* mean?" Romi asked, apropos of nothing.

At least in Maxwell's viewpoint.

"Little bear, though there's nothing little about my son," his mother answered, appearing as confused as Maxwell felt. "It is a childhood nickname that stuck."

Maxwell winced. Only with her had the nickname stuck and she only used it when she was reminding him that he would always be her son.

Romi's smile was too sweet in the current situation. "I like it."

Maxwell stared between the two women. His mother was

staring at Romi with an unexpected measure of respect. What had just happened?

Maxwell looked around the table to see if the others seemed to have more of a clue than he did. Viktor gave him a commiserating look tinged by clear confusion.

It was good to know Maxwell wasn't alone in his reaction to Romi.

Madison didn't look bewildered at all. Romi's sister-by-choice looked ready to strangle his mother.

And he couldn't blame her.

"I apologize if what I said offended you," his mother offered to Romi with the first sign of real warmth that evening.

"It did, but then I consider the source." Romi's words took a second to register for both Maxwell and his mother.

She gasped, but instead of getting angry as he expected, she smiled. "Touché. He is my baby, even if he is a business tycoon."

"Corporate Tsar. It's more fitting, don't you think?" Romi asked, no anger in her tone.

"He can be very imperious." Natalya looked at him with an expression that said maybe he was being that right now.

"I'm sure he doesn't get it from a stranger." Romi's smile took some of the sting from her words, but not all. "There's more than one flaw floating in our gene pool I guess."

Incredibly, his mother laughed.

Romi reached out, took his wrist and tugged. "Sit down, Mr. Tsar. Your mom will behave and we've got wedding plans to make."

"Your fiancée is a very confusing woman," his mother said. "I like her."

"I do, too. Very much."

"More than that, I think," Viktor said with that smug superiority Maxwell always wanted to knock off is his face.

Surprisingly, Mama didn't start in on one of her antilove tirades. She was busy asking Madison where she thought they should go shopping for Romi's wedding gown.

"I've asked our favorite boutique to get in a selection of vintage bohemian chic."

"You are not going to wear your mother's gown?" Viktor had asked what Maxwell wanted to.

Admittedly, he knew little of this type of thing, but Jeremy Archer had happily proclaimed to anyone who would listen that Madison was wearing her mother's wedding dress.

"Maddie's dress is a family heirloom," Romi explained. "My mom's was a typical 1980s monstrosity. Poufy sleeves, layers and layers of polyester lace and about four inches too long for me."

"Oh," Max said as if he'd asked the question.

"It's really not Romi at all. Besides, her dad doesn't need the reminder," Madison declared.

Romi grimaced and Maxwell reached down to squeeze her thigh in support. "He will be delighted to see you in your finery, whatever it ends up being."

Her smile in appreciation of his support was worth any amount of firm talks he would have to have with his mother.

"Where are we having the reception?" Natalya asked.

"We will host it, it's the bride's family's prerogative," Madison replied with no room for question.

"You and the Graysons are related?" Mama asked.

"She's my sister-by-choice," Madison said firmly.

Romi nodded. "We chose each other before we knew people didn't just get to pick their family."

"They do if they want," Madison opined.

"I would have liked to have chosen my family," his mother said with more feeling than she usually showed. "Mine soured me on any familial relationships but mother and son."

"Do you miss them?" Romi asked.

"I do." His mother's face took on a faraway look. "I didn't realize that neither of us was all wrong or all right until *Maxika* was a boy in school and I was too proud to write and tell them where I was."

"So, they don't know?" Romi pressed.

His mother shook her head. "I will never know if my own mama could forgive me and accept the woman I have become. She would have been proud of *Maxika* in any case."

"I'm sure your whole family would admire the man *Little Max* has become." Viktor's tease on Maxwell's other nickname didn't negate his words.

And Maxwell found himself oddly moved by the other man's approval.

"As your family is," Natalya said with a pat to Viktor's hand. "To think you two were once little boys together."

"It's hard to imagine either of them as little anything," Madison said with a laugh.

Romi gave them a droll look. "For me, too."

"I assure you. While he's always had a voice worthy of the little bear I called him, my *Maxika* was a small baby."

"His dad must have been a giant," Romi said with a smile for his diminutive mama.

Large in spirit, at a scant five foot nothing, her stature wasn't nearly as imposing.

"Oh, he was. In so many ways." Natalya winked at Romi.

And Maxwell started wondering again about how soon he could take her home.

"He would be so proud to know how well our son turned out."

"You never said that," Maxwell blurted before thought.

His mother looked more shocked by his blunt admission than he was by her forthright speech.

She reached out to pat his hand. "I never saw the point talking about a man you could never meet."

Maxwell was surprised when not a single person at the table asked why he *couldn't* meet his father.

"I'm sure he would be proud," Madison said.

It was Romi's turn to offer comfort with a caress on his thigh. "I think you got the best of his gene pool anyway."

He grinned down at her. "I am glad you think so."

"Oh, he did. My *Maxika*, he is a son to make any mother proud."

"He's always been a good stick to measure my own success by," Viktor said.

And Maxwell felt the first blush in memory heat his face with uncomfortable prickles. "It has been mutual."

And that was enough admissions for the night. Week. Month. Year. Lifetime maybe. "You wish to host the reception?" he asked Madison.

"Definitely. Have you two chosen accent colors?"

"Blue," he said without hesitation.

"And I bet I know just the shade," Natalya said indulgently as she looked at Romi.

"We could do a metallic pewter with the blue," Madison offered and Romi nodded, looking unaccountably emotional.

Pewter was close enough to black that Maxwell approved the choice. They discussed wedding and reception plans late into the evening.

Maxwell found the domestic scene unexpectedly enjoyable.

Romi couldn't believe how quickly the time leading up to her wedding flew. She, Maddie and the often acerbic Natalya Black went wedding-dress shopping, met with the caterers and tasted more cakes than Romi knew had flavors.

Max was often too busy with work to involve himself in the day-to-day preparations for the wedding. However, he had surprisingly strong opinions on things like whether she wore a veil—he wanted her to wear one—or if there was a ring bearer: Max insisted on one as well as a flower girl.

Romi's oldest cousin's children were going to fulfill the duties. Her grandparents and all her aunts and uncles and their children were coming to the wedding despite the short notice.

Romi was delighted, but sick with nerves at the thought of promising love and fidelity to a man who wasn't making the same lifetime commitment.

She clung to the memory of that one night when he'd said there was no expiration date.

It was easy when he held her at night, or made love to her. During the day while she and Maddie worked on bringing their dreams of a charter school to fruition or the wedding plans, and he was too busy to meet them for lunch or attend yet another cake testing—she hadn't found the right flavor yet—it wasn't so simple.

Her dad was doing well. They'd spoken on the phone again and he sounded so much like the dad of her childhood, she'd cried for an hour after hanging up.

Max had found her and seduced her tears into passion.

She still hadn't brought the blue silk scarves out, but he never mentioned them. There was a little part of her brain that said she'd let him use them after he told her he loved her.

Then she could trust him completely, right?

And she just wasn't sure those blue silk scarves were ever going to see the light of day.

Their sex life was plenty exciting without them anyway. Max wasn't complaining and neither was she.

She had asked him about the fact that Maddie's shares would only revert to her father if Grayson Enterprises was under threat from AIH.

"Jeremy Archer had already begun the initial steps of the takeover. It would have taken some effort on my part, but it could have been manipulated to look like he was the one threatening Grayson Enterprises."

"You're so Machiavellian, it's scary," she said, not sure if she was impressed, or horrified.

Maybe a little bit of both.

"It is a gift." His expression dared her to deny it.

"Some gift," was all she said.

"Grayson Enterprises is already improving."

"With you at the helm, I have no doubt."

"I am not exactly at the helm. I kept on the main management as I agreed to do for your father."

"But you've given them both direction and limits, right?"

"Naturally."

"Being your normal tsar-like self."

"If you say so."

"Oh, I do." She leaned up and kissed him. "I have a strange desire to make love to a tsar. Do you know anyone who might fit the bill?"

He had and the time that followed had left them both replete and winded.

But memory of those blue scarves niggled at the back of her mind, reminding her that he wasn't the only one holding something back in the emotions department.

Maxwell's wedding day dawned bright, the sunshine burning through San Francisco's morning fog.

Romi had spent the night before at her childhood home with Madison Beck.

Viktor had called to complain. "I don't know why I have to spend the night before *your* wedding alone."

"Because we will always give those two whatever they ask." Which did not mean Maxwell loved Romi.

Just that he recognized how necessary her happiness was to his contentment.

Viktor didn't bother denying the truth. "I have to admit I'm surprised you're getting married, Maxwell."

"Yes?"

"Business was always your mistress."

"The same could be said of you."

"Yes, well, as strange as it is to admit, there are things more important than business." Viktor still sounded a little bewildered by that realization.

"I have always known it." Recognition. Respect. These things were as important as his business success.

"I think we're talking different things here."

"You are happy with Madison." Maxwell hadn't made it a question because the truth was there for the most dull-witted to see and he was an astute observer of human nature.

"Happier than I knew it was possible to be." Viktor did not sound embarrassed to admit it, either.

Giving Maxwell the impetus to make his own admission. "Romi fits me and my life perfectly."

"That is good to hear. So, do you have someone to stand up with you?" Viktor asked.

Maxwell had not even considered it. "Do I need someone?"

Viktor made a comment about oblivious bastards.

"I do not suppose it is a task you would care to take on?" Who else would Maxwell ask?

Other than Viktor, he had no friends. Just business contacts and acquaintances.

"I would be honored."

Maxwell breathed out a sigh of relief. "Thank you."

"Romi would have been unhappy if you'd been standing up there alone. She would have felt sorry for you."

"No one ever need pity me."

"Don't I know it? But women see things differently."

Maxwell chuckled. "You are barely married and suddenly you are an expert."

"My grandmother told me."

"Why did Mama not realize this?"

"I don't know, I think your mom is still adjusting to *her Maxika* having another woman at the top of your priorities."

"She is too pragmatic for such sentiment."

"You don't really believe that," Viktor said pityingly.

And Maxwell realized the other man was probably right. "She *wanted* Romi to be sad?"

"Give Natalya the benefit of the doubt. Has she ever even attended a wedding?"

"Not since we emigrated."

"There. She didn't know."

"Isn't it common knowledge?"

"You didn't know."

There was a lot about social niceties Maxwell chose not to learn. If it didn't enhance his business, he wasn't interested.

"Thank you for telling me."

"You are welcome. Just be grateful you don't have to deal with the father-in-law from hell."

"I thought you and Archer were friends."

"We were, until he threatened to commit his daughter. He apologized, but I have random moments when I want to drop him from the windows in his top-floor corner office."

Maxwell laughed. "Romi's father is not mercenary. At all."

"No."

"He's not weak, though." Maxwell had thought at first the man was nothing *but* weakness.

He'd come to appreciate the strength it took to give oneself so completely.

It wasn't in *his* makeup, or at least he'd always believed it wasn't.

"Madison thinks he's Mr. Dad."

"Her and Romi both."

The men shared a silent moment of understanding.

"Just think—you have something to look forward to," Viktor said as they were preparing to hang up.

"What is that?"

"Considering how close Madison and Romi are, we will probably spend most major holidays together."

The idiot was still laughing when the call disconnected. But Maxwell wasn't sure that was such a bad thing. Having a friend rather than friendly rival might actually be worth something.

He was remembering that conversation as he waited in the front of the church for Romi to enter.

A love song popular back in the seventies began to play and then Romi was there on her father's arm.

The older Grayson looked a little rough around the edges, but better despite that. Romi was so beautiful, Maxwell's heart tightened in his chest and it was not a new experience. He still wasn't sure how to handle it though.

She wore a straight gown of pale ivory. It hung straight to the floor with daisy appliqués that were so *her*. She'd worn a veil like he asked, but it was attached to a 1920s-style headpiece.

Romi carried a bouquet of white daisies tied together with ribbons of blue and dark gray.

He was sure Madison would insist the color was pewter.

It was only in that moment seeing the two colors entwined symbolically that he realized the gray ribbon was the color of his eyes.

Romi's were shimmering with the love she told him of at least once a day. His favorite was when she called him *my love* while they were having sex.

It always made the experience hotter and more intense for him.

She looked nervous, too. And happy. And so completely focused on him, he actually started forward to join her rather than wait for her to come to him.

The titters that washed through their guests barely registered.

He only stayed in place because Viktor had grabbed his arm. "Don't worry, she's coming to you, *Maxika*."

Even the diminutive use of his name was not enough to make him turn from the vision of his bride to glare at his best man and only friend.

Romi's smile was blinding as she reached him. She leaned forward and whispered. "A little eager there, *Maxika*?"

Oh, hell. His mother had a lot to answer for. That name was never going to leave him. He just knew it.

"Very eager to make you mine," he replied, making no effort to keep his own voice down.

Even the priest cracked a smile at that.

The wedding went by in a blur. Everything except the promises.

He soaked in every word of Romi's vows, pulling them deep into his soul.

She seemed to be doing the same and when he ended his vows with a "No expiration date," she started to cry.

Thank goodness he got to kiss her then. He hated to see the woman cry. Even if it was in happiness.

Romi danced in Max's arms at their wedding reception.

Madison had gone all out and the ballroom at Parean Hall was decked out in white linen, the fixtures polished to a golden shine, the marble floor pristine. The accent décor and centerpieces were beautiful and every single one of them reminded Romi that she and her gray-eyed man had promised one another fidelity, honor, and to cherish the other. With *no expiration date*.

Her dad looked more peaceful and happy than she could ever remember. He'd even brought Mrs. K to the reception. Romi had invited the housekeeper as a guest, but her dad didn't have to be her escort.

That was all on him and she was proud of him for making the effort.

Jeremy Archer was there, but he was keeping a wide berth of pretty much everyone who mattered in his life.

Romi took pity on him and told her dad to go make nice. They'd been friends for years. Jeremy Archer wasn't perfect, or even nice, but he was a human being and his estrangement with his daughter clearly hurt him.

"You are too softhearted," Maxwell said.

Romi smiled up at him, not worried in the least. "You think?"

"Does he deserve your consideration?"

"Do any of us deserve the second chances we are given?"

Max's smile melted her to her toes. "Perhaps not, *lyubimaya*."

"What does that mean?" He'd never used it with her.

"I will tell you some day."

"But not today?"

He shook his head, the expression in his dark gaze flashing briefly with a vulnerability she could not push against.

She tipped her head back and waited. His kiss came less than a second later.

"Later," she whispered as he pulled his mouth away.

He kissed her a second time and promised against her lips, "Later."

They spent that night glamping, sleeping in a tent at one of the luxury camping resorts that had sprung up around the country. Their accommodations would have made any pasha proud.

In the morning, at the unholy hour of 5:00 a.m., because apparently they had a takeoff slot at six-thirty—though she had no idea where they were going—she asked with a yawn, "So, we spent our wedding night in a tent because why?"

Not that it hadn't been amazing, but even glamping wasn't something she would expect her Corporate Tsar to aspire to.

He smiled enigmatically. "We were practicing for the next two weeks."

"Practicing what?"

But he refused to answer. They spent the private plane ride talking, making love and sleeping cuddled side by side in the leather seats of his private plane.

She started to get a glimpse when the door of the plane opened to reveal the private airfield on Haiti. They joined a group from a worldwide charity that built houses and spent the next two weeks building homes for people who wouldn't have them otherwise.

Watching him pour concrete in a pair of designer jeans and long-sleeved Calvin Klein T-shirt, his head protected from the sun by a San Francisco Giants gimme cap, she realized that even if he never said words of love, and she was starting to suspect *lyubimaya* meant something in that regard, her heart was safe with this man.

And it always would be.

What other man in Max's position would give his new wife a honeymoon that required him to get dirty, sweaty and exhausted every single day and not one of them from really athletic sex?

Okay, so they had their own tent and bodyguards in the one right next to them, but that was hardly the privacy most men dreamt of for their honeymoon.

Not to mention that exhaustion thing. Building a house?

Not for the faint of heart, especially on the schedule they had.

It was neat seeing Max respond to the other members of their group, too. He was the unquestionable leader in any situation, but he took direction when he didn't know how to do something. And he *did not* know how to build a house.

He'd provided the building materials for the house they were working on, though. All of them. Apparently the cargo hold of his plane had been full and he'd had others shipped earlier.

She loved this man and even if he never told her he returned the feelings, she knew he would never walk away from her.

Not after building a house for a family in need to commemorate their wedding.

* * *

Maxwell critically surveyed the sturdy, simple three-room house.

Two small bedrooms, a slightly large living area and tiny bathroom would house a family of three generations and six people. He wanted to add a second story, but the charity coordinators had been clear. They had more houses to build and the family was thrilled. They'd been sharing a smaller space with another family of five.

He had to rethink how much of BIT's profit he donated to charity.

He didn't have to rethink his decision to marry Romi. Any woman who would want to do something so worthwhile for their honeymoon was a keeper.

For life.

And that didn't even scare him a little.

He hadn't said the words, but what others could describe the way he felt about her? The way he just felt happy to be next to her? The way he wanted to make everything better in her life? The way even his own mother stood second to his need to protect Romi's feelings?

He'd called her *lyubimaya* and he was almost ready to tell her what that meant.

CHAPTER THIRTEEN

THE BEDROOM WAS dappled with afternoon light as Romi lay naked on her and Maxwell's bed. Naked in more ways than one as she waited for her husband to join her for the afternoon tryst she'd set up.

Lying beside her on the bed were the two blue silk scarves.

She'd decided on her honeymoon that the time had come to show Maxwell she trusted him completely.

Footfalls made by Italian leather against hardwood announced his arrival.

"Now that is a beautiful tableau to come home to." He stood in the doorway, his eyes fixed on Romi.

She didn't think he'd even seen the blue silk yet.

She lifted it toward him. "I'm glad to hear you think so."

He stopped in his forward progression as he took in what she held in her hand. His pewter gaze locked on the silk for long, silent seconds before shifting to her face. "Are you sure?"

"Absolutely."

"But I'm still that same guy. The one who blackmailed you into marriage."

"The one who *tried* to blackmail me. You know why I married you Max and it wasn't because of your empty threats."

"They were not empty."

"Are you so sure about that?" she asked, her tone soft

with the love she had no desire to ever hide. "Because I'm not."

"I'm not like your dad."

"Oh, I know." But for the first time, she thought maybe Maxwell wished he could be like Harry Grayson.

"And still you love me."

"And trust you."

He nodded toward the scarves. "Completely. Those say so."

"Yes, they do."

The lovemaking that followed was earth-shattering, but not because he brought her to the pinnacle of pleasure over and over again before allowing her body to complete the journey. And while she learned she absolutely loved being bound by him, that wasn't why, either.

It was the tender way he touched her, the way he treated this like as important a gift as her virginity as her agreeing to marry him. None of which did her Corporate Tsar husband take for granted.

Romi walked into her childhood home, listening for voices.

Max had told her to see him here and she assumed they were having dinner with her dad.

She and Max had been back from their honeymoon for a month.

The charter school was taking shape and Maddie had been thrilled to find out that BIT would be making such a large yearly donation.

It was about half what Max had originally thought because after seeing the way he reacted to the people in need in Haiti, Romi had talked him into donating the rest to projects like the one they'd worked on.

He'd been so moved by the family moving into their new home, Maxwell had insisted on buying them all new bedding and cookware. He'd told them it was his way of honoring the woman who had married him.

Romi had cried. Unashamedly and unreservedly.

It had been an amazing moment.

She walked into the living room startled by the dearth of furniture. Some pieces still remained, but the sofa and her dad's favorite leather armchairs were gone. Was he redecorating?

Fifteen minutes later, she'd searched the house and found several rooms in similar states. Her father's study was totally empty, even the bookshelves.

Mrs. K was nowhere to be found and Romi's father hadn't shown, either.

He'd only been out of the treatment facility for a week, but he'd gone back to work and showed a passion for his company he hadn't in longer than she could remember.

"Romi! Where are you, *lyubimaya*?" Max yelled from the bottom of the stairs.

Her dad would never have done that, but Romi liked her husband's lack of submission to certain polite behaviors.

She rushed out to let him know she was there. "What's going on, Max? Is my dad remodeling?"

She would understand if he was. The house hadn't been changed since Romi's mother died. If Harry were willing to alter it, that would be a really good sign that he really was making strides in moving forward with his life.

Maxwell reached for her, even though he wasn't anywhere near enough to complete the intent. When he was within touching distance, he touched her. All the time.

It was kind of amazing.

His hand dropped by his side. "Not exactly, *lyubimaya*."

"Well, what exactly?" She stood at the top of the stairs, crossed her arms and tapped her foot.

He waggled his brows at her, showing a playful side he

had just started letting come out. "Come down here and I will tell you."

"You have that look on your face."

"What look is that?" he teased.

Oh, he knew. "Like you're about to make love to me."

"How astute you are."

"Not in my dad's house!" She laughed, though, really pleased that he wanted to, that nothing got in the way of Maxwell's desire to be as near her as he could get.

And most times that meant ultimately joining their bodies.

"Not his house," Max said with a secretive smile. "Not anymore."

"What?" Her dad had sold the house? "Whose house is it?"

"Ours."

"Are you serious?"

"Have I ever lied to you?" he asked, all humor gone.

"No." Not once. She loved this man so much.

He grinned up at her, the playful *Maxika* back. "Now, are you coming down here or am I coming up there?"

"You'd better come up here. There's more furniture." Specifically the bed in her former bedroom.

He took the stairs two at a time and swept her into a truly stellar kiss.

She reveled in his affection, but broke the kiss to ask. "So, you bought me my childhood home?"

Maxwell nodded. "Your dad needs a change."

"Yes."

"So, this is a good house to raise a family."

"I always thought so." Oh, gosh…she was ready to just melt. "Is there anything not perfect about you?"

"How long it has taken to admit I love you?"

"You love me?" She'd hoped, thought…but she couldn't be sure.

"With my soul and the heart I was so sure was dormant."

"You say the cheesiest things."

"But I am sincere."

"And that makes them poetic."

"I should have realized I loved you when I was plotting your downfall and that included you becoming my wife."

"You're used to seeing everything like a business to take over."

"I was scared of what you made me feel, so I hid behind a blackmail attempt. I can't believe you agreed."

"How could I say no? I loved you, too. I love you. So much, Max."

"Yes, well, you are married to a man who is perhaps not as smart as he always assumed."

"Why is that?"

"I wanted a church wedding. That prenup was more a set of strings than arrangements for me to get out of our marriage when I was ready to move on. As if that could ever happen."

"I noticed that." She could be forgiven for a moment of smug reflection.

This man had been worth every risk and she just loved him so much sometimes it hurt how much.

"And the church wedding?" he asked.

She agreed. "A definite sign."

"Did you know?"

"I suspected in Haiti." But she couldn't be sure. Not without the words.

"Because I built you a home to give away."

"Exactly. You're an incredible man, Maxwell Black. My man. My superhero."

"Your tsar maybe."

"Did the tsars love passionately and forever?"

"Some of them."

"Then you are my tsar."

"And you are my wife, the love of my life."

"With no expiration date."

"No."

The kiss that sealed their vows was filled with their love and sparked their passion, exactly how they lived their lives together.

EPILOGUE

MAXWELL HELD TIGHTLY to Romi's hand as he followed his mother into the hotel's restaurant.

Inside, waiting to meet him was a group of his family.

Viktor's was there, too.

Like so many things Romi and Madison did, they'd planned this reunion for their husbands with their Russian families.

Two men raised in a new country with a different life here to meet and connect with a heritage they'd never left completely behind.

His mom had been talking to her family for months. All Romi's doing. They were thick as thieves now.

Which was a good thing.

He loved his mother, but he adored his wife.

Her father was with them as well. As moral support, he'd called it.

Harry Grayson had remained sober and started dating his housekeeper two months after getting out of rehab. They were engaged to be married in the fall.

His family still wasn't speaking to him, but they'd made overtures to Romi.

She'd shown something of a ruthless streak herself in refusing anything to do with the rich and powerful Graysons because of the way they treated her father.

Maxwell looked over at where Viktor was hugging a distant cousin, his expression pained, and smiled.

Neither man had gotten any more adept at physical expressions of affection with anyone but their wives. That would change, too, soon.

Because Romi and Madison were doing something else together.

Carrying their first children.

The future stretched out in front of Max in a long winding road that glowed with promise, paved with emotion that might bring pain, but the happiness was worth it.

Very worth it.

* * * * *

If you enjoyed Max's story,
don't miss Viktor's story in
AN HEIRESS FOR HIS EMPIRE
by Lucy Monroe

Daisy ignored the red flag that warned against spending too much time with the wickedly charming Luiz Valquez. She had asked for four days and now she had the chance to have four weeks. She'd wanted a walk on the wild side, hadn't she? This was her chance to make it one to remember.

'OK. You're on.'

Luiz took her by the shoulders and pressed a blisteringly hot kiss to her mouth. Daisy leaned into him, unable to help herself from responding with burgeoning passion. He only had to touch her and she erupted into flames. She could feel the heat rushing through her veins, sending electric sensations through every cell in her body.

His hands cupped her face, his fingers splaying out over her cheeks as he deepened the kiss. His tongue played cat and mouse with hers, teasing and taunting hers to fight back. She flicked her tongue against his, doing her own little teasing routine, delighting in the way he groaned in the back of his throat and brought his pelvis hard against hers. She felt the hard ridge of him, the pressure of his blood building as his desire for her escalated.

'Relax for me, *querida*,' he whispered against the skin of her neck.

THE PLAYBOYS OF ARGENTINA

Introducing the untameable Valquez brothers...

The Valquez brothers are living legends.

Alejandro's business prowess is staggering,
Luiz's success on the polo field is unparalleled,
and their reputations in the bedroom are scandalous!

But they're both about to face their biggest challenge yet...

Alejandro must marry—
but he never anticipated desiring his convenient wife!

And notorious playboy Luiz finds his match
in the delectably innocent Daisy Wyndham!

You won't want to miss this scorching new duet
from Melanie Milburne!

You read Alejandro's story in:
THE VALQUEZ BRIDE
October 2014

Now read Luiz's story in:
THE VALQUEZ SEDUCTION
November 2014

THE VALQUEZ
SEDUCTION

BY
MELANIE MILBURNE

MILLS & BOON

Published in Great Britain 2014
by Mills & Boon, an imprint of Harlequin (UK) Limited,
Eton House, 18-24 Paradise Road, Richmond, Surrey, TW9 1SR

© 2014 Melanie Milburne

ISBN: 978-0-263-25025-1

From as soon as **Melanie Milburne** could pick up a pen she knew she wanted to write. It was when she picked up her first Mills & Boon® at seventeen that she realised she wanted to write romance. Distracted for a few years by meeting marrying her own handsome hero, surgeon husband Steve, and having two boys, plus completing a Masters of Education and becoming a nationally ranked athlete (masters swimming), she decided to write. Five submissions later she sold her first book and is now a multi-published, bestselling, award-winning *USA TODAY* author. In 2008 she won the Australian Readers' Association most popular category/series romance and in 2011 she won the prestigious Romance Writers of Australia R*BY award.

Melanie loves to hear from her readers via her website, www.melaniemilburne.com.au, or on Facebook: www.facebook.com/pages/Melanie-Milburne/351594482609

Recent titles by the same author:

THE VALQUEZ BRIDE
  (The Playboys of Argentina)
AT NO MAN'S COMMAND
PLAYBOY'S LESSON
  (The Chatsfield)
NEVER GAMBLE WITH A CAFFARELLI
  (Those Scandalous Caffarellis)

To Fiona Lowe, who is always at the end of the phone
to talk me down from the ledge!
Thanks for your warm and supportive friendship. XXX

CHAPTER ONE

IT ONLY TOOK Daisy Wyndham three and a half blocks to shake off her father's bodyguard. She grinned as she joined her two teaching friends inside the Las Vegas hot spot nightclub where they planned to kick off their half-term holiday before the winter school term in London resumed. 'See?' She high-fived Belinda and then Kate. 'I told you I'd make it before the first round of drinks. That's a new record too. It usually takes me at least five blocks to lose Bruno when I'm abroad.'

Kate, recently appointed to teach Year Three, handed her a glass of champagne with a frown pleating her brow. 'Is this going to happen *every* night we're here on holiday?'

Belinda from Grade Four rolled her eyes. 'I did warn you, Kate. Travelling abroad with Daze means excess baggage in the shape of a big hairy scary guy carrying a concealed weapon. Get used to it. It ain't going to change any time soon.'

'Oh, yes it is.' Daisy set her posture in a determined line. 'I'm sick of being treated like a little kid. I'm plenty old enough to take care of myself. And this holiday is the perfect chance to prove it.'

Once and for all.

Her father would have to get over it. She wanted to live her life the way she wanted to live it. Not be answerable to her dad, who thought she was still twelve years old.

'Why's your dad so protective anyway?' Kate asked.

Daisy took a sip of her drink before she answered. She hadn't told anyone of her father's former and thankfully brief connection with the underworld. It was far easier to pretend he was overly protective because she once went missing for half an hour as a child. That her disappearance had been nothing more than a case of her hiding from her mother behind a rack of dresses in Marks and Spencer was beside the point. 'My dad watches too many scary movies. He thinks as soon as I step foot in a foreign country someone is going to kidnap me and demand a ransom.'

Kate raised her brows. 'I realised you came from money but—'

'Pots and pots of money.' Belinda held her glass out for a refill. 'You should see her dad's estate in Surrey. Massive. He has villas in Italy and the South of France too. I didn't realise being an accountant could be so lucrative. Maybe I should've done that instead of teaching.'

Daisy chewed the edge of her lower lip. She had always believed her father's wealth was gained through hard work and discipline, building up his London accounting firm from scratch. She *still* believed it…sort of. How could she believe anything else? He was a loving dad who consecrated the ground she walked on. So what if he had once done a teensy weensy accounting job for a Mafia boss? That didn't make *him* a criminal. He had assured her it had been years and years ago and there was no reason to be worried now, although why he insisted she have top level security at her flat and always travel abroad with a bodyguard did make her feel a smidgeon of disquiet if she were to be perfectly honest. But that was something she had always put up with because it was easier than arguing with him about it. Arguing with her father was an exhausting and pointless exercise, which her mother, Rose, had found out the hard way when she'd tried to divorce him.

'If you've got so much family money why bother teaching?' Kate asked.

'I love teaching,' Daisy said, thinking of her kindergarten class with their sunny and earnest little faces. 'The kids are so innocent and—'

Belinda gave a half snort, half laugh as she wiped up a dribble of bubbles off the side of her glass with her fingertip. 'Yeah, like you.'

Daisy sent her a mock glower. 'Just because I'm technically still a virgin doesn't mean—'

'Technically?' Kate frowned in puzzlement. 'What? You mean you haven't actually *slept* with a guy?'

Here we go, Daisy silently groaned. Why was being a virgin such an oddity these days? Plenty of girls didn't sleep around. What about Amish girls? Or girls from other religious persuasions? Nuns, for instance. Anyway, having an overprotective father was like being raised in a convent. He'd practically strip-searched every suitor she'd ever had. He did background checks on them too. It was beyond embarrassing. Which was how she had ended up twenty-six years old without having done the deed.

But this holiday was going to change all that. Or so she hoped. Away from her father's watchful eye, she would be able to stretch her dating wings. Flirt a little. Relax instead of being uptight about the whole process in case her father suddenly appeared, waving a warrant for her date's arrest.

'Not yet,' Daisy said. 'But I'm not going to do it just for the sake of it. I want it to mean something. I want it to mean something for the guy too.'

'I hate to be the one to tell you this but you're unlikely to find your soulmate in Vegas,' Kate said.

'Don't feel too sorry for her,' Belinda said with a naughty grin. 'Our Daze has a toy. I gave it to her when we did Secret Santa with the staff at school last year. Didn't I, Daze?'

Daisy laughed it off but she hated that she still blushed over that wretched sex toy. She'd only taken it out of the box a few times… OK, well, maybe more than a few times. Truth be told, she hadn't put it *back* in the box. It was currently in her make-up bag in her hotel room because she hadn't wanted her new nosy flatmate to find it in her bedside drawer while she was away. Anyway, it had an absolutely brilliant massage attachment that was really handy when her neck or shoulders got tense.

'Hey, check out two o'clock.' Belinda jerked her head

towards the right hand end of the bar. 'The guy standing next to the girl in the dress that looks like aluminium foil. Do you know who it is?'

Daisy studied the tall black-haired man leaning indolently against the bar as he chatted to a young woman dressed in a tight sheath of a shimmering dress that clung to every curve of her supermodel-perfect body. The man's open-necked shirt was startlingly white against his deep tan and his eyes were so dark they looked as black as molasses. His hair was long enough to curl against his collar and was tousled, as if he'd not long tumbled out of bed or run his hands through it, or both. His mouth was nothing short of mesmerising. A sculptured sensual curve surrounded by a day or two of dense black stubble, the top lip curved upwards in a smile that looked more cynical than amused, and a bottom lip that hinted at a dangerously healthy sexual appetite. In spite of the heat in the crowded nightclub Daisy felt an involuntary shiver run over her flesh. 'No, who is it?'

'Luiz Valquez,' Belinda said. 'He's a famous Argentinian champion polo player. He's nicknamed in the press as the king of one-night stands. There's not a playboy out there who can change partners as fast as he does. He's practically turned it into a sport. Talk about smoking-hot.'

Hot wasn't even close, Daisy thought. She hadn't seen a man who looked anywhere near as heart-stoppingly handsome as him. He looked like one of those male magazine models, the ones who advertised designer eyewear or expensive aftershave. Oozing testosterone and sex appeal. Simmering with sensual energy that radiated out from him in soundless waves. She couldn't seem to drag her gaze back to her friends. It was glued to the man as if invisible wires had tethered her eyeballs. There was something about him that was so…hypnotic. Captivating. It wasn't just his staggeringly gorgeous good looks. There was something about his aura of supreme confidence she found intensely intriguing. She could see it in the arrogant tilt of his head, the hawk-like blade of his nose, the sharply intelligent gaze. It was as if he knew he was in command of the room and was biding his time to demonstrate it.

'Stop drooling, Daze,' Belinda said. 'He doesn't associate with mere mortals like us. He only ever dates supermodels or Hollywood starlets.'

Daisy was about to look away when he suddenly turned his head and his dark-as-night eyes met hers across the crowded nightclub. An electric jolt shot through her as his black brows lifted in blatant male appraisal. A hot spurting sensation arrowed between her legs and she almost fell off the bar stool she was perched on. She quickly crossed her legs but his gaze followed her right thigh as it hooked over her left one. Then his gaze came up ever so lazily the whole length of her body from ankle to hip, from her waist to her breasts, stalled there for a pulse-thundering pause, before coming up to her mouth.

He paused again. Longer this time.

Daisy felt her lips burn as if he had pressed a hot brand to them via his sexily hooded gaze. He then moved his gaze from her mouth to do a leisurely sweep of her chestnut hair, which she had bundled into a half-up, half-down do that framed her face and brushed her shoulders at the same time.

Then he came back to her eyes.

Daisy had heard the expression 'time stood still' many times. She had even used it on occasion. She knew it wasn't logically possible but this time it really *did* stop. She felt it. It was as if every clock in the night-club, every clock on every smartphone, every watch on every wrist shuddered and then stopped.

Tick. Tock. Stop.

Belinda snapped her fingers in front of Daisy's face. 'Earth to Daze.'

'Oh, my God.' Kate nudged Daisy in the ribs. 'He's coming over!'

Daisy sat with her heart pounding like a piston in an engine long overdue for a service. Her skin felt tingly all over. She could even feel the backs of her knees fizzing like sherbet trickled into a glass of soda. She felt giddy. She had to grip the edge of the bar with one of her hands to stop from tumbling to the floor in an ungainly heap.

She couldn't remember a time when a man had looked at her like…like *that*. As if she was the only woman in the room. As if he could see through her little black dress to the black bra and lacy knickers she was wearing underneath. As if he could see how her body was responding to him of its own volition, as if he had cast some kind of magic spell over her. It was shocking and yet somehow wickedly thrilling to feel as if she had no control over her body or her senses. It was as if the universe had heard a whisper of her desire to step out of her good girl shoes and was offering her up the most tempting bad boy man on the planet. No man had ever singled her out in such a brazenly sexual way. No man had ever triggered such a primal need in her. It pumped through her body like a potent steroid, making her aware of every inch of her flesh.

As he walked across the dance floor Daisy was reminded of Moses parting the Red Sea. Not that this particular Moses would be taking any notice of the Ten Commandments, she thought wryly. He had probably broken every one of them before breakfast. She watched as people stepped back in unison like a standing Mexican wave, and even the strobe lighting seemed to highlight his progress as if his coming over to speak to her was the main event of the evening.

He came and stood in front of her, so close her crossed over right knee was almost touching his trouser zip. Her kneecap began to twitch, the nerves beneath the skin doing frantic little somersaults at the thought of brushing against that hard and potent male body.

His mouth curved upwards in a smile so arrantly sexy it should have had an Adults Only rating. '*Hola.*'

Daisy practically melted into a pool of molten wax at his feet when she heard his deep baritone voice greet her in his native tongue. Spanish was delightful to hear from just about anyone's mouth but never more so than from an Argentinian's. The influences on Argentina from large migrations of Italians in the nineteenth century gave the accent in some regions an Italian flair that was as lyrical as music. But reading such information in a travel guide hadn't prepared her for the real thing.

She sat spellbound and speechless for five full seconds as the sound of his voice moved its way through her body like a seductive caress. She felt a slow blush creep over her cheeks and finally managed to get her voice to come out of her throat. It was a little mortifying it came out like a mouse squeak, but still… 'Hi… erm…hello.'

Luiz Valquez's eyes were even darker up close. She couldn't find his pupils in that glinting sea of bottomless black. His mouth was even more tempting now she could see its contours so intimately. His philtrum running down from beneath his nose was so well defined she could have placed her pinkie fingertip in the dish between the stubble-coated lines. She curled her fingers into her hand to stop from actually doing so. The force field of his body was so strong she felt like a microscopic iron filing in front of an industrial strength magnet. Pull. Pull. Pull. It was all she could do to remain upright on the bar stool.

'Would you like to dance?' He asked the question in English but with that distinctive accent wrapped around every word it made her spine feel as if someone was unbolting each vertebra.

But the confidence and self-assurance she had admired just a moment before now began to annoy her. He *expected* her to say yes. Kate and Belinda expected her to say yes. The whole nightclub crowd expected her to say yes.

Physically she wanted to say yes, but her rational

mind snapped back to attention like a soldier click-
ing his heels in front of a drill sergeant. The one thing
she loathed in a potential date was cocksure arrogance.
Who the hell did he think he was? He could go and
crook his little finger someplace else. If and when she
got involved with someone it would be with someone
who had the decency to treat her as an equal, not like
some desperate little sports star groupie looking for a
quick trophy shag.

'No.' Daisy softened it with a brief smile that didn't
show her teeth. 'Thanks anyway.'

Something in his pitch-black eyes sharpened. His
nostrils widened as if taking up the challenge of getting her to change her mind privately excited him. His
charming smile, however, didn't falter. 'You're with
someone?'

'No…I mean yes. My friends from school. The
school I teach at. *We* teach at. In London.' Daisy pointed
at her friends, only to find they weren't there. They had
slipped off the bar stools next to hers and were currently dancing on the dance floor with two men she'd
seen them chatting to as she'd come in from shaking
off her bodyguard.

Thanks a bunch, girls.

He followed the line of her gaze. 'They look like
they're having fun.'

What did he mean? That she wasn't? That she was
too strait-laced and uptight to have a good time? She
might not be used to colouring outside the lines but she
had her crayons sharpened. But she was going to use

them on someone a little less self-assured than him. 'Yes, they are.' Her chin went up. 'So am I.'

The meshing of his brown-black gaze with her blue one felt like a taser shock to her system. Her whole body reacted with a zinging fizz that whizzed through her blood like a missile. 'Is this your first time?'

Daisy felt her blush spread a little further until her whole body felt as if it was being engulfed by fire. How could he know that? How could he possibly know *that*? 'Erm…in Vegas, you mean?'

His slow smile tilted the side of his mouth. It tilted her stomach as well, like a paper boat on a tidal wave. '*Sí.*'

Oh, God, please don't keep speaking in Spanish or I will sleep with you. Here. On the floor right in front of everyone. 'It's my first time to the US, and yes, to Vegas as well.'

'What do you think of it so far?'

Daisy kept her gaze locked on his, not that she had any choice in the matter. Her eyes weren't responding to the message from her brain to stop staring at him like a star-struck fan in front of a Hollywood superstar. 'It's bold and brash and in-your-face. Vegas, I mean. Not the States in general. I haven't been anywhere else except LA and that was only when we landed at the airport.'

'Did you fly or drive down?'

'We came by bus.'

His half smile was still doing weird and exciting things to her insides. His smell was doing equally weird and exciting things to her senses. His citrus-based co-logne had grace notes of a rain-washed cypress pine forest that was powerfully intoxicating. For a tiny moment Daisy wondered if she'd done the wrong thing in knocking back his offer of a dance. She was supposed to be fluttering her flirting wings. What better way to get off the ground than with a bad boy who did nothing but flirt and have fun? But then she saw the anticipatory glint in his eyes. He thought he had her in the bag—erm, bed. *Damn him.*

'How long are you staying in Vegas?' he asked.

'Four days.'

His eyes moved over her face again, as if memorising her features. He lingered a little too long on her mouth, making her itch to send out her tongue to moisten her lips. Daisy had never been more conscious of her body language. She knew it had the potential to contradict every word she said. If it hadn't already.

'If you change your mind about that dance I'll be over there.' He jerked his head towards the area of the bar he had come from.

She raised her chin again, giving him a pointed look. 'With your date?'

He gave a negligent shrug of one of his broad shoulders. 'She's someone I just met.'

'And will sleep with just the once before you move on to the next candidate?'

His smile widened. 'You've heard about me?'

Daisy gave him the sort of look she would give one of the naughtiest boys in her kindergarten class. 'It's not a reputation to be proud of. Sleeping your way around the world with a bunch of nameless women you'll never see again.'

His eyes glinted wickedly. 'It's a tough gig but some-one's got to have the stamina to do it.'

Do it. The words triggered a flood of erotic thoughts to her mind. Him doing it. Her doing it. *With him.* Their naked bodies wrapped together, his hair-roughened thighs entrapping hers, his hands cupping her breasts, touching her in that secret valley between her thighs.

Daisy suppressed a whole body shudder, somehow keeping her features in her best haughty schoolmis-tress mask. But, looking at his dancing black eyes, she suspected he knew exactly the effect he was having on her. It was the same effect he had on any woman with a pulse. He was utterly gorgeous. Über-sexy. Terrify-ingly irresistible.

She gave him another one of her stiff on-off smiles to disguise the torment of temptation currently assail-ing her. 'Will you excuse me? I'm falling behind my friends in the having-a-good-time stakes.'

He didn't move a millimetre, which meant she had to sidle down off the stool and brush past his tall mus-cle-packed frame. The shock of his body against hers was like coming into contact with an electric fence. She glanced up at the laughing gleam of his gaze and an-other fiery blush swept over her entire body.

'A word of advice before you go.'

Daisy pursed her lips. 'Go on.' *If you must.* She didn't say that bit out loud. She didn't need to. Her folded arms and rolled eyes said it for her.

He pointed to the drink she had left behind. 'Don't leave your drinks unattended.'

She gave him an irritated glance. How galling to

have him point out her oversight. It made her feel all the more foolish and gauche. 'I *have* been out at night before.'

'Maybe, but some of the nightclubs along the strip have had a problem with drink spiking. Better to be safe than sorry.'

'I know how to take care of myself.'

His eyes had the most annoying habit of staring at her mouth, which made her want to stare at his. She fought the impulse but within a heartbeat her gaze had tracked to the sensual seam that was no longer smiling but set in more serious lines. For some reason it made him even more stop-the-traffic gorgeous. She drew in a breath that felt as if it had thumbtacks attached. The ear-throbbing music faded into the background. The sweaty, gyrating crowd on the dance floor might have been in another state for all the notice she took of them. In spite of all the competing aftershaves and expensive perfumes, she could still smell him. The sharp fresh tang of his cologne was imprinted in her brain and she knew she would never be able to walk past a cypress pine without wanting to hug it. It was a shame he was so arrogant. A little fling with someone like him would have been fun to talk about with the girls when she got home.

But a one-night stand?

Out of the question.

Daisy gave him an arch look. 'Do I have lipstick on my teeth or something?'

'Why don't you smile so I can check?'

She pressed her lips together. *Where was a naughty*

*step when you needed on*e? 'Why did you come over to talk to me?'

His eyes twinkled as they held hers. 'I saw you staring at me.'

'I wasn't staring!' Daisy spluttered. 'My friends pointed you out and I merely glanced at you to see if I recognised you, which I didn't. Sorry if that upsets your ego.' She wasn't one bit sorry.

A hint of a smile still lurked in the black ink of his eyes. 'It doesn't.'

'No, I imagine not.' She knew she sounded ridiculously prim but she couldn't seem to help it. The words kept coming out in a steady stream—sounding scarily like Miss Edith Cassidy, her starchy soon-to-retire headmistress. 'I expect you're used to young women the world over dropping into a swoon when they see you but I'm not one to be impressed by outward appearances.'

'What does impress you?'

Daisy paused as she thought about it. 'Erm…'

He leaned back against the bar and crossed one ankle over the other as if prepared to settle in for the night. 'Money?'

She frowned. 'Of course not.'

His mouth curved in a cynical arc. 'What, then?'

'Manners. Intellect. Morality.'

His smile became an amused chuckle. 'An old-fashioned girl hanging out in Vegas. Who would've thought?'

Daisy was sure she would have permanent lines around her mouth from all the lip-pursing she was doing. 'Were you born naturally obnoxious or is it something you've worked on over the years?'

He pushed himself away from the bar and ran an idle fingertip down the length of her bare arm from her shoulder to her wrist, still with that mocking smile curving his mouth. 'Save the last dance for me, *querida*.'

Daisy gave him a withering look as she brushed past him to join her friends, 'Dream on.'

Luiz decided to leave the nightclub at 3:00 a.m. He'd lost sight of the English girl when he'd stopped to chat to someone he knew on the polo circuit. By the time he'd turned around again she had disappeared. He refused to acknowledge the strange little pit of disappointment in his belly. Easy come, easy go. There were plenty of other girls he could pick up if he could be bothered.

He wasn't sure what it was about her that fascinated him so much. She wasn't his usual type with her girl-next-door looks and prim goody-two-shoes manner. But her chestnut hair had highlights that shone like spun gold and her darkly lashed intensely blue eyes reminded him of the Aegean Sea. Her skin had that roses and cream bloom young English women were famous for and her mouth was generous and full, suggesting a passionate nature behind the haughty I'm-too-good-for-the-likes-of-you air she affected.

He'd spent most of the evening watching her watching him. It amused him to see her try and disguise her interest. Hiding behind a drink she barely touched or the shoulder of one of her friends. Pretending to be having a good time when clearly the nightclub scene was not her usual stomping ground. For all that she'd dressed for the part in a little black dress and high heels, she looked out of place. She reminded him of Bambi pretending to be Barbarella.

Luiz walked back to his hotel room alone. He'd had plenty of offers he could have taken up but for once he wasn't in the mood. He was still shaking off the jet lag from when he'd flown in from Argentina, where he'd spent some time with his older brother and his new wife, Teddy. Seeing his brother so happy had triggered a restless feeling he couldn't block out with endless partying. It used to be just him and Alejandro. They were a team. The playboy Valquez brothers, notorious the world over for having a good time. Women flocked to them wherever they went.

Now Luiz was on his own, wandering around the globe in search of the next victory on the polo field. Trophy after trophy lined the bookshelves at his villa—the villa he only ever visited when the polo schedule allowed. He lived out of an overnight bag; he didn't stay long enough in one place to warrant a suitcase. He checked in and checked out of hotels like he checked in and out of relationships. One-night stands were his speciality. What was the point of hanging around for someone to do the check out on you? He had seen his mother do that to his father. He had seen his brother suffer the public humiliation of being jilted at the altar ten years ago. Sure, Alejandro was happy now, and Teddy seemed like a top sort of girl, but that sort of commitment wasn't for him.

No one was *ever* going to have the power to hurt him. Again.

Luiz was five doors away from his suite when he saw her—the English girl with the cut-glass accent. She was with a man who was leading her by the hand towards a room on the other side further down the corridor. However, something about the little tableau didn't seem right. The English girl was not steady on her feet and her blue eyes were no longer clear and bright but glazed and disoriented.

'What are you looking at?' the man with her snarled at Luiz.

Luiz glanced at the English girl. 'Are you all right, *querida*?'

The girl looked at him vacantly, her head lolling to one side. 'I need to go to bed…'

'In here, sugar,' the man said as he shouldered open his door.

Luiz put his arm across the door jamb like a blockade. 'You want me to call the cops or will you let her go quietly?'

The man breathed alcohol fumes over Luiz's face. 'She wants to be with me. She said so earlier.'

Luiz wanted to punch the man's teeth into the back of his preppy pretty boy head. 'She's not capable of saying anything and you damn well know it. Did you do this to her? Give her something in her drink to make her come with you?'

The man gave him a *cool it* look. 'Hey, man, what's your problem? Is she yours or something?'

Luiz felt a sour taste come up in his mouth. Anger came

up with it, moving through his body like a bloated tide. What sort of man treated a woman like a toy they could pick up off a shelf? *You do*, a little voice piped up. He brushed aside the pricking arrow of his conscience and directed his ire where it belonged right now. 'I'm going to ask you again. Did you do this to her?'

The man's eyes darted either side of the corridor. 'Is this a sting or something? Are you undercover?'

Luiz grabbed the man by the throat and pushed him back against the wall so hard all the pictures hanging along the corridor rattled in their frames. 'I'm going to give you three minutes to check out of this hotel. After that I'm calling the cops. Got it?'

The man swallowed against the heel of Luiz's hand. 'I didn't do it. It was my mate. He said it wouldn't hurt her. He put a few extra shots of vodka in her drink when she wasn't looking. I wanted her to loosen up a bit. She was acting all stuck-up. Said she wasn't interested, but I know she was. They all are in Vegas. That's why they're here. To have a good time.'

Luiz bared his teeth like a wolf against a rival. 'You come anywhere near her again and I'll make sure you're sipping your meals through a straw for the rest of your life. Understood?'

The man nodded as he rubbed at his throat, slinking away like a cowed animal until he disappeared into one of the elevators.

Luiz muttered a curse and bent down to where the English girl had slumped to the floor. He touched the side of her creamy cheek with a light fingertip. She was a ghastly shade of white and her skin was clammy but her breathing was normal. 'Are you staying in house?' he asked.

She blinked owlishly at him. 'Have we met before?'

'Briefly.'

She cocked her head and narrowed her gaze as if trying to place him. 'You look kind of familiar...'

'Your room number?' he prompted.

Her smooth brow wrinkled for a moment as he helped her to her feet. Luiz tried not to notice the way the skin of her hand felt against his, soft as the petals of a magnolia.

'I think it has a seven in it.' She gave him a bright smile. 'That's my lucky number. I once won a day spa package in a raffle we had at school. It was so relaxing I didn't want to leave. It was the first time I had a Brazilian. Belinda talked me into it. It hurt like hell. Funny thing is I get them all the time now. I guess my pain threshold has risen or something. Normally I'm the biggest coward out. I cry when I take a plaster off. It's pathetic.' Her dazzling smile faded a little as she added, 'I blame it on losing my mother so young. She died in an accident when I was ten...'

'I'm sorry to hear that—'

'My father never remarried,' she went on as if he hadn't spoken. 'I thought he would replace her as soon as he could, but no. He never did. Not that he hasn't had lovers. He's had lots and lots of them. No one ever likes to think of their parents doing it, do they? It's gross. My dad is over sixty. I mean, what *is* he thinking? Isn't it time to put his tackle away and have a rest?'

'I guess boys will be boys, no matter what their age.'

She gave him another angled look. 'Am I keeping you from something? Someone?'

'No.'

'No hot date?'

'Sadly, no.'

She scrunched up her forehead again. 'Why not?'

'I asked a girl to dance with me but she turned me down.'

She made a sympathetic sound. 'Oh, poor you. Were you terribly crushed?'

'Irreparably.'

She put a hand on his arm, sending a shock of electricity straight to his groin. 'Never mind. I'm sure you'll find someone some day. I think there's a soulmate out there for each of us. We just have to be patient and wait until the planets align. Or at least that's what I keep telling myself.'

Luiz momentarily lost his train of thought as he looked at the soft and generous bow of her mouth. Her lips were still glossy from a recent coating of lipgloss, making them look even more luscious and tempting. He could smell the flowery scent she wore, a mixture of gardenia and honeysuckle that teased his nostrils and made him think of sultry summer nights. 'How much did you have to drink?' he asked.

'Hardly anything. I'm not a big drinker. I talk too much when I have wine. I guess that's why it's called truth serum, huh? *In vino veritas.* That's Latin, by the way. The truth is in the wine.' She gave him another megawatt smile. 'That's why I stuck to vodka. One shot with orange juice and I didn't even get to finish it because I was too busy dancing. Did you see me? It was awesome. I've never been able to do the Macarena before.'

Luiz felt like a parent handling a wayward teenager after a night out on the town. 'Do you have your room key with you?'

She fished around in her purse, her brow doing that little crinkly thing again, her teeth embedded in her lower lip. After a fruitless search she dropped her purse and reached inside the left hand cup of her bra and handed him a card key with another broad smile. 'I knew I put it somewhere safe.'

Luiz could feel the heat of her breast on the card. His fingers moved over its surface in a stroking manner as he locked gazes with her. 'This card isn't from this hotel. Do you know which one you're staying at?'

She wrinkled her nose like a child refusing to eat spinach. 'I don't want to go *there*. This is much nicer.'

'Do you know where you are? What floor you're on?'

She gave him a vampish look, batting her impossibly long eyelashes coquettishly. 'I'm on *your* floor.'

He ignored the wanton come-on in her gaze on principle. He could have any woman he wanted. He didn't have to resort to drunk or stoned ones. He might be considered an irascible rake but even *he* had some standards. 'Listen, *querida*, you need to lie flat in a dark room until you sober up.'

She pushed her lush mouth out in a pout. 'I'm not drunk. Look, I can walk in a straight line.' She tottered off along the corridor, arms out wide to stabilise her passage. She turned and came back towards him but the fourth step was her undoing. Her legs suddenly tangled and she came down in a heap and would have fallen badly if not for him catching her in time.

He gathered her slim body in his arms, trying not to notice the sweet cinnamon of her breath on his face as she snuggled up close with her arms flung around his neck. 'I'm soooo tired…' She gave a huge yawn and dropped her head against the wall of his chest and closed her eyes with a soft little sigh.

He gave her a gentle shake. 'Hey, you didn't tell me your name.'

She made another soft purring sound and burrowed closer to his chest. 'Need to sleep now…'

Luiz caught sight of himself carrying his rescued damsel in one of the gilt mirrors hanging above the hall table. Her shiny shoulder-length hair was swaying loose in a soft cloud over one of his arms, tickling the skin where he had rolled back the cuffs of his shirt. Her conservative black dress had ridden up, revealing slim legs and thoroughbred-narrow ankles, and a soft dreamy smile curved her mouth as her cheek settled against the steady beat of his heart as if she had finally found home.

He let out a low rough expletive. 'Now what, Sir Galahad?'

CHAPTER TWO

DAISY WOKE WITH a construction site hammering inside her head. Her mouth felt as if she had been sucking on a gym sock all night and her stomach was churning so fast it could have spat out pats of butter.

She cranked open one eye to find herself in a plush penthouse suite instead of her budget book-three-nights-get-one-free hotel room. Chandeliers dripped from the high ceiling in a waterfall of sparkling and twinkling crystal. The walls were papered in a luxurious satin-embossed two-toned stripe that was unapologetically masculine and yet opulently stylish. The lighting was softly muted but she could see a sliver of bright sun-light through the gap in the brocade curtains, suggest-ing it was well past dawn. The acre of carpet looked so thick she was sure if she took one step on it she would be knee-deep. Maybe neck-deep. The pillows behind her were as soft as clouds and the sheets that covered her naked body were super-fine Egyptian cotton.

Her stomach swooped. *Naked* body? She lifted the sheet and peeked beneath it. *Eek!* She'd had sex with someone? No. Not possible. Not in a million squillion

years. She was not the type of girl to go to bed with
a stranger. She hadn't even gone to bed with a friend.
Flirting was one thing. Sharing her body with someone
was something else again. But why on earth would she
be naked in bed if she hadn't?

No. No. No.

Surely she hadn't. *Had* she? She pressed her legs together. *Nope. Doesn't feel any different.* She checked
her breasts for any love bites. Scrambled up onto her
knees to glance in the mirror to see if her neck had any
signs of foreplay.

Nothing.

The door of the bedroom opened and Daisy choked
out a shocked gasp and quickly cupped her hands over
her breasts as Luiz Valquez with his laughing black
eyes entered the room. '*You?*'

He gave a mock formal bow. 'At your service, *mi
pasión.*'

His...passion? Double eek! Daisy dived under the
sheets, pulling them right up to her chin. Oh, dear God.
What had she done? Or, more to the point… What had
he done? Anger came to her rescue, filling her voice
with fulminating rage. 'Where are my clothes?'

The half-smile that tilted his mouth had a glint of
devilry about it. 'Where you left them.'

Her eyes widened in horror. Had he—*gulp*—stripped
her? Stolen her clothes? Was she to be sold into sex
slavery? Never to be heard from again? Where was her
damn bodyguard when she needed him? She threw Luiz
a combative glare, determined not to show how terrified
she was. 'I won't let you get away with this. You don't

know who you're dealing with. I have connections that could wipe the floor with you.'

He had the gall to chuckle. 'You mean those two travelling companions of yours?'

Daisy felt her flesh shrink on her bones. Oh, dear Lord. What if Belinda and Kate had been kidnapped as well? Were all three of them to be shipped off to some ghastly foreign hellhole where disgusting men would paw and slaver over them? She could already see the headlines. *Three London Infant Teachers: Tragic Victims of International Sex Slave Ring.* 'Wh-what about them?'

His dark eyes gave nothing away other than amusement. 'They weren't the least bit interested in coming to your rescue.'

She narrowed her gaze to slits. 'What do you mean?'

'I asked them to fetch you from my suite last night but they refused.'

Daisy shot him a look of pure venom. 'I don't believe you. They would never leave me to fend for myself.' *Hmm, maybe Belinda would.* 'Anyway, how did you contact them? You didn't have their numbers or names.'

He inspected his square and buffed nails in a casual manner. 'I sent a staff member to find them. Apparently they were too busy with their dates to come and collect you.' He looked at her again and added, 'Their message to you was—and I quote—"Have fun".'

I am so going to kill you, Belinda.

Daisy huddled further up the bank of pillows under her shroud of luxury sheets. He looked so…so unlike a sexual predator. He was too sophisticated. Too clock-stopping handsome. Why would he have to resort to kidnap when he could crook his little finger and have any woman he wanted? *Except you*, she thought as she recalled her haughty rejection of him in the bar. She swallowed to clear the ropey knot of part dread, part excitement currently clogging her throat. She had spent the night with one of the world's most notorious bad boys. How had he changed her mind? And why couldn't she remember a single second of it? 'What happened last night?'

He hooked an ink-black eyebrow upwards. 'You don't remember?'

She frantically hunted through her memory but it was like rifling through a file that hadn't been organised properly. Nothing made sense. She could only remember watching him for most of the night, feeling annoyed he was never without a partner. He seemed to be flaunting them before her every time she looked at him, doing raunchy dance moves with an array of nubile young women.

It was nauseating.

Daisy had staunchly remained a wallflower—her default position—until a compatriot from Ealing had asked her to dance. She hadn't really wanted to dance with him but she must have changed her mind for she remembered being on the dance floor and at one point cannoning into Luiz. The shockwave of touching his hard male body had sent her senses spinning like a top. His dark eyes had run over her partner in a sizing up look and his top lip had curled as if to say, *Is that the best you could do?* But after that her memory was a blank.

She gave him a caustic glare. 'Why did you bring me here?'

He sent his gaze over her in a long lazy sweep. 'You can't guess?'

In spite of her trepidation, Daisy felt every pore of her skin flower open in response. Heat rushed along her veins, lighting a fire that fanned out from her core. Damn the man for being so attractive. How shameful of her to be so turned on by such a fiend. No wonder her father thought she needed a bodyguard. Clearly she was a ticking time bomb when left to her own devices. One night let loose on the town and she hooked up with the world's most wicked playboy. 'Did you—' she swallowed tightly again '—undress me?'

His expression was now deadpan. 'No.'

Daisy looked at him blankly. 'Then who did?'

'You did.'

Her eyes were so wide with shock they felt as if they were going to pop out of her head. She hadn't been naked in front of anyone since she was twelve. She was twenty-six years old and she still got dressed under a towel at the gym. Body issues had plagued her since she hit puberty. Small breasts, a jelly belly if she didn't do a hundred sit-ups a day and thighs that had a tendency to look like cottage cheese if she didn't stick to her diet of cottage cheese. 'I don't believe you.'

A glimmer of a smile came back in his eyes. 'I thought you said you were a teacher. Where did you learn the stripper routine?'

'You're lying!' she choked. 'I would never do something like that!'

'It was the best lap dance I've ever had and I didn't even have to tip for it.'

Daisy felt a blush move over her face like a flame let loose beneath her skin. 'I don't believe you. You're making this up.' *You must be. You* have *to be.*

He shrugged as if he didn't give a damn either way. 'You want some breakfast before you leave?'

Daisy frowned in a combination of confusion and an inexplicable sense of disappointment. *He was letting her go?* 'You mean you're not going to keep me here chained to the bed to have your wicked way with me?'

Those sinfully dark eyes roved over her huddled form once more, sending another wave of heat to her core. 'Thanks, but no.'

She knew it was inconsistent of her to feel slighted but surely she hadn't been that much of a flop in bed? Sure, she might have been unconscious, but still... 'Fine. I'm leaving.' She scrambled off the bed, taking the sheet with her. 'If you'll lead me to my clothes I'll be right on my way.'

'They're on the coffee table near the sofa. I took the liberty of having them cleaned while you were sleeping.'

Daisy swung around to face him, a dangerous manoeuvre given she was mummy-wrapped in one of his sheets. She would have gone over except one of his hands shot out to steady her. It was warm and strong against her flesh, his fingers like velvet-covered steel. Something flashed through her brain...a vague memory of strong arms holding her close. Protectively close.

Fresh-smelling laundry detergent and lemon-scented male flesh close to her face. A rock-steady heartbeat. A sense of being carried to safety... She frowned to bring the memory closer but it floated away like an apparition that no longer wanted to be seen.

She craned her head right back to look into his eyes, her stomach folding over at the satirical gleam that permanently shone there. 'Why did you do that?'

'Have your clothes cleaned?'

'Yes.'

'Seemed the right thing to do under the circumstances.'

'What...erm, circumstances?'

His mouth had that half smiling slant to it again. 'After the lap dance you had an episode of dispensing with the contents of your stomach in my bathroom. Unfortunately, your aim was off.'

Oh, dear Lord above. Could this nightmare get any worse? 'I was...sick?'

'Spectacularly so.'

Daisy chewed her lower lip, desperately trying not to picture how *that* might have played out. No one looked their best when being sick. But it was the ultimate humiliation to have disgraced herself in front of *him*. He was so self-assured. So suave. How he must have gloated over her misfortune after the way she had rejected his offer of a dance. He couldn't have asked for a better comeuppance for her. She had been so dismissive of his warning the night before. Arrogant even. How had she been so stupid and trusting to let something like that happen? *Ugh!* She was not some silly young girl on her first night on the town. She had a university degree, for God's sake.

She rummaged inside her purse for a handful of banknotes, thrusting them at him. 'I'm terribly sorry for any inconvenience I've caused. I hope this covers the expense of…erm, seeing to my needs.' *Bleah. Bad choice of words.*

He pushed her hand back with a gentle but firm pressure, his eyes locked on hers. 'I don't want your money.'

Daisy was having trouble concentrating. Her thoughts were flying all over the place. The energy coming from his hand where it was holding hers back was making her whole body fizz with reaction. It was like being plugged into a power outlet with too high a voltage for her sensitive wiring. She was going to short circuit for sure. He was so intensely male. So unbelievably handsome it made a hollow space inside her belly vibrate. Her eyes kept tracking to his mouth. Had he kissed her? How annoying she couldn't remember. That was a mouth that would know how to kiss. There would be no teeth scraping and nose bumping and awkward repositioning of lips and tongues. That was a mouth that knew how to seduce, to slay her senses with one brush of those hard male lips against hers. She drew in a shaky little breath and pushed back against his hand. 'Take it. I insist.'

He pushed back a little harder. The uptake of tension triggered something deep and low in her pelvis. She felt it between her thighs, a tight ache that was part pulse, part contraction. A frisson shimmied down her spine as his fingers wrapped around hers, tethering her to him.

His hands were not smooth but slightly calloused, which was strangely arousing. His thumb found her pulse and measured its frantic pace. 'I have plenty of money.'

Daisy gave him an imperious look to disguise the catastrophic effect he was having on her senses. 'Is that supposed to impress me?'

A lazy smile teased up the corners of his mouth. 'Nothing else has so far.'

She raised one of her eyebrows. 'You mean I wasn't left breathless and gasping by your…erm, attentions last night?'

He gave a deep chuckle, which combined with that toe-curling stroking along the thumpety-thump-thump-thump of her pulse, made her senses career off into another tailspin. 'Your honour was safe with me, *dulzura*. I didn't lay a finger on you.'

Daisy pulled out of his hold, blinking at him in surprise. 'Y-You didn't?'

He shook his head with mock gravitas.

'Why not?'

'I prefer my women sober.'

She glared at him again, stamping her foot for good measure. 'I was not drunk! I've never been intoxicated in my life.'

'You were legless last night. Just as well I came along when I did. You were about to get down and dirty with the man in Suite 1524.'

Daisy stopped glaring at him. Another fragmented memory filtered through the haze of her brain. The guy from Ealing pressuring her to have a drink. Refusing his offer but finding he had bought her one while she had gone to the restroom. He insisting he keep her company while she drank it. She had suffered his company because she'd become so irritated with seeing Luiz Valquez working the room like Casanova with catnip. Surely a single vodka and orange wouldn't have caused her to lose all sense of control? 'How do you know I was going to…erm, become intimate with that guy? I might've just been going to his room to—'

'Look at his etchings?'

She gave him a look. 'Not all men have one-track minds, you know.'

He moved over every inch of her sheet-wrapped body with the smouldering heat of his gaze. 'They do when someone looks as gorgeous as you.'

Daisy knew it was a throwaway line but she couldn't help feeling a little thrill all the same. It wasn't that she wasn't used to compliments. She knew she wasn't model-thin or billboard-beautiful but she was pretty enough in a girl-next-door sort of way. But hearing him say it made her feel all fluttery and feminine. It made her want to flirt with him, which was rather surprising as she never flirted.

She shuffled over to where her clothes were folded in a neat pile on a coffee table next to one of the plush sofas. 'I have to get moving. The girls will be waiting for me.' She scooped up her clothes with her free hand, turning back to glance at him. 'Do you mind if I use your bathroom to get changed?'

His eyes had that laughing glint in them again. 'Be my guest.'

Daisy sniffed the air in the luxuriously appointed

bathroom for any trace of sickness. To her very great relief it smelt of citrus with a hint of lemongrass and gin-
ger. She unwrapped herself from the sheet and quickly
donned her clothes, her fingers tracing over the lace of
her bra and knickers as she thought of Luiz handling her
intimates, even to pass them over to the laundry staff.
Had he put her to bed? Had he carried her or had she
walked/stumbled/crawled on her own? Had he tucked
her in? A shiver passed over her flesh at the thought of
his hands on her naked body. Damn it. Why couldn't
she remember the most exciting moment of her life? If
he hadn't acted inappropriately given the way he said
she had, then why not? Wasn't he supposed to be a bad
boy or something?

Or did he have some scruples after all?

When Daisy came out of the bathroom he was standing with his back to her, looking down at the Vegas strip
in all its crazy madness. 'Are you decent?' he asked.

'Hardy-ha-ha.'

He grinned as he turned around to face her. 'Don't
you like your men with a sense of humour?'

Her men? What a laugh. If only he knew the only
men in her life were her father, her bodyguard and Robert, the elderly gardener at Wyndham Heath.

Daisy was afraid she was starting to like Luiz
Valquez a little too much. His uncharacteristic chivalry was potently attractive. If what he had said was
true about her having been in danger of being taken
advantage of by the Ealing guy, she owed him a huge
debt of gratitude, not censure. Anything could have
happened to her last night but he had stepped in and

made sure she was safe, possibly putting himself at risk in the process. She'd had him pegged as a hard partying bad boy and yet he had acted with honour and propriety.

Had the world got it wrong about him? Or did he cash in on his racy reputation because it fitted the image of the sporting superstar? Who was he behind that mask of sophisticated playboy? If she had offered herself to him so shamelessly and he'd refused, then he must surely have far more to him than met the eye.

She held her purse in front of her stomach with both hands, suddenly feeling terribly gauche...well, even more so than usual. 'About last night...' she began.

'Don't mention it. I won't.' Another glinting look. 'It can be our little secret.'

She gnawed her lip as she thought of all the thousands of followers he would have on Twitter or other social media. He could make an absolute fool of her with a couple of hash tags. What if he'd taken pictures of her without her knowing? Her stomach dropped. The stripper routine. *Oh, God.* What if he'd recorded it? Uploaded it? Sent it out to cyberspace. What if he blackmailed her? What if—?

He reached into his trouser pocket and handed her his phone. 'You can check it if you like.'

Daisy stared at his phone as if it were a grenade with the pin pulled out. 'I really don't think that's—'

'Here, I'll show you.' He came and stood shoulder to shoulder with her, accessing the camera roll on his phone. 'See?'

She peered at the images he was scrolling through,

conscious of the way his light lemony and citrus cologne sharpened the air. She could feel the slightest brush of his hair-roughened arm against her smoother one. Her traitorous mind began assembling images of them in bed together, limbs entangled, lips locked, tongues mating. 'Good gracious, is that a dress that girl is almost wearing?'

He gave one of his deep rumbly chuckles that sent her senses spinning all over again. 'For a simple scrap of fabric it was damn hard to get off.'

Daisy gave him a wry glance. 'What? She didn't offer to help you?'

'Can't remember.' He carried on thumbing through another few photos.

'How long ago was it—erm, she?'

'Ages ago.' He flashed her a sudden grin. 'A couple of weeks at least.'

Daisy rolled her eyes and then pointed to a picture on the photo stream of a slightly older woman standing next to Luiz at what looked like a cocktail party. 'Who's that?'

'My mother, Eloise.'

Something about the way he said his mother's name alerted her to an undercurrent of tension. 'She looks very beautiful. Very glamorous. Like a movie star.'

His lips moved in the semblance of a smile. 'Yes, she likes the spotlight, that's for sure.'

'You're not close?'

He looked at her briefly, his eyes meshing with hers in a moment of silence. There was a vacancy in the back of his gaze, as if he was looking in the past for something but was having trouble finding it. 'We were once, or so I thought.'

'When was that?'

He clicked off the screen of his phone and slipped it back into his pocket in a *subject closed* manner. 'What do you normally eat for breakfast?'

'*Well*…ideally, I would eat an egg white omelette and drink a herbal tea.'

His brow lifted. 'Ideally?'

She gave him a self-deprecating look. 'I'm rubbish at sticking to diets. I last about three days and then I cave in and eat everything that isn't nailed down.'

'How does bacon and eggs, pancakes, maple syrup and a side of hash browns sound?'

Daisy swayed on her feet as if about to go into a swoon. 'Like heaven. I'm so hungry I could eat a horse and chase the rider.'

He stood looking down at her with a gleaming look in his dark as pitch eyes. 'I've heard there are some riders out there who like to do all the chasing.'

Daisy held his look with an aplomb she had no idea she possessed. Who knew flirting could be so much fun? 'Then perhaps those riders should make sure they never get caught.'

He picked up a lock of her hair and twirled it a couple of times around his tanned finger. She felt the gentle tug as one by one the roots of her hair lifted off her scalp. His eyes slipped to her mouth, lingered there as if he was weighing up whether to kiss her or not.

Do it. Do it. Do it, a voice chanted in her head.

His head came down in a slow motion action, block-

ing out the light shining in from the window. He stopped
a mere millimetre away from her mouth, close enough
for their breaths to mingle. His smelt of toothpaste.
God alone knew what hers smelt like after a night on
the tiles. Bathroom ones included. *Ack!*

Daisy put a fingertip against his lips, her voice coming out as little more than a husky whisper. 'Wait.'

He nibbled her fingertip with his lips, making her
legs unlock at the knees. 'What for?'

'I haven't even told you my name.'

He turned her hand over and kissed a tickling pathway from her wrist to her elbow. 'So, tell me.'

She shivered as his lips came back down to the sensitive skin on the underside of her wrist. 'Daisy...Daisy
Wyndham.'

He held her wrist to his mouth as his eyes meshed
with hers. 'Nice.'

Daisy had trouble breathing. His eyes were so dark
she felt as if she were drowning in their bottomless
depths. His stubble-surrounded mouth against her skin
was making her belly do somersaults worthy of a Cirque
du Soleil performance. She even heard the rasp of his
skin as he moved his mouth to the heel of her hand as
his tongue made one flicking lick against the ridge of
flesh. A flashpoint of heat triggered a tumult of sensation in her core. She hadn't even realised that part of
her hand had an erogenous zone.

The doorbell sounded behind him and he dropped
her hand with a regretful smile. 'Breakfast.'

CHAPTER THREE

FOOD HAD NEVER been further from Daisy's mind, which was saying something as normally it was *always* on her mind. Forbidden food. The yummy stuff she secretly craved but rigorously denied herself in fear of losing control. Her father had drummed it into her from early childhood that being in control of one's mind and body and physical appetites was the mark of a well-disciplined person. In order to win his approval she denied herself anything that was the slightest bit sinful. But the years of self-denial hadn't made her stronger and more disciplined. If anything, they had made her all the more conflicted and confused about what she wanted and why she wanted it.

She watched with her mouth watering and her stomach rumbling as Luiz opened the door to the hotel attendant, who wheeled in a loaded trolley of silver domed dishes. The delicious aroma almost knocked her off her feet. Crispy bacon, soufflé-soft scrambled eggs, deep-fried hash browns, fluffy buttermilk pancakes, the sweetness of maple syrup—not the cheap imitation but the real stuff—a platter of tropical fruit, coffee and even a bottle of champagne in an ice bucket.

The attendant left with a sizeable tip in his hand, closing the door on his exit.

'*Wow.*'

Luiz tossed his wallet on the sofa. 'Hungry?'

'I meant the tip.' Daisy's eyes were still out on stalks. 'Did you really give that young man two hundred dollars?'

He shrugged a loose shoulder. 'I can afford it.'

'Do you light your cigarettes with a fifty?'

He flashed her a quick smile. 'I don't smoke.'

Another point in his favour, she thought as he began to take the lids off the food. He handed her a plate. 'Help yourself.'

Daisy tried to be circumspect. She *really* tried. But the food was so scrumptious and she hadn't had a proper cooked breakfast in years. Before she knew it, her plate was loaded with a mountain of monstrously wicked calories that would at some time in the future have to be worked off. But it would be worth it.

She took the chair opposite his at the table near the window overlooking the Nevada desert in the distance. She unwrapped her silver cutlery from the snowy white napkin it was encased in and then glanced across at Luiz but all he had in front of him was a steaming cup of black coffee. 'Aren't you hungry?'

'I'll have something later.'

'But there's so much here.' *Most of it on my plate.*

'I like to work out first.'

The gym or the bedroom? Daisy blushed as the

thought slipped into her mind. 'I suppose you have to be super fit to be a polo player.'

'If you want to be the best then that's exactly what you have to be.'

She looked up from her forkful of eggs. 'I've never been to a polo game. Is it fun?'

A smile kicked up the corner of his mouth. 'I enjoy it.'

'So…that's all you do? Fly around the world to play polo?'

'I have business interests with my older brother Alejandro. Resorts, investments, horse breeding, that sort of thing. But yes, I mostly fly around the globe to play polo.'

Daisy took a mouthful of the delectable bacon, trying not to groan in ecstasy as it went down. 'Don't you ever get bored?' she asked after a moment.

He cradled his coffee cup in one hand, the handle pointing away from him. 'How do you mean?'

'Living out of hotel rooms all the time. Doesn't that get a little boring year after year after year?'

Something about his expression subtly changed. The half smile was not so playful. The chiselled contours of his jaw not so relaxed. His eyes a little more screened than before. 'Not so far.'

'Don't get me wrong—' she scooped up some more egg '—I love hotel rooms, especially ones as nice as this. But there's no place like home.'

'Where do you live?'

'London.'

'Want to narrow that down a bit?'

Daisy gave him a coy look over her loaded fork. 'Why do you ask? Are you thinking of visiting me?'

His eyes didn't waver as they held hers. 'I don't do relationships, especially long distance ones.'

She squashed a little niggle of disappointment. Last night she had thought him the most obnoxious upstart. But now…

She gave a mental shrug and loaded up her fork again. 'I live in Belgravia.'

His brow lifted ever so slightly. 'So you're no stranger to money in spite of your comment about the tip earlier.'

Daisy gave him a sheepish glance. 'It's not my flat. It belongs to my father. I pay him a nominal rent. He insists I live in a high security complex. He's kind of overprotective, to put it mildly.'

He leaned forward to refill his cup from the silver percolator on the table. 'You're lucky to have someone watching out for you.'

Daisy wondered if he'd think she was so lucky if she told him the rest. Like how her father often turned up unannounced at her flat, checking her fridge or pantry for contraband food. Not to mention dates. Making comments about her clothes and appearance or the amount of make-up she was wearing. Offering his opinion on every aspect of her life. She had put up with his controlling ways for too long. The trouble was she had no idea how to get him to change without hurting him. So many of her friends didn't have fathers, or had fathers who weren't interested or involved in their lives. She had already lost one parent. The thought of losing another—even through estrangement—was too daunting.

She studied Luiz's face for a moment. 'You mentioned your mother. What about your father? Is he still alive?'

His expression gave the tiniest flinch as if the mention of his father was somehow painful to him. 'He died a couple of years ago.'

'I'm sorry.'

'Don't be.' He stirred his coffee with a teaspoon even though she hadn't seen him put sugar or cream into it. 'He was glad to go in the end.'

'Was he ill?'

'He had a riding accident when I was a kid. He wasn't expected to survive but he did—much to my mother's despair.'

Daisy frowned. 'But surely—?'

His expression was cynical. 'It wasn't my mother's idea of marital bliss to be shackled to a quadriplegic who couldn't even lift a cup to his mouth. She left six months after the accident.' He swirled the coffee in his cup until it became a dark whirlpool. Daisy watched with bated breath for some to spill over the sides but it didn't. It told her a lot about him. He was a risk-taker but he knew exactly how far he could push the boundaries.

'Did she take you and your brother with her?'

He laughed a brittle-sounding laugh. 'She hadn't wanted kids in the first place. She only married my father because her family pressured her into it once she got pregnant with my brother.' He put the cup down again with a precise movement before he sat back, hooking one ankle over the top of his muscled thigh. 'She came back a couple of years later to get me but our father wouldn't hear of it.'

'Would you have wanted to go?'

His lips rose and fell in a shrug-like movement. 'It was no picnic being brought up in a sickroom. My brother did his best but he wasn't able to be both parents and a brother to me. But I wouldn't go unless he came too and there was no way he would ever leave my father.'

'So you stayed.'

'I stayed.'

A silence crept in from the four corners of the room.

There was no outward sign on his face but Daisy got the impression he regretted revealing so much about his background. His fingers began to drum on the arms of the chair he was sitting on. It was barely audible but it spoke volumes. He wasn't a man to sit around chatting. He was a man of action. He lived life on the edge. He didn't sit on the sidelines and ruminate about what might have, could have, or should have been.

'Why did you come to my rescue last night?'

His eyes took on that teasing glint again but she noticed his smile looked a little forced. 'You seemed like a nice kid. I didn't want you to come to any harm on your first night in Vegas.'

'So you tucked me safely up in bed and gallantly slept on the sofa.'

'Correction. I didn't sleep.'

She frowned. 'What did you do?'

'I kept an eye on you.'

'Why?'

'Your drink was doctored. I heard it from the horse's mouth.'

Daisy's mouth dropped open. 'You mean a drug of some sort?'

'He only confessed to getting a friend to put a couple of extra shots of vodka in your glass while you weren't watching,' he said. 'I asked the hotel doctor to give you the once-over. He seemed pretty confident it was just a case of a little too much to drink. Your pupils and your breathing were normal.'

She stared at him with burgeoning respect. How had she got it so wrong about him? He had acted so responsibly last night. Taking care of her. Protecting her. Sacrificing his evening to stay with her. How had she thought he was shallow and arrogant? He wasn't the devil she had taken him for. He was a guardian angel. *Her* guardian angel. 'I don't know how to thank you for watching out for me.'

'Yeah, well, how about being a little more careful when you're out on the town? They're a lot of opportunistic guys out there who'd not think twice about taking advantage of a girl who's three sheets to the wind.'

Daisy chewed her lower lip. 'I can see now why my father always insists I travel with a bodyguard.'

His brows snapped together. 'You have a bodyguard?'

She gave him another sheepish look. 'I did up until last night. I slipped away from him to join the girls in the nightclub downstairs.'

'Where is he now?'

'Probably handing in his notice to my father.'

His frown cut into his forehead like a deep V. 'Don't you think you should call him to let him know you're safe?'

'I guess…'

He snatched up her purse where her phone was stored. 'Better do it before the cops put out a missing person's alert—if they haven't already.'

Daisy took out her phone to find thirty-three missed calls from her father. She had forgotten she'd put her phone on silent before she met the girls last night and hadn't got around to turning it back. She pressed the call button and mentally counted to three to prepare herself for the fallout. 'Dad?'

'Where the hell are you?' her father blasted. 'I've been worried sick. I was about to get every cop in Vegas out looking for you. Are you all right? What happened last night? Bruno told me you gave him the slip. Just wait until I see you, young lady. Do you think I'm not serious about your safety? There are creeps out there just waiting to get their hands on a good old-fashioned girl like you. I swear to God if anyone's hurt my baby girl I'll have their balls for breakfast.'

'I'm fine, Dad, please stop shouting.' Daisy tried to cover the mouthpiece but it was obvious Luiz had heard every word because he was grinning. 'I'm fine, really I am. Nothing happened. Nothing at all.'

'Where are you?' her father demanded.

'I'm at a hotel with a…a friend.'

'Which friend? You don't know anyone in Vegas apart from those silly girlfriends of yours.'

'A new friend.' Daisy looked at Luiz with a can-I-mention-your-name? look but, before he could give her an answer, she told her father, 'I'm with Luiz Valquez, you know, the famous polo champion?'

'*What?*' her father roared.

'I met him last night. He was terribly nice and took me to his—'

'That profligate time-wasting party boy?' Her father was apoplectic. 'Wait till I get my hands on him. I'll tear him limb from—'

Luiz signalled for her to give him the phone. 'I'll talk to him.'

Daisy gingerly handed the phone to him as her father continued his audible tirade. 'Sorry,' she mouthed.

'Mr...er...Wyndham? Luiz Valquez. Daisy was a little under the weather last night so I—'

'Drunk?' her father exploded. 'How dare you suggest such a thing? Do you have any idea of whom you're dealing with here?'

Luiz's mouth developed a smirk, which Daisy was eminently glad her father couldn't see. 'Yes, sir, I do. You're a loving father who is concerned about his daughter's welfare.'

She grimaced. Her father *hated* being patronised. She waited for the fallout. Any second now... She exchanged a quick look with Luiz. He wasn't looking unduly worried. If anything, there was a glint of amusement in his dark gaze.

'*Parli italiano?*' her father demanded.

'*Sì.*'

The rest of the exchange was conducted in rapid-fire Italian and, while Daisy was moderately good at languages, she wasn't *that* good. Whatever was said was short and to the point. Luiz showed little emotion on his face but she noticed the smirk had gone by the time the call ended and he handed back her phone. 'Quite a guy.'

'He's really sweet when you get to know him.'

There was a pregnant silence.

'What did he say to you?' Daisy asked.

'Nothing much.'

She chewed her lip again. Her father could be quite threatening at times. He was all bluster, of course. He wouldn't hurt a fly if push came to shove. She reached for her purse again. 'I guess I should let you get on with your morning.'

Luiz's hand on her arm stalled her. 'There'll be press out there.'

'Press?'

His look was grim. 'Paparazzi. They follow me everywhere.'

'Oh...' Daisy hadn't got as far as thinking beyond leaving his hotel suite before she made a complete fool of herself and begged him to kiss her. Being in his company had been far more pleasant than she'd expected. He was funny and charming and his gallantry towards her had totally ambushed her determination to dislike him. 'What should I do?'

'Leave all the talking to me.'

Daisy had spent most of her life having her voice silenced by her father. She wasn't going to let another man, even one as gorgeous and sexy as Luiz Valquez, speak for her. For the moment she'd play along but he would soon find out she wasn't as wet behind the ears as he thought. 'What will you say to them?'

'I'll think of something.'

Something that might not reflect too well on her, Daisy thought. His scandalously racy reputation was well known. Being found in his room was not going to do hers any favours. She would be painted as one of his groupies for sure. No way was she going to be portrayed as yet another one of his one-night stands. She would have to think of something a little more fitting for a London kindergarten teacher who had the school board to consider.

Luiz reached for the champagne in the ice bucket. 'Have a drink with me.'

'At this hour?'

He popped the cork and poured the delicate bubbles into the crystal long-stemmed flutes. He handed her one, clinking his against hers in a toast. 'What happens in Vegas stays in Vegas.'

Daisy took a sip of the champagne, feeling decidedly decadent on top of her calorie-rich breakfast. 'Hair of the dog, huh?'

'Works for me.'

She watched as he took a measured sip of his drink. His smile had faded and two pleats had formed between his brows. 'Is something wrong?'

His features relaxed but she could still see a faint line of tension around his mouth. 'What are your plans for the rest of your stay? Have you booked any tours?'

'No, the girls have but I wanted to do my own thing.

I hate structured tours. I like to mooch around and get a feel for the place on my own.'

'Fancy me as a guide for the next couple of hours?'

Daisy fancied him full stop. Big time. The longer she spent in his company, the more tempted she was to relax her good girl standards and take a walk on the wild side with him. Besides, hadn't he already demonstrated his trustworthiness? What would be the harm in hanging out with him for the rest of the day? Maybe even a few days?

A little thought took hold in her mind… She could have a holiday fling with him to get herself out there. He wasn't interested in anything permanent. And there was no way she could ever be serious about someone so unsuitable as husband material. But for a few days of flirting and fun…who better than a man who really knew how to lay on the charm? 'Are you sure you're not too busy?'

'For you, *querida?*' He clinked his glass against hers once more, his black eyes gleaming. 'I am more than happy to clear my diary.'

'Well…if you insist.'

'I do.'

She smiled at him. 'You know something? When I first met you I thought you were brash and arrogant and ridiculously shallow.'

'And now?'

'I think underneath that easy come, easy go exterior you're a really nice guy.'

A dangerous light came back on in his eyes as he trailed a lazy finger down the curve of her cheek. 'Don't be fooled, little English girl. Your white knight has the blackest of hearts.'

'At least you have one.'

He studied her mouth for a heart-stopping moment. Daisy felt her breath come to a screeching halt as his fingertip traced the outline of her lips, the top one and then the bottom one. The movement of his finger stirred every nerve into a happy dance. She could feel her lips buzzing as if a swarm of bees was trapped beneath their surface.

'Are you going to kiss me?' Had she *really* asked that? She really needed to work on her flirting lines. But hey, this might just be the opportunity to do it.

His mouth curved upwards in an enigmatic smile. 'Let's say I'm measuring the risks.'

'Just so you know…I don't bite.'

'No.' He took a fistful of her hair in his hand and pulled her close as his mouth came down towards hers. 'But I do.'

CHAPTER FOUR

HER LIPS WERE soft and pliable and she tasted of a heady cocktail of champagne and innocence. Luiz had wanted to kiss her from the moment he'd laid eyes on her in the nightclub. Her feisty little brush-off had amused him. He knew he could take her down given enough time. Now he had her in his arms but taking it a step further was giving him some pause. Her father had issued a thinly disguised warning. Sully his little girl's reputation and there would be unpleasant consequences. Luiz would have told him where to stick his threats but the name Charles Wyndham rang a faint alarm bell in his head.

But that didn't mean he couldn't indulge in a kiss with Daddy's little princess first.

Except that kissing her was proving to be far more addictive than he had bargained for. Her soft lips opened on a breathless sigh as he deepened the kiss with a smooth stroke of his tongue against the seam of her mouth. She pressed herself closer to his body, triggering a molten fire inside him as he recalled every deliciously naked inch of her last night as she had wantonly stripped off her clothes and danced and jiggled her breasts around him. In spite of his moral stance, it had taken a monumental amount of willpower to resist her clumsy attempt to seduce him. She had gorgeous curves that were womanly and yet delightfully youthful. Her breasts were small but perfect globes of feminine flesh with rose-pink nipples that had made his mouth ache to taste their budded peaks. Her waist was tiny in comparison to the feminine swell of her hips, small enough for his hands to span, which had been one temptation he hadn't been able to resist. He had done it as an experiment…or so he told himself. But feeling her push against him in nothing but her creamy skin had all but disabled his willpower. A backdraught of heat had shot through his system when her pelvis came in contact with his.

Luiz felt it again as she moved against him now and, even though this time she was fully clothed, just knowing that under that little black dress and those little lacy black knickers she was waxed clear made him throb with a fireball of lust.

He plunged deeper into her mouth, seeking the hot sweet wetness of her, as if that in some vicarious way would suffice. Her tongue approached his with a teasing little flicker that made him go after it with ruthless intent. He drew it into his mouth, cajoling it into submission as his hands gripped her hips and held her tight against the swell of his pounding erection. Need roared inside him like a wild animal on the prowl. Earthy need. Primal need that would not be assuaged any other way than with monkey sex at its most animated.

He brought his hands to her head, spreading his fingers through her hair as he held her mouth to his in a passionate duel. Not that she was fighting him or anything. She was with him all the way, making it impossible for him to pull back and get perspective.

Damn perspective.

He wanted her.

But, for all that, her father's threat sent a cube of ice scudding down his spine. It was one thing to make a threat to have his legs broken—which he didn't for a moment take seriously because last time he looked he wasn't in an episode of a mob drama—but how far did her old man's influence reach? During the course of the brief conversation Charles Wyndham had chillingly mentioned Alejandro and Teddy's upcoming wedding. They had married a few weeks earlier in a marriage of convenience arrangement to secure Teddy's inheritance and some land next to the Valquez family estate—now Alejandro's property—which had been swindled off their father by Teddy's father twenty years ago.

How much did Charles Wyndham know about the way Alejandro and Teddy had come together? Luiz knew Alejandro was at great pains to give Teddy the best wedding day imaginable, given he had marched her off to a register office for a civil ceremony that had no hint of romance or fairy tale about it. Charles Wyndham had implied Alejandro and Teddy's special day would be sabotaged if Luiz didn't play by the rules.

Rules. Schmules. No one told him what to do or how to do it.

But this wasn't just about him now. His older brother

had sacrificed years of his life—the best years—to salvage the family business and to bring Luiz up. Alejandro had forfeited fun for duty. Now he was finally happy with the lovely Teddy and all that could be undone if Luiz didn't watch his step.

As much as it galled him to appear to be kowtowing to a tyrannical dictator, he knew it was in his interests to keep things cool until this particular storm cloud blew over. All he had to do was hang out with Daisy for a few hours before getting her back on her way with her girlfriends.

After he finished kissing her, of course.

When had a kiss tasted so tantalising? Her arms were around his neck, her mouth pressed hotly to his, her fingers playing with the ends of his hair that brushed his collar. Shivers coursed up and down his spine at her touch. He imagined those soft little hands exploring other parts of his body: down the muscles of his back and shoulders, his chest and abdomen and lower, where he throbbed and pulsed the hardest.

He groaned deep in the back of his throat as her teeth nipped at his lower lip before salving the sting with a moist stroke of her cat-like tongue. His erection painfully hardened at the thought of that clever little tongue teasing the length of him, tasting him, taking him to the limit of human control and beyond.

Her body rubbed against him invitingly, from chest to thigh, ramping up his desire to a level that was quickly slipping out of the bounds of his normally cool and measured control. He prided himself—some would say arrogantly so—on being a supremely competent lover who always made sure a good time was had by all. But with Daisy's soft little mouth and her perky little breasts and her curvy body wreaking such havoc on his senses he felt like a trigger-happy teenager.

He pulled back reluctantly, his body instantly wailing at the loss of the teasing friction of hers. 'This might be a good time to put the brakes on.'

Her cheeks were flushed a deep shade of rose. Her lips were swollen from the press of his; even her chin had a little red patch where his morning stubble had caught her. She had a dazed look in her beautiful blue eyes. He suspected it might match the one he was doing his level best to disguise in his own. 'Oh…yes, right. Good idea…'

'Do you normally kiss like that?' he found himself asking.

Her forehead puckered. 'Was I totally rubbish at it?'

'Hell, no. I'm just saying…' What *was* he saying? That she knocked him off his feet with a kiss? Yeah, right, like he was going to tell her that. *Anyone* that.

She, it seemed, had no such scruples. 'You're an amazing kisser. No wonder you've got the reputation you have.'

Why did his reputation feel like something to be ashamed of when he was with her? He couldn't imagine her leaping from one bed to the other, barely taking enough time to register a sexual partner's name before moving on to the next.

Not that he wasn't happy with his life. His life was fun. He liked being on the move. Putting down roots was for trees. Not for him.

But something about the way she was looking at him made a space creak open inside his chest. A tiny fissure along a fault line, barely enough to send a beam of light through, but he felt a spill of warmth flow from it and brush like a puff of a hot breath against his chilled heart.

'What was wrong with the way I was kissing you?' she suddenly asked.

'Nothing. It was great. You were great. Fabulous, in fact.' He stopped gushing long enough to draw a breath to rebalance. 'You might want to hold back on the enthusiasm a bit. A less principled guy might take advantage of it.' *Jeez, he was starting to sound like a parent again.*

'But what if I wanted you to take advantage of it?'

Luiz blinked. 'No, you don't… *Do* you?'

Her face was so youthfully open and fresh it made something deep inside his chest pinch. 'I didn't before but I've changed my mind. I like you. I'd like to spend some more time with—'

'No. No. No. A thousand times no.' He practically frogmarched her to the door. 'You, young lady, need to go and join your friends. Go do a tour of the Grand Canyon or go shopping or book to see a show or something.' He scooped up her purse and thrust it in her hands before opening the door. 'Out.'

A blinding flash hit him in the eyes as a round of paparazzi cameras went off.

'Luiz, tell us about your mystery date,' a journalist said. 'Everyone's talking about her. Who is she?'

'Are you going to see her again?'

'What's your name, sweetheart?'

Luiz took Daisy's arm and pulled her back behind him. 'Don't tell them.'

'Ooh!' a female journalist crowed. 'It must be serious. He's never done *that* before.'

'Her name's Daisy,' someone offered from the back of the assembled press. 'I spoke to one of her friends earlier. She's a kindergarten teacher from a posh school in London.'

'Can we expect a double wedding with your brother, eh, Luiz?' one of the old regulars asked.

Luiz laughed it off. 'We're just friends.'

'How about we hear what Miss Wyndham has to say?'

Luiz's fingers clamped down on Daisy's wrist. 'She has no comment to make. Now, if you'll excuse us—'

'Yes, I do.' Daisy poked her head around his shoulder before he could stop her. 'I'm in love with Luiz and he's in love with me.'

Somehow Luiz kept his composure but it was a near thing. Thank God for the improvisation drama classes way back in his boarding school days. He smiled stiffly and put his arm around Daisy's waist, tugging her close to his body; registering again how neatly she fitted against him. 'That's right.' He swallowed to get his next words out without choking. 'We're officially a couple.'

The cameras went crazy. So many flashes and clicks it sounded like rounds of artillery on a battlefield.

But this was one battle Luiz was determined to win. No one—not even a pretty little English girl or her overbearing father—was going to manipulate him into a relationship. He was a free agent and he was going to stay that way.

He shepherded Daisy back inside his suite and closed the door firmly, hoping the paparazzi would get the message and move on. When he was certain they had left he nailed her with a hardened look. 'Want to tell me what that was all about?'

She stood before him, straight-backed and defiant. 'I didn't want them to think I was one of your groupies.'

'*In love?*' Saying the words felt as if he was coughing up a fur ball.

Her cheeks stained with spreading colour. 'OK, I admit it might've been a bit over the top but I had to say something.'

'No, you did not.' He didn't bother softening his tone. 'I told you to keep quiet. But no. You go and announce to the world you're in love with me. *Seriously?*'

A combative light came into her eyes. 'It's all right for you. You don't care what people think of you, but I have to think of my reputation. I don't want to be seen as another one of your trashy one-night stands. I have children who look up to me.'

He looked at her blankly. 'Children?'

She whooshed out a flustered breath. 'My pupils. You heard what the journalist said. My school's not just your common or garden variety one. The parents pay extortionate fees to have their little darlings educated. As a staff member I have standards to uphold both professionally and personally. Kindergarten kids are highly impressionable. If word got back to the school board that I was cavorting in Vegas with a layabout play—'

'Hey, watch your language.'

She rolled her eyes. 'Whatever.'

Luiz raked a hand through his hair. Did she really think he was—? No, don't even go there. He didn't care what she thought of him. Why would he? He didn't have to explain himself to her or to anyone. 'I don't care if you want to pretend to be in love with me, but why throw in that porkie of me being in love with you?'

She gave him a pert look. 'How do you know I'm pretending?'

He narrowed his gaze. 'You're…you're not serious?'

She flashed him a teasing smile. 'No, of course not. You're the last person I'd ever fall for.'

'Why?' *You so should not have asked that.*

She put a finger to her lips, tapping them thoughtfully. 'Let me count the ways…' She held up each finger as she ticked them off. 'You're arrogant. Overly confident. Egotistical. Self-serving. Morally corrupt.'

Luiz let out a hissing breath, following it up with a choice expletive. 'I should've left you to that sleazeball last night. That's who I'd be calling morally corrupt.' Along with her mob-connected father, a fact he declined to mention because, as angry as he was, he wasn't the type of guy to judge her for who her parents were or what they did.

'Why are you so upset?' she asked. 'It's not as if I'm rushing you to the nearest wedding chapel for an Elvis-themed wedding or something.'

He swung round to fix her with another glare. 'I'm the one with the reputation being trashed here. You're making me out to be some sort of soppy, heartsore

Romeo who's gone gaga over a girl he didn't know from a bar of soap this time yesterday.'

'What did I tell you?' She flickered her eyelids upwards again. 'Self-serving and egotistical.'

He jabbed a finger towards her. 'Hey, wait a damn minute. I've a right to be a little pissed. I did the right thing by you and now it's coming back to bite me.'

Her pert look was back. 'Maybe you should've taken advantage of me when you had the chance.'

A vision of her gloriously naked and trying to climb into his skin flooded his brain. His groin remembered it all too well. It was responding in the only way it knew how. Instinctively. Urgently. He sent her a smouldering look and watched as her cheeks darkened. 'Don't tempt me, *mi pasión.*'

The tip of her tongue crept out to leave a shiny film of moisture over her youthful mouth. His mouth recalled every passionate movement of hers underneath his: the soft fullness, the sweetness, and the ripeness. 'It'd be fine if you want to,' she said. 'Sleep with me, I mean.'

He frowned at her. 'I thought you said I was a self-serving, egotistical jerk?'

'You are, but that doesn't mean I don't fancy you.'

Luiz shook his head, hoping it would get his addled brain in order. 'Let me get this straight… You *want* me to have a one-night stand with you?'

She put her hands on her hips as if she were addressing one of her infant charges. 'You're not listening to me, Luiz. I'm not interested in a one-night stand. I'm not that sort of girl. I will, however, agree to a short-term holiday fling.'

His frown was so deep it was making his forehead hurt. 'So what was with the sweet little romance thing just now? Why give the press the impression we're in—' he refused to say the word *love* again in case it jinxed him '—an item? Why not say we're having a fling?'

'It's not just the school board I have to consider. I have my father to think about. If the press wrote that I stumbled out of your suite and never saw you again he'd be after your blood. Not literally, of course. But he'd be furious if I were to waste myself on someone who didn't appreciate me. He's old-fashioned like that.'

'You don't say.' He sent his hand through his hair again. If this farce got any crazier he'd be pulling it out by the clump.

'I'm only here for four days,' she said. 'That's long enough to have a holiday romance and then move on. Dad will understand these flash in the pan things don't always last. And hopefully now we've made our announcement to the press they'll leave us alone.'

He studied her for a long moment. 'So, let me get this straight. You want to have a fling with me. For four days and nights. No strings?'

She smiled brightly as if he had just explained relativity to her after a painfully slow lesson. 'Exactly.'

'But why?'

'Why what?'

'Why me?'

'I told you before. I like you.'

'Even though I'm a morally corrupt layabout?'

She gave a tinkling bell laugh that did serious damage to his resolve to send her on her way as soon as he could. It was a champagne laugh. A bubbly, happy sound that made him think of fun and celebration. Her smile was the same—bright and positive, a smile that in full force made the hot Nevada desert sun look dull.

'I guess lust doesn't discriminate, does it?' she said.

It certainly does not, Luiz thought. If he'd known she was going to be this much trouble he would never have asked her to dance, much less come to her rescue.

Maybe that wasn't strictly true…

He could have no more left her in that corridor than fly to the moon on a paper aeroplane. Daisy was the sort of girl he instinctively wanted to protect. His brother had done a good job on him. Alejandro was the master at the white knight gig; the way he cosseted his wife Teddy was proof of it. Luiz was happy for his brother finding love. He hadn't thought it would ever happen. But that didn't mean *he* was looking for a similar happy ending. He didn't do happy endings. He couldn't rely on them. He was all about living in the moment.

And right now he had a hell of a moment to get through.

Luiz strode over to the window to check if any more press had turned up outside the hotel complex. He could feel Daisy's clear blue gaze studying him from behind. Never had a woman's presence disturbed him so much. She was sweet and innocent and yet impossibly sexy, a potent combination he had never encountered before. The taste of her kiss lingered in his mouth like a delectable dessert he hadn't had enough of. His taste buds were zinging, his lips buzzing, his blood thrumming. Last night had been the first time he had spent the night with a woman without making love to her. The need to do so was still thundering in his body. But it wasn't just the lust that worried him. The spill-all conversation over breakfast… *Why had he done that?* What was it about her that made him reveal so much about his past?

'So, what's the plan?' she said in an eager voice. 'What are we doing today?'

He twitched the curtains back across the window and faced her. 'How many lovers have you had?'

She momentarily sank her teeth into the pillow of her lower lip. 'Depends what you mean by lover.'

His brows met over his eyes. 'Have you had sex?'

'Technically, yes, but not with a human.'

No wonder her old man didn't let her out without a SWAT-trained security team, Luiz thought. 'Want to elaborate?'

Her cheeks were a fiery red but her blue eyes were unapologetic as they held his. 'A girl has the right to pleasure herself if there's no one else about. You men do it all the time. It's perfectly normal. A vibrator is good practice for the real thing…or that's what I'm hoping.'

Luiz was having trouble keeping his jaw off the floor. 'Are you saying you've never had sex other than with a vibrator?'

She gave him a huffy look. 'What of it? It's safe. At least I won't pick up any nasty infections. And he doesn't cheat on me.'

'He?'

'Edward.'

'You called your vibrator *Edward?*'

'What's wrong?' she said. 'It's a good old-fashioned

name. I admit it's a bit on the conservative side but I didn't want to sleep with a nameless object. It's... dehumanising.'

Luiz couldn't hold back a laugh. 'You are such a crazy girl. I don't think I've ever met anyone quite like you.'

'Same goes.'

'Meaning?'

She gave him a forthright look. 'You're so confident and upfront about what you want. Some would say brazen.'

'I thought you didn't like that about me?'

'Not if you were to be my life partner, but as a casual fling candidate you're perfect because it would be well-nigh impossible to damage your hubris.'

Luiz wasn't sure if she was insulting him or complimenting him. He wasn't sure why he even cared either way. 'So you ultimately want a life partner?'

Her expression was completely guileless. 'Doesn't everyone?'

'Not me.'

'Why not you?'

He lifted a shoulder. 'You said it yourself. I'd make a terrible husband.'

'You could be trained.'

He gave a wry laugh. 'You make me sound like a wild animal.'

Her beautiful blue eyes twinkled. 'Don't worry. I won't be in your life long enough to domesticate you.'

Something about the way she was calling the shots sat uncomfortably with him. He was the one who did the checking in and checking out. He didn't leave it to other people to come and go in his life. That was his prerogative. 'Why me?' he asked. 'Why not the other guy?'

'The Ealing guy?'

'Yeah. Him.' Luiz could barely think of that creep without wanting to punch something. Preferably him. Hard.

'I can't have a holiday fling with a compatriot. It's not half as exciting or exotic.'

'I'm not sure I've been called exotic before,' he muttered drily. 'Exciting, yes.'

She grinned at him. 'You're exotic to me because I've never even talked to an Argentinian before.'

'I can assure you we're situated on much the same level on the evolutionary chain as you Brits.'

'Oh, I wasn't implying you're not civilised,' she said sweetly. 'Look at how you conducted yourself last night. You were the perfect gentleman.'

'You only have my word on that.'

'Exactly my point.'

'I could be lying to you,' he said.

'But you're not.'

'You can tell that, how?'

'Your eyes,' she said, looking straight into them. 'You have the darkest brown eyes I've ever seen. But they don't shift about as if you're trying to hide something. And they laugh a lot. I find that really attractive. You look like a man who really enjoys life.'

Yeah, well, I was enjoying it just fine until a few hours ago, Luiz thought.

But had he?

Hadn't he come back to his suite alone because he *wasn't* enjoying himself?

He shrugged the thought aside. He had to find a way to get himself out of this entanglement before some serious harm was done.

Hadn't cute little Daisy Wyndham already got more out of him in a few minutes than anyone had in years? He *never* spoke of his childhood. To anyone. But for some reason he had spilled out his whole back story to her over breakfast. It had come pouring out…sentence after sentence, buried hurt after buried hurt. Little Miss Daisy Wyndham, with her sweet and engaging manner, had stumbled upon his Achilles heel. The pain and bitterness he concealed behind a laugh-at-life façade. He laughed his way through life because it was a damn sight more comfortable than whinging about the stuff he couldn't change.

He had been young—only eight years old—when his father had the accident, but not too young to understand that life would never be the same. He had spent day after day waiting for his mother to return from her 'holiday', as she'd termed it. He had almost worn out the end of his nose pressing it to the window whenever he heard a car come up the long driveway to the villa.

But no, each time he'd been bitterly disappointed. He hadn't shown it on his face, but for years that disappointment had burned and festered inside him like a fetid sore. One conversation with Daisy and it had all come bubbling to the surface. How much more would she get out of him if he let her too close?

He had watched his older brother painfully struggle

to keep the family together, taking on responsibilities that no child of ten should ever have to shoulder.

He had seen his strong and capable father reduced to a skin-wrapped skeleton in a chair, wearing nappies like a baby. The indignity of it had been stomach-churning. The suffering of his father had been like a brooding presence in the villa—haunting, maudlin, tortured.

From as young as he could remember, Luiz had chosen to enjoy life in the fast lane because he knew how quickly things could change. He pushed the limits but only as far as he knew he could go. The adrenalin rush of a new challenge energised him. Hadn't that been the most alluring thing about Daisy? She hadn't fallen at his feet as he'd expected. Even now she wasn't playing by his rules.

What would happen if he dared to relax them just this once?

CHAPTER FIVE

'OF COURSE, IF you don't think you're up to the task of taking me on then I'm sure I'll soon find some other guy to—' Daisy began.

'No, you won't.' Luiz's tone was strident. 'From what I've seen so far, you'll probably pick up some sleazy creep who'll take more than your virginity off you. Your credit card details, for instance. Or your passport. No wonder your old man won't let you out alone. Do you have any idea of the danger you could get into in a place like this?'

Daisy was finding his protective streak rather endearing. Underneath that suave and sophisticated übermodern exterior he was as old-fashioned as her father. Which was why she wanted him to be the one to make love to her for the first time. He ticked all the boxes for a holiday fling. He was gorgeous and fun-loving. He was respectably dissolute—a bad boy from a good family. He wouldn't make demands on her past the time frame of their fling. Who could be better to give her the experience she longed for than a man who was a professional playboy? It wasn't as if she was in any danger of falling in love with him. He was the total opposite of what she wanted in a long-term partner.

Besides, Belinda was always ragging her for not stepping outside her comfort zone. A red-hot fling with world champion polo player Luiz Valquez would win her some serious bragging rights.

Not to mention she was *seriously* attracted to him.

Daisy smiled up at him. 'So you'll do it?'

He was glowering as if she'd asked him to skin a spider before swallowing it. 'Aren't you being a little cold-blooded about this?'

'What's wrong? Surely you don't expect me to wrap it up in flowery language? I bet you don't when you se-lect your next sleepover partner.'

He stalked to the other side of the room, one of his hands rubbing at the back of his neck as if he had a knot of tension bothering him. 'This is crazy. I can't believe I'm having this conversation.'

'Is it because I'm not a supermodel? I've heard you're really picky over your partners.'

'Not picky enough, it seems,' he muttered not quite under his breath.

'Yes, well, now that you mention it, you were the one who started this by approaching me in the nightclub,' she said. 'Who knows? If you hadn't been so full of yourself I mightn't have gone off with the Ealing guy and then none of this would have happened.'

His top lip curled. 'Is that your version of logic? If so, it's a little short of the mark.'

Daisy gave a small shrug. 'I'm just saying…'

He came back over to her, standing right in front of

her so she had to crane her neck to keep eye contact. His eyes moved between both of hers, back and forth, as if he were waiting for her to reveal some other motive other than pure unadulterated lust. After a moment he lifted his hand and stroked his fingertip across her jawline. His touch was mesmerising, light as air, and yet every nerve of hers twanged with awareness. 'I should send you packing.'

'That would be the sensible thing to do if I had indeed anything to pack before I left,' Daisy said. 'I don't suppose visiting the Grand Canyon in a little black dress and heels is sensible either.'

His half smile made her stomach slip. So did his touch as he cupped her cheek in one of his broad hands. His thumb moved over her cheek in a stroking motion that was as hypnotic as his dark chocolate gaze. 'No. It isn't.'

Daisy looked at his mouth, wondering if he was going to kiss her again. Never had a kiss been so exciting. Every pore of her body had responded to him. It was as if he had turned a switch on inside her body. Her inner core pulsated with the need to feel his thick male presence—a real flesh and blood man, not a cold and clinical machine. She could feel the twitching of those delicate nerves in anticipation of his intimate invasion. 'Maybe I should head back to my hotel and slip into something a little more touristy.'

'You should.'

She looked at the way his eyes became sleepily hooded, the dark fan of his lashes shielding half of his gaze as it focused on her mouth. 'Should I bring my things back here, do you think?'

His eyes sprang open again. 'What for?'

'Well, if we're going to hang out together for the next four days it would make sense, wouldn't it?'

He frowned as if he hadn't considered that angle before. 'How far away is your hotel?'

'It's down the budget end of the strip. It's what the girls could afford.' Daisy nibbled at her lip before adding, 'I guess I could cab it back and forth…'

'And make me look like a tight-fisted jerk?' he said. 'No. You can move in here with me.'

'Are you sure?'

'I'm not sleeping over in some flea-bitten dive.'

'It's not *that* far down the strip,' Daisy said. 'Mind you, this place must cost a packet. Do you always stay on the penthouse floor?'

'I like my space.'

'For all your wild parties?'

He gave her a stern look. 'I'm a professional sportsman. If I partied as hard as everyone made out in the press I wouldn't be able to win a single game.'

She angled her head as she surveyed his frowning expression. 'And winning is everything to you, isn't it?'

'I don't play polo to lose.'

'What about life?'

'That too.'

Daisy acknowledged that with a thoughtful nod. 'Which is why you don't invest in relationships, right?'

His lip curled mockingly again. 'Is the psychoanalysis part of the deal or is that a bonus?'

Daisy ignored his sarcasm as she tilted her head like a dealer assessing a unique work of art. 'You love your brother and you loved your father, but you hold your mother at arm's length, as you do all women. Your relationship with her is on your terms, not hers. You have attachment issues. Textbook case, in my opinion.'

Two lines of tension ran from his nose to his mouth. 'If you want your four days of fun then maybe you should keep your opinions to yourself.'

'Fair enough.'

His brow was deeply furrowed. 'That's it?'

'What?'

'You're going to do what you're told?'

Daisy gave him an innocent-as-pie look. 'Sure. That's what you want, isn't it? You only sleep with women who don't stand up to you—correct? They're not allowed to have a mind or opinions of their own. You just want their body, not their intellect. I can do that. Mind you, four days is about my limit, though.'

He let out another curse as he thrust a hand through the thickness of his hair. 'You are un-effing-believable.'

The sound of his phone ringing from the desk where he'd left it broke the silence. Daisy watched as he snatched it up and barked out a curt greeting. She couldn't hear the conversation but his expression went from dark and stormy to a slowly spreading smile that made the corners of his eyes crinkle attractively.

He ended the call and slipped his phone in his trouser pocket, sending her a glinting look. 'It seems there might be some fringe benefits for me in this crazy scheme of yours after all.'

'Oh?'

'That was one of the big time sponsors I've been chasing for months. He wouldn't play ball. Until now.'

'Why now?'

Luiz took her hand and entwined his fingers with hers, drawing her a step closer to his tall hard frame. 'Because up until now he thought I was a reckless playboy who would bring nothing but disrepute to his precious company's name. But a tweet's just gone out about us being a couple.'

Daisy could feel the electric zing of his touch racing all the way to her armpit and beyond. 'You mean he'll back you now? Because of me?'

His eyes shone with triumph. 'Apparently one of his goddaughters goes to your school. She's not in your class but he's heard nothing but praise for you. He figures if you're involved with me then I must be worth backing. This is exactly what I need to win the Argentine Open Championship.'

'Why do you need his sponsorship? Don't you have plenty of money of your own?'

'It's not about the money,' he said. 'It's the show of confidence in my ability I'm after. Look at the top sportsmen and women in golf and tennis or skiing or snowboarding or whatever. Their sponsors build their image. They brand it. The better your brand, the more confidence people have in your talent. That show of confidence boosts your own. It feeds off it.'

Daisy was pleased for him but she could see the pitfalls even if he couldn't. 'What are you going to say to your sponsor when we break up at the end of the week?'

She could almost see the cogs of his brain ticking over. His triumphant expression faltered momentarily before he beamed her a confident smile. 'We can always extend our fling. It's only a month till the Grand Slam.'

Daisy frowned at him. 'Aren't you forgetting something? I live in London. I have a job to go to. I'm only here now because the girls wanted me to come to Vegas with them for half-term break.'

'The Argentine Open is on the first Saturday in December,' he said. 'I could fly you over for it.'

It sounded wonderfully exotic. A trip to Buenos Aires, all expenses paid. A box seat to see one of the most talented polo players in the world battle it out for the ultimate crown. It would be something to remember when she was just another suburban wife and mother trying to juggle work and family.

'But what about the other three weeks?' she asked.

'The sponsor is based in London so I'll be back and forth,' he said. 'We can meet up often enough to keep the press from thinking anything's amiss.'

Daisy ignored the red flag that warned against spending too much time with the wickedly charming Luiz Valquez. She had asked for four days and now she had the chance to have four weeks. She'd wanted a walk on the wild side, hadn't she? This was her chance to make it one to remember. 'OK. You're on.'

He took her by the shoulders and pressed a blisteringly hot kiss to her mouth. Daisy leaned into him, unable to help herself from responding with burgeoning passion. He only had to touch her and she erupted into flames. She could feel the heat rushing through her veins, sending electric sensations through every cell in her body.

His hands cupped her face, his fingers splaying out over her cheeks as he deepened the kiss. His tongue played cat and mouse with hers, teasing and taunting hers to fight back. She flicked her tongue against his, doing her own little teasing routine, delighting in the way he groaned in the back of his throat and brought his pelvis hard against hers. She felt the hard ridge of him, the pressure of his blood building as his desire for her escalated. She stroked her hands down over the taut curve of his buttocks, bringing him in closer so she could feel the imprint of his erect flesh on hers.

His hands left her face; one went to her left hip, the other to the zip at the back of her dress. He rolled it down, exposing her spine from the base of her neck to the crease at the top of her bottom. He slid his hand over her skin, discovering every one of her vertebrae in turn. His touch evoked a delicious shower of reaction, especially when he came to the curve of her bottom. She immediately tensed her buttocks, hoping he wouldn't think her fat.

'Relax for me, *querida*,' he whispered against the skin of her neck.

'I'm not good at getting naked with people.'

He sent his tongue over her top lip and then her bottom one in a barely-there caress that made her lips sing with delight. 'You were pretty relaxed about it last night.'

Did he have to remind her? 'Yes, well, I was apparently off my face, which would have helped.'

He eased back to look at her with a slight frown. 'You're embarrassed about your body?'

What was he implying? That she had something to *be* embarrassed about? The cruel chant of one of the mean girls at boarding school rang in her ears: 'Lazy Daisy... Fat Daisy'. Not a natural sportsperson, Daisy had used every excuse in the book to avoid playing team sport. A sudden increase in weight during puberty had made her ashamed of her body, a shame she had never been able to shed. Even though she was more or less average weight for her height and build, there was still a mean girl's voice in her head that taunted her every time she stepped in front of a mirror. 'Let's put it this way. The only catwalk I've been anywhere near is my neighbour's moggie stalking a bird in the garden.'

There was a smile in his eyes as he slid his hand underneath her knickers, exploring her curves with the warm palm of his hand. 'Did he catch it?'

'The bird? No, I stepped in before it got to bloodshed.'

Still holding her gaze, he sent his finger down the crease of her bottom, a shamefully erotic caress that triggered a firestorm in her core. 'You have a beautiful body.'

'I wonder how many times you've used that line.'

His slight frown reappeared. 'I mean it, *querida*. You have a womanly figure. Curves in all the right places.'

'My breasts are too small.'

'Says who?'

Daisy felt a rush of heat as his gaze went to the modest cleavage he uncovered as he slipped her dress from her shoulders. She stopped breathing altogether when he slowly traced his finger over each upper curve of her breasts that were pushed up by her lacy bra. He touched her nipples through the lace, which somehow intensified the sensation. The lace abrading her erect flesh made something deep and low in her belly roll over.

'So beautiful.' He brought his mouth to her right breast, kissing the cupped flesh until she was writhing with the pleasure of it. He did the same to the other one, stroking his tongue over the exposed curve. Her breasts were tingling all over. She could feel them swelling inside the cage of her bra, peaking against the lace cups as if desperate to get out so they could feel his mouth and lips and tongue directly.

As if reading her mind, he deftly unhooked her bra and it fell to the floor along with her dress. She was standing in nothing but her knickers and her heels and for once in her life she couldn't give a damn. He made her feel beautiful with his dark lustrous eyes roving over her form as if he wanted to eat her alive. Everywhere his gaze rested burned and tingled. Everywhere his hands touched made her flesh shiver and dance in delight.

But she couldn't have him doing all the touching and caressing.

Daisy wanted to touch and caress him. To devour him. She started on the buttons of his shirt, undoing them one by one, leaning into him to press a kiss to the hot musky satin of his skin. She used her tongue to anoint him. Little stabs. Little flicks. Little licks. Feeling thrilled as he sucked in a breath as if her ministrations excited him like no other.

She slid her hands over his rock-hard pectoral muscles, exploring his flat male nipples with her fingertips, pressing a moist kiss to each one, following it up with a hot swirl of her tongue.

'You're a dangerous woman,' he growled against her neck, taking a nip of her sensitive skin like a wolf did to control an overly amorous mate.

Daisy felt something wild and primitive inside her break free. She stepped up on tiptoe and put her mouth to his neck, taking a section of his flesh and biting down just hard enough to feel the tension of his skin. She released it to sweep her tongue over the spot, lulling him into a false sense of security before she bit him again.

He swore playfully and came back at her with a bite on her breast that was just shy of painful. Pleasure exploded like firecrackers under her skin.

But he wasn't done yet.

He sucked her nipple into his mouth. Gently pulling on it with his hot wet mouth, drawing on it until she was hovering in that tantalising place somewhere between pleasure and pain. He moved to her other nipple, rolling his tongue over it, circling it, teasing it, and then gently sinking his teeth just enough to pinch the flesh.

Daisy pressed her burning pelvis against the scorching heat of his. Rampant need was crawling all over her skin, making her breathless and mindless in her pursuit of ultimate pleasure. Never had her body felt more electrically alive. Never had it ached with such relentless want. Never had she been so desperate to come apart. The tension was like a pressure cooker inside her body. Building. Building. Building.

He slid his hands back over her buttocks, cupping her to his body, letting her feel the outline of his arousal. 'I want you.'

'I want you too.'

He walked her back towards the nearest wall, hooking his fingers into her knickers, but somehow in the haste to get them off his fingers tore through the fine cobweb of lace. He glanced at them ruefully, a frown pulling at his brow. 'Sorry.'

'It's fine.' Daisy kicked them away with her foot. 'Now, where were we? Oh, I remember. We were doing something about all these clothes you're wearing.'

She proceeded to tug the tail of his shirt out of his trousers. But suddenly his hands came down and stalled her. 'Wait,' he said, breathing heavily.

She raised her brows in surprise. 'What for?'

He stepped back from her and pushed one of his hands through his hair. His gaze went back to the tiny scrap of torn lace on the floor at his feet, his brow furrowing tighter as he bent down to pick them up. He handed them to her, his expression now inscrutable. 'I'll buy you a new pair.'

What did she care about a silly little pair of chain store knickers when her body was screaming for release? But then a host of self-doubts flooded her system. It was like throwing a bucket of ice cubes on her nascent sexual confidence. She wasn't like his usual conquests. She wasn't catwalk-skinny. She wasn't beautiful enough for the likes of him. She gathered what remnants of pride she could and set about getting back into her dress and bra, all the while conscious of him silently watching her, still with that unreadable expression on his face.

'Was it something I said?' she asked after a painful silence.

'No.'

'Something I did?'

'No.'

'Something I didn't?'

'No.'

Daisy pushed her lips out on an expelled breath as she smoothed down her dress. 'You really know how to leave a girl hanging.'

'I'm sorry.' His hand went through his hair again, this time from front to back, leaving it all sexily tousled as if he'd just got out of bed. 'I'm not used to doing things this way.'

'Which way is that? We're both adults who are attracted to each other. What other way are you talking about?'

He drew in an audible breath before slowly releasing it. 'You're a virgin, for one thing.'

Daisy wrinkled her brow in a frown. 'What's that got to do with it?'

'Having sex for the first time can be an intensely emotional experience.'

'Was it for you?'

He frowned as if the thought was ludicrous. 'No, not at all.'

'So why should it be intensely emotional for me?'

He looked at her for a moment without speaking, his eyes surveying every feature on her face as if she was a complicated puzzle he couldn't quite figure out. 'It's different for women. It's harder for them to separate their emotions from the physicality of sex. Especially the first time.'

'How many virgins have you slept with?'

'None that I know of.'

'So how can you speak with such authority?'

He let out another long breath. 'Look, I don't want you to get hurt, OK? You're a good girl, and in my experience good girls and bad boys don't mix.'

Daisy wasn't sure what he was saying. Was he saying their fling wasn't going to go ahead after all? Disappointment felt like a weary ache in her bones. 'So what happens now?'

He rubbed at his shadowed jaw before dropping his hand by his side. 'We'll hang out together as planned.'

'And what about sex?'

'I think it's best if we leave sex out of it.'

Daisy blinked. 'No sex?'

A tiny muscle beat a one-two rhythm at the side of his mouth. 'No sex.'

She ran her tongue over her lips, wondering why he was suddenly baulking at the idea of becoming intimate with her. Surely this wasn't just about her looks. He had been as turned on as her just moments ago. She had seen and felt the evidence with her own eyes and hands. Was it the thought of the time frame that was putting him off? He was used to one-night stands. He didn't have relationships with women. He had hook-ups. Quick, temporary transactions that involved their bodies, not their minds or their emotions or, indeed, his. 'So, let me get this straight… You want me to *pretend* to be your lover until after the Grand Slam but we're not going to have sex?'

'Correct.'

'Will we kiss?'

The muscle near his mouth started beating again. 'If the occasion demands it.'

'What occasion might that be?'

'A public one.'

'Oh, right. Silly me. I thought maybe you'd want to kiss me because you found me irresistibly attractive and just couldn't help yourself.' She scooped her purse off the coffee table and slipped her knickers inside and clipped it shut. 'Let's not forget *you* were the one to give me the biggest come-on in the nightclub.'

'I'm doing this for you, Daisy.'

She clutched a hand to her heart theatrically. 'For *me*? How incredibly sweet.'

He gave her a black look. 'Don't be like that.'

She pressed her lips tightly together as she studied him. 'Is this because of my father?'

'He's got a right to be worried about you. You're a loose cannon.'

Daisy decided right then and there she would show him just how loose she could be. He might want to keep things on a platonic level but she had other ideas. She wanted her holiday fling and she wanted it with him and no one—not even his newly invented moral code—was going to stop her. 'I'm going back to my hotel to get my things.'

He reached for his room key. 'I'll come with you. The press will be—'

'No, don't do that. I'll meet you back here in ten or fifteen minutes.'

A frown was beetling his brows. 'I might as well come with you and wait until you're ready.'

'Erm, I don't think so.' She gave him a cryptic little smile. 'Edward might not like that.'

His frown deepened. 'Who the hell…? Oh…'

Daisy lifted her hand in a cheery fingertip wave. 'See you in fifteen.'

CHAPTER SIX

Luiz caught her before she got into the elevator. Thankfully, the press had moved on now they had their story. And what a story it was. How had he ended up in this melodrama? One act of chivalry and he was in so deep he didn't know whether he was coming or going. Well, he definitely hadn't come, but it had been a close shave. Closer than he cared to admit.

The shock of seeing that torn scrap of lace had reminded him of what he'd been about to do. Deflowering virgins, even ones with attitude, was not on his agenda. Especially ones with fathers with agendas of their own. He had to do the right thing by her and not just because of her old man. She was a nice kid. A bit ditzy and naïve, but in a way that was what was so darned refreshing about her. She didn't treat him as if he was a demigod. She hadn't even known who he was when she'd first met him. It was only his protection of her that had changed her mind about him.

Now she had her mind set on him being her first lover...apart from her mechanical boyfriend, that was. He might be a thoroughly modern guy and chilled about all things sexual, but there was no way he was going to stand outside the door and let some battery-operated device do what he ached and throbbed to do. If he had to be celibate for the next couple of weeks, then Daisy could damn well join him.

He slipped in before the elevator doors closed and faced her squarely. 'You can't go haring off by yourself. We're supposed to be a couple. Couples do everything together.' *Or so I'm told.*

Her bright blue eyes with their dark fan of lashes looked up at him guilelessly. 'But the press have gone now.'

'That's not the point.' He reached over to stab at the ground floor button as if it had personally insulted him. 'There are people with camera phones everywhere. One shot of one of us without the other and the gossip will start. There'll be speculation that we're over. I can't afford to let that happen until the paperwork is secure on my sponsorship.'

'Fine, I'll stick to you like glue.' She closed the distance between them and looped an arm through his. 'I'll be your little shadow.'

Little tormentor, more like, Luiz thought, as the soft skin of her arm brushed against the hairs on his. He looked at her mouth, that delicious curve that was always on the verge of smiling, the cute little dimples that appeared when she did.

How had she lasted this long without someone snapping her up? She was gorgeous and super sexy and she kissed with such passion his body was still thrumming with the aftershocks.

How was he going to keep his hands off her for the duration of their 'relationship'? The sensation of her soft creamy breasts against his mouth, the way her tender skin caught against his stubble, the feel of her tightly budded nipples against his tongue and the soft little gasp she gave with each of his caresses made his body writhe with sexual hunger.

He would have to fly in icy water from Antarctica to douse the heat she had stirred in his blood.

'Stop looking at me like that,' he growled.

'How am I looking at you?'

He put his hands on her shoulders and turned her so she was facing the mirrored panel on the elevator. 'Like that.'

She leaned back against him, the sexy cheeks of her bottom brushing against his still swollen erection. There was a secret smile playing about her mouth and her sparkling eyes were full of mischief. 'Like this?'

Luiz's hands slipped down to hold her hips. His rational brain said, *No! Don't do it!* But his body was acting of its own volition. His blood ran hot and urgent with the need to press against her. Her light and delicate fragrance wafted past his nostrils—cottage flowers this time, with the alluring and exotic grace notes of sun-warmed honeysuckle. Her lips were without lipgloss or lipstick but they were as red as spring's first rose. Her complexion had not a single blemish. Not even a freckle. He had never seen skin so pure and untainted. The comparison with his was stark. His was olive-toned and tanned from a lifetime of playing polo and other outdoor sports.

His hand moved up to sit just below her right breast.
He could feel the slight weight of it resting against the
line of his thumb. She brought one of her hands over his,
her small, slim fingers looking as small and dainty as
a child's compared to his. She danced her fingers over
the back of his hand, and then started toying with the
coarse masculine hair that fanned from his hand and
down each of his fingers.

'You have nice hands,' she said.

Luiz couldn't help himself. His hand came up and
settled over her breast, her tight little nipple pressing
against his palm. He heard her draw in a breath, saw
the flash of pleasure on her face. Felt the thunderous
roar of his lust charging through his body like a wild
bull on a stampede.

He spun her around and brought his mouth down to
hers in a crushing kiss, heat exploding like a volcano
as his tongue found hers. The hot, sweet wetness of her
mouth made his longing for her body all the more intense. He could feel his erection straining against the
zip on his trousers. He pulled her as close to him as it
was possible to be while still clothed. Her breasts were
jammed against his chest, her hips flush with his, her
thighs tangling with his in a desperate attempt to get
even closer. She made soft little mewling sounds of approval in her throat, her arms snaking up around his
neck, her clever little fingers spreading through his hair,
tugging and pulling and caressing.

He could feel the scrape of his stubble along her skin
as he shifted position, reminding him again of her soft-
ness against his hardness. His tongue found hers again,

coiled around it, danced with it, taunted and teased it until it finally gave in to his command.

He sucked on her lower lip, and then he used his teeth to nip and tug at the tender flesh, following it up with a sweep of his tongue and then repeating the process.

Her tongue flicked against his, a sexy little payback that heated his blood to sizzling. Her teeth got into the action, biting him like a tigress did an aggressive mate, showing him she was not going to submit without a fight.

Luiz had never experienced a more enthralling kiss. His whole body was feeling the supercharge of it. Nerve endings were firing in his lips, sensations were racing up and down his spine, and his thighs were trembling with the pressure of holding himself in. He knew if she so much as put her hand on him he would blow.

The doors of the elevator sprang open and he had a deer-in-the-headlights moment as a camera flashed in his face. He smothered a rough curse and dropped his hands from Daisy's hips.

'Get a room!' someone jeered.

Luiz grabbed Daisy's hand and pulled her behind him. 'Let's get out of here.'

Daisy was bundled into a limousine within seconds of leaving Luiz's hotel. He was still holding her hand, his long calloused fingers wrapped around hers in a bruising grip. High on his aristocratic cheekbones two flags of dull colour were showing beneath his tan. His coal-black eyes were fixed straight ahead but she had a feeling he wasn't registering any of the lurid colour and excitement and craziness of the strip as they traversed the length of it.

'Are you angry with me?' she asked.

He glanced at her as if he had forgotten she was there. 'No. Why do you ask that?'

She indicated her hand trapped within his. 'You're cutting off my circulation.'

He immediately relaxed his hold but he didn't release her hand. Rather he began to caress it in slow, soothing strokes. 'I'm sorry. I didn't realise.'

Daisy looked at his brooding expression. 'Do the press follow you everywhere?'

'Just about.'

'Don't you find it…annoying?'

'Sometimes.'

She moved her fingers over the length of his index finger, circling each of his knuckles and then the neat square of his fingernail. 'Why don't you do something about it?'

He glanced down at her. 'Like what?'

'You could wear a disguise.'

He gave a short laugh. 'As if that would work.'

'A lot of celebrities do it. You'd be surprised how effective it is. A wig or a hat or a different style of clothes can make all the difference. When my kindy kids get in the dress-up box it's impossible to tell who is who. Sometimes even their parents don't recognise them.'

He looked back at their joined hands, his thumb moving over the back of hers in a rhythmic fashion. 'It bothers my brother more than it does me. I guess I'm like my mother in that regard. I've never shied away from the limelight.'

'What's your brother like?'

His thumb found the heel of her hand and began to massage it. 'He's strong. Determined. Focused.'

'Like you, then.'

He smiled a half-smile. 'I'm not sure he would agree with you on that.'

'Why?'

'He doesn't say it upfront, but he thinks I'm chasing a dream that will only disappoint in the end.'

'The Championship?'

He met her gaze again. 'Winning is everything to me. It's always been my main motivation. Being the best.'

'I guess what your brother's saying is one day someone will come along who's better than you,' Daisy said. 'You can't win for ever.'

His gaze went to her mouth. 'No, but I like to think I'll know when it's time to hang up my hat.'

'You mean go out on a high?'

His eyes searched hers for a long moment. 'Did you always want to be a teacher?'

Daisy grinned. 'Always. I used to line up my dolls when I was about three or so and play schools with them for hours.'

There was a serious light in his gaze. 'Did you have a happy childhood?'

Her smile faded as she thought about her mother's restlessness and her father's controlling ways. 'In the early days, but then my mum's accident changed everything. She died when I was ten. A car ran into her as she was coming home from bridge club. My father was always a bit of a control freak but after that he was unbelievable. I couldn't go anywhere without a nanny or babysitter. I had heaps of them over the years. Dad would always upset them over something and they'd storm out in tears. Fear does terrible things to people, doesn't it?'

He gave her hand an absent squeeze. 'Yes, indeed it does.'

Daisy glanced out of the window as her hotel came into view. 'Oh, look. The girls are waiting for me outside. I texted them while I was waiting for the elevator.'

'What did you tell them?'

She gave them a mad wave. 'The truth.'

'Which version?' His tone was dry. 'I'm having a little trouble keeping up.'

Daisy looked at him again. 'Oh, they know I'm not really in love with you. That would be taking things to ridiculous extremes.'

His expression was deadpan. 'Quite.'

'But they're the ones—Belinda in particular—who encouraged me to put myself out there and find myself a holiday romance.' She grinned at him. 'How lucky am I? I asked for four days and you're giving me four weeks. Cool, huh?'

His smile looked a little tight. 'Way cool.'

Luiz stood back as Daisy was reunited with her friends. There was a group hug and lots of excited chatter and a few sideways glances in his direction and some nudging and winking. He took it in good spirit because he wasn't going to risk his sponsorship deal before it even got off the ground. Once it was done and dusted he could distance himself from the engaging Miss Daisy before she drove him crazy. The more time he spent with her, the more he wanted her. Now he had four weeks with her. *Four weeks!* He had trouble being celibate for four hours, let alone four weeks. Once they parted in Vegas he would keep things to a minimum. He could take her out to dinner in London but he wouldn't stay with her or have her stay with him. That would be testing his resolve a little too far. If he kept their dates public he would be home free.

While Daisy was collecting her things, Luiz organised a helicopter for the Grand Canyon. He figured a day outside in the fresh air was another good way to distract himself from the temptation of taking her to bed.

Once they were on their way in the limousine he told her what he had planned. 'We'll fly over Hoover Dam first and then on to the Grand Canyon. You'll get a good view of both.'

'Oh, lovely,' she said. 'But you shouldn't have gone to any trouble.'

'It's no trouble.'

'But what did you have planned for today?'

Luiz wasn't used to his dates being concerned about him, only what he could do for them. Daisy's concern was not only refreshing but it was surprisingly genuine. Her blue eyes had a worried light in them as she waited for his reply.

'Nothing much,' he said. 'A bit of time in the gym, a few games of poker. Chilling out.'

'So is that why you're here in Vegas now? Just for a holiday?'

Why did he go anywhere when he wasn't competing? To distract himself from moping around his huge empty villa in Argentina. If he didn't fill his spare time with parties and people he got restless and bored. His older brother enjoyed solitude. Luiz didn't. Time alone reminded him too much of how he had felt as a child.

Abandoned.

'I come over a couple of times a year. It's a great place to blend into the crowd.' He realised too late the irony of what he'd just said and sent her a wry smile. 'Well, maybe not always.'

She gave him a sympathetic look. 'I'd hate to be famous. It must be awful to have cameras thrust in your face all the time. Never being able to go anywhere without someone tailing you.'

'Having a bodyguard must be similar.'

She rolled her eyes. 'Tell me about it.'

Luiz glanced out of the back window of the limousine. 'Is he still following you?'

'No. I called my father when I was packing my things and made him promise. I think he finally accepts I'm safe with you.'

You're not safe, he thought. *But then, I'm not safe either. Damn it.*

The helicopter was waiting for them when they arrived. Luiz handed Daisy the headset and went through the safety features.

'But what about the pilot?' she asked.

He adjusted her earphones so they sat correctly. 'I'm your pilot.'

Her eyes rounded. 'You're a pilot?'

He couldn't help touching her chin where the red mark from his stubble was still faintly apparent. 'Got my licence years ago.'

Her eyes began to sparkle. 'Do you have any other secret talents I should know about?'

'None that I can show you right now.' Do *not* flirt with her. Do. Not. Flirt. With. Her.

Her smile had a touch of naughty girl about it. 'I bet you have lots of tricks up your sleeve.'

Right now my biggest trick is not up my sleeve, Luiz thought as he helped her into the passenger seat. His hand inadvertently brushed against her breast as he pulled the seat belt into place.

Her eyes met his in a little lock that made his blood hurtle through his veins. Her eyes had tiny flecks of slate in amongst the intense blue, reminding him of an ocean with hidden depths. Her lashes were spider leg long and spiky with a coat of mascara. The point of her tongue darted out to sweep over her lips, making it impossible for him not to stare at the soft shiny lushness of her mouth.

He brought his mouth closer, pausing within a whisker of her slightly parted lips. Her sweet cinnamon and honey breath danced over the surface of his lips, her signature fragrance of old-fashioned cottage flowers teasing his senses into an intoxicated stupor.

'Is someone watching?' she said.

'Not that I know of.' He nudged his nose against hers. 'Why?'

'You're about to kiss me.'

'So?'

'So I thought someone must be watching.'

He couldn't pull himself away from the lure of her soft mouth that tantalisingly brushed against his lower lip every time she spoke. 'Can't I kiss you when no one's watching?'

'Sure. But I thought—'

'Stop thinking.' Luiz wasn't sure if he was saying it to her or himself. 'Just feel.'

He closed the distance between their mouths with a soft press against hers but as soon as her mouth flowered open he was gone. He drove his tongue into her mouth to meet hers; tangling with it in a passionate duel that made the base of his spine shudder and his groin fill with pulsating blood.

Her hands came up to cradle his face, a tender gesture that was at odds with the heated fervour of her kiss. But that was the complexity of her—the beguiling mix of passion and innocence that so knocked him off kilter.

He encircled her wrists with his hands, reluctantly pulling away before things got too out of hand. He needed to stay in control. It was what he did best. He pushed the boundaries as far as he could but no further. He knew his limits and Daisy Wyndham was testing every damn one of them.

She looked at him with a quizzical expression, her mouth all soft and glistening from his moistness and hers. 'Is something wrong?'

Before he could stop himself, he gently brushed her cheek with his index finger. 'We should get going. I've only booked this helicopter for a couple of hours.'

'Oh…right, of course.' She settled back in her seat, wriggling her shoulders and testing the strength of the seat belt, a little frown pulling at her smooth brow.

Luiz brought her chin around so her gaze met his. 'You're safe with me, *querida*.'

Her blue eyes were as clear and pure as a mountain stream. 'But what if I don't want to be?'

CHAPTER SEVEN

IT WAS A breathtaking experience, winging over the engineering marvel of Hoover Dam, but it was nothing to the vista of the magnificent Grand Canyon a short while later. The majestic height of the layers of richly coloured sandstone, the seemingly endless sinuous curve of the Colorado River so far below and the wheeling of a lonely bird of prey and the whistling silence was such a stunning contrast to the madcap noise and frenetic activity of Las Vegas.

Luiz pointed out various landmarks to Daisy, such as Eagle Point, the Grand Canyon Skywalk and Guano Point, telling her some of the history of the first people, the Hualapai tribe. But, rather than land amongst all the tourist buses and cars, he flew her to a quiet gorge where he'd organised special permission to land.

Daisy held her breath in wonder as he brought the helicopter down the face of the canyon into a deep shaded gully where the river flowed as it had done for millions of years. Once the helicopter engine had turned off and the whirling blades ceased, the sense of timelessness struck her as she stood with Luiz in the cool green valley between the huge rock walls of the canyon. The lonely cry of a red-tailed hawk added to the sense of peace and serenity. She didn't want to speak for fear of breaking the spell of mystical silence.

Luiz stood shoulder to shoulder with her. He didn't speak either. He just stood there with a hand shading his eyes as he surveyed their surroundings.

She stole covert glances at him from time to time, watching as he bent down to pick up a little piece of sandstone, turning it over in his fingers before tossing it in the direction of the river, where the *plop* of the pebble as it went down sounded as loud as a rifle shot.

Daisy sensed a deep loneliness in him. He was so popular, so capable, so much the man about town, but out here in the quiet of the timeless canyon he reminded her of one of the birds of prey circling overhead. Solitary. Alone.

Without a word he led her back to the helicopter, guiding her back into her seat and helping her with the headset. She studied his concentrated expression, wondering what he was thinking as he got back behind the controls for take-off. His hands dealt with the controls with the expertise of a pro. He was as at home in the cockpit as he was working the floor at a nightclub or working his way around a woman's body. She hadn't seen him live on horseback but she had looked at some footage online on her phone. He was a natural sportsman, athletic, strong, capable and fiercely competitive.

She glanced at his strongly muscled thighs, so close

to hers in the cockpit. She only had to reach out her hand to touch him. Her fingers opened and closed, warming up for the first caress of that denim-clad thigh.

'Not while I'm flying.'

Daisy looked at him in surprise. 'You knew what I was thinking?'

He glanced at her wryly. 'I thought you were a good girl?'

'Not when I'm with you.'

He made a grunting sound in his throat as he turned back to face the front. 'Fancy a swim when we get back to the hotel?'

Daisy pictured a private pool off his suite with a bubbling Jacuzzi and champagne in an ice bucket close at hand. Fragrant lotions and potions on tap for hours of sensual massage. She smiled a secret smile. Just as well Belinda had slipped her that racy little Brazilian-style bikini earlier. Body issues aside, her conservative one-piece would look totally out of place. It was time for her inner naughty girl to come out to play.

Luiz was keeping her at arm's length but she knew he wanted her. Every time he looked at her she felt the burn of his hungry gaze. She imagined how it would feel to make love on the deck by the pool in the bright sunshine, his hard body driving hers to paradise. She wanted to make love with him. Desperately. But not like all his other partners. She wanted to be different. To be someone he remembered with a special fondness. She wasn't asking for love. She didn't want to fall in love with someone like him. He was not part of her long-term plan. But she did want him to care enough about her to spend more than one night with her.

She smiled at him. 'Sounds wonderful.'

Luiz waited for Daisy to get changed once they got back to his hotel. He checked his emails on his phone. Scrolled through Twitter. Read a couple of blogs he had zero interest in—anything to distract himself from the thought of spending the next hour or two with her dressed in a swimsuit. But at least going downstairs to the public pool area would be his insurance policy. He could hardly make out with her with all the other hotel guests milling about. He looked up when she came out of the bathroom. She was wearing one of the hotel bathrobes tied neatly at the waist and it was far too big for her. It covered her from neck to ankle.

So far, so good.

'Ready?'

'Sure.'

She untied the waist and the white robe fell to a puddle at her feet. Luiz felt his jaw clang to the floor. The soft mounds of her breasts spilled out from behind two tiny triangles of fuchsia-pink. The triangle that covered her pubic area was even tinier, the strings that held it in place barely thicker than dental floss.

'You can't wear that!'

Her brow puckered. 'Why not?'

'Everyone will see your...er...assets.'

'But I thought we were swimming in your pool?'

'The one downstairs is bigger.'

She toyed with one of the strings on her bikini bottoms. 'I don't care if it's small. I'd rather stay up here. I don't like swimming with crowds of people.'

Luiz had to think on his feet and fast. 'There's way too much chlorine in this one. It'll ruin your bikini. It'll make the colour fade.'

'That's easily fixed.' She tugged at one of the strings holding her top in place. 'I won't wear it.'

He feasted his eyes on the creamy globes of her breasts with their twin points of rosy pink. He slid his gaze down to her slim waist, then to the tiny cave of her belly button. He snatched in a breath as she gave her bikini bottom ties a tug. The scrap of fabric fell away to reveal her feminine form. She was like a closed orchid, soft delicate petals folded together.

She came towards him with a swinging catwalk gait, her hips swaying, her beautiful breasts jiggling tantalisingly, her good-girl-turned-naughty smile on her mouth and dancing in her eyes. 'You sure you want to go downstairs and swim in that crowded pool with all those other people?'

He swallowed thickly as she looped her arms around his neck, pushing her naked breasts against his chest. Even through the cotton of his shirt he could feel her nipples poking him. Lust charged through his body with rocket-force speed. His hands were on her waist before his brain had even registered the command. His mouth came down and covered hers in an explosive kiss that made his spine tingle from top to base.

Her tongue met his in a frenzied dance, moistly coiling and retreating, stabbing and darting around his until he had to ruthlessly take charge. He thrust deeply into her mouth, swirling his tongue over every corner of her mouth until, with a breathless little gasp, she succumbed. She melted against him, hands threading through his hair, her mouth a soft yielding pliancy beneath his.

He stroked his hands down her body, skirting over her breasts, sliding down her hips and back up again. Her skin was as smooth as cream and as soft as satin, every inch of her so perfectly feminine his body throbbed with the need to possess her.

He slid his hands down over the curve of her bottom, cupping her to him, relishing the feel of her so close to the pulsating need of his body. He continued to kiss her, deeply, thoroughly, delighting in the feel of her lips and tongue wrangling with his.

Her teeth made a series of kitten nips against his, thrilling his blood to fever-pitch. He did the same to her, pulling and tugging her lower lip with his teeth, reminding her he was the one with the greater strength.

Her hands went to the buttons of his shirt, undoing them with fumbling haste as her mouth played with the skin of his neck, over his collarbone, and down his sternum.

She smoothed her hands over each part of his chest as she uncovered it, sliding over and stroking him until he was so worked up he was having trouble keeping control. His erection strained, tight and aching, against the prison of his jeans.

Once he had shrugged off his shirt, she started on

his waistband fastening, releasing it and sliding his zip down. He watched as she peeled back his underwear, her small white hand stroking his length with tentative shyness. He held his breath as she smoothed the pad of her finger over the bead of pre-ejaculatory moisture at his tip. Her caresses became bolder as she saw the way he was responding.

He put his hand over hers, halting her movements before he disgraced himself. 'I need a minute.'

'You need me,' she said. 'I need you. I want you.'

'I want you too.' There. He'd admitted it. What was the point of trying to pretend otherwise? He hadn't a hope of holding out. She was too distracting. Too engaging. Too everything.

'Then why are you stalling?'

The irony didn't escape him. When had he ever been concerned about going too fast? Normally he was all for the faster, the better. He didn't hang around too long in case his casual partners got any funny ideas about taking things more seriously.

He didn't do serious.

He was in it for fun, not for ever.

But something about Daisy made him think of taking his time, indulging in an affair that lasted longer than an orgasm. She was like a good wine. It would be a sin to scull a fine wine without lingering over the bouquet, tasting the subtle nuances and reflecting on the aftertaste.

But even a good wine lost its appeal over time. There was always another variety waiting in the wings. He was like his mother in that way, always on the lookout for something or someone more exciting.

Although right now there was nothing he could think of that was more exciting than having Daisy Wyndham naked in his arms. Her body was so nubile and feminine he wanted to lose himself in her delectable curves.

Luiz brought his mouth back down to within a breath of hers. 'I'm not stalling,' he said. 'I'm just warming up.'

'So what was that about only kissing in public?'

Yeah, what was that? His attempt to control a situation that was never going to be in his control.

'I've changed my mind.'

He walked her backwards to the bed, his mouth locked on hers, their tongues duelling, their bodies straining to get as close as humanly possible. He quickly shucked off his jeans and shoes and socks and joined her on the bed. 'I don't want to hurt you.'

'How will you hurt me?'

He brushed a strand of hair away from her face, looking into the clear blue of her gaze. 'The first time can be painful.'

She gave him a twinkling look. 'Well, you *are* a little bigger than Edward.'

He pressed a hard kiss to her mouth. 'Wicked girl.'

She grinned at him. 'I'm learning.'

He brought his mouth to her breast, suckling at the tight nipple while she expressed her pleasure in little moans and gasps. He took his mouth further down her body, lingering over her belly button, dipping his tongue in and out before going lower. He traced the seam of her body with the tip of his tongue, once, twice, the third time gently opening her to taste her. She arched up in delight, her hands clutching at the bedcover either side of her. He felt her every tremble against his tongue, her breathless gasps like music to his ears. He varied his speed and pressure, encouraging her to relax into the rhythm of his caresses. She pulled back a couple of times as if shying away from the powerful sensations. He calmed her with slower movements, placing his hand on her belly, close to her mound to anchor her. She sighed deeply and he resumed his caresses, feeling the exact moment when she lifted off. He watched the spasms of ecstasy play out on her face; the intimacy of watching someone having an orgasm had never really struck him quite that way before. She was so open and free, so uninhibited, so perfectly natural it made his breath catch.

She opened her eyes and looked at him with a smile. 'It didn't hurt a bit.'

'Not yet, but it might.' Luiz took one of her hands and pressed a kiss to the middle of her palm. 'I'll take it slowly just in case.' He reached past her to retrieve a condom from the bedside drawer.

She turned her head to watch him. 'How many do you have in there?'

'Enough.'

'I suppose you buy them in the hundreds.'

He glanced at her to see if there was any sign of censure in her expression but, surprisingly, there was none.

Unless she was doing her best to disguise it, which was more likely. 'It's not good to hold on to them for too long. They have a use-by date.'

'Like your partners?'

He searched her gaze for another moment. 'Yes. Exactly like them.'

She trailed a fingertip down the length of his forearm. 'What's been your longest relationship?'

'Two weeks.'

Her brows lifted. 'That long?'

Luiz gave a rueful twist of his mouth. 'Yeah, it's a record. It was when I was a teenager. I fell madly in love at sixteen. She was a year older and had much more experience.'

'Who broke it off?'

'She did.'

'Ouch.'

He traced a slow circle on the back of her hand. 'She had a boyfriend she forgot to tell me about.' He met her gaze again. 'I was a fling to make him jealous.'

She frowned. 'That was pretty mean of her.'

'Quite.'

She lifted her hand to his face, stroking his lean cheek, her blue eyes holding his. 'So you've used women ever since.'

He pulled back from her hand and frowned. 'I don't use women.'

'Yes, you do. You hook up with them for sex. You don't spend any time getting to know them. If that's not using then I don't know what is.'

He pushed up off the bed and got to his feet, slamming the bedside drawer on the way. 'No one's complained so far.'

'No, because you buy them off with a flashy bit of jewellery or flowers.'

He sent her a cutting look. 'I see you and Mr Google have been getting up close and personal. What else have you found out about me?'

She sat up and hugged her knees to her chest, her teeth giving her lower lip a chew, her eyes now downcast. 'I think I just ruined the moment... Sorry.'

Luiz found it impossible to be angry with her. He let out a slow breath and came back to the bed and sat beside her. He took her hand and turned it over in his, playing with each of her fingers in turn. 'You don't approve of my lifestyle, do you?'

Her blue eyes were clear and open and honest as they met his. 'I don't know much about it, other than what I've read. You might have a completely different take on it. But one thing I do know. You can't live your whole life without connecting with other people on more than a physical level.'

He moved his thumb over the knuckle of hers in a slow motion caress. 'How come someone who's only had sex with a toy knows so much about connecting with people?'

Her cheeks blushed a faint pink. 'I've had sex with you...sort of...'

He watched as her gaze dropped to his mouth, her tongue sneaking out to moisten her lips in a darting sweep. He pressed the pad of his finger to her bottom lip, watching as the blood retreated and then flowed back in when he lifted it away. 'Want to pick up where we left off?'

He heard her draw in a quick little breath. 'Do you want to?'

He pressed her back down on the bed. 'Do I really need to answer that?'

She smiled as his body bore down on hers. 'I think you just did.'

CHAPTER EIGHT

Daisy sighed in bliss as his mouth sealed hers in a searing kiss. His tongue stroked for entry in that commanding way he had, making her stomach turn over like a flipped pancake. His hand came down on her hip and pulled her up against him, one of his thighs coming over the top of hers in an intimate entrapment that made her skin pepper with goosebumps. His erection was pressed hard against her belly, a tantalising reminder of all the differences between them.

She reached down to stroke him, loving the feel of him pulsing with desire under her fingertips. He was oozing moisture and she felt her own beading inside her body in preparation for him.

One of his hands cupped her breast, his thumb pressing against her nipple, pushing it in and out, and then circling it. He bent his head to take it in his mouth, laving it with his tongue, tracing every inch of her flesh with soft but sure movements.

Daisy felt the rise of her need for him like a tremor before an earthquake. It moved through her flesh with every scorching touch of his mouth and hands on her body.

He rolled her over on her back, leaning his weight on his elbows. His mouth moved with erotic intent over hers, drawing from her a fevered response she hadn't realised she was capable of giving. She felt as if she would die if he didn't make love to her. She opened her legs and felt her stomach swoop as he settled between them. Somehow he'd managed to slip a condom on. She felt him at her entrance, hard, swollen, ready. She arched up to receive him, urging him to possess her without language but with unmitigated primal need.

He slowly entered her with a deep guttural groan of pleasure. Her body wrapped around him, holding him, delighting in him. Needing him like she needed air to breathe.

He steadily increased his pace, taking his time so she could find her own rhythm. She moved with him, lifting her hips to each of his downward thrusts, shuddering with pleasure as the friction targeted the most sensitive spot. The pleasure built to a crescendo. She could feel the tension in her body building like the overstretching of a violin string. Her body was singing, humming and thrumming with delicious shockwaves of feeling. A shiver coursed over her skin as he upped the pace, his thrusts deeper, harder and more frantic, as if he too was close to the summit of human pleasure.

He slipped one of his hands between their bodies to heighten the pleasure. It was all she needed to tip over the edge. The orgasm smashed into her in a giant wave that sent her flying higher than she had ever flown before. The combination of human touch, the musky fragrance of male arousal, the stroke and glide of clever hands and the expertise of his lips and tongue made a mockery of everything she had experienced on her own.

Daisy floated down from the heights with a rapturous sigh just in time to feel his release power through him. He tensed over her, poised in that nanosecond between control and freedom. He gave a primal growl and surged deep, shuddering his way through his orgasm, the skin on his back and shoulders rising in the fine gravel of goosebumps beneath her fingertips.

She heard him give a long, deep sigh before he collapsed on top of her, his head buried beside her neck, his breathing still racing.

It was so different being held in a man's arms. Being *wanted*. Her body was still tingling with the aftershocks of his possession. She hadn't expected it to be so utterly consuming. Her entire body had been swept away with the rushing sensations of pleasure. Was it because it was him, not some other man? Was it his experience or something else? Every step of the way he had made sure of her comfort and pleasure. He had taken extra care of her. How could that not have an impact on her reaction to him? He had made her first time not only special but also memorable. How would she ever forget this moment? He had taught her the secrets of her body. Coaxed her into the most amazing orgasm that she could still feel trembling underneath her skin.

He had said the first time could be emotional and she had laughed it off. But her emotions were shaken. Tumbled about. Confused by the storm of passion that had powered through her. Her body felt different. Her senses were turned to a different radar frequency. The glow of satiation fanned out over every inch of her flesh, each muscle and sinew softened in lassitude.

Daisy ran her hands up and down his spine, stroking and caressing the strongly muscled flesh, wondering if he had experienced anything out of the ordinary or if this was another day at the office, so to speak. She knew it would be foolish indeed to put too much significance on their lovemaking. Chemistry was chemistry. Some people connected well physically. It didn't mean they were necessarily ideal partners, for so many other factors came into play in order to sustain a long-term relationship. That she had connected so well with Luiz might just be her inexperience clouding her judgement. He had so many partners to compare her to. He was probably measuring her by them even now.

After a long moment he lifted his head to look down at her. 'I know what you're thinking.'

Daisy traced the stubble that surrounded his mouth with one of her fingertips. 'So tell me.'

His gaze went back and forth between each of her eyes. His eyes were so dark they looked like pools of black ink. 'You want to know if it was different for me.'

She made herself hold his gaze but hoped she gave little away in her own. 'Was it?'

He pushed back her hair from her face with a hand that was so gentle it felt like a feather. 'It was.'

'Because I was a virgin.'

'Not just that.'

'Then what?'

He sent his fingertip down the slope of her nose. 'I've never made love to a woman like you.'

'Fat, do you mean?'

He frowned. 'Why are you so hard on yourself? You're beautiful.'

Daisy wanted to believe him but years of self-doubt were not going to be erased that easily. She might have pranced around in that tiny bikini as if she didn't have a care in the world but she had been sucking in her tummy the whole time. 'I'm probably taking up twice the space in your bed as your other partners.'

His expression darkened as he moved away to deal with the condom. 'That's ridiculous.'

She rolled over to her stomach to watch as he went in search of his clothes. 'You're angry.'

He pulled on his jeans and zipped them up roughly. 'No, I'm not.'

'Then why are you frowning so heavily?'

He blew out a frustrated-sounding breath. 'So I date models. Is that a crime?'

Daisy propped her chin on her folded over hands, seesawing her bent legs behind her. There seemed no point hiding her nakedness now. He'd seen all there was to see. Besides, lying on her tummy meant she didn't have to concentrate on holding it in. 'Why do you date them?'

He gave her a worldly look. 'Why do you think?'

She rolled her lips together as she studied him thoughtfully. 'I don't think it's about their looks. It's their lifestyle. They're on the move like you. Another city. Another hotel. Another catwalk. They're free agents like you. That's the appeal. They won't make any demands on you.'

He gave a laugh as he reached for his shirt, thrusting his arms through and loosely buttoning it. 'I must've been mad to approach you in the bar last night.'

Daisy widened her eyes. 'Was it only last night? Gosh, I feel like I've known you for ever.'

He snatched up his phone. 'I have a couple of calls to make. Excuse me.'

'That's another thing I've noticed about you.'

He turned from the door leading into the lounge area, his expression tight with tension. 'I don't suppose you'll refrain from telling me even if I expressly ask you not to?'

She smiled sweetly. 'See? You know me so well too.'

He leaned one shoulder on the door jamb in an indolent fashion. 'Go on. Tell me what you've noticed.'

Daisy looked at the pulse that was beating at the side of his mouth. 'Intimacy scares you. And no, I'm not talking about sex. That requires very little intimacy. It's just bodies rubbing up against each other. Anyone can do that.'

His top lip curled. 'Or a machine.'

'Excellent point.'

The cynical gleam was back in his eyes. 'One would hope you enjoyed the man more than the machine?'

Daisy rolled over onto her back and tilted her head over the edge of the bed to look at him upside down. 'Are you fishing for compliments, Luiz Valquez?'

His eyes feasted on her hungrily. She had never felt such feminine power before. It made her forget her doubts about her body. He made no secret of the fact her body delighted him. The way he looked at her heated her flesh in anticipation of his touch. He wanted her even though he was trying to distance himself. It was what he did when he felt cornered. He didn't want to want her more than once. She saw the battle play out over his face as his gaze ran over her naked breasts and beyond. Stay or go. Stay or go.

'You want to play some more, *querida?*'

She gave him a vampish smile. 'Edward can go as long as I want him to.'

'Did you bring him with you?'

She sent him an arch look. 'What do you think?'

He came back over to her and traced a lazy pathway from her sternum to her mound, stopping just above the seam of her body. 'You are the most bewitching woman I've ever met.'

Daisy basked in the compliment like a fur seal in the sun. His finger was tantalisingly close to where she most wanted him. The ache was building deep inside her, all of her nerves dancing in anticipation of that first delicious stroke of his finger. His eyes grew darker and darker with desire as they held hers. Then, ever so slowly, he separated her folds, slipping one finger into the silky wetness of her body. She arched her spine like a cat, all but purring as he began to stroke her. It was impossible not to come. She didn't even have to concentrate or empty her mind of distracting thoughts. The sensations triggered by his magical touch were so intense they took over her body as if she were a rag doll, shaking her senseless.

But he didn't stop there.

He unzipped his jeans, stepping out of them roughly before reaching for another condom. She watched as he peeled it back over his length, proud and strong and virile.

He came over her, nudging her legs further apart, his eyes black and glittering as his hands pinned her arms above her head in a masterful manner, making everything that was female in her shudder in primal pleasure. She gasped as he sheathed himself to the hilt, the sensation of him stretching her to capacity sending her senses reeling. There was no slow and considerate pacing this time. He set a ruthlessly fast rhythm that made her nerves come vibrantly alive. Her body welcomed the sensual assault, delighting in the way he was thrusting with such relentless vigour as if the desire he felt for her was an unstoppable force. His face was clenched tight as he fought for control, his breathing rough and hectic.

She cried out loud as the first wave of her release hit her. It ricocheted through her body, shaking her, rattling her, sending her spinning off into a vortex that was beyond the reach of all thought and reason.

But she was still conscious enough to be aware of him as he spilled. He gave one deep sound that sounded as primitive as a feral growl, his face contorting with pleasure as he emptied.

Daisy released a shuddering breath as he released his grip on her arms. 'You really know how to give a girl a good time.' She rubbed at her tingling arms, wondering if she would bruise.

He frowned as his gaze went to the reddened marks on her skin. 'Did I hurt you?'

She suddenly felt embarrassed. She didn't want to come across as fragile. She wanted to be his equal, not some vapid wimp who didn't know how to play the casual dating game. 'Not at all.'

He ran his fingers over the marks in a barely-there touch. 'I'm sorry. I lost my head there for a bit.'

Daisy tiptoed her fingers up and down his chest. 'You don't like losing control, do you?'

'It's not a habit of mine.'

She circled each of his nipples in turn. 'There are some things in life you can't control.'

'Young, smart-mouthed Englishwomen being one of them.'

She smiled at him. 'The more I get to know you, the better I like you.'

Something flashed over his face. A camera shutter quick movement that left a nerve ticking in his jaw. 'Let's stick to the rules, shall we?'

'Oh, I'm not changing the goalposts,' she reassured him. 'Why would I? You're not what I'm looking for in a husband.'

'So you keep reminding me.'

'Why does that annoy you?'

His frown brought his brows together. 'It doesn't annoy me.'

Daisy reached up and smoothed out the crease between his eyes. 'Yes, it does.'

He pushed her hand away and got off the bed. 'I have to—'

'I know, I know,' she said with a knowing smile. 'You have to make some calls or check some emails, right?'

He shifted his lips from side to side as if wondering what to do with her. 'What is it you want from me?'

'I told you. A holiday fling. Sex without strings.'

He raked a hand through his hair, releasing a harsh-sounding breath. 'You expect me to believe that?'

'Why not?'

He stepped back into his jeans and pulled up the zip. 'Because it doesn't usually work that way.'

'You mean because women usually want the fairy-tale ending?'

'Don't you?'

'Yes, but not with you.'

He looked about to ask something but changed his mind. His mouth slammed shut as he glowered at her. But, for all that, the unspoken words rang in the silence: *Why not me?*

Daisy decided to answer anyway and ticked off her fingers as if checking off a list. 'One. You're a player, not a stayer. Two. You live in Argentina and I live in England. Three. You're—'

'Spare me the rest,' he muttered. 'I think I get the picture.'

She swung her legs off the bed and reached for the bathrobe, making a little moue with her mouth. 'I thought men were supposed to be all soft and mellow after sex? You're a big old grouch.'

He let out a just audible curse. 'I'm going to have a shower.'

'Is that code for "you're pressing my buttons"?' she asked innocently.

He caught her by the ties of the bathrobe and pulled her roughly to him. 'No,' he said. 'It's code for "I haven't finished pressing yours".'

Luiz left Daisy sleeping while he read through the sponsorship contract that had come through on email. But his gaze kept tracking back to the bed, where she lay with her cheek resting on one of her hands. Her hair was spread out over his pillow, her kiss-swollen mouth slightly parted. His groin tingled at the memory of her mouth beneath his, the way her tongue played and flirted with his.

He glanced at the bedside clock. Midnight. The second night he'd spent with her. The first one he'd spent watching her sleep. The second one he'd spent making love with her and wondering how he was going to let her go at the end of their affair.

Was this how his brother felt watching Teddy sleep? This inexplicable feeling of tenderness he couldn't shake off, no matter how much he wanted to?

Daisy didn't belong in his life. He had no time for a relationship. He wasn't relationship material—a fact she kept reminding him of at annoyingly regular intervals. He was the first to list his inadequacies. He didn't need her to spell them out for him. He knew he was unreliable in a relationship. He got bored easily. He liked to get out first before someone left him.

But for the first time in a long time—possibly ever—he didn't want to leave. He wanted to see Daisy wake up in the morning, blink those big baby-blues at him a couple of times and then smile that radiant smile that made something in his chest squeeze tight. He wanted to sit opposite her and watch her eat her breakfast like a child who had been let loose in a candy store. He wanted to see her embrace her sensuality even more, to indulge her senses without the hang-ups she had about her body. How she could doubt her physical beauty astonished him. She might not be as reed-thin as some of the models he'd dated but she had an inner beauty that was even more alluring.

He liked her sense of playfulness. She could be serious when she needed to be but a smile was never far away. He liked the way her smile lit up her eyes so they danced and sparkled.

She burrowed further into the pillow, her eyelids flickering, just like they'd done the first night he had watched her sleep. Her skin was free of make-up, as pure and as smooth as milk. He could spend hours watching her. The peacefulness of her when she slept calmed him. It soothed that restless energy deep inside him.

He came over to the bed and touched her creamy cheek with his fingertip, tracing the aristocratic slope, watching as her eyelids flickered again before opening to meet his gaze. 'What time is it?' she asked.

'Just gone midnight.'

She sat up and pushed her hair back over one shoulder, holding the sheet up to her chest to cover her nakedness. 'Have I missed dinner?'

He couldn't hold back a smile as he traced her cheekbone again. 'Do you think of anything but food?'

Her cheek bloomed pink under the brushstroke of his fingertip. 'I do now.'

Luiz bent down to press his mouth against the lush bow of hers. It never failed to amaze him how soft her lips were. Soft and pliable as they moved against his in a kiss that spoke of physical yearnings that simmered under the surface. He cupped her face and deepened the kiss, putting his knee on the bed beside her as he pressed her back down on the bed. Her arms went around his neck, her mouth hot and tempting beneath his. He explored every corner of her sweetness, the taste of her like an intoxicating elixir. He wondered if he could ever satisfy his craving for her. He was trying not to overwhelm her with too much too soon. Her body would be tender and sore if he made love to her too vigorously and too often. It was strange territory for him to be feeling so protective.

It was strange for him to be *feeling*...

He pulled back as she reached for him. 'You need food.'

'I need you more.'

He stood and put some distance between himself and her tempting body. 'Food first.'

While he was on the phone ordering room service he watched her slip on a bathrobe. She gave a little wincing movement as she walked away from the bed. Something slipped in his stomach. He'd hurt her. 'Are you OK?'

She gave him one of her bright smiles. 'Of course.'

He put the phone down and came over to her, tipping up her chin to look deep into her clear blue gaze. 'I was too rough with you.'

Her forehead pleated in a protesting frown. 'No, you weren't.'

He stroked her reddened chin where his stubble had prickled her soft skin. He heard her breath softly catch. Saw her pupils dilate. Watched as the tip of her tongue came out to dart over her lips. Felt his own body quake with want as she put her hands on his chest. Her pelvis was within a millimetre of his. He could feel the magnetic pull of her body drawing him inexorably towards her. His erection swelled, tightened, ached. It was all he could do not to crush her to him and slake the wild lust that threatened to overwhelm him.

He put his hands over hers and gently but firmly removed them from his chest. 'You need to pace yourself, *querida*. We have plenty of time.'

'Three days…or is it two now that today's over?'

Luiz ignored the odd little ache below his heart as he selected a bottle of champagne from the minibar. He popped the cork and poured two glasses, handing one to her. 'It's two.'

She took a sip of the champagne, wrinkling up her nose like a bunny as the bubbles fizzed. 'I really shouldn't be drinking this. Before you know it, I'll be spilling all my secrets.'

'Feel free.'

She laughed and set her glass down. 'Not unless you tell me one of yours first.'

Luiz leaned against the arm of the sofa. 'I don't have any. The press take care of that.'

He was acutely conscious of her gaze as it rested on him as if she were peeling back the mask of indifference he wore. He had spent most of his life pretending not to care what people said or thought about him. He had especially perfected the art in the company of his mother. He never let his mother think she had the power to hurt him. While Alejandro silently brooded over their mother's critical comments, Luiz actively encouraged them, laughing them off as if life was one big game. He enjoyed the lovable bad boy role. He'd been doing it for so long it felt normal…and yet, when Daisy looked at him with that thoughtful gaze, he wondered if she could see a tiny glimpse of the sensitive boy he had once been.

'All right,' Daisy said. 'I'll go first. I once ate a whole block of milk chocolate and burned the wrapper in the fireplace so my father wouldn't find out.'

'How old were you?'

She gave him a sheepish look. 'Twenty-three.'

'Are you joking?'

'Sadly, no.'

Luiz frowned. 'What is his problem?'

'Control is his problem. He finds it hard to love someone without controlling them. It drove my mother nuts.'

'Why do you put up with it?'

She dropped her shoulders on an expelled breath. 'I think deep down he means well. Besides, he's the only family I've got.'

'Yes, but this is the only life you've got. You can't live it according to his standards.'

'I know. That's why I came to Vegas with the girls. He didn't want me to go but for once I put my foot down.'

'Clearly not hard enough if he sent a bodyguard.'

'Yes, well, that's my dad for you.'

There was a knock on the door, announcing the arrival of the midnight supper Luiz had ordered. He tipped the young staff member and closed the door.

Daisy was staring at the tray of food as if she hadn't seen a meal for a year. 'Is this all for us?' she asked.

'It's just a snack.'

She touched a tentative hand to the tiered plate of ribbon sandwiches and buttery savoury scones. 'I swear I'm going to chain myself to the treadmill when I get home.'

Luiz watched as she picked up a salmon and asparagus sandwich, biting into it with her small white teeth, her eyes closing in bliss. There was something so sexy about the way she ate. She savoured every mouthful, licking her lips and groaning in pleasure.

She caught him watching her and blushed again. 'That's the problem with denying yourself something. Whatever's taboo is the thing you end up wanting the most.'

Isn't that the truth? Luiz thought. He hoped his expression was giving nothing away of the struggle he was enduring to keep his hands to himself. He wanted her so badly it was a throbbing ache. Worse than hunger. Worse than thirst. It was like being addicted to a potent drug. The craving ate away at his self-control until he could think of nothing but sinking into her hot, warm tightness. 'Isn't that what holidays are for? Relaxing the rules a bit?'

'Maybe.' She picked up a wedge of Camembert

cheese and looked at it balefully. 'There's more fat in this piece of cheese than in that whole plate of sandwiches.' She gave a deep sign and put the cheese back down. 'No. I'd better be good.'

Luiz picked up the cheese and held it in front of her mouth. 'Be bad. Be very bad.'

Her eyes twinkled as she opened her mouth for him to pop the cheese in. 'Mmm. That is *soooo* good.'

He wiped a tiny crumb from the corner of her mouth with the pad of his thumb, trying his best not to think of her mouth feasting on him. His attempt to keep a lid on his desire for her was taking a battering. Everything about her turned him on. The way she spoke in that husky tone. The way her eyes kept slipping to his mouth as if she couldn't help herself. The way she stood so close to him he could feel the warmth of her body and could smell the fragrance of her perfume like a sensual mist teasing his nostrils.

He gave himself a mental shake and reached for the champagne bottle. 'Top up?'

She put her hand over the top of her glass. 'And have me spilling all my secrets without you telling me one of yours? Play fair. How about you tell me something you haven't told anyone else before?'

Luiz pushed his lips from side to side, weighing up whether to take up her challenge. Hadn't he already told her more than he'd told anyone else? But something about her cute dimples and pretty blue eyes made him give in. 'OK.' He took a deep breath and slowly released it. 'I hate spiders.'

Her eyes rounded. 'Really? Like totally freaked out, stand screaming on a chair hate them?'

He gave her a look. 'No. I can actually manage to remove them without any outbursts of hysteria.'

She screwed up her nose. 'You mean like…pick them up?'

Luiz suppressed the urge to brush the skin of his arms. Talking about spiders always made him feel as if a dozen of them were tiptoeing over his flesh. 'Not with my bare hands. That's what a vacuum cleaner is for.'

'But you're six foot four tall. What's a teensy weensy little spider going to do to you?'

'Some of them are poisonous.'

She perched on the arm of the sofa, her mouth wreathed in a teasing smile. 'Don't worry. If a big, bad old spider comes sneaking in I'll save you from it.'

He drained his glass and set it back down. 'Thanks. Appreciate it.'

'I suppose you don't run across them all that often in penthouse suites.'

'You'd be surprised.'

She twirled her glass for a moment. 'I guess you must have felt so frightened and anchorless when your mum left.'

Luiz shrugged. 'I got over it.'

'I was devastated when my mum was killed.' She put her glass down and looked at him again. 'I didn't believe it at first. I thought my dad was lying. I thought she'd left him as she'd threatened to do a couple of times.' Her gaze fell away from his. 'But then I saw the police arrive…'

Luiz put a hand on her shoulder and gave it a gentle squeeze. 'I'm sorry.'

She looked up at him again. 'Do you know what was really awful?'

'What?'

'My father refused to allow me to go to the funeral. I begged and pleaded but he wouldn't listen.' Her frown was so heavy it made her look fierce in a cute and endearing way. 'He said a funeral was no place for a child. So I held my own for her. I got all my dolls and toys and took them down to the rose garden. I even made a special shrine for her out of modelling clay. I had to make the gardener, Robert, promise not to tell my father. We hid it behind her favourite rose bush. It's still there.'

'You must have loved her very much.'

She smiled a sad-looking smile. 'Yes, but don't all children love their mothers?'

Luiz thought of the shallowness of his mother. Of the way she cut down his brother every chance she got. Of the way she had insulted Teddy at the cocktail party Luiz had held recently, seeming to enjoy the hurt and cruelty she inflicted. How she publicly fawned over him as if he could do no wrong, treating him like a favourite toy instead of a son she would give her life for. 'Not all.'

Daisy put her hand over his on her shoulder. 'You hate your mother?'

Luiz gave her a rueful look. 'So, Miss Daisy, you've uncovered another well-kept secret.'

She brought his hand down to her lap, stroking the back of it with her soft fingers. 'Maybe she can't help being the way she is. Some people are not good at being parents. I see it all too often. They have this idea of how their child will be but the child is someone else entirely. They're not blank slates when they're born. They're their own little person. You can't make them into something they're not.'

Luiz suddenly had a vision of Daisy with a brood of kids around her. Not just the ones she taught, but her own children. He could imagine a little girl with a dimpled smile and bright eyes and chestnut hair and creamy skin. He thought of a little boy with—

He jerked back from where his thoughts were heading. Kids meant commitment. Long-term commitment. A lifetime of commitment and care and concern and responsibility.

But, even so, an image kept popping into his head of a little boy with black hair and brown eyes, with a little starfish hand reaching for his...

'You shouldn't hate her, Luiz.' Daisy's soft voice jolted him out of his daydream. 'Hate is such a destructive emotion.'

Luiz took a tendril of her hair and curled it around his finger. 'I should let you get back to bed.'

'Aren't you coming too?'

He tucked the hair behind her ear. 'You need a rest.'

'But I'm not tired.'

'I saw you wince when you got off the bed.'

She suddenly scowled at him and pushed his hand away to fold her arms across her body. 'I wish you wouldn't treat me like I'm made of glass. It reminds me too much of my father. Telling me what's good for me as if I couldn't possibly know myself.'

Luiz drew in a long breath through his nostrils. 'I'm sorry for being so considerate. Maybe I should just throw you down on the bed and take my pleasure without any thought of yours, like that creep you picked up the other night would've done if I hadn't stepped in.'

Her scowl fell away and her teeth bit down on her lower lip. 'I'm sorry.'

'Forget about it.'

She came over to him and put a hand on his arm, looking up at him with those beautiful lake-blue eyes. 'You let everyone think you're a caddish man-about-town but you're the most gentle and considerate man I've ever met.'

He put his hands on her upper arms, tensing his fingers just enough to remind her of the strength he had at his disposal. He felt her shiver under his touch and his body responded with a rocket blast of lust. He brought his mouth down to hers, shocked at the heat that exploded as his lips came into contact with hers. Her tongue tangled with his in a sexy duel that made his whole body vibrate with longing. Blood surged hot and strong to his groin, swelling him against the urgent press of her body.

He slipped her robe off her shoulders, letting it fall to the floor at her feet. His hands moved over her silky flesh, cupping and shaping her until she whimpered her delight into his mouth. He moved his hands down over her hips, holding her to the throb of his need. She moved against him, wriggling her body to get closer.

He picked her up and carried her back to the bedroom, sliding her down the length of his body as he lowered her feet to the floor. Her mouth stayed locked on his, her tongue playing with his in an erotic dance that fired his blood. Her hands were everywhere—in his hair, moving up and down his back and shoulders, cupping his buttocks, touching him and stroking him until he was so primed he had to fight for control.

He bent her back down on the bed, rolling her over so she straddled him. Her hair cascaded over her shoulders, half covering her breasts in a sexy pose that thrilled his senses. He reached for a condom from the bedside drawer and sheathed himself. 'This way you can control the depth,' he said.

She placed her hands either side of his head and lowered herself onto him, her mouth opening on a soft little gasp as her body accepted him. He kept his movements to a minimum, letting her do the work so she could control how much of him she took in. She began to move, slowly rocking, then building the pace as she found her sweet spot.

He began to move with her, taking her with him on a wave of pleasure that travelled through his body until he could hold back no longer. He felt her contract around him in tight spasms of release that triggered his own. He lost all thought as he gave himself to the moment of exhilaration, that wonderful moment when his body broke free from all restraints and soared.

He held her to his chest as she collapsed over him, her hair tickling his face and chest. He stroked his hand in lazy circles up and down her spine, over the curve of her bottom and then back up again. Breathing in the scent of her skin, the summer flowers and sensual woman fragrance that thrilled his senses in a way no other woman had before.

'Your hands are like exfoliation gloves,' she said against his ear.

Luiz felt a smile tug on his lips. 'Glad I'm proving to be so useful.'

She raised herself up to look at him with a playful expression. 'Are we done?'

'Not yet.'

Her eyes danced in anticipation. 'You mean you can go another round?'

Luiz rolled her off him and got off the bed and held out his hand to her. 'Come on.'

'Where are we going?'

'I scrubbed your back. Now it's time for you to scrub mine.'

Before she knew it, Daisy was in the shower recess with him, naked and slippery with bath gel. Her mouth was locked beneath his in a searing kiss, his hands moving over her body in caressing waves that made her skin tingle all over. The combination of the stinging needles of water as well as his calloused hands was enough to send her senses haywire. He came to her breasts and subjected them to a torturous massage, stopping only to suckle on each of her nipples before resuming his mind-blowing stroking. He moved down her body, dipping his fingers between her thighs, tantalising her with little touches and fleeting strokes that stirred her desire to fever-pitch. She shamelessly rubbed herself against his hand, whimpering as the water coursed over her face and shoulders.

He slipped a finger inside her but it wasn't enough. She wanted him. All of him.

She reached for him, holding him in her hand, stroking the velvet-covered hardness until he had to brace himself against the shower stall. Emboldened by his response to her touch, she slipped to her knees and traced her tongue over him from base to tip. He shuddered and smothered a groan and she became bolder, using her whole mouth this time to draw on him. She felt his blood thundering as she moved her mouth up and down, varying the speed and suction, testing what he liked, going purely on instinct and being rewarded by his passionate response.

'Enough,' he groaned and pulled away, breathing heavily as he hauled her upright.

Daisy looked into his lust-glazed eyes and a frisson of excitement washed over her. 'I wanted to make you come.'

'I don't think there's any danger of that not happening.' He took a handful of her wet hair, bringing her head closer to kiss her deeply.

She moved against his hard body, wriggling so his erection was against her folds. She reached for him again and guided him towards her.

He suddenly stalled. 'Are you on the Pill?'

'Yes.'

He seemed to be hesitating, his body poised at her entrance. 'I don't usually do this.'

'It's not as if I've been with anyone else, so if that's what's—'

'It's not that.' He brushed the wet hair back from her

forehead, his gaze trained on hers. 'It's a boundary I've never crossed before.'

Daisy placed her hand on his chest where his heart was thumping. 'So it will be your first time too. That kind of makes us even, doesn't it?'

His mouth kicked up at one corner. 'There's something really screwy about your logic but I'm going to go with it for once.'

She smiled back and moved closer, enticing him with her body, rolling her hips and brushing her breasts against his chest, watching in delight as his eyes darkened even further.

He hooked one of her legs over his hip as he drove into her with a strong thrust that made the breath whoosh out of her lungs. Pleasure shot through her as her body surrounded him tightly. He began to move within her, each thrust delivering more friction against her sensitised nerves. The water poured down over their bodies in a warm flow that added to the eroticism of the moment.

His hands cupped the cheeks of her bottom firmly as he increased the pace, holding her in a sensual lock that she caught sight of in the mirror out of the corner of her eye. The image of their bodies locked in passion was so arousing she felt every erogenous zone on her body quake in reaction.

He caught her eye in the mirror and gave her a bad boy smile that made her inner core clench. He turned her so she was facing the mirror full on with him behind her. He entered her again, this most alpha and primitive of positions making her legs tremble as she saw the glinting delight in his gaze. Feeling his powerful thrusts from behind heightened her pleasure in a way she hadn't thought possible. The slight tilt of her hips, the sexy rocking in his body, the sheer wildness and wickedness of doing it in front of a mirror made her senses sing with rapture. The orgasm came upon her like a thrashing wave, rushing through her like a bullet train, spitting her out the other side until she felt limbless.

But Luiz was still holding her upright, his strong thighs braced either side of hers as he prepared to let himself fly free. Daisy watched him as he pumped his way to a cataclysmic release. All of his facial muscles tensed, his breathing deep and heavy as he gave a series of surging thrusts that tipped him over the edge. He gave a wild groan as he emptied himself, his hands still fastened like manacles on her hips. She felt the warm spill of his essence between her thighs, such a raw and intimate coupling with her own moisture.

He turned her to face him and took her mouth in a long deep kiss as the water cascaded over their faces and their bodies.

Daisy stroked her hands over his warm wet chest, angling her head so he could take his kiss down the slope of her neck. The scrape of his stubble on her skin made her shiver in delight. Was there no end to the magic this man could do to her? She had gone from being a sexually shy, body issue plagued virgin to a steamy, flirty wanton in less than forty-eight hours.

But in four weeks' time her exotic fling would be over and so too would her walk on the wild side. Facing

the long, cold bleakness of winter would be even worse
now she had experienced such scorching heat. Would
her new confidence disappear under layers of winter
woollies or would the part of her Luiz had brought out
stay out?

Luiz threaded his hands through the wet curtain of
her hair, holding her head steady as he meshed his gaze
with hers. 'So, we're even.'

Daisy pressed her belly against his iron-hard abdomen. Oh, for muscles as toned as that, she thought.
'You've never done it uncovered before?'

'No.'

She outlined his mouth with her fingertip. 'That's
very responsible of you.'

A shadow passed through his gaze. 'How long have
you been on the Pill?'

She gave him a self-deprecating look. 'Five years.
How's that for wishful thinking?'

His deep frown gave him an intimidating air. 'I can't
believe what's wrong with your countrymen. If it'd been
up to me I would've sorted you out at the age of con-
sent.'

She sent him a provocative smile. 'Sort me out? What
on earth does that mean?'

He reached for her again and brought his mouth
down to hers. 'I'll show you.'

CHAPTER NINE

'So HOW'S THE hot fling going?' Belinda asked Daisy when they met up briefly for a quick shop on day three of the holiday.

'Too fast.' Daisy allowed herself the smallest of shoulder slumps at the thought of flying home in the morning.

The last three days had gone past in a whirlwind of late breakfasts and long, lazy lunches and dinners and spectacular shows and late suppers. Dancing in night-clubs until the wee hours, a drive out to the desert in an Italian sports car with a gourmet picnic and a rug to indulge in a champagne supper under the stars. Passion-ate nights in Luiz's arms, making love in every room, in every position and even inventing some of their own.

How was her quiet ordinary life in London ever going to compare?

'But you're seeing him back in London, right?' Kate said.

'That's the plan…'

'If you ask me, I think you're crazy to continue with him,' Belinda said. 'A holiday fling is meant to be just that. Once the holiday is over, that's it. *Finito*. You're not supposed to see each other again.'

'But what if they're in love?' Kate said.

Belinda gave Daisy a beady look. 'Are you?'

Daisy laughed it off. 'Of course not.'

'Sure?'

No. 'Yes.'

Falling in love with someone like Luiz Valquez would prove once and for all how ridiculously naïve she was. Thinking for a moment someone like him would be interested in spending the rest of his life with her was about as deluded as anyone could get. He was ready to move on. Sure, he'd been charming and sweet and caring but she'd seen him watching her with a frown one too many times. He was probably planning to ditch her before she left for London. Why wouldn't he? He wouldn't want the inconvenience of a long distance relationship, even if it were only for another four weeks. He would want to get back to his fly-in, fly-out lifestyle.

'What about Luiz?' Kate asked.

'What about him?' Daisy said.

'What does he feel about you?'

'Lust,' Belinda said with an eye roll. 'Didn't you see that video clip on Twitter someone posted last night? I didn't know you could do the tango, Daze. It looked like you were having sex with him on that dance floor.'

Daisy could feel a blush stealing over her entire body at the thought of how she and Luiz had burned up the dance floor late last night. He had turned it into a form of foreplay. Her whole body had been vibrating with lust by the time they got back to his suite. Their need for each other had been so explosive they hadn't even bothered removing their clothes but shoved them out of the way instead. 'He's an excellent teacher.'

'Not just on the dance floor, one presumes,' Belinda said. 'You've got that look.'

She was almost afraid to ask. 'What look is that?'

'The I've-just-had-the-best-sex-of-my-life look.'

'All I can say is good on you, Daisy.' Kate leaned forward to refill her wine glass. 'It's not like we've been so lucky, have we, Belinda?'

'Just because neither of us has been wined and dined and seduced out of our senses by a hot Argentinian play-boy doesn't mean we haven't had a good time,' Belinda said with a little scowl.

'But what about those guys you were dancing with the other night?' Daisy asked.

Belinda gave a snort. 'Turns out they were married.'

'Oh...'

Kate raised her glass in a toast. 'To Daisy's first fling.'

Belinda clinked her glass against Daisy's. 'Let's hope you end it before it's too late.'

Luiz took a sip of his drink as he waited for Daisy to join him in the bar. She had spent a couple of hours that afternoon with her girlfriends shopping, claiming she couldn't possibly go back home without a quick trip to the outlet mall. After appearing in that skimpy fuchsia-pink bikini the other day, he was starting to wonder what she might come back with. As much as it thrilled him to see her in such a racy little number, or indeed nothing at all, he had other concerns right now. After the smoking-hot clip someone had loaded on social media of them doing the tango last night, he was expecting someone to sneak up behind him with a baseball bat. If word got back to Charles Wyndham that Luiz was corrupting his baby girl with raunchy dancing and porn star bikinis and God knew what else, he would be limping around on crutches for sure.

What had happened to his determination to keep his hands off her? What a joke. He hadn't lasted twenty-four hours. The last three days had been some of the most sensually pleasing of his life. *The* most sensually pleasing. Who was he kidding? No one came close to rocking his world the way Daisy did.

A vision of them in the shower together flashed through his brain. His body hardened at the memory. His skin shivered beneath his clothes, his desire for her ramping up until it was all he could think about. Her gorgeous and totally natural body, her breasts and womanly hips, the soft feminine swell of her belly that was such a contrast to the toned strength of his. The way she had stroked and worshipped his body with such honesty, responding to him with her whole being, her shyness melting away as she discovered the intimate secrets of her womanhood. He had seen it all played out on her face—the wonder, the joy, the rapture. He felt a part of it in a way he had never felt with another partner. She gave herself to him in a way no one had ever done before. And not just because she was a virgin, although he'd be lying if he didn't admit that had triggered some Neanderthal-like pleasure deep in his psyche.

Daisy was an old-fashioned girl with a wicked and playful side he found enormously attractive. The only thing he found a little irritating was her candour. She had a tendency to speak her mind, most particularly her observations about him. He'd made the fatal error of revealing too much to her over that first breakfast. Somehow, watching her gobble up that meal like a kid in a candy store had made him lower his guard. She might have the appearance of being a little naïve but underneath that guileless dimpled smile was a smart young woman who knew much more than she let on.

But was she being straight with him about what she wanted out of their relationship? She claimed she only wanted him for sex. It was the same claim he had made to all the women he'd slept with over the years. Why then did it niggle him so much she didn't want more? This was their last night together. She hadn't said a word about wanting more from him. Most women would have dropped a hint or two by now. But she had said nothing. Zilch. He wasn't even sure if she was going to agree to see him in London. What if she changed her mind? What if she decided what happened in Vegas had to stay in Vegas?

Not that he was thinking of settling down any time soon. He supposed there might come a day in the distant future when he would get around to thinking about acquiring a suitable wife, maybe having a couple of kids to keep his branch of the family tree going. But it wasn't on his radar at the moment. Besides, Alejandro and Teddy would see to all that traditional stuff, which would leave him with a little more breathing room.

In the past, whenever he'd thought of settling down he'd got a claustrophobic feeling. A cold dread would fill him. He would feel suffocated by the thought of being tied down to one woman.

But that was before he'd met Daisy with her sparkling smile and winsome ways.

As soon as he'd laid eyes on her he had felt something thump him in the chest. Her clear blue eyes had met his across the crowded room and her uppity little nose had inched ever so higher. The rush of his blood had almost knocked him off his feet. Lust had rocketed through him as soon as he saw the defiant way she looked at him. The denial of her attraction to him had been a potent turn-on. The fact she hadn't known who he was had been a bonus. He was growing weary of the groupies who trailed after him and his mates for the sake of bedding a professional sportsman. They weren't interested in him as a person. They didn't know a brass razoo about him. They knew nothing about who he was beneath the brash, fun-loving mask.

There were times when he didn't know himself...

Luiz drowned the thought with another sip of his drink but, as he lowered his glass, he saw Daisy enter the bar. It was like a bizarre rerun of the first night they had met. He felt the same knockout punch to his chest as her eyes met his across the floor. But this time she didn't put her nose in the air. Instead, she gave him a smouldering come-and-get-me look that made the back of his neck fizz and prickle in excitement.

His eyes nearly popped out of his head and landed in his drink when he ran his gaze over her outfit. So too did every other man's. Gone was the conservative little black dress.

Her dress was a tight-fitting leather sheath that clung to her body like a sleek evening glove. The neckline plunged between her breasts, giving cheeky little glimpses of the gentle curves of her breasts. The hemline was mid-thigh but it looked even shorter because she was wearing hooker-high heels.

Also gone was the prim and conservative schoolteacher make-up. In its place was smoky eye shadow, scarlet lipstick, bronze blush and thick black mascara and eyeliner that gave her a free love, Sixties look to match her teased, high ponytail. She was wearing dangling earrings and carrying a tiny silver evening purse and her arms were bare apart from a metallic bracelet that jangled as she sashayed towards him.

She sent a fingertip over the back of his hand in a teasing brushstroke and batted her eyelashes at him. 'Want to buy me a drink?'

'Sure.' He liked this game. If this was her idea of dress-ups he was in. 'What will you have?'

'Champagne.'

'French?'

She gave him a worldly look. 'Is there any other?'

Luiz had never felt more turned on by a woman. She was vampish and yet underneath all the war paint and costuming he could see the essence of purity and wholesomeness that made her so unique. He ordered the champagne and when it arrived he ushered her to a more private area where velvet sofas were stationed in a cosy nook.

She sat down opposite him and elegantly crossed one leg over the other, her dazzling smile brighter than the surrounding lighting.

He handed her a bubbling glass of champagne. 'I see the shopping trip was successful.'

'Very.' She took a sip and wrinkled up her nose as the bubbles danced. That was another thing he adored about her. All those little mannerisms she didn't try to hide in order to appear sophisticated. 'How did you spend your time?'

'I had a Skype call with the sponsors.'

'It went well?'

'Extremely.' He raised his glass to hers. 'I have a meeting with them in London the week after next. The whole board want to meet me, thanks to you whitewashing my reputation.'

She clinked her glass against his. 'To reforming irascible rakes.'

He held her gaze with smouldering heat. 'To debauching good girls.'

She laughed a tinkling bell laugh. 'Belinda can't believe the change in me. She's always told me off for being so staid and conservative. Just shows what meeting the right man can do.'

The right man? He was totally wrong for her. Hadn't her father made that clear? He hooked an eyebrow upwards. 'I'm not sure your father would think that.'

Her smile slipped away as she looked at the leaping bubbles in her glass. 'For years I've always done what he said. I was happy to do it. It was easier than arguing with him. But over the last few months I started to feel like life was leaving me behind.' Her gaze came back to his. 'That's why this trip here was so important. I had to shake off the old Daisy and embrace the new. I'm not sure I would've been able to do it at home.'

'So what happens when you go back tomorrow? Will you slip back into good habits again?'

Her dimples appeared as she smiled. 'There's always that danger, I suppose.'

Luiz ran his eyes over her outfit again. 'You look hot tonight.'

She pulled at her lip with her teeth. 'You don't think it's too over the top?'

'For Vegas, no. For teaching five-year-olds in London? You may have a problem.'

A little frown flitted over her forehead as she glanced around. 'Gosh, I didn't think of that. What if someone sees me?'

'Wasn't that the whole idea?' he asked. 'To get noticed?'

'By you; not by the rest of the world.'

'It comes with the territory of hanging out with me. I attract the world's attention.'

She looked at him thoughtfully for a long moment. 'Why is being the centre of attention so important to you?'

Luiz thought of all the times as a child when his needs went unnoticed. The constant struggle to be heard in a house that had to remain quiet for the sake of his father's health. His brother had done what he could but he hadn't been able to meet the emotional needs of a young insecure child. Who would have expected him to? His mother's desertion had made Luiz act out in a variety of ways that had tested his older brother's patience. Alejandro had used work and study and doing whatever he could to keep the family together as his way of coping with the pain of their father's accident and their mother's leaving. Luiz had used any number of attention-seeking behaviours. His reputation as a tearaway began early and even though there were times when he'd wished he could reinvent himself, he'd never quite managed to do it. Although he was more than competent academically, his love and natural aptitude for sport was the thing that stood him apart from his peers. Over the years the adulation of the crowd had become more and more addictive. It made him all the more competitive and ruthlessly driven to be the best.

But it was lonely at the top and there was only one way down from it—the word he dreaded more than any other—failure.

'I'm just a ratbag,' he said lightly. 'Ask my brother. He'll tell you.'

A wistful smile curved her mouth. 'I would've loved a sister or a brother. I think my mum would've had another child but for the fact that she wasn't happy with my father.'

'Why didn't she divorce him?'

'She asked him once or twice but he always talked her out of it.' She traced her fingertip around the rim of her glass before she added, 'Arguing with my father is not for the faint-hearted. He can be very persuasive.'

Tell me about it, Luiz thought. 'What sort of husband was he to your mother?'

She looked at him with her clear blue gaze. 'Do you mean: was he abusive?'

'Is that why she wanted to leave him?'

'No, he wasn't abusive. He loved her too much, if that makes sense.' Her finger did another circuit before she looked at him again. 'He expected her to be a certain type of wife. But my mother wasn't the type of person to be boxed in.'

'Is that what he does to you? He expects you to act and behave a certain way?'

She sighed. 'Yes…I hate disappointing him. I really do. I'm all he has, when you think about it. He wants me to be happy. I totally understand that. It's what all parents want for their kids. He doesn't want me to mess up my life with being with the wrong person, I guess because of how things turned out between my mother and him. But how can I find out who's right for me if I don't put myself out there? It's not like you can just know in an instant if someone's perfect for you.'

Luiz studiously examined the contents of his half-empty glass. 'My brother said as soon as he met his wife Teddy he knew she was the one.' He met her gaze again. 'So I suppose it must happen occasionally.'

'So you believe in love at first sight?'

'I didn't say that.'

'But that's what happened with your brother.'

'Doesn't mean it will happen with me.'

She angled her head in that cute way she had. 'But it could. Statistically speaking.'

'What have statistics got to do with it?'

She shrugged and picked up her drink again. 'Your

brother sounds like a romantic. You've got a fifty per cent chance of being one as well.'

'I don't think so.'

She gave him a teasing smile. 'How do you know? You haven't met the woman of your dreams yet. But when you do—whammo—you'll be done like a turkey at Christmas.'

He gave a wry chuckle. 'The woman of my dreams doesn't exist.'

She sat back in her chair and recrossed her long legs, gently kicking one dainty ankle up and down as her gaze held his. 'Describe her to me.'

Luiz gave her a crooked smile. 'Chestnut hair, blue eyes, creamy skin, hot body and legs up to—'

She leaned forward and tapped his thigh with a playful hand. 'I'm being serious.'

So am I, he thought with a jolt. Wasn't Daisy everything he wanted? She was funny and smart. She was fun to be around. She was sweet and yet strong enough to speak her mind. She was sexy and yet she could be a perfect lady when the need arose. She had class. She was the most thrilling lover he'd ever had.

But...

He wasn't going to fall in love and have his feelings trampled over. He wasn't going to make himself vulnerable. Not to her. Not to anyone. Not again.

'What about you?' He tossed the question back. 'Describe your dream lover.'

Her gaze flicked up to the right as if she was picturing her ideal man in her mind. 'Tall, because I would hate to tower over a man when I put on a pair of heels.

Smart, because I find intelligence the biggest turn-on. Funny, because life is so serious anyway and it's important to be with someone who makes you smile. Sexy, because chemistry is so important and who wants to be with someone who doesn't make your heart go pitter-patter?'

'Anything else?'

She tapped her index finger against her lips. 'Let me see now... Ah, yes. Eyes. He has to have nice eyes.'

Luiz lifted a brow. 'What about money?'

'Not important.'

He gave a cynical laugh. 'It's always important.'

'Not to me.'

He held her gaze for a beat. 'Isn't the possession of money a sign the man has got his act together? That he has drive and ambition?'

Her clear blue gaze didn't waver. 'He might have got it through inheritance or luck, such as winning the lottery.'

'So you don't mind if he's got money as long as he's earned it himself?'

'I would overlook his affluence for other far more important qualities.'

'Such as?'

'Moral fortitude.'

Luiz laughed again. 'I guess that rules me out.'

A tiny frown tugged at her brow as she sat looking at him in silence.

'What?'

She blinked and cleared her gaze. 'Nothing.'

'Why were you frowning?'

She put her drink down and flashed him a smile. 'What does a girl have to do around here to get a guy to ask her to dance?'

Luiz led Daisy to the dance floor but, instead of the thumping music of all the nights before, there was a pianist playing a slow tempo romantic ballad. Right now she could have done with some head-banging music to knock the sprouting foolishness out of her head. What was she thinking? Luiz wasn't marriage material. He might be funny and charming and sexy and intelligent and have the nicest eyes she'd ever seen, but he was way out of her league. He was an international sports star. He was the epitome of the freedom-loving playboy. Men like Luiz Valquez did not settle down to suburbia and raise two-point-two kids. He was not the type of man to fall in love, let alone with someone like her.

No, she would be sensible and stick to the plan. She would have her fun and then it would be over. After the Grand Slam he would go back to his life and she would go back to hers. They would never meet again and she would be fine about that. She would have to be fine about it. She had no business conjuring up unrealistic scenarios. Luiz might be a lot deeper than she had first thought him but that didn't mean he would suddenly morph into ideal husband material. He would hate to be tied down to one woman. He was used to a banquet of them. She'd be lucky to even see him once during the next month. Surely he would find someone more exciting than her.

Luiz's hand rested in the small of Daisy's back. 'You've gone quiet.'

'I'm thinking.'

'About?'

She looked up at him. 'Will you see anyone else during the next month?'

His brow was deeply furrowed. 'What sort of question is that?'

'It's not like you'll be in London full-time. You might get lonely and—'

'I might seem a little loose with my morals to someone like you but I don't fool around when I'm in a relationship.'

'But we're not really in a relationship. It's just a fling.'

'Same difference.'

She looked at his frowning expression. 'I didn't mean to upset you.'

'I am *not* upset.'

She touched the corner of his mouth, where a knot of tension had gathered. 'You're grinding your teeth. I can hear it over the music. It's really bad for your molars.'

He suddenly laughed. 'I need my head read.'

Daisy peeped up at him again. 'Why? Because you're enjoying yourself and you didn't expect to?'

He brought the tip of his finger down the slope of her nose. 'I've never met anyone like you before.'

'You really need to get out more.'

He was still smiling as he pulled her close. 'Maybe I do.'

Because it was their last night together before she flew home with the girls, Luiz took Daisy to an exclusive restaurant where the chef had won numerous awards.

He had booked a private dining room for them, which added to the decadence. She drooled at the delicious food as each dish was brought to their table. A seafood starter in a delectable piquant sauce, prime fillet steak with a colourful vegetable stack and crusty bread rolls with fresh butter for mains. All artfully presented and cooked to perfection, complemented with fine wines that burst with flavour with each sip.

'My thighs are going to hate you for this,' Daisy said as she finally put down her knife and fork. 'I've eaten more in the last four days than I've eaten in the last four months. Years, even.'

He sat watching her like an indulgent uncle. 'I like to see a woman with a healthy appetite.'

'Yes, well, if only my appetite for exercise was as robust.'

His dark eyes smouldered. 'Maybe you've been doing the wrong sort of workouts.'

Daisy felt a shiver go down her spine. 'I hate exercising alone.'

'So you prefer contact sports?'

'Not until very recently.'

His mouth tipped up in a sexy smile. 'Do you want dessert and coffee or should we go and get some exercise?'

Daisy pretended to think about it. 'Hmm, let me see now…dessert or a hot, sweaty workout?'

His eyes glinted some more. 'Can I tempt you with your own personal trainer?'

She tossed her napkin on the table and pushed back her chair. 'Sold.'

* * *

Luiz pushed back the bedcovers at two a.m. and wandered over to the windows to look at the busy strip below. He hated not being able to sleep. Hour after hour of tossing and fidgeting and ruminating made his head pound. Normally he would work off his restlessness in the gym but he hadn't wanted to leave Daisy. He scoffed at his uncharacteristic sentimentality. It wasn't as if this was the end of the affair. He would be seeing her on and off in London. He was still in the driving seat. He would say when and where and for how long. The Grand Slam was supposed to be his focus, not a slip of a girl who was looking for the fairy tale. The closest he got to the fairy tale was the role of the big bad wolf. He was good at being bad. He'd spent most of his life playing up. It was his trademark.

He turned from the window to look at Daisy. She was still sleeping soundly, clearly not worried this was their last night together. She was curled up on her side, her cheek resting on one of her hands in that childlike manner she had and her hair splayed out over his pillow. The scent of her was on his sheets, on his skin, burned in his memory. He would never be able to walk past honeysuckle without thinking of her.

How had he got himself in this situation? He was feeling sick to his stomach at the thought of saying goodbye to her at the airport. He *hated* goodbyes. He loathed them with a passion. He still remembered the way his mother had swept him up in a goodbye hug and poured kisses all over his face as she left for her 'holiday'. He hadn't seen her for two years. He had spent every single day of them waiting. Hoping.

What if he never saw Daisy again? What if she changed her mind when she got back to London? Would the intimacy they'd shared be enough to keep her tied to him until the Grand Slam was over?

And then what?

He brushed the errant thought aside. His credo was 'for fun, not for ever'. He was only interested in the here and now.

Not the, then what?

CHAPTER TEN

DAISY WOKE IN the night and found the space beside her in the bed was empty. She brushed her hair out of her face and swung her legs over the side of the bed. The bedside clock showed it was almost five in the morning and while down below on the strip there was a seething mass of revellers still spilling out from hotels and clubs, the suite felt unnaturally, eerily quiet. She slipped on a bathrobe and loosely tied the waistband, and pointedly ignoring her packed suitcase in the corner, padded out to the lounge area.

Luiz was sitting in front of the large-screen television with the sound turned off. He was watching a twenty-four-hour sporting channel—she would rather watch paint dry—or at least he had been watching. Right now, he was soundly asleep.

Daisy took the opportunity to soak in his features. His dark hair was still tousled from where her fingers had threaded through it. He had slipped on a pair of boxers but the rest of his body was gloriously naked. She had run her hands over every inch of his body, worshipping him with kisses and caresses, imprinting his scent and the feel of his skin on her senses so she could revisit them when their affair was finally over.

She drifted over to the sofa, drawn to him like a magnet drew metal. Her fingers lightly touched his hair, moving through the thick dark strands as lightly as fairy feet. His breathing was deep and even, but there were shadows beneath his eyes, as if he'd taken a long time to get to sleep. His stubble was heavily shadowed along his jaw and she couldn't resist placing her fingertips on it to feel the sexy rasp of it. His eyelids flickered but his breathing remained steady.

She couldn't stop herself from touching him. He was a temptation she had no power to resist. Forget about forbidden food. *He* was her new vice.

Just as well she was leaving this morning…

She traced the outline of each of his eyebrows. She travelled her finger down the length of his nose. She leaned in close and pressed her lips to his in a kiss as soft as a moth's wing.

His eyes opened and locked on hers. 'What are you up to?'

'Watching you sleep.'

'I wasn't sleeping.'

'Yes, you were.'

His brow lifted. 'On the contrary, I was watching golf.'

Daisy gave him a wry smile. 'Well, I would be sleeping too if I had to watch that.'

His gaze went to her mouth. 'What time do you leave?'

'Eight.'

He traced her mouth with a lazy finger for a long beat of silence. 'You could stay a couple more days. I don't have to fly back to Argentina until the weekend.'

'If I didn't have a classroom of kids to worry about I might take you up on that.'

He held her gaze with an unreadable look. 'What if I cover your wages?'

Daisy pulled away to stand with her arms folded across her middle. Hurt knifed through her with shame closely on its tail. He was reducing her to *that?* Nothing more than a plaything he was prepared to *pay* for? 'You know, for a scary moment there I thought you were asking me to be your kept mistress.'

There was another beat of silence.

'Would that be a problem?'

She dropped her arms and blew out a breath. 'Of course it's a problem. I'm not one of your good time floozies. I have a career that's important to me.'

'It's only for a month.'

'A month is a long time in a child's life,' she said. 'This is the winter term. There's the Christmas pageant to organise. I have heaps to do and I can't just drop everything because you want to party a little longer.'

He rose from the sofa and shoved a hand through his hair. 'Fine. Go back to London. I'll see you when I see you.'

Daisy looked at the tight set to his back and shoulders as he faced the windows. A wall had come up and she was on the wrong side of it. 'You're asking too much, Luiz. Surely you can see that?'

He turned to look at her with an inscrutable expression. 'It was just an idea. Forget about it. Let's stick to the plan.'

'It's not that I don't want to—'

'Can I ask you to refrain from speaking to the press?' He gave her a formal smile that didn't involve his eyes. 'They have a habit of twisting things.'

Daisy turned back to the bedroom, her spirits sinking like a ship's anchor. She could feel the dragging weight of it in the pit of her stomach. How could he dismiss her so casually after the passionate night they'd spent together? Or was this the way he ended all of his hook-ups? Cleanly and coldly and clinically.

When she came back out, showered and dressed, Luiz informed her he had a taxi waiting.

She hoped she wasn't showing anything of the disappointment she was feeling. It was a tight ache in her chest like a band of steel squeezing against her heart and lungs. 'You're not coming to see me off?'

'I have a conference call with the sponsors.'

Daisy could see which way his priorities lay. She would be out of sight and out of mind. How soon before he found a replacement? Her spirits plummeted even further. How had she let this happen? Why hadn't she seen it coming? Her four days of fun had set her up for a lifetime of misery.

He handed her into the taxi and leaned down and kissed her on the mouth through the open window. 'Be safe, little English girl.' He tapped his hand on the rim of the window and then stepped back, his expression as blank as if he was seeing off an acquaintance.

Daisy waved to him as the taxi pulled away from

the hotel concourse, her heart feeling as if it was being pulled in a vicious tug-of-war. She wanted to stay but she had responsibilities she couldn't drop on a whim. But even if she had stayed, how could she agree to his terms? He wasn't offering her a future. He was offering her a position. A temporary one. A tawdry one. He wanted to grease the wheels with his sponsors. She was nothing more than a means to an end. He would achieve his goal and she would be out of his life, just like every other woman he had associated with before.

How had she been so foolish and naïve to expect anything else? Was this why her father felt she had to have someone to watch over her twenty-four seven? She couldn't be trusted to run her own life. She was too gullible. Not street smart enough to know when she was being used. Luiz Valquez wasn't the sort of man to suddenly fall in love, certainly not after only four days. How could she compete with the women who took his fancy? She was so ordinary compared to them. He would probably hook up with a replacement while she was on her way to the airport. Las Vegas was full of girls looking for a good time with a bad boy.

She had stupidly been one of them.

Belinda and Kate were waiting outside their hotel as the taxi swept in to collect them.

'Where's lover boy?' Belinda asked. 'I thought he'd be seeing you off.'

'He has more important things to do.'

Belinda gave her a probing look. 'Uh-oh.'

Daisy glowered. 'Don't start.'

'Have I taught you nothing, Daze?' Belinda's tone

was exasperated. 'How many times do I have to drum it into your thick head? You're not supposed to fall in love on a holiday fling.'

'I'm not in love with him.' If she said it enough times maybe it would be true. How could she have fallen in love with him? It was the last thing she wanted. The last thing she expected.

'Sure you're not.'

'I just think he could've had the decency to say goodbye at the airport like everyone else does.' Daisy hugged her handbag against her stomach. 'I mean, how hard is that?'

'Maybe he doesn't like saying goodbye,' Kate said.

Daisy thought about Luiz's mother leaving when he was a small child. Had she explained to him where she was going or had she just left? Had he waited for her day after day, not sure if she would ever return? She thought of him being brought up by his older brother, only a child himself, struggling to keep the family together. Their tragically injured father living out the rest of his days in sickness and dependency. Was that why Luiz was so restless and rootless? He hated being tied down. He shied away from commitment. He didn't bond with people because people always let him down one way or the other.

Wasn't that why he always had a call to make or an email to check? He used business to distance himself. It was a barrier he used to keep himself separate from anything emotional. Was he developing feelings for her—fledgling feelings he didn't know how to handle? Like the feelings she wasn't even game to name? Was that why he'd put the drawbridge up, making her think his conference call was far more important than seeing her off? Was it foolish to hope she would be the one person to dismantle the defences he had built around himself?

The last four days had been much more than a sex-fest. He had taken her to dinner and shows, spent hours with her, talking about everyday matters. He had told her things he had told no one before—secrets and confidences. He had allowed her in. He seemed to enjoy her company in whatever context. All those times she'd found him looking at her with a contemplative expression on his face were surely not the product of her imagination. It was as if he was imagining the possibility of a future with her.

Or had that been just wishful thinking on her part?

As they were checking in a young man dressed in the uniform of Luiz's hotel came rushing over. 'Miss Wyndham? This is from Luiz Valquez. He asked me to give it to you.'

Daisy took the small square package. 'Thank you.'

'Aren't you going to open it?' Belinda asked.

'What is it?' Kate peered over her shoulder. 'Is it a ring?'

Daisy peeled back the giftwrap to find a small lingerie box inside, tied up with a scarlet bow. She undid the bow and opened the box and lifted out of the bed of tissue a pair of dainty lace knickers as fine as a silky cobweb. There was a card poked in amongst the tissue.

'What does it say?' Belinda jostled against her shoulder.

Daisy looked down at the dark scrawl of the letter *L*.

Belinda gave a cynical exhale. 'His initial.'

'What if it stands for love?' Kate asked.

Daisy folded her fingers over the card, her heart lifting on a faint breath of hope. 'Come on. That's our boarding call.'

It was raining when Daisy landed in London. Her father was there to meet her and ushered her out of the arrivals hall with a hand firmly at her elbow. 'You have some explaining to do, young lady,' he said. 'That clip of you dancing with Luiz Valquez has gone viral. I didn't sacrifice everything to bring you up to act like a slut the first moment I turn my back.'

'I was dancing, Dad. I was enjoying myself. You should try it some time.'

He frowned at her. 'Why him? Why not some decent guy who'd do the right thing by you? This is not what I wanted for you. You could do so much better.'

So much better than what? Daisy thought. Who could be better than Luiz? He was everything she wanted. She couldn't imagine wanting anyone else. He had awakened her with his touch. Her body responded to him as if it had been waiting for him all this time. How could she settle for anyone else with the memory of his caresses still echoing throughout her body?

'Attraction doesn't work that way,' she said. 'You should know that. Remember how you chased after Mum until she finally gave in? Yes, I thought you might.'

'That's not the same at all,' he said. 'I loved your mother.'

She stopped walking to look at her father. 'What if I told you I was in love with Luiz?'

He looked at her for a long moment. Then he threw back his head and laughed so hard his eyes watered. He brushed the moisture away with the back of his hand, still chuckling but with a cynical tone to it that made her stomach feel uneasy. 'Did he say he was in love with you?'

'No, but I think he's coming round to—'

'He's looking out for himself, that's what he's doing,' he said. 'And I'm not referring to his big sponsorship deal everyone is talking about.'

Daisy didn't care for the snide expression on her father's face. Suspicion began to chill her blood until every hair on her head pulled away from her scalp. 'What do you mean?'

'I told him what I'd do with him if he didn't do the right thing by you.'

Something heavy lurched in her belly. 'You…you *threatened* him?'

'Not much, just enough to make sure he toed the line. I wasn't going to stand by and watch him trash my little girl's reputation with a one-night stand. He knew which side his bread was buttered. I made sure he ate it.'

Daisy couldn't believe it. Didn't want to believe it. The whole time Luiz had been with her he had been acting out of fear of her father? Had none of it meant anything to him—not one kiss, not one caress, not one passionate interlude—except as a way to save his own back? The man she had thought so gallant and kind was acting out of cowardice? How could it be true? It couldn't be true. He had been so convincing. She had fallen so hard and so fast. Was she really *that* naïve?

'I don't believe it. He wanted to be with me. I *know* he did. He wanted me to stay longer. He asked me to but I said no because—'

'He won't see you again,' her father said. 'He'll have someone else in his bed by now. You mark my words. Before you know it, someone will post a photo of him on social media with a new lover on his arm.'

Daisy didn't want her father to be right. It was too painful to think of Luiz replacing her before her plane had got off the ground. But what else was she to think? He had only been with her because of the pressure her father had put on him. It tarnished everything they had shared. Every moment they'd had together was tainted. Spoiled by the machinations of her father, who wanted to control every aspect of her life. His constant need to control her had ruined her one chance at finding happiness.

She had connected with Luiz. Not just physically, but emotionally. And it had happened right from that first breakfast. She had *seen* him. The *real* him. Without the mask he wore for everyone else. How could that have been an act on his part? Why would he let her in like that if he was only pretending to enjoy her company?

She had fallen in love with him. He had come to her rescue and kept her safe. Every time he had smiled at her she had fallen a little harder. Every time he touched her, kissed her or made love to her she had given him another piece of her heart. She had denied it to herself, not wanting to admit how much he had affected her. But he was everything she was looking for in a partner because without him she felt only half alive.

But he hadn't been with her for *her*.

He had been pretending the whole time. Acting his way through their four days together like an actor did a role he'd been assigned. Had *any* of their time together been real or was it all one big fake? What about that morning? Why had he asked her to stay? That surely couldn't have been because of what her father had said?

Daisy felt as if a blade had carved right through her heart, leaving it in shredded pieces hanging from her ribcage. Why couldn't he have flown with her back to England if he'd wanted more time with her? Surely he could have postponed his trip back to Argentina by a couple of days.

No. He would never do that because she was meant to fit into his life as if she had no life of her own. Just like her mother had been expected to fit into her father's life. To be what he wanted, when he wanted, where he wanted.

To be controlled.

'Come on,' her father said as he shepherded her towards the exit. 'I've got a special dinner planned. You know that new accountant I put on a few months ago? I'd like you to spend some time with him. I'm thinking of making him a partner. He can take over the business once I retire. He's exactly the sort of man I want as a son-in-law.'

Daisy stopped in her tracks and shook off her father's hold. 'What?'

'I don't think he'll be put off by your little fling in Vegas—' her father carried on as if she hadn't spoken '—he's probably sown a few wild oats himself. If I offer him a partnership to sweeten the—'

'Stop it right there,' she said through clenched teeth. 'I do *not* need you to organise my life for me. I do not need to find me a husband or bribe someone to have dinner with me or anything else. How can you be so... so ridiculously obsessive about controlling everything I do? I'm not a kid any more. I'm an adult, Dad. I want to be in control of my own life. When are you going to finally accept that?'

Her father frowned as people glanced at them on their way past. 'Don't make a scene. You're acting like your mother, getting hysterical over nothing. I'm just trying to help you because I love you.'

'Do you?' Daisy asked. 'Do you really? You said you loved Mum but you never let her be herself. If you love me so much then why aren't I good enough the way I am?'

Her father's frown was dark and forbidding. 'What's got into you? Have you been eating too much sugar or something? You know how it makes you tetchy.'

Daisy repositioned her handbag strap over her shoulder. 'Maybe I've finally grown up.'

'You're letting one silly little fling go to your head,' he said. 'You'll forget about him soon enough. Once you meet Laurence you'll see what I mean. He's perfect for you. He reminds me of myself at that age.'

Great. Just what she needed. Another control freak in her life, hand-picked by her father.

Daisy kept walking towards the exit. 'Make my apologies. I have other plans.'

'You're jet-lagged. You always get irrational when you're over-tired. I can make it next week. How about that?'

She rolled her eyes as she faced him again. 'Dad. Read my lips. Stop controlling me.'

'A coffee?'

'No.'

He sucked in his lips and then pushed them out on a sigh, giving her the little boy lost look that normally would have seen her cave in. 'Does this mean you'll be moving out of the flat?'

Daisy gave him a determined look. 'I think it's time, don't you?'

Luiz stood a few metres away from the school gate, where an assortment of mothers and fathers and nannies or au pairs were collecting children. The icy wind was boring holes in his chest and making his eyes sting but he barely noticed. He had flown in that day after a week of playing charity matches in towns throughout Argentina. He had sent Daisy a few texts over the last few days but her replies had been distant and impersonal. He could hardly blame her, given how clumsily he had handled their parting back in Vegas. He hadn't had enough time to prepare for her leaving. He'd put it to the back of his mind, not wanting to face the fact their relationship would be on hold until he could free up some time to be with her. Offering to cover her wages… He still kicked himself over that. Of course she would be offended. Could he have thought of a worse way to insult her?

But he had a surprise for her that would make up for it. It had taken him this time apart to realise she was the only woman he could ever love. Perhaps a part of him had known it right from the start. Wasn't that why he had relaxed his guard? He had told her of his deepest hurts and she had listened with that gentle look on her face that made him feel as if a soothing balm had been spread over his raw wounds, finally giving them a chance to heal.

The last of the children were collected and the wind got icier as sleet started to fall. And then he saw her. She was dressed in a smart wool dress with a cashmere coat over the top and knee-high boots. A scarf was wound around her neck and her hair was in a tidy chignon at the back of her head. She had her head down against the wind-driven sleet but she must have sensed she was being watched for she suddenly glanced his way. Her eyes blinked and she touched the scarf at her throat with a nervous flutter of her hand. But then she gripped the strap of her bag a little tighter and stalked out of the school gates and towards the tube station a couple of blocks away.

He caught her before she got to the last wrought iron post of the school fence. 'Daisy. Wait.'

She swung around to face him, her cheeks rosy-red and her blue eyes flashing. 'I have nothing to say to you. I think my father said it all, don't you?'

He frowned. 'What has your father got to do with anything?'

She stood staunchly before him. 'Why don't you tell me?'

He took in her tightly set mouth and glittering eyes. 'I'm here because I need to talk to you.'

'I think you should find someone else to help you butter up your sponsors,' she said. 'I'm no longer available.'

A sharp pain seized him in the chest but there was no way he was going to let her see how much her cold statement hurt him. 'That didn't take you long. How long's it been? A week?'

She raised her chin. 'I'm sure you've filled my position seven times over.'

'Is that what you think?'

'It's what I expect from someone like you.'

Luiz drew in a breath and slowly released it. 'Right, well, then. I guess I should cancel my arrangements for the weekend.'

She glared at him. 'How *could* you?'

'How could I what?'

'Sleep with me because of what my father said.'

'Hang on a minute. I did not sleep with you because of anything your father said. I slept with you because I couldn't help myself.'

She threw him a scornful look. 'You expect me to believe that?'

'It's true,' Luiz said. 'I wanted you from the moment I laid eyes on you. Your father had nothing to do with it.'

Her forehead crinkled in an even deeper frown. 'But he told me he threatened you.'

'He did but I didn't take it seriously. Well, only a bit. But it didn't stop me from wanting you. I don't think any threat could do that.'

She chewed her lip for a moment. 'Why are you here?'

'We had an agreement, remember?'

She moved her gaze to look at a point in the distance, both of her hands gripping her bag strap so tightly he could see the small white bulges of her knuckles. 'I'm not sure I can go through with it… Not now…'

'Why not?'

She shifted her weight on the cobblestones and met his eyes. 'I think it's unwise to extend a holiday fling.'

'Why?'

'Because people aren't the same when they're back in their real worlds.'

'I came all this way to see you, *querida*,' he said. 'I've booked a luxury hotel. I've got a helicopter on standby to take you there. We can have the weekend together and shut out the rest of the world. Come on. What do you say?'

Her eyes hardened as they held his. 'Did you think to *ask* me if I'd like to be whisked away to a hotel for the weekend? What if I had other plans? What if I had already made my own arrangements?'

'You can cancel them, can't you?'

She blew out a whooshing breath. 'You're unbeliev-able. You think you can do anything you like by waving a fistful of money around. You're exactly like my father. You think you can control people by dangling big car-rots under their nose. Well, you can find someone else to have your weekend with. I'm sure you won't have too much trouble. I'm not available, nor am I interested.'

Luiz stopped her spinning away by grabbing her arm. 'Wait a damn minute. I've rearranged my whole schedule to get here. I forfeited a training session with my team. That's a big deal so close to the Grand Slam.'

She looked at him with a steely glare. 'Why are you here, Luiz? Why are you *really* here?'

He thought about telling her but how could he do it like this? Not out on a cold and gloomy rain-sodden street with people looking on. He wanted to take her away and romance her, to show her just how much he loved her by treating her like a princess. 'I told you. I wanted to see you. We agreed to see each other for the next—'

'So you've seen me. Now you can go.'

His heart jerked with a spasm of pain so sharp it felt like someone had ripped it out of his chest. Disappointment chugged through him, making his legs feel numb and useless.

He'd been wrong.

Stupidly, gullibly wrong.

She didn't feel anything for him. She couldn't have made it clearer.

The blood was pounding in his head and his ears to a repetitive and sickening beat: *It. Is. Over. It. Is. Over.*

He let his hold fall away from her arm. 'Fine. If that's the way you want to play it. We'll leave it there.' He stepped back from her. '*Adios, querida.*'

She stood with soldier-straight shoulders, her lips barely moving as she said, 'Goodbye.'

* * *

Belinda scrolled through her Twitter feed. 'Nope. Not a thing about him anywhere. He hasn't posted anything since he was playing those charity matches in Argentina.' She put her phone down and gave Daisy a pointed look. 'Makes you kind of wonder, doesn't it?'

Daisy flattened her lips. 'He's probably too busy seducing some skinny supermodel.'

'Maybe.' Belinda leaned forward. 'Are you going to eat that cheesecake or just scowl at it?'

She shoved the plate in Belinda's direction. 'You have it.'

Belinda took a mouthful and then swallowed it before saying, 'Turning your nose up at cheesecake is a bad sign.'

'I'm not hungry.'

'Boy, you have got it bad, haven't you? I've never seen you like this before.'

Daisy dropped her head into her hands and squeezed bunches of her hair until her scalp stung. 'I'm so stupid. What was I thinking? A holiday fling with a career playboy? *Me?* God, what a pathetic joke.'

Belinda downed another mouthful of raspberry cheesecake. 'What exactly did your father say to him?'

'Does it matter?' Daisy sat back and folded her arms crossly. 'He expected me to drop everything and go with him. What planet is he from? I have a career. I have commitments. I have responsibilities I take very seriously. What does *he* do? He flies around the globe to sit on a horse and whack a ball with a mallet.'

Belinda scooped up a dollop of cream. 'He raised a lot of money for homeless kids in Argentina.'

'So?'

'Come on, Daze. You've got to admit that's pretty decent of him.'

Daisy let out a long breath. 'I wish he'd asked me first, you know? I mean, what sort of guy just *assumes* you've got nothing better to do than to wait for him to call?'

Belinda licked some raspberry coulis off the end of her fork. 'A guy in love doesn't always think. They act first.'

Daisy frowned. 'What do you mean?'

'Think about it. On the spur of the moment he asked you to stay with him a little longer but you declined. Then he flew to London after organising a surprise weekend getaway for you, which you also declined. Which, by the way, must have cost him a bomb. My guess is he's not going to ask again.'

'He didn't ask.' Daisy scowled. 'He *told* me.'

Belinda dug into the cheesecake again. 'Maybe you should ask him this time.'

'Ask him what?'

Belinda gave her a level look. 'If he's not in love with you, then why hasn't he been seen with anyone since?'

Luiz went through his warm-up routine in the changing room but his heart wasn't in it. His head wasn't in the right space. He couldn't concentrate. He couldn't think of anything but of how angry Daisy had been. How she had looked at him with such icy coldness. How she had frozen him out when all he had wanted was to whisk her away to tell her how he felt. He'd pinned so much on that trip. He had organised it down to the finest detail. Roses, champagne, gourmet food—everything a girl with her heart set on romance would want. How had he got it so wrong about her? Had he been so blindsided by his feelings he hadn't seen what was right under his nose?

She hadn't wanted *him*. Not the real him. She'd wanted a fling, an experience to look back on, just like all the other women who trailed after him.

It infuriated him to think that all those chatty little exchanges to get him to reveal his innermost secrets had been a ruse. She'd probably been laughing at him the whole time. She'd had no intention of continuing their affair. Not with her posh school board turning their noses up at her choice of partner. She probably had some stuck-up merchant banker by now. Someone her father approved of.

His gut twisted at the thought of her in another man's arms. It sickened him to think of another man kissing her. Touching her. Marrying her. Having babies with her.

He spun away and raked his head with his fingers. He had to stop thinking about her. It was over. He had to accept it. He thumped his fist on the lockers as if it would drum it into his skull. He. Had. To. Accept. It.

The crowds were milling into the stands. Alejandro and Teddy were being entertained in the sponsors' corporate marquee while he prepared for the game. The game he had spent years of his life training for; the game he was expected to win. The trophy was as good as his if he could just force himself to get out there and do what needed to be done.

He swore as he kicked his boot against the bench seat. What was the point of playing when the one person he was playing for wasn't here? Wasn't this for Daisy? Everything he had worked for he now wanted for her. She had shown him the shallowness of his life. His endless pursuit of pleasure without strings had all but strangled everything that was good in him.

Could he be wrong about her motives? Hadn't she made him see how much richer life could be when you lived it for others? Like she did. Devoting her life to the education of children. Sacrificing what she wanted so they could have what they needed. So different from his mother, who hadn't bothered to sacrifice anything for anyone.

Was he foolish to think he could try again with her? That this time he could ask her—*beg her*—to see him instead of assuming she would drop everything? She was proud and defiant. Hadn't he loved that about her from the moment he'd met her? She wasn't a pushover. She wasn't yet another sycophant. She was a genuine girl with a big heart who wanted the fairy tale. A fairy tale she deserved.

She had spent most of her life being controlled by her father. Why hadn't he realised his approach was exactly the same? He hadn't given her a choice. He had told her what he wanted as if she had no say in the matter. Of course she would cut him loose. Why would she sign up for more of the bulldozing tactics of her overbearing father?

Alejandro suddenly appeared in the doorway. 'There's someone here to see you.'

Luiz turned his back as he leaned his hands on the washbasin. He couldn't give a press interview now. Not now. Not while his emotions were so churned up inside his chest he couldn't breathe without it hurting. 'Tell them to go away.'

'I'm not sure she'll appreciate being told what to do.'

She?

His heart skipped a beat as he whipped back around. 'Who is it?'

'It's me,' Daisy said, stepping forward.

Luiz stared at her. He opened his mouth to speak but he couldn't get his vocal cords to respond. They were jammed by emotion so thick it paralysed his throat.

She was here?

He blinked to make sure he wasn't imagining her standing there. Like all those times as a kid, pressing his nose to the glass as he waited for his mother, only to have his heart plummet in disappointment when she didn't show up.

His mouth was dry. His heart was pounding so hard he could feel the echo of it beating in his fingertips.

'Aren't you going to say something?' Daisy said.

'Hello.' *Hello? Is that the best you could do?*

'I liked it when you said it in Argentinian.'

Luiz cleared his throat. '*Hola.*'

'I really like your brother.'

'He's married.'

'I know. I like his wife too. She's awfully sweet. You didn't tell me she was Theodora Marlstone, the brilliantly talented children's book illustrator. I've got all of her books. I use them in my class. My kids love them.'

Luiz swallowed again. Best not to get too ahead of himself. He wasn't going to let her rip his heart out again. 'Why are you here?'

'Why do you think I'm here?'

He searched her expression but she was playing him at his own game. He thought he was good at a poker face but she took it to a whole new level. 'I have no idea.'

For the first time a tiny crack appeared in her composure. 'Really? No idea at all?'

'You wanted to see a polo game?'

She let out a little breath. 'I guess you're still angry.'

'What gives you that idea?'

She chewed at her lip. 'You're not making this easy for me...'

'Did my brother set this up?'

'No. I came because I wanted to see you.'

'Why?'

Her blue eyes meshed with his. 'I wanted to ask you something.'

'Ask.'

She pressed her lips together for a moment, her gaze lowering slightly. 'Do you love me?'

Luiz watched the way her throat tightened, just as his had earlier. He watched as her teeth tugged at the inside of her mouth as if trying to control the urge to cry. His heart swelled in his chest until he could feel it pushing against his lungs. 'Yes.'

Her eyes flew back to his. '*Yes?*'

He smiled and closed the gap between them, reaching for her and hugging her close to his chest. 'Yes, you little goose. How could you think I didn't?'

'But my father—'

'Was right to warn me to keep my hands off his little princess, but do you think I could do it?' He cupped her face in his hands. 'I fell in love with you that first night. You put your nose in the air and gave me such a haughty look I was instantly smitten.'

'*Really?* That early on?'

He laughed as relief and joy spread through him. 'Of course it only made it worse when you did that stripper routine. What hope did I have after that?'

Her cheeks flushed in the way he adored so much. 'I think I fell in love with you when you came to my rescue. I didn't want to admit it, but when you stayed up all night watching over me I saw you in a completely different light. Of course, the way you kept plying me with delicious food only made it worse.'

He stroked her face. 'I'm sorry for how I handled things back in Vegas. It was such a crass offer. Not one of my proudest moments, that's for sure. I wanted you to stay but I didn't think of how you would take it. I stupidly assumed you'd jump at the chance. I should've known you'd do the opposite.'

She looked at him earnestly. 'It wasn't that I didn't want to be with you. I did. So much. But I couldn't bear to be just another one of your girls. I wanted to be special.'

He held her by the upper arms. 'You are, *mi amor.* So special I can barely find the words. I love you. I want to spend the rest of my life with you. Say you'll marry me.'

She gave him a teasing smile. 'Are you asking me or telling me?'

He grinned back. 'I'm begging you.'

'Well, that's different.'

'Is that a yes?'

Daisy linked her arms around his neck. 'How could I ever say no to you?'

He kissed her for a long breathless minute before pulling back to look at her glowing face and sparkling eyes. 'So, you've come all this way to see a polo game. I guess I'd better go out there and get that trophy.'

She gave him a look of mock reproach. 'Aren't you being terribly arrogant to assume you're going to win?'

He pressed another kiss to her lips. 'It would be if I was playing for myself.'

Daisy stood next to Teddy and Alejandro in the stands as Luiz came round for a victory lap after the thrilling game. He held the trophy high above his head as he sought her gaze in the stand, his dark eyes glinting as he mouthed the words, 'This one's for you, *querida*.'

* * * * *

MILLS & BOON®

Want to get more from Mills & Boon?

Here's what's available to you if you join the exclusive **Mills & Boon eBook Club** today:

✦ *Convenience – choose your books each month*
✦ *Exclusive – receive your books a month before anywhere else*
✦ *Flexibility – change your subscription at any time*
✦ *Variety – gain access to eBook-only series*
✦ *Value – subscriptions from just £1.99 a month*

So visit **www.millsandboon.co.uk/esubs** today to be a part of this exclusive eBook Club!